Realm of Fire

Realm of Fire

Marauder Book III

D.W. Roach

Acknowledgements

First and foremost to my loving wife. I can't thank you enough for taking this journey with me. When I was ready to give up you encouraged me, when I thought it wasn't good enough you said it was! You are my better half, my bridge to Valhalla, my answer in the stars...

To my children, I hope that one day when you grow up that you can come to read and love these books. When my days were long I often thought of you to keep going.

To my family, thank you for your continued support. It takes a village to raise a Viking.

To my Editor and USA Today Best Selling Author Cara Lockwood, this is the third time you have rescued a warrior on his quest for literary greatness. Thank you!

To my Cover Designer Miguel Parisi, your creative skills continue to bring my story to visual life. Thank you for your hard work and dedication.

To Author and fellow Viking C.J. Adrien who took special interest in me from a very early stage in my writing career, thank you for your continued support. Your support came at a much needed time!

Lastly to the many fans of my work. Thank you, thank you, and thank you! I would not have written a second book let alone a third book without you. Your interest and inspiration for my writing is the greatest reward I could have asked for.

"Think lightly of yourself and deeply of the world."

- Miyamoto Musashi

Contents

One
Fenrir

When does the loss become too great a toll on the soul of a man? The mind itself is not without its injuries through the journey of life. It is torn, shredded, maimed, and dare I say, altered. When a man loses the things in his life that make him complete, make him whole, he becomes one of two things: a broken man, or something else entirely. You see, pain can infect a man's mind, pain can dull the senses and emotions. The man turns away from familiar things and gazes back to the darkness, back to the wilds.

The wild, being what it is, accepts all manner of creature without favoritism, without judgement, and without remorse. The man enters the wild once more and is no longer a man. He becomes an animal; he learns to exist in the wild but the pain remains and cuts deeper still. Twisting his innards, poisoning his heart, damaging his soul into a black and unnatural thing.

The being who was once a man, who then became an animal, transformed to something the wild itself fears, something the wild conceals itself from. The man became the monster...

* * *

"Audan!" a hoarse voice called out to me. "Audan, wake up!" My head fell in the direction of the voice as my eyes remained shut. I felt strange, warm and comfortable but heavy like a stone pressed against my chest all at once. Beneath my heals, the earth moved. "Audan! Audan, you must wake!" the voice called out again but this time more clearly. My eyes opened partly to a mass of objects strewn about the ground as my body moved backwards pulled by someone or something. Everything was blurry. Blinking rapidly, I opened my eyes wide to see myself being dragged through a field of corpses. Vikings, Draugr, and Valkyries lay motionless, staring at me with their dead eyes, their blood still warm upon the ground as I felt it soaking through my armor and tunic. My eyelids felt heavy once more and so I allowed them shut.

"Audan!" The voice brought me back from the depths and I tilted my head back to see a large dark gray figure pulling me up a wet grassy hillside.

"Odin…" I mumbled. The old man gazed down at me with a worried but relieved look. He quickly stopped pulling and placed me flat on the ground.

"Audan, can you stand?" I blinked a few more times and slowly lifted my head. Suddenly a rush of noise found me and the battle that still raged all around was now very apparent; the clash of steel and iron was deafening. Men cried out in agony from their wounds and the Draugr made their usual ghastly blood curdled screams. I nodded towards Odin and with his help slowly lifted my weak body upright.

"What happened?" I asked quietly. My head pounded on the inside with the drums of war.

"Freya has taken your brother to the depths of hell; the Draugr are now rampant and pushing your forces back, Audan."

"Jareth…" My eyes opened wide as my heart raced deep inside my chest. I had promptly remembered what had transpired no more than a few moments ago. "Jareth!" Odin pressed his large hand against my chest and held me back from running towards the barricaded hallow where Freya had made good her escape.

"Audan, your brother is gone, the battle is all but lost. You must get what remains of your forces back to Bjorgvin and retreat to the sea with your people." The ground now rumbled at my feet, taking my attention away from Odin. In the distance just beyond the main melee were warriors of Asgard in brilliant shining armor adorned in glowing runes, pulling at great ropes and chains on the massive beast that was Fenrir the wolf. The enormous cavern in the ground next to him had closed behind Freya and Jareth, limiting the number of Draugr that had reached the battlefield. I watched helplessly as many of my warriors were slaughtered without mercy. They crawled through the mud darkened by the bloodied and bile-covered ground. The smell was putrid with entrails. I looked up at Odin who swung a great sword cutting down vast swaths of undead that approached from the side.

"Odin, where shall we go?" I yelled. Odin turned to me, gripping me by the tunic and lifting me to my feet.

"Now is not the time, Audan! Go! Valhalla will hold off the forces of hell for as long as we can but you must retreat! Your people need you!" The very word tasted foul in my mouth: retreat…but I dared not disobey the All Father and his ancient wisdom. I surveyed the battlefield and watched as the Valkyries descended from the air weakening our lines. As they plummeted downward, they would pluck men from the shield wall and throw their bodies from the sky at their comrades. With each falling warrior, a gap opened within the lines and the Draugr would pour inside like the rising tide. They hacked and slashed without mercy at my warriors giving no quarter until their flanks were fully engulfed by the undead. All the men of Bjorgvin would be cut down if we did not fall back to the village now. I reluctantly raised my axe high into the air and waved it back and forth in hopes to catch the attention of my men.

"Men of Bjorgvin! Retreat! Retreat back to the village! We must protect our home!" Without hesitation, the beleaguered warriors fell back covered under a hail of arrow fire followed up by throwing axes that kept the Draugr line from advancing. Odin and his Asgardian warriors melded together hastily creating a shield wall to ensure our escape. We ran back up the hill bloodied and cleaved with our feet slipping relentlessly on the wet grass. Just before reaching the top of the mound, my legs began to give out and I braced my thighs with my hands under each step. Finally reaching the top, I turned around to witness the valley of absolute carnage below. The ground which had once been a serene grass valley now stood a darkened pit of mud, bile, and blood. Pieces of flesh were strewn about mixed in with an arm, leg, or head every few paces. The wounded screamed and cried out in relentless agony, begging for the All Father to take them away from this wretched scene. I stepped forward back towards the field of battle in hopes to lend aid to these poor souls.

"Audan!" I turned to gaze upon the bloodied face of Gunnar who pulled urgently on my shoulder. "We cannot help them now. We must save our people. Let's go, Audan!" Hesitantly, I turned away and followed my warriors back through the thick forest. The Valkyries pursued us from the air as we ran like rabbits being hunted by hawks. The thick forest lent little comfort as we were mercilessly smacked in the faces by twigs and branches that stood between us and survival. One by one, the winged creatures descended upon us plucking men from the earth with their bird like talons and carrying them high up into the air.

"Keep up, men! We must protect the village!" I yelled weakly.

"Audan!" a voice yelled from behind me. I turned my head back only to see a blur rushing from behind. My back was struck by a pair of hands and I fell quickly to the dirt, rolling into a tree lying prostrate on my back. A body flew over my eyes kicking dirt into my face. I blinked rapidly and wiped the soil off my face until I could see once more. High in the air, a Viking warrior struggled against the talons dug deep into his shoulders. It was Uncle Valdemar!

"Valdemar!" I yelled as I watched helplessly from the ground. An archer no more than a farm field from me raised his bow into the air with an arrow nocked in the string. "No!" With all my strength I sprinted towards the archer and pushed his arms away just as he let loose his arrow. The stinger flew upwards with great speed but missed its mark widely. "What the hell are you doing?" I yelled. The warrior pushed me back with a look of frustration on his face.

"Somebody has to help him! That demon is going to tear him apart."

"You'll hit Valdemar! He still has a fighting chance."

"Then, you help him!" The archer reluctantly lowered his bow and continued running toward Bjorgvin. Most of the men who had survived, passed me up by now and only the warriors of Asgard kept me from being overrun by the hordes of hell. Suddenly, a scream erupted from overhead; there was Valdemar with a knife buried in the thigh of the Valkyrie filling the sky with her spattering blood. She loosened her grip of him and he slid down gripping the dagger tighter.

"Die, you devil creature! Die!" yelled Valdemar as he appeared to twist the blade in the winged beast's leg. "Valhalla will know my name!" The Valkyrie began to slowly descend as her wings faltered under the pain of the knife. Soon, they were just above the canopy and I followed them as best I could while dodging tree limbs.

"Valdemar, jump!" I urged. "Valdemar, let go! Let go!" He looked down at me and released his grip falling into the side of a tree. Smacking against the limbs, his body fell loudly and I rushed towards Valdemar to brace his fall to the earth. Uncle gripped a branch and his body slowed but swung quickly around until his backside hit my shoulder. Before I knew it, I was already on the ground with a heavy warrior lying motionless on top of me. "Uncle?" I moaned but he did not move. "Uncle?" A wheezing sound escaped from his lips and his head turned towards mine.

"What is it, boy?" he asked weakly.

"You're fucking heavy, old man. Get off me…" Uncle Valdemar rolled off and we helped each other back to our feet. Just then, a large crash erupted from behind us. Valdemar turned around before I did and leapt atop the Valkyrie that had pulled him into the air. Appearing weakened, the Valkyrie had returned to her more pleasant human form; Uncle Valdemar did not descend with blade or iron but with his bare hands. He gripped around her throat tightly and she lifted her hands to his, barely putting up a fight until the last of her life left her bloodshot eyes. The Valkyrie kicked and shook until she went limp and even still Valdemar continued to choke her. I pulled at his back side and he took a halfhearted swing at me.

"Go away, boy. This she devil is mine!" The bloodlust had overcome him and I needed to pull him away before more arrived to shorten his victory.

"We must go." I urged. "More are on the way." Valdemar looked to the skies and quickly released his fresh kill. Spitting on the corpse he grabbed his knife from her thigh and pulled it out. He stood and walked past me brushing my shoulder and giving me a pat on the back.

"Let's go then. We're not done yet." We reached a dense part of the wood just outside our village. The Valkyries could no longer see us and thus they did not descend upon our heads. Moving leaves from my gaze I could see the clearing to the gates of home. The fortified palisades of Bjorgvin were in sight at long last. The villagers lined the walls with bows at the ready. Gunnar was crouched with other warriors in the underbrush and I quickly joined him with Valdemar at my side.

"Alright, we're going to have to make a run for it." Gunnar lifted his sword and pointed towards the guarded palisades that lay an entire field away. The clearing had no cover from the talons of the corpse goddesses making us easy prey. "I'll go first," Gunnar remarked.

"No! If we go one at a time they will pick us off. We must move together keeping our blades in the air. We need to get in range of the archers on the wall. If we make it that far they can provide us some cover. We just may have a chance but only if we do this together." Gunnar nodded.

"It's your call, Audan. We will move on your word." I looked up through the cracks in the trees watching the dark shadows circle quickly above waiting to dive down on anything that moved. Turning my head to each side I could see that the men were ready I lifted my arm into the air and then pointed forward towards the palisades.

"Forward!" Warriors darted from the bushes and tree line straight ahead for the main gates. Not a word was uttered save for the pounding of heavy footsteps on the trodden paths. We heard terrible screams from above and we turned back to see the Valkyries closing in on us with their dark wings tucked back. "Don't look back! Keep running!" I urged. Desperately looking ahead, the villagers atop the palisades scrambled loudly to their positions.

"Loose!" I heard commanded in the distance. Arrows shrieked towards us dotting the sky in a dark moving haze. Just as the winged beasts caught up with us and fell upon our heads, so, too, did the sharp iron fly above us creating some temporary cover. The Valkyries did not seem to think much of the danger and descended upon us regardless. A corpse goddess fell heavily to the ground in front of me littered in arrows; her body rolled in the dirt, snapping the arrow shafts in half as I jumped over her. I looked to my left and right at the chaos that now ensued. The Valkyries plucked what men they could while others fell to their death under the unrelenting hail of stingers. They quickly gave up chase as we came closer to the village and the volley of arrows only intensified, cutting their sisters down with ease. I reached the gates and pounded my fist on the door.

"Open the gates! Open the gates!" I yelled in desperation. Suddenly, the wooden wall was opened; spearman with shields rushed forward providing more cover and those of us left standing flooded into the village.

"Audan!" a women's voice called from overhead; it was Kenna. She leaned over the back of the palisade with a sword in the air and shield at her side. "What happened?"

"Fenrir! Fenrir has been freed from his chains!" Kenna slowly dropped her sword upon her side; the look of fear had overcome her.

"How can it be?" she asked. I rushed up the steps to mother's side.

"It was Freya, that damned vile creature. She has released the gates of hell; Draugr flood the valleys below and Valkyries the sky above. The war bands are not far behind them." Archers continued their relentless onslaught as the last of the men arrived within the shelter of the gates.

"Then we haven't much time. Where is your brother? Where is Jareth?" Still breathing heavily, I looked away towards the tree line. "Son? Where is your brother?" Kenna had quickly caught on to my delay in response and now sounded very much concerned. I dreaded the words that would follow.

"Freya..." I mumbled. Kenna approached closer placing her hand heavy on my shoulder.

"Is he... is he dead? Has my son fallen in battle?" Kenna's voice cracked and shook. I quickly lifted my head.

"I don't know, Mother. Fenrir appeared from below the earth. Freya followed with an army of undead at her back. Jareth was knocked to the ground motionless and in the struggle she lifted him upon her shoulder and retreated back into the hallow." In great shame, I fell to one knee lowering my head. "I tried to save him Mother, I'm so very sorry." Kenna's fingers wrapped around my chin tugging my beard upwards. Her eyes bloodshot and swollen with tears, she embraced me tightly.

"It's not your fault, son. I know you did your very best." I gritted my teeth and braced myself for the next volley of terrible news that I was about to unleash upon her. Through the tears and spit I forced out one word.

"Father..." Kenna pulled back quickly, her mouth left wide open and her eyes wide with fear. She dropped her sword to the ground this time and knelt down next to me.

"Is he?" I looked at mother once more, the words that would cut her deeply sat on the tip of my tongue. Try as I might, I could not keep this darkness from her. She had to know the fate of our beloved Rurik.

"Father fell in battle. He fought bravely and earned his place in Valhalla. I watched as his soul was carried off to the heavens." Kenna swallowed back her tears placing a hand on her waist and quickly composed herself.

"Who did it?" she asked with vengeance in her voice. "Who slayed my husband?"

"Steinar," I replied without hesitation.

"And did you avenge your father?"

"I did, Mother. Steinar is dead. He shall not cause our family any more heartache." Kenna turned away to walk down the palisades; she faltered after three or four steps falling to one knee. I rushed to her side and she gently pushed me away.

"No. I'm fine, son. I just need a moment to myself is all. Take watch over the walls." Kenna walked down the wooden steps and made her way back to the Great Hall. A loud bang startled me and I turned back to see the gates slammed shut. Icy water fell atop my head and I looked up to see terrible and dark storm clouds pushing towards Bjorgvin. A crack of lightning erupted in the valley above the tree line. I hoped desperately that Thor was watching over us this day. Another bolt of lightning erupted and in the distance above the trees was a formation of winged beasts staying just beyond our archers range, the Valkyries. They were waiting, holding back their assault. A strong hand suddenly grasped my arm from behind.

"My boy! It is good to see you not yet among the gods." The short and eccentric fat man brought comfort to my shaken soul.

"It's good to see you, Eygautr, alive and unscathed." Eygautr laughed and carefully lifted the crimson cloak covering his right shoulder.

"Not entirely, my young friend." The cloak now lifted revealed three deep cuts into his upper chest that stretched across his shoulder. "The foul beast tried to carry me like a hawk carries a mouse. She came for more than she had bargained for. The wretch barely lifted me from the ground before I pierced my sword into her belly and spilled her innards to the ground." Eygautr covered his wound back up securing his cloak in place. "My only regret is that my mouth was open when I gutted the bitch. Their blood tastes rotten, diseased." The short fat man spit, wiping his mouth with his bloodied sleeve. The storm picked up its strength and the lighting struck closer. Eygautr leaned against the outer palisade and pointed to the Valkyrie formation in the distance. "Why do they wait, brother Audan? Why do they not press their attack?"

"The Clans and Draugr will be here soon. They wait to finish us off." Eygautr gripped his belt and pulled it tightly under his fat stomach.

"Well, then, perhaps I will join your father in Valhalla after all. It would be a shame for him to drink without his friends." Just below us the warriors gathered in the village center. Orbrecht arrived without delay treating the wounded with a handful of thrall at his disposal. Those who were still able-bodied rested as they waited for the next battle. Two pairs of footsteps came up the steps noisily behind me. Gunnar and Uncle Valdemar had also survived the first battle.

"Audan, my brother." Gunnar approach quickly and we embraced in a hearty handshake. "Our forces have suffered heavy losses but we will be ready to fight them off when they assault the village. We can save Bjorgvin." I shook my head at the young warrior's false optimism.

"No," I said quietly.

"No?" replied Uncle Valdemar in surprise. "Why would we not save Bjorgvin? This is our home." In frustration I swung my bearded axe and planted the blade into the wooden planks below my feet.

"The village is beyond saving. It is wood and stone and memories. Nothing more. The people, our people, are all that matters," I replied.

"So what would you have us do nephew? The clans are on our heels. The Valkyries will not wait outside our gates forever." I looked at the tired faces before me that waited eagerly for an answer, one that would perhaps give them hope. For me, the path was clear and I only hoped that they were confident in my actions. I pointed rigidly towards the docks.

"Load the ships, prepare the boats, get every woman and child to the docks with only food and weapons. If we cannot hold off our enemies, then we must flee to fight another day."

"How long would you have us wait until the ships leave?" Asked Gunnar.

"When they knock down the gates a small force will stay behind to give everyone a chance to escape. We will hold them off until all the ships have left."

"So we go to Valhalla," Gunnar remarked with a wide grin on his face. Eygautr punched Gunnar in the shoulder.

"You're too young, lad. It's my turn and mine alone to go to Valhalla. Rurik waits for me there and I don't intend to disappoint him." I sat there quietly for a moment surrounded by my family and friends. My thoughts dwelled upon my fallen father and that of my brother taken against his will.

"Audan?" asked Valdemar. I blinked rapidly and nodded my head.

"Eygautr will man the palisade with me and the warriors already on the wall. I want the rest of you to ready the ships and our people." Gunnar and Valdemar appeared reluctant to take my orders, no doubt wanting to fight with me until the very end.

"I don't wish to disobey you, brother, but I would prefer to stay here and die with you," replied Gunnar.

"And I," said Uncle Valdemar enthusiastically.

"I am honored by your loyalty and love. My decision has no bearing on your honor. Our people need good warriors to lead them in the harsh days ahead. I would not trust them under the care of anyone else."

"But, Audan, you are Chieftain now. Our people need a leader." I looked down at my muddied feet, watching the rain wash away the blood from my clothes. The crimson liquid flowed down between the planks and below to the trodden earth. I thought for a moment on how I might still serve my people, but I saw no better way than with my blade.

"And that is why I must stay. A Chieftain does not forsake his people." I opened my eyes wide and unblinking stared at my comrades to drive my point. "These are my final orders, brothers. Now go." Gunnar stepped closer and extended his rune covered tattooed hand.

"It has been an honor to know you in this life. I will be honored to see you again in the halls of Valhalla."

"And you, Gunnar," I replied warmly. Valdemar approached next with a look of reluctant pride.

"You're a stubborn son of a bitch, just like your father. I am proud to call you nephew." Valdemar embraced me tightly for a moment and then quickly backed away. "Odin watch over you in your final moments! Die well." They turned away and I watched the pair walk down the steps and head toward the hall to make preparations. Gunnar turned back to give me one final look. I did not move, nor give him any sign of weakness. He needed to know I was resolute in my decision or he may disobey me in an effort to save the village. I turned my back on them and gazed back out to the open field.

"So, it's just you and I then," remarked Eygautr, crossing his arms with sword in hand.

"And nearly one hundred men." Eygautr nodded at my reply and breathed in heavily through his nose.

"Against the Clans." I nodded. "And the Valkyries." I took in a deep breath and nodded again. Silence fell upon us for a moment until Eygautr spoke once more. "And all of hell..." I turned to the short fat man in frustration giving him a sinister look.

"What's your point old man?" I asked.

"I'm just making it clear that we are heavily outnumbered is all. It would be agreeable to get the gods help in this time of need." I sneered at Eygautr's jest.

"Odin has his hands full. We must bear the burden of this on our own." Eygautr kicked the wooden wall in front of us.

"Well, that's just great now isn't it? I hope were not too late for supper in the halls of Valhalla." Just then a loud voice called out.

"Someone's at the gates!" I pulled my axe from the wood plank and rushed to the heavily guarded entrance.

"Who goes there?" a guard commanded.

"It's Hilgrid," a hoarse voice called out. "I carry the fallen Chieftain upon my back." My heart quickened at this surprising news.

"Open the gates!" I ordered. I sprinted down the palisade followed closely by Eygautr. Hilgrid rushed inside carrying a cloaked body on his right shoulder. He knelt to the ground and placed it down gently. Hilgrid remained on one knee, his breath hot against the cold air. The guards slammed the gates shut and the men circled around the cloaked figure.

"I'm…" Hilgrid was utterly bereft of breath. I placed my hand upon his shoulder to calm his nerves.

"Take a moment, brother. Catch your breath." Hilgrid slowed his breathing and took in deeper gusts of air. He exhaled slowly and then looked up at me with his blood shot feral eyes.

"I'm sorry, Audan. I ran here as quickly as I could. The Valkyries! They closed in from all sides." Hilgrid slumped over further to the ground; Eygautr and I rushed to brace his fall. His claw-like fingertips dug into my arm as he tried to hold himself up. "We have failed, brother," Hilgrid said in a soft and remorseful tone. "Hell is unleashed upon these lands. We are all doomed." I looked up at the men who now stared wide eyed and frightened at the sight of Hilgrid; like a hare being hunted by the fox. Without delay, I snapped at them.

"All of you, back to your posts!" Lifting Hilgrid to his feet, I barked once more at those who did not immediately obey my orders. "Freya is coming; she comes for all of us. Hell and Fenrir come for us. Make peace with the gods you favor, for this will be our final battle! And when it is over, I will raise a horn of mead in the halls of Valhalla to each and every one of you!" The men lifted their weapons into the air and cheered proudly before returning to their posts. Soon after, Orbrecht approached covered in blood not of his own and carrying crimson-soaked rags.

"May I be of assistance, brother?" I gripped Hilgrid's shoulders and slowly pushed him towards Orbrecht.

"Take Hilgrid and give him whatever aide he desires. He has done more than his share today." The half beast violently pulled away from me. His hood fell back, revealing his disfigurement to the men of the village. Orbrecht stepped away frightened at the very sight of our brother now transformed by the venom of the Ulfhednar.

"Leave me be! I can take care of myself!" Hilgrid gripped his hood and angrily pulled it back down over his head to cover up his face, storming off to the Seers

11

hovel where he could hide from the world. Orbrecht brought his face close to mine with a worried look upon his brow.

"What in the name of Odin was that?"

"That, my friend, is our brother, Hilgrid." Orbrecht turned his head back towards where Hilgrid had gone and then quickly returned to my gaze.

"Well that's impossible. Hilgrid… Hilgrid is dead." I lowered my head and swaying it from side to side.

"No, no. Not dead, just not precisely Hilgrid." A fist suddenly found its way into my chest. Orbrecht gazed fiercely upon me and for a brief moment I thought he may lunge.

"You told us all he was dead! Who the fuck do you think you are?" I looked up with a stern face and cool temper.

"I apologize, my friend. A lie had to be told to serve a greater good. Hilgrid would have been shunned by our people. I thought it to be the right thing to do and I stand by that decision." Orbrecht pulled a clean rag from his shoulder, wiping the blood from his hands he lifted the soiled linen and threw it at my feet.

"I'm tired of cleaning up your messes." Orbrecht stormed off after Hilgrid. This whole time, the cloaked figure lay below me motionless. I looked down and began to daydream that perhaps if I remove the cloak, father would be alive once more, that maybe Odin could put to good use his sorcery. I bent my knees and knelt down, watching the ripples of rain land in the puddles that surrounded his body. How serene they seemed in all this darkness. I squeezed my eyelids tightly and then blinked rapidly to return to present affairs. Slowly, I reached for the corner of the cloak nearest the bodies face and gently pulled it back. There he was, my father, in all his splendor— with eyes wide open and bereft of the spark that once filled them. I placed the palm of my hand softly against his cheeks, his skin now cold and hard to the touch. Removing my hand quickly, I covered my mouth to conceal a quivering lip.

"I'm sorry, Father," I said as I spoke through my fingers. "I'm sorry I could not be there to save you." A tear streamed down my face and I quickly captured it and wiped away the trail. "Jareth is gone. I have failed you, my father. I have failed you." A shadow over came me and I looked back to see Kenna leaning over me. I rose quickly and gripped her arm, hoping to brace her in her moment of intense grief. In my surprise, she stood there motionless, like a great rune stone from ancient times she did not falter. Her face was calm and she turned her head towards me slowly staring at me with eyes as cold as the glaciers themselves. Placing her hand atop my head, I felt like a child once more and not the man I had become.

"I will tend to your father. Now go. The men need you." I nodded slowly in agreement.

"See to it that he ends up on Valdemar's ship. I'd like to bury him on the island where Uncle's trading post lies." Kenna nodded.

"Very well, son. Gods be with you." Several thralls, young and old quickly lifted the fallen Chieftain above their heads. Kenna gazed upon her lifetime love one last time, leaned in kissing his lips before covering his face back up with the cloak and followed her servants down to the docks where they would load his body on to the ship for his final voyage. I watched silently as he was carried off in the icy rain and did not turn away until he was gone from my sight. I turned my attentions back to the defenses and marched to the guards at the gates.

"You there!" I said sharply to the guards.

"Yes, Audan?" the young warrior replied.

"We're making our final stand. Get everything you can to brace this gate. Do you understand?" The boy nodded quickly. "Good. When the horn blows, return to your post. The enemy will be at our gates shortly." The three guards at the gate quickly dispersed to find what they could. I ran back up the slick steps of the palisades and reunited with Eygautr once more.

"Your father was a great man, Audan. A king amongst Chieftains. He will be greatly missed by all that knew him. I will make sacrifices to Odin in his name." The hurt was too great; no longer wishing to speak of my father I quickly diverted the conversation.

"How many archers?" I asked. Eygautr took in a deep breath and looked down both sides of the wall.

"Nearly fifty," he replied.

"And arrows?"

"Plenty. We could lay waste to two armies if needed." I nodded and looked over the edge of the walls to inspect the random placement of wooden spikes just on the outside. These defenses would not do; Freya and her minions would quickly overwhelm the fortifications. We needed something else, but what? I turned back towards the village to see the chaotic activity below. Women and children scrambled through the muddy paths to the docks escorted by warriors carrying the heaviest of cargo. The many thrall moved livestock, heavy crates, and jars filled with food stores. The ships would be completely weighed down from the combination of ships passengers and supplies. Then, I noticed grey smoke coming from the fires of the blacksmiths workshop. Njord was still hard at work. From the palisades, I could see the fiery coals burning brightly. The flames consumed my gaze entirely and sparked my imagination. "That's it..." I muttered.

"What was that?" Eygautr asked curiously.

"That's it!" I ran down from the palisades like a crazed man and Eygautr chased after until stopping at the base of the steps.

"What is it, Audan?"

"I have an idea. Get the men to pile as much wood in front of the walls as possible!" I yelled excitedly.

"To what end?" the short fat man pressed on to understand my orders.

"We're going to start a fire. The biggest one that Bjorgvin has ever seen!" I sprinted across the courtyard darting past the scurrying village people. I stopped quickly several paces in front of the forge until I lost my footing; my right foot slipped out from under me and I landed in the thick mud on my backside. "Shit!" I exclaimed slowly lifting my head from the ground. A large hand found its way in front of my face; it was Njord covered in ash offering to help me to my feet.

"I thank the gods you are alive, my brother, but you'll do us no good if you slumber with the boars." I reached out and gripped his forearm; Njord lifted me effortlessly to my feet. A lifetime of smithy work had made him unnaturally strong.

"Njord, I need your help. The entire village does." Njord squinted his eyes and seemed perplexed by my request.

"I still have not finished all the arrows you asked for." I looked down at Njord's hands, cracked and bleeding. He had not stopped working since before the battle.

"Your efforts have not gone unnoticed brother. For now I need your coals." He looked back at the roaring fires and again seemed confused by what I was asking of him.

"Of course, Audan, anything for Bjorgvin. But, without the coals how will I work my iron?" I placed my hand on his shoulder and spoke softly.

"We need your coals to start a fire. The icy rain will make it difficult to start one otherwise." Njord nodded.

"Where shall I take them?" I turned and pointed to the gates.

"The men are laying firewood several paces from the palisades. I want a wall of flame when Freya's main force arrives. Get the coals to the top of the palisades. The warriors will drop them from on high when it is time." Njord nodded and gripped my forearm.

"It shall be done, brother!" he quickly grabbed a shovel and ordered the Thralls assisting him at the forge to do the same. They buried their shovel blades deeply in the coals pulling out the hottest of embers. Sparks flew high into the air and they poured them into buckets. A wall of flame emerged. Perhaps Bjorgvin had a chance after all.

* * *

Nightfall came upon us quickly and we staggered torches along the fortified wall. Sada stood at my side with her head leaning against my shoulder as Eygautr paced the walls nervously, his chainmail shifting loudly in the darkness. "Eygautr," I said quietly. He did not reply but merely grunted in my general direction. "Calm yourself." He took three more steps until stopping directly in front of me.

"Do I appear nervous to you?" he said angrily.

"You look like an old fart waiting for a fight," I said only half joking.

"When you reach my age you'll be begging the gods to take you to Valhalla. Every morning I wake up feeling stiff as an oak. The bones in my body crack and ache. The soul is willing, but the body, well, let's just say the body becomes a pile of horse dung." I cracked a smile for the first time that day. "Think it's amusing do you? Well, at least you will go to the never ending halls a beautiful corpse. I'll still be old and the Valkyries will have to take pity on me for an evening romp." Footsteps approached once more from behind; it was Gunnar and Uncle Valdemar.

"The ships are ready; nearly everyone is waiting at the docks to board. Shall we give the order?" The ground suddenly shook underneath foot.

"Did you feel that?" I asked.

"Feel what?" asked Sada. Again, the ground shook.

"Guards! What do you see?" I asked urgently. Torches leaned over the palisade walls lending what light they could to the endless darkness. There was no moon and no stars to speak of. The clouds hung low this evening pinning the fog against our faces. Little would be seen on this most dangerous of nights.

"I see nothing, my lord," the guard replied. A quiet whip in the air sounded overhead and the light of a torch fell from the top of the palisade to the other side of the wall. I heard the shuffle of feet and then a rush of several men to another warrior's aid.

"Arrows! Guard yourselves!" a watchman yelled out. Suddenly, the air was filled with whips and cracks followed by the falling shafts of hundreds of arrows. I ran to the wall with Eygautr at my side. Iron stingers stuck loudly to the wooden palisades; volley after volley they came until the silent death quieted. I stepped out from my hiding place and motioned to the men at the wall.

"Light it up!" Several warriors stood quickly lifting buckets of glowing hot coals and poured them gracefully over the wall. Falling like stars from the sky they sunk deeply into the piles of wood left for them and rapidly lit the oil soaked timber below. Almost instantly heat grew to flame. The valley floor lit quickly and the tree line could now be plainly seen, *but where was the enemy?* I stood upright and gazed upon the dark wood that appeared vacant. In my frustration I gritted my teeth and pounded my fist against the wall.

"Why do they wait?" Eygautr asked.

"Freya!" I yelled violently as I ran to the very top of the palisade. "Freya! Come and get me, you cowardly bitch! Stop playing games. I'm ready for you!" I lifted my axe high above head gripping the handle tightly. A rush of hot air streamed across my face and in the distance a pair of giant glowing orbs appeared.

"In the name of Odin..." Eygautr muttered. A great and powerful howl erupted from the beast that stood beyond the walls. A beast that would consume us all. My fury at the loss of my father and the capture of my brother had all but taken over; in spite of this monster I beat my chest wildly with the broad side of my axe and lifted it into the air once more. The beast dug at the group with its terrible claws and snapped madly with its fangs.

"Fenrir! Fenrir, come for me!"

Two
The Fall

A great roar erupted from the colossal Fenrir as he took another step forward with his massive paws outside the dark wood. Glowing haunting eyes emerged out of the forest and darted the spaces between the trees as they moved in front of the great wolf forming a solid battle line. My nose caught the offensive stench of rotting flesh that carried on the wind, and I gagged briefly and now there was no doubting that the Draugr took up the center line. The decrepit warriors held their stance firmly and showed no sign of advancing on our village. Eygautr slapped me on the shoulder, spitting on the ground and taking a large step forward with his belly against the palisade.

"Archers ready your bows!" commanded Eygautr through his beard. Bows were quickly raised in the air with arrows nocked and strings drawn to the rear. A deafening silence fell over the valley floor below until the march of footsteps could be heard coming from the right flank of Freya's main force. Great shadows that were light of foot emerged, reflecting the light off the wall of flame. Mounted warriors placed themselves at the front of this formation and stopped at the center.

"Death to Bjorgvin! Death to Audan, son of the coward Rurik!" A voice called out. His insult enraged me, causing my blood to boil but I did all in my power to hold my temper for the fight to come. The warriors of the right flank cheered and a clamor of arms erupted in the sky. A mounted warrior raised his arm and silence came upon the field once more and again the sound of footsteps caught my ear. This time it was on the left flank; a much smaller mass of warriors emerged in a meager and loose formation. They appeared leaderless but none the less showed up for a fight. A low growl emerged from behind me, a cloaked figure stood close by with a small hand axe ready in each hand.

"Hilgrid?" I asked curiously. He turned his gaze upon me and nodded.

"I am here, brother. Let's finish what we started. We must slay these cowards where they stand or send them running back to hell." I nodded in agreement and turned to Sada who stood fearlessly at my side.

"What is it, my love?" she asked.

"Get to the ships as fast as you can, help everyone onboard and do not turn back. The battle will begin soon and I will not have you here to witness it." My love looked up at me with deep and great sorrow in her eyes.

"You're not coming, are you?" I reluctantly shook my head knowing full well the heartache my answer would cause. "So this is where I leave you?" I could not hold back my sadness but the battle was near and I needed to be strong if we were to hold off our enemies long enough for our loved ones to escape.

"I don't, I don't have the words..." Sada placed her fingers gently against my lips tracing my mouth until she reached the corner. She gripped my beard and pulled my face down to hers.

"You don't have to." She leaned in and pressed her lips heavy against mine. She tasted of spring and smelt like the blossoms on a warm summer's day. I pulled my face from hers and embraced her tightly one last time. She leaned in to my ear gently and whispered, "Save a place for me in Valhalla, my love..." I nodded and squeezed her body all the more.

"Go. Take care of my mother for me. See to it that my father receives the burial he deserves." Sada slowly began to back away, running her fingers across my body. Her feet seemed heavy as if stones had been tied to them. It was clear she did not wish to leave my side, nor I hers.

"I will. I love you, Audan." Tears ran down her face and despite the utter sadness I felt inside I could not bring myself to cry in this moment. Like a stone, I stood strong, unmoving, the way I wanted her to remember me, a true and noble warrior of Odin.

"I love you Sada." Another volley of arrows came screeching past and without ducking for cover I stood there watching my love run back to the docks, her long braid bouncing off her back in the wind. I felt the air whip past the back of my neck and lifted my hand to rub the feeling away. It was wet and warm, I pulled my hand in front of my face to see it covered in blood; a stinger had grazed me from behind leaving its gentle kiss of death.

"What are you doing boy?" yelled Eygautr, as he pulled me down by my belt. "You want to get yourself killed already? We need fighting men, not corpses!" The volley ceased once more and I stood upright to observe the battlefield. The Draugr remained at the center, at both flanks what remained of the clans, Fenrir at the rear, and the Valkyries suspended above. A fearsome scream erupted from the skies and at the center of the formation another Valkyrie emerged with arms wide open. It was the worst of them all, the bringer of death and chaos, Freya.

"Audan!" she called out in a fury. The skies above erupted with lightning and the rain began to fall heavy atop our heads. "Audan, are you still alive?" I climbed to the very top of the palisades swinging my axe back and forth in the air to get her attention. It was time to draw her forces in for a fight. The hail of arrows would only whittle away at our small band of warriors.

"Where's my brother, you senseless bitch?" Freya flapped her midnight black wings faster and leaned forward pointing her steel at me.

"Your brother is in hell along with your father. Tonight, I will drink from your skull and feed your blood to that sweet little woman of yours! Your doom is upon you, Audan! Upon you all! Ragnarok is approaching!" I pointed my bearded axe toward Freya and her minions, the light from the fires shining brightly from the polished blade.

"Come and get it!" A terrifying sound erupted from the formation of the Valkyries above. The center line of undead warriors moved forward at a steady march but Fenrir remained in place at the rear. Freya did not appear willing to yet sacrifice her mortal warriors; instead, she unleashed the rotting corpses upon us. Eygautr stood now appearing taller than ever.

"Enough of this shit! Archers make ready!" Bows rose quickly to the air, the glint of bolt tips hinted at the death that would follow their release.

"Hold!" I called out. Eygautr gave me a perplexed look. "You must take off their heads. Arrows will not slow them. Focus the archers on the clans." Eygautr nodded and quickly barked out my orders.

"Archers aim for the flanks! Do not loose your arrows upon the Draugr." He turned about, motioning to the band of warriors below in the village center. "I need swords and axes on the walls, get the fuck up here or by the gods we will all perish on this day." Like a stampede of wild beast, warriors rushed up the steps to line the tops of the walls. Shields of every color and design ran past me in a blur that resembled the telling of the Bifrost Bridge, finding a place in front of the archers. As the demon spawn of Freya approached, their horrific appearance became even more apparent to the men on the wall; fear, it seemed, was beginning to settle in to their hearts and heads. I raised my axe and called out to rally the men and assuage those fears.

"Men of Bjorgvin! Men of Bjorgvin! Hear me now!" The warriors turned their heads away from the approaching corpses and focused in on me. "Do not despair on this day. Freya descends upon us but Valhalla is not on her side. We, the brave men of Bjorgvin, do not just fight for the people, our home. We fight, we fight for Odin, we fight for Valhalla!" The men cheered smacking their weapons loudly against their shields. I peered over the soaked palisades and saw the Draugr had reached the wall of flame below. "Men of Bjorgvin, earn your place in Valhalla on this day! Fight with honor! Fight with courage in your hearts! There is nothing they can do this day to defeat us for we are sons of Odin!" Passing the wall of flame, the beasts caught fire but managed to clear small paths through the many barriers we had left for them. Engulfed in fire, they reached the bottom of the palisade and began to pile on top of one another. I shook my head and fixated my eyes on the wall waiting for the first of the Draugr to ascend to the top. "Sons of Odin, what makes the grass grow and the rivers flow?" The warriors replied in unison yelling loud enough for all of Asgard and the Aesir to hear.

"Blood, blood, blood!" The ground shook under our war cries and the air around us felt electric. My eyes fixated forward, unmoving, waiting for the slightest presence of my enemy to appear.

"And how do we get blood?" I called out with great fury.

"Kill, kill, kill!" The first of the Draugr ascended to the top of the palisades, head and hands engulfed in flame. Warriors descended upon him with many blades decapitating him and sending his fiery corpse down to his decrepit brothers below.

"For glory!" Many more monsters rose to the top of the wall, hacking and slashing with their rusted and pitted blades. I rushed to the center wall to aide my brothers where most of the Draugr amassed. A shield painted with a skull appeared in front of me and I pushed the end of my bearded axe into it to knock the beast down. A small axe came over the shield glancing my axe handle, knocking it away. I pulled my axe higher and hooked the top of the shield pulling it to the side. The creature tried to pull his shield back to the front and screamed furiously in frustration until Eygautr struck at an angle with his sword on the right. I unhooked the axe, swung around over my head and struck the opposite side of the beast's neck, taking his head clean off. Dark blood spattered our faces and Eygautr laughed wildly.

"Keep them off the walls. They must not gain a foot hold!" A horn bellowed loudly from on high and the right flank of Freya's forces began to march forward.

"Now, Eygautr! To the archers!" Eygautr stepped back from the wall to command the line of archers. He stood rigid in his position despite blades and shields swinging just inches from him.

"Archers! Archers! The right flank!" Eygautr took another step back from the bloody fight to command the arrows. Bows rose skyward once more. "Make ready!" Eygautr lifted his sword high into the air. "Loose!" The snap of bow strings sent the air around us rushing past. Arrows screamed and shrieked wildly towards the sky, reaching their highest point until arcing downward for their final death fall. I watched with great anticipation as the stingers descended against the enemies of my father. The arrows hit their mark as the once orderly mass began to falter and their ranks became splintered. The groans and screams of injured men echoed against the rocky hills sending a pleasing chill down my spine. Their once-solid battle line had become porous and I sought to send them all to their demise.

"Again!" I urged in wicked fury. As the bodies piled up outside the walls my actions and words felt like fire and I wished to unleash it upon everything that stood in my way.

"Make ready!" Eygautr commanded gallantly. The right flank of mortal warriors increased their speed hoping to avoid the next volley. I watched the arrow tips closely waiting for their release. "Loose!" Eygautr called out. The arrows shrieked skyward, falling rapidly on our adversaries. The warriors at the center of the right flank held ranks holding shields above their heads; they survived. Some warriors on the edges of the formation tried to outrun the hail and quickly found themselves pinned to the ground to bleed on the earth. My eye caught the glimpse of one bearded warrior in particular. An arrow had pierced his thigh, knocking him to the ground. As he stood, another arrow cracked into his skull sending him face first into the mud. I laughed aloud at this man's terrible fate, feeling warmed at his failure.

"Audan!" Eygautr called out in a strained voice. "The walls! The walls, Audan!" Draugr now covered every segment of the wall, clawing their way to the top and finally making it to the other side. Several of our fighters began to falter under their blades but for every one of our men who made their way to Valhalla we sent back at least ten of the rotting corpses to hell. I rushed to aid Eygautr when an unfamiliar figure on the battlefield rushed past me like lightning along the wall. Wearing a thick dark leather apron and an iron helm, Njord the blacksmith ran.

"For Brokkr!" he cried out. Njord lifted his arms high into the air with heavy hammers in each hand and mercilessly fell them upon his victims, crushing their heads. He worked the line vigorously even jumping in front of other warriors until a portion of the wall had cleared of enemy combatants. Covered in murky blood, he wiped it from his eyes and shouted a war cry up to the heavens then rushed to the aid of a beleaguered warrior who lay prostrate beneath a Draugr wielding a dull weapon. The monster swung downward over and over again, striking the Viking warrior's shield and preventing him from standing to fight. Njord threw one of his hammers, hitting the Draugr in the back. He spun round quickly to find Njord leaping towards him and striking him square in the head. Dazed, the beast fell and Njord continued his assault, hitting relentlessly until his enemies blade slipped from hand. The warrior blacksmith had left his mark amongst the veteran fighters. He lowered his tattooed arm and opened his hand lifting the warrior upright.

"Well done, Njord!" I called out. He nodded and returned to the fight. Another horn called out from above and now the left flank advanced as well. Freya had nearly committed all her forces to battle, all except the Valkyries and Fenrir.

"Archers!" Eygautr was still plenty in the fight and prepared to give the order to decimate the last of our rival clans. "Make ready!" A Draugr reached the top of the wall and leapt for Eygautr, swinging a sword across the fat man's chest. Eygautr fell, bracing himself with one arm; I feared him mortally wounded. The corpse prepared to deliver the final blow when I took off his arm at the elbow. He stared at his hacked limb that twitched on the floor boards and slowly turned his head charging towards me with a terrible scream. Too close to strike down, I pushed him back with the point of my axe, took a step back and swung down with both hands giving a mighty blow. The blade cut deep into his shoulder cutting his collar bone in half. My blade would not release from his rotting carcass so I kicked him to the ground to free it. With my axe released, I swung again landing the blade on the top half of his skull; the contents of which spilled out to the earth covering the walkway beneath.

"Foul beasts." I ran to the short fat man and knelt next to him. "Eygautr, Eygautr! Are you well, old friend?" He sat up slowly, laughing with a hoarse voice and coughing. Slipping his hand into the cut of his crimson tunic he revealed the bright chain mail that lay beneath. The blow of the blade had knocked the air from his chest but had not pierced his flesh.

"I always hated wearing mail; it's too damn heavy." He laughed again and I helped him to his feet.

"Finish your order, old man." Eygautr lifted his sword. "Archers, ready!" Without delay, he lowered his sword. "Loose!" The sweet melody of death rang out in the sky above and fell to the left flank. Already a sparse and loose formation, their numbers quickly thinned.

"Do you see that, brothers? They flee! Steinars puppets are no more!" Those that still drew breath ran back for the tree line to make their way through the mountains. The Valkyrie's released their terrifying shriek and I saw the unmoving beast Fenrir leap towards the retreating troops, causing the earth to tremble beneath his paws. He roared, barked, and snapped viciously at the retreating men. The fleeing forces stopped in their place. Fenrir reached down with his massive jaws gripping a spearman in his jaws and ripped him in half, sending half of his body flying into the formation. A line of Draugr moved in front of Fenrir with shield and spear pushing the deserters forward back toward the battle. The warriors reluctantly turned back around and marched slowly towards the walls of Bjorgvin with spear tips at their backs. They would die a coward's death this day.

Just then I heard the countless screams of Bjorgvin warriors along the right side of the wall. The mortal warriors had at long last made their ascent and taken some ground along the palisade thanks to the piled up remnants of Draugr beneath their feet. Our warriors dashed headfirst but were held back by a line of well-placed spears. An old man with long grey hair and beard burst forth through the spears swinging axes wildly. He struck four of our warriors before a sword pierced his belly and sent him falling into the courtyard. Arrows struck the spearmen and the warriors who lined up behind them. I looked back to see Eygautr had pulled the archers down from the palisades and began forming warriors just on the other side of the gate. Several fighters held firm atop the palisade but the spearmen fell to their deaths and I stepped forward to clear the walkway. A man with sword and shield embossed with a raven approached quickly thrusting his blade forward. I knocked it to the side with my axe handle and gripped his shield with my axe pulling it from his grasp. The shocked warrior, now bereft of his defenses, lunged forward and found himself pinned to the palisade floor by axe, spear, and sword. He gripped several of the blades in his gut lifting his head upward. A river of blood shot out from his mouth and the warrior's head fell to the floor. The last of the warriors behind him were killed by the archers below. The palisade had been cleared.

"Victory is ours!" a young warrior called out with axe and shield in the air. A spear pierced him through the back with the tip protruding through his chest. His tunic quickly turned the color red and a shadow descended gripping the man by the shoulders and throwing him down from the walls.

"Valkyries! Protect yourselves!" Njord yelled out. The winged banshees plummeted downward towards the palisades. One by one the warriors atop the wall fought back against claw and fang. Hilgrid lifted a spear from the group and stood atop the wooden pikes.

"Here! Here!" he taunted bravely. A Valkyrie heard his call and flew down towards him. Faster and faster she came until her face was nothing but blur and shadow. Just before reaching Hilgrid, he raised the spear clipping the wing of the corpse goddess and sending her rolling downward and smashing into an old barn house. Hilgrid turned and ushered the other warriors down from the palisades. I too turned away and jumped down as the wind rushed overhead. A Valkyrie had narrowly missed me and returned to her kin outside the walls. I quickly reunited with Eygautr just opposite the main gate.

"Shield wall!" I commanded. The men were exhausted but ready to make their final stand. I looked to the dock and noticed the last of the boats had not yet left and it was on us to ensure they made good their escape. "Close ranks! Close ranks! Keep it tight." The warriors in front and behind me closed in tightly and I peered through our defense at the front gate. Fire now consumed the palisade walls entirely. The black smoke prevented us from seeing anything above or beyond. The battlefield became silent and so we waited for our enemies to come for us. Sweat stung my eyes and I wiped it from my brow. I loosened the grip from my axe to let the palm of my hand cool and the sweat dry. Then, the ground shuddered beneath our feet. My blood ran cold sending a chill crawling up my spine. The ground shook again and I watched the muddy puddles in front of me as ripples broke the surface. No doubt the footsteps of the realm eater, the destroyer of souls, Fenrir was coming to finish us off.

"This is it, young man. I will see you again in the halls of the honored slain." A deafening crash erupted at the front gate sending a cloud of dust in its wake. One of the massive gate doors flew past, knocking down a fish hut behind us. Dirt flew into my eyes and I blinked rapidly, wiping my face against my shoulder. I looked back up through the shield wall only to see the cloud of earth and so we waited with bated breath. The ground trembled once more and now the air around us seemed to quiver until silence fell upon us. A quiet growl began to grow louder, an unnerving and sinister sound that made the hairs on a man's arms stand upright. I looked upward as a massive shadow caught my eye. The dark image, nearly as wide as the gate entry, lowered itself and opened its glowing yellow eyes. Several of the men quietly gasped and readjusted their grips upon their weapons now knowing the terror that was about to unfold. The black wolf took a step forward shaking the ground beneath foot. More dark figures appeared under Fenrir, walking between his legs and forward into a loose formation.

"Audan," a gentle voice called out. "Are you still alive, Audan?" Emerging from the smoke and dust, Freya strutted about clad in shining plate armor. "Ah," she said as she fixated her gaze upon us. "Men of Bjorgvin, a once proud people fighting for your lands and freedom, you now huddle behind your shields like children hiding from their angry parents." She stepped further forward flanked by her monstrous Valkyrie horde that slowly transformed from their ghoulish forms back into their preferred goddess-like states. "Is your leader amongst you? Audan? Or does he lay in ruin with the rest of your village?" In anger I lowered my shield, stepping outside of the formation. Shields quickly closed behind me as I took a cautious stance in front of our enemy.

"I am here, Freya!" I said boldly. Freya cracked a crooked smile as she leaned her head to one side.

"You are foolish to leave the protection of your shields, Audan." Several Valkyries on the flanks raised their bows ready to loose their arrows upon me.

"Who is the greater fool? The man who defends his people or the goddess who turned her allegiance from Odin?" Freya gracefully lifted her arm into the air pressing two of her fingers together.

"With the snap of my fingers I could end your life." I took one half-step forward and drew in air, sticking my chest outward in defiance.

"So do it! Let loose your arrows! End this, Freya. My people have suffered enough." Freya lowered her hand back to her side placing it on her hip.

"Well, where would be the fun in that, Audan? You have made it this far in the game; perhaps, you should see the ending?" I lowered my axe in frustration. Freya appeared to be in a boasting mood and I longed for her to bleed like a river under my blade.

"What ending, Freya?" I extended my arms outward, gesturing to the destruction of Bjorgvin. "Is this what you want? Death? There is no ending here where you succeed, Freya. You have fought but one village, Bjorgvin, and look at the toll your forces have taken. All of Midgard will turn against you and end your reign of terror. Odin will return with all the Asgardian forces and wipe you from existence." Freya placed her hand on her stomach and a dark and sinister laugh erupted forth.

"Odin? The old man with one eye? Do you really think he will have a chance at stopping me? This world will be consumed in fire and ash choking the very life from your kind. The elementals will walk the earth once more as they did in ancient times." The fires at the walls grew higher, ash and embers flew past my face; it appeared as if she was right, as if the whole world was doomed.

"Who is it, Freya? You are not all powerful! Who is the master that controls the puppet?" She lifted her sword and rested the blade on her shoulders.

"Clever as always, Audan. No, I am not the creator of this plot but I serve its purpose fervently. If you had listened to me in the beginning you to could have joined me, but now it's too late. You will suffer the same fate as so many brave men."

"Tell me, Freya, who is it!" I furiously demanded.

"All will be revealed my love. In due course…"

"What about my brother? What have you done with Jareth?"

"He is my guest, for now. However, if he acts in a manner that displeases me, I will cut off his head and fashion his skull into a cup." Tired of her threats I raised my shield and slowly stepped back into the formation.

"Finish this, Freya. I grow weary of your games." The goddess turned away walking towards her monster, Fenrir. She reached upward gripping the bottom of his chin she began to stroke his dark fur back and forth ever so gently.

"Fenrir, my sweet. Kill the people of Bjorgvin, swallow them whole, every last one of them. Save Audan for me. He still needs to watch me kill his woman and wretched mother." Fenrir lifted himself upward and slowly opened his mouth; growling as he made his way towards us. I looked back to see the last of the ships had left and the water's edge just behind us. We had no room to maneuver.

The only way out was forward, forward into the fangs of the beast. Fenrir, the world eater, would now bare down upon us with all the fury of hell.

"Stand fast, boys! We're not going to let this mutt stop us!" Eygautr yelled. I began chanting at the top of my lungs and the men joined in.

"Hah, hah, hah, hah, hah, hah, hah, hah, hah!" Our warriors' call only seemed to enrage the beast further. Fenrir slowly lowered his head fixating his deathly gaze upon us. I caught my reflection in his eye. Fenrir had focused on me. He blinked his massive eyes slowly, lifted his enormous head and let out a blood curdling howl that made my bones ache. The sound was so deafening that I could only hear the ringing in my ears.

He charged, tooth and claw descending upon us, but we held firm within the shield wall. We cried out furiously and extended our weapons forward as far as we could. The beast collided with our shields and blades, sending a great and terrible din echoing throughout the village. Falling back, I saw our center line folding, spear, axe, shield and sword flew about as warriors were knocked off their feet. The flanks of the lines collapsed on Fenrir and attacked his sides feverishly. With shield still in hand I looked for my axe and found it just beyond my reach. I leaned over to grab it when a dark shadow came over me. The sheer weight of the thing was all too apparent; Fenrir had placed his paw on top of me. No doubt to keep me from the fight and save my fate for his master. Using both arms, I pushed against his immense foot and he closed his claws around me digging into the dirt. I stopped fighting for a moment and witnessed the carnage in front of me.

Fenrir was bleeding from all sides, but despite his wounds, he overwhelmed the battle field. Warriors rushed in and out, hacking wildly at the wolf's flesh. Fenrir snapped and bit tearing men in half and throwing their parts all about. A warm and wet feeling came over my arms and back as a river of blood piled up from the docks. A warrior that had been knocked down rushed past me with spear in hand. Fenrir swiped at him with his other paw, knocking him unconscious in front of me. Then, my eyes fixated on the blade of a seax firmly tucked into the warrior's brown leather belt. I stretched out my left hand, my fingertips barely touching the pommel of the seax. With every last bit of strength, I breathed outward and reached for the handle stretching as far as I could and just reached it. Gripping it firmly, I pulled the blade from its holding place. In desperation I reached back with both arms gripping the blade tightly and yelled as I buried it into the beast's foot.

"Valhalla!" The seax plunged deep to the hilt and the wolf monster swiftly pulled up his foot in sheer agony with his blood trickling down on me. Fenrir, the world eater, wailed and cried in great pain. Without hesitation, I rolled my body to the right, grabbing my bearded axe and stood to my feet. Fenrir took a weak step backward, hobbling as his did so. Eygautr began swinging his sword in a circle at the center of the formation.

"Shield wall!" commanded Eygautr. "Get back in line! The beast bleeds! The world eater bleeds!" I ran towards the hasty defense and joined my brothers. With Eygautr at my left and Njord at my right, we held firm.

"Loose!" I heard a woman's voice call out. The Valkyries began taking aim at us, intending to keep our formation from moving forward. The stingers landed heavy against our shields, some of the arrow heads even piercing through our defenses, barely missing our bodies. Fenrir took a step forward under the cover of arrows and swiped out our lines. His paw was met by a dozen blades and again the Valkyries pinned us down with a hail of arrow fire.

"We can't hold out like this much longer," Njord cried out. "If we do nothing, they are going to cut us down one by one." A hand gripped my shoulder from behind and I gazed upon our very own Ulfhednar warrior.

"I have an idea," said Hilgrid. "When I give the signal, place your shields atop your heads. Do you understand?" Eygautr, Njord and I nodded and quickly returned our attentions to the front of the line. Fenrir swiped at us again and leaned in sideways with his jaws open. A spear flew forward over my head, striking the monster's tongue. Fenrir yelled again and bit down on the shaft snapping it in half.

"Now!" Hilgrid cried out. I lifted my shield over my head with my brothers; Hilgrid leapt atop our defenses and jumped from our shields landing on the snout of Fenrir. With an axe in each hard he buried them into Fenrir's cheeks and blocked his eyes from sight. My face lit up with excitement and I cheered our brother on in his assault.

"You mad bastard!" I yelled excitedly. Fenrir was furious and swung his body about uncontrollably trying to throw off Hilgrid. He jumped in the air and twisted his body, knocking down most of the line of Valkyries with his tail behind him. Smoke, dirt and ash flew all around. The Valkyries lifted themselves from the ground and took to the air above the melee. Freya pointed her sword towards us and let out a terrifying scream.

"Finish them!" The corpse goddesses descended with their blades drawn, falling at great speed. We braced for the impact behind our shields when without warning I heard the air above our heads whip and snap. Looking upward, I saw thin, dark shadows gracefully hurl themselves towards our foes planting stingers deeply into their flesh. I spun back to see a massive shadow pushing its way towards the docks through the thick fog.

"Again!" a familiar voice called out. The snap of bow strings could now be clearly heard and a Drakkar emerged like a serpent from the mists. "Blood, glory, and Valhalla!" It was Uncle Valdemar! The front prow of the ship quickly turned to the port side with its starboard side lined with archers. A relentless barrage of stingers was unleashed, the likes of which the remaining Valkyries were not ready to confront. "What are you waiting for? Get aboard, lads, before that overgrown dog sinks us!"

"Back up!" Eygautr commanded. With our shield wall intact, the remaining twelve warriors walked backward slowly down the dock towards the Drakkar.

"No! Don't let them escape!" From the air archer Valkyries drew their bows and worked their strings in a fever.

"Withdraw to the ship! Withdraw!" One by one, the men turned about, throwing their shields over their backs and jumping the gap from the dock to the Drakkar. Eygautr, Njord, and I waited until the others had boarded.

"Njord, go brother! Run!" Njord turned quickly lifting his shield over the back of his head just as an arrow buried itself in the wood planking. I heard him land heavily on the ship and so I nudged Eygautr with my shoulder. "Go, old man!" Without delay, Eygautr turned and ran.

"Come on, you fat fuck! Jump!" yelled Valdemar. I looked back to see Eygautr jump and land his belly against the rail of the ship. Valdemar and two other men reached over to pick him up and dragged him into the ship by the back of his leather belt. I turned my gaze back over my shield to see Hilgrid still holding on for dear life against the face of Fenrir.

"Audan!" Eygautr yelled. "What are you waiting for?"

"I won't leave Hilgrid behind!"

"We can't save him! Now, let's go!" Eygautr urged.

"No!" I ran forward under a hail of arrow fire until I was directly under Fenrir. I slung my shield on my back, gripped my axe with both hands as I swung it behind my body and dropped the blade with all my fury into the beast's ankle. Fenrir's weight buckled under the pain and he fell to the ground. "Hilgrid, jump!

Jump, Hilgrid!" Our Ulfhednar friend leapt and rolled to the ground. I rushed to him and picked him up off the earth and pulled him towards the Drakkar. I looked ahead and saw our brothers gesturing us to come to the ship. Arrow heads followed closely to our footsteps, landing behind us until we reached the edge of the dock and leapt. As I hung in the air something cold and sharp tapped me on the back. My legs went cold and I landed hard against the deck of the ship. Hands gripped my shoulder and lifted me upright.

"Are you alright, lad?" asked Valdemar. I stood, gazing down the docks to see Fenrir hobbling towards the edge barking and snapping in a fit.

"Push off!" Valdemar commanded to the men on the oars. Without delay, we drifted back into the fjord and paddled away from Bjorgvin. I stumbled and fell down to my knee. I looked up at my kin that surrounded me and watched as their faces turned dark. The weight of the world fell upon my shoulders and the cold abyss took me under.

"Audan!"

Three
A Most Dangerous Voyage

Gulls...

Gulls called loudly overhead, crying and yelling down at me. I felt warm and safe in this shadowy place and cared not to leave it, but something beckoned to me to wake and be present in this very moment. I gradually opened my eyes and the light painfully flooded my skull. I closed my eyes quickly and then began to gradually open them again. Lying on my side against the cold, hard wooden deck I saw the base of the mast in front of me. The sound of rushing water filled my ears and was suddenly all around. My lips felt dry and coarse so I stuck my tongue out to wet them; the overwhelming taste of sea salt awoke the senses as I blinked rapidly. Placing my hand on the deck of the ship I pushed myself up quickly but was stopped by the rushing and overwhelming pain on the right side of my upper back. I gritted my teeth and stopped moving about to calm whatever this terrible discomfort was.

"Slow..." a gentle voice called out. "Take it slow, nephew. You're lucky, the arrow stopped against your shoulder blade. A few more inches to the left and you would be a beautiful corpse. You'd be drinking in the great halls with your father and he'd be blaming me for not keeping a better watch over you." I rubbed my face coarsely to wipe away the sleep and scratched at my head that itched terribly from dried sea salt. My entire body ached, my arms, back, and neck popped and cracked at every move. Valdemar sat just across from me leaning comfortably into the hull of the Drakkar.

"How long have I been under, uncle?" Valdemar reached for a wooden mug and handed it to me. Grasping it eagerly I looked down at the contents of the cup and to my dismay saw water instead of golden mead. I cared not for the plainness of water at the moment and wanted something to dull the pain.

"Drink, nephew," Valdemar urged. "You need to regain your strength if you are to be of use to us. The crossing to Fani is known to be a treacherous one and we will need more men at the oars." I lifted the mug and took a small sip to wash the salt away. As my dry lips and the back of my throat were wetted by the drink, a sudden thirst came over me and I quickly finished what was left. Dropping the mug in front of me, I lifted my right arm and felt a terrible burning shock travel throughout my back. The stinger had done a fair bit of harm and so I lowered my right arm and used my left to wipe away the water that was falling down my beard. Gazing upward at my weary-looking uncle, I asked again.

"How long have I been asleep, uncle?" Valdemar pulled at his beard and gave me a warm look as he shuffled his body closer to mine.

"Nearly a day. You had us all worried when you took on a fever, but when the sun came up the fever broke. Hilgrid kept a diligent watch over you until your head cooled. He now slumbers peacefully. Perhaps I should be thanking Sol for bestowing these blessings upon you and ridding you of your ailment. You were pale, covered in sweat, but like magic, the rising of the sun healed you."

I opened my eyes wide in amazement. "An entire day? Where are we?"

Valdemar gently removed a soaked wool cap from his head and scratched his hair vigorously. He looked up at the position of the sun through his fingertips and then plotted the horizon carefully with his arm. He lowered his arms and then raised them once more to take another measurement. He tugged his beard and nodded his head several times gazing out towards the sun.

"I'd say about half a day's sail from the Isle of Fani, if the seas are in our favor that is. Perhaps it's time for you to give an offering to one of your friends on high. I'm sure Aegir would honor anything you have to sacrifice to the depths below. He may even steer the tides for us." I shook my head in disagreement as I looked upward through my dirty blond hair.

"I don't believe it works that way, uncle. The gods do not grant favors upon a request. Nor do they always show in our times of need. Rather they do what they can, in their own time. Even great feats of bravery do not always attract their gaze." Valdemar rolled his eyes in frustration.

"Well, that's a shame then, isn't it? A damn shame! We fight off the demons and Odin won't even fart to change the wind. In any case, once we reach the trading post, we can have a proper ceremony for Rurik. Your father, my beloved brother, deserves only the very best. There will be song, dance, sacrifices and a roaring fire. We shall feast for days and make the gods envious of this mans life." Valdemar stood and approached me uncomfortably close. "Now, then, let's have a look at that bandage." He laid me back down against the deck, rolled me higher up on my side and I felt the cloth strip on my back being gradually pulled from my skin. "Ah, good! The wound is clean. There does not appear to be any disease to speak of."

He placed the cloth back in its place and allowed me to sit up again.

"In a few weeks, you should feel like yourself once more. Just don't go fighting Fenrir any time soon. If you tear the wound open it may become diseased without the proper care." My clouded mind began to clear itself of the fog and just the mention of his name, Fenrir, brought the terrible glowing eyes to the fore front of my thoughts. It all seemed like a dream but the world-eater was very real indeed. His claws had ripped the lives away from many of my people and his fangs were stained with the blood of legions of Norse warriors. I knew in my heart that the beast would return to finish what he had started. Fenrir would run wild in the lands of Midgard killing more and more. His bloodlust would only grow with each soul he devoured. Freya would march the beast to the very heart of Midgard, to the hall of kings itself and set it ablaze. The destruction of Bjorgvin would no doubt bring her greater control along the coast and instill fear in any who would dare oppose her.

"Fenrir?" I asked. "What happened to the wolf?" Valdemar placed his cap back on and leaned back gently against the mast with his legs crossed.

"After you slipped away, the mutt came towards us but he was badly wounded and could not close in before we pushed off from the dock. Those bitch Valkyries tried to drop a few more arrows on us, but they seemed more concerned with tending to their dog and gave up their chase. If not for Hilgrid I think the lot of you would have been torn to pieces before we got there. He's a brave man; brave but cursed by the poison of the Ulfhednar." I lamented at Hilgrid's new found torment, to live his life in this manner. My only hope was that he may find his abilities a strength, and not the curse everyone thought it was.

"I told you to sail on. What made you turn back for us? Fenrir could have killed you all. Why risk so much?" Valdemar smiled and gazed downward at the soaked decks.

He placed his hand on my forearm.

"I went many years at my trading post without anyone to call kin. Then, one day you ploughed your ship onto my lonely shores. That day I reclaimed a brother, a sister-in- law, and two handsome nephews to call family. The sun shined brightly that day like none before it, but now my brother is slain and my nephew Jareth is missing. I could not bear to suffer the loss of another of my kin, not while I still had it in me to save them. If we are going to survive whatever this is, we will need to stick together and keep our blades sharp." I slowly extended my left arm and placed it on Valdemar's shoulder patting it roughly several times.

"I am grateful to you, uncle. I shall never forget what you have done for us. Not just for our family but for the people of Bjorgvin. Our people will know your name and we will sing of your deeds in every hall we visit." Valdemar shrugged his shoulders and returned a wide, crooked smile.

"You would have done the same thing had our fates been traded. Had your father still been around it would have been you on that ship while I stood at the gates with Rurik. The gods smiled on us this day. Many warriors went willingly to Valhalla and some of us survived to find our glory another day."

"And what of Freya?" Uncle's face turned bitter and angry at the name. He gazed on the horizon once more, seeming cautious about his words that would carry on the wind.

"Freya! A piece of work that one is. Of all the gods and goddesses I never thought that Freya would be the one to unleash her fury on the likes of us. Midgard is full of wicked people, but I would not count our household amongst them." I nodded slowly and turned my gaze to the deck.

"Nor would I, uncle. Nor would I." Valdemar leaned forward and tapped my chest lightly with two of his fingers.

"So, then, tell me, dear nephew. What did you do to vex a goddess so? What makes her hate for our kin with such fervor that she would gather the local clans against us?" I smirked and laughed quietly under my breath. I pondered whether to tell Valdemar the short or long tale of Freya. With all my heart, I hated that creature but in some ways I admired her more human traits.

"I made the mistake of believing that all gods had the best of intentions for men. That just because they are gods that we could not question their motivations." Valdemar scooted closer to me, tucking his shoulder gently into mine with a shit-eating grin on his face.

"And what were her intentions, nephew?" He gazed at me with wide eyes, no doubt waiting to be given the story of a lifetime.

"Freya desires to sit at the throne of Odin in his place. She seeks to usurp him by any means necessary. Helheim and Folkvangr already reside under her control. Midgard has been set in her gaze for some time now. Once she rules the three realms entirely, she should have all the power she needs to move on the other five and conquer them." Valdemar leaned back and did not speak for several moments. His eyes bounced back and forth in his skull, perhaps trying to understand what I had told him.

"And what was your role in all of this? Why does she hate you so? Surely, you did something to offend her? Do the gods not favor those who love them and condemn those who do not?" I could feel the blood rush to my cheeks and I tried as best I could to conceal the blush upon my face.

"Freya took a fondness to me, uncle. Odin knows I gave her reason to think I cared for her, but I would not turn on the wanderer nor Sada. I betrayed Freya when I learned of her terrible plans for Midgard." Valdemar eyes opened wide in shock, his mouth hung open as if he waited for the flies to land.

"You mean to tell me you slept with a goddess? You, my little nephew?" I rubbed my face again coarsely and spoke through a partially clenched jaw.

"Yes..." Valdemar jumped to his feet and spun in a circle performing an odd kind of dance I had never seen before. He stopped himself and bent down placing his smiling face next to mine.

"And how was she?" I blushed at the question and thought how best to cleverly respond to my uncle. He was seeking the raw details of my conquest but in my shame I chose to forget them and speak in riddles.

"She was like many powerful women. Beautiful, confident, and full of rage." Valdemar's grin quickly faded at his disappointment to my short and colorless tale.

"Is that all you're going to share with your dear uncle? Selfish!" Valdemar shook his head but smiled as he did so. "Well, then, I'll have to ask you again after a few horns of mead swim in your gut. Perhaps that would loosen your tongue?" I smiled at his persistence but cared not to continue the discussion of my immortal adversary.

"Perhaps," I replied.

"Oh, and I saved this for you. I thought you might want to keep it. Perhaps create a necklace out of it." Valdemar extended his closed fist placing it over mine. I opened my hand and he dropped a small metal object into it. It was the arrowhead that had pierced my back. I lifted it up holding the stinger between two of my fingertips.

"It's strange," I remarked.

"What's strange?"

"The arrowhead. It's not made of iron, nor is it made of steel."

"So what is it, then?" Valdemar asked.

"I'm not sure." The arrowhead was flawless, craftsmanship like nothing I had ever seen in Bjorgvin or Midgard. The metal gleamed brightly in the sunlight without any pits or rust to speak of. The blade itself seemed razor sharp. I touched it as lightly as possible and still my flesh split to bleeding. The center of the arrow was hammered inward, perhaps to make it lighter than other arrows. "If I am so lucky to see Odin again I shall ask him." Reaching over my legs I grasped a small leather pouch that had been removed from my belt and carefully placed the arrowhead inside for safe keeping. I then looked over my hands that rested in my lap and saw them still stained with blood. The stain was thick and dark and would probably not come out for several days. The wind abruptly picked up and I could smell my own stink about me. Surely, I looked worse than I smelled. Valdemar pointed eagerly towards the front prow.

"There's a bucket of salt water at the bow if you wish to clean off. You may find Hilgrid under a spare sail. Last I checked, he was sleeping off the battle." Using the wooden mast to guide me to my feet, I stood slowly as I swayed with the ocean. The sea was a dark blue this day and my eyes fixated on the rolling waves in the distance. The rocking of the ship twisted my stomach so, I felt my face awash with sweat and I ran to the rail of the ship, emptying the contents of my gut into the frothy waters below. I looked upward, wiping my face clean with my sleeve. I stood upright once more and gazed out to the horizon. "That should make you feel better," remarked Valdemar. "Now, go wash up; your smell offends my nose."

"Fuck off, uncle." He laughed at me as I made my way to the front prow of the Drakkar. With the sails up the oars were in and tucked neatly away against the inside of the deck. Women and children of the village slept or rested quietly as I walked past. The warriors, however, had been awake for some time. Some tended to their wounds; others sat quietly eating small pieces of rations while playing with their seax. I walked past Njord, who lay outstretched on the hard deck soaking up the sun. He slapped my leg as soon as his eyes caught a glimpse of me and rose quickly.

"So it's true. The dead do rise from the grave." He pulled his long hair out from his face quickly holding me in a warm embrace. Pushing me back, he looked carefully over my body.

"What is it?" I asked curiously.

"Just checking you for more holes. The Valkyries are good fighters but tenacious archers. When you fell to the deck I was sure that Freya had pierced your heart as you did hers." I shook my head and began to hobble forward again.

"Not this time brother, not this time." I reached the front prow finding the bucket of salt water. I lowered myself down cupping my hands in the salty liquid and splashed myself several times until my face was covered. I rubbed the water quickly into my face, hair, and beard wiping away what dirt and blood I could. When finished, I sat down hard against the deck and felt something pull away from me. A quiet growl grew from under the sail and a hand pulled back under the cloth. Sharp eyes looked up at me angrily and then softened.

"You should watch where you sit, little brother. You never know when you will run into a wolf." It was Hilgrid, ill-tempered that I had disturbed his rest.

"Thank you," I said. Hilgrid lifted his head slightly with a surprised expression on his face.

"For what?" Hilgrid grumbled.

"For watching over me in my time of need."

"It was the honorable thing to do. You still had a lot of fight in you. I did not wish to see you pass so soon to Valhalla."

"Hilgrid, you are a brave man." Hilgrid scoffed and turned to his side facing away from me.

"I am nothing of the sort and I won't have you speak of me that way."

"Hilgrid, if not for you, we never would have made it to the Drakkar. None of us would be alive today to tell the tale." Hilgrid laid his head back down and breathed deeply outward.

"I am a warrior, Audan, simple as that. I played my part just as our fallen brothers had. I'm no better or worse than any man."

* * *

We sailed on for a time ahead with the wind and waves pulling us effortlessly closer to Valdemar's trading post. Soon, I would be reunited with what remained of my family. My only question was what to do beyond just surviving? When the burial and celebration ended, what then? Would we stay at Fani for the rest of our lives or strike out to build a new home? Bjorgvin was my home, my only home, and I wished to one day return and rebuild my father's legacy.

"Dark clouds on the horizon. It's a bad omen, Audan." Valdemar exclaimed. Many of the men had a worried look on their faces. I pretended not to notice and dismissed their concerns.

"It's a storm, nothing more, Valdemar." The winds picked up fiercely as the sea spray began to cover my face. The passage to Fani would now be a perilous one. More than half the ships occupants were women and children; they would not weather the storm as well as the men. "Will the ship hold up?" I joked as Valdemar gave me a cross look.

"Will the ship..." He stomped on the deck loudly with his big feet; he gazed up at me and smiled. "My ship has never lost a man at sea. I'm not about to tarnish that reputation. She is the finest Drakkar in all the northern realm. You would do good to recognize that and show her some respect." I chuckled at Valdemar's constant description of the ship as a *her*.

"Her, is it? So you found yourself a wife after all. Does she have a name or do you just call her ship?" Eygautr arose from his slumber and chuckled loudly.

"Or perhaps it's the name of a goat he became, overly familiar with." Eygautr cracked. Valdemar paid no attention to the short fat man's insults.

"She does, nephew. I named her Ginna."

"Ginna? Someone you knew?" Valdemar paused for a moment and looked outward towards the brewing seas.

"An old friend from long, long ago. A tale for perhaps another time, my nephew." It wasn't long before the sea turned into a field of white caps cresting above the blue waves. The waters broke over the ships front prow and those people of Bjorgvin, not of a sailing nature, huddled nearer the mast underneath a wool cover. The rain now swept gently across the decks and I reached for a hooded wool cloak to protect me from the coming cold.

"Alright, uncle, if you say so."

"You best be careful, boy. A ship has a soul you know. If she hears you, she might decide to throw you to Aegir just in spite of you." I wrapped the wool cloak around my body tighter and carefully took a seat at the stern against the rails. The seas began to churn now and all I could hear was the sound of the wind and waves. Eygautr held the helm in place, leaning his girth against the rudder stick and gave an apprehensive stare.

"What's the matter, old man? Haven't you sailed through a squall before? You look pale." Eygautr glanced downward and quickly returned his gaze to the front of the ship.

"I don't like it, Audan. This storm crept up on us from out of nowhere. This is Freya's doing, I swear it. That vile woman has turned the seas against us." Lightning cracked in the distance, striking the water below as it forked in different directions. "We should seek shelter before things get worse."

"I thought you said the ship would hold up in the storm. Fani can't be more than a sea mile away." Eygautr pointed above his head.

"Look at the skies, Audan. I've never seen anything like this. It's unnatural. The gods are toying with us." Overhead black clouds swirled and swung angrily back and forth. The wind would not choose a path to blow as it sputtered from side to side. The dark mists pushed downward as the skies cracked wildly with blue and white light.

"Odin will not have me this day," I replied confidently. Eygautr scoffed at my remark and pulled the wool cloth tightly over his head.

"Maybe not you, Audan, not the chosen one. But the rest of us? Midgard still has much in store for me. Valhalla can wait!" The small waves outside the ship gave way to rolling hills that now blocked the view of the horizon. I gripped a line leading up to the mast and bent my legs to move with the sea. A large wave rolled towards the front of the ship and the Drakkar climbed upward to great heights until I could see the horizon and mountains in the distance. The Drakkar dipped down and then roared forward at reckless speed.

"Hold on!" I called out. Winds whipped past my face blowing my hood clean off my head. The front prow crashed into the water submerging much of it underneath until the next wave lifted us upward. The sail was tight being pushed up the hill of water faster than I had ever seen. We ascended to the top of a watery mound once more and this time much higher. As we reached the top my heart slowed and I heard nothing except for the wind as I looked down the canyon that lay before us.

"Everyone hold on for your lives!" yelled Eygautr. The women and children aboard the ship cried and screamed at our warnings. Ginna dipped down again following the steep backside of the wave. We rolled down the surf even faster this time and crashed hard at the bottom. The water collided heavy over the front prow reaching halfway across the deck. The next wave approach but our ship had stalled and turned slightly to port. The wave caught us on the starboard side and slowly pulled us upward.

"Turn the rudder! Turn the rudder!" I yelled in a panic. Digging my feet firmly into the deck, I pushed against the rudder stick with all my strength as Eygautr pulled from the other side. We ascended to the top of the wave and looking over Eygautr's shoulder I saw the massive drop on the other end.

"Odin help us!" Valdemar cried out. I gripped the rudder stick tighter and found a line to wrap around my wrist.

"It's too late, hold on!" The ship roared down the other side and we were helpless to steer it in the right direction. "Everyone hold on..." I closed my eyes, bracing for the impact and we collided into the water and the icy mist swallowed the decks whole. I held onto the rudder as tightly as I could until the sea subsided from the ship. I found myself lying on the deck of the craft completely weighed down by my cloak that had been drenched. Some of the travelers were in a panic as several of the women and children had been washed overboard, never to be seen again. Slowly, I rose to one knee when I heard a loud crack that shook the hull. At first, I thought it was Thor pounding against his anvil sending down bolts of lightning but as I gazed up a line snapped and the timber of the ship's mast began to sway.

"The mast! Lookout!" yelled Hilgrid from the front prow. A loud and violent crack erupted on the deck of the ship. The top of the mast bent hard to the port side and finally snapped near the base of the deck. "Lookout!" All hands scrambled to avoid the crash of timber as the massive log fell hard to the ships deck dragging line and bits of the railing with it. Chunks of wood and iron flew in all directions, bouncing off the floor. I jumped out of the way pulling several thrall with me who had ran from the falling timber. Standing quickly, I saw the masts top end leaning into the sea; it was pulling the Drakkar in with it.

"Cut the lines! Cut the lines!" I called out in a dread. Warriors drew axe, sword, and seax to cut away the mast that now acted as an anchor dragging us to Aegir's kingdom. Water began to pour in quickly and the decks were ankle-deep in sea. I unlashed my bearded axe from its resting place at the stern and fell the blade upon a line quickly cutting it away. The other lines gave way to the warrior's blades until one remained tied off from the bow to the top of the mast. Eygautr lifted his sword blade and cut the line against the deck until it snapped. The mast and sail tipped over and fell on the port side. With a great crash the lines that were still attached followed the mast into the sea. A yell erupted from the center deck and a line had caught the leg of a thrall pulling him face down.

"No!" the young man cried out. With barely a warning the boy was whipped over the side of the rails and thrown into the merciless ocean. I picked up a mass of rolled up line and ran to the edge of the rails hoping to catch a glimpse of the young thrall and perhaps to save him from an icy demise. The mast bobbed up and down for a moment and then quickly sank into the depths taking everything else with it. The boy was nowhere to be seen.

"He's with Aegir now," said Eygautr. Perhaps the water god shall see to it to take the boy to Odin." I looked up at the sky and hoped that the old man would do just that.

"Everyone grab an oar! Quickly!" called out Valdemar. "If you want to live, you will row." I found a place on the starboard side and gripped an oar ready to put in my fair share. A hand came down heavy on my shoulder and I could see Hilgrid gazing down on me.

"No brother. Take care of that wound. Man the rudder. I'll put my back to the oar." I did not argue with brother Hilgrid. My shoulder still hurt greatly from the arrow that had been removed from it and I would not last long trying to keep up with the others. I stood and gave him a nod of thanks for his offering.

"Thank you, Hilgrid. I will be sure to repay you." Hilgrid sat quietly and gripped the oar waiting for Valdemar to call out the cadence.

"Alright, you sons of Bjorgvin, on my command. Row! Row! Row!" I turned the rudder to lead us directly into the oceans waves but kept our heading towards Fani. As the time passed and the men would tire they traded off with thrall, free women, and even children who felt strong enough to row as one. Waves crashed without mercy over the bow and I struggled to keep the Drakkar from rolling over in the fierce sea. Valdemar took a much needed respite from rowing and stood from his sitting place. His beard was soaked in sea water and hung low to his belt.

"You look like a wet cat, uncle, sour-faced and angry!" I remarked. I laughed for a moment until a wave slapped the side of my face.

"You are none the better!" Uncle leaned back against the rear prow and placed his arms on the rudder to give me aid.

"How much longer until we reach your island?" Valdemar wiped the water from his brow and gazed at the horizon trying to spot the few dark signs of land still visible. Each time the waves came over us all we could see was water, legions and legions of sea that hunched over us like the great mountain sides of the fjords. He pointed just to the left of the front prow, pulling his arm back in just before another wave came over us.

"You see that finger of land there?" I stood on my toes, trying to see over the mounds of sea. There in the distance I could see dark rocks jutting out into the ocean. The waves slammed hard against these rocks sending sea spray high in the air.

"I do, uncle."

"The island lies just beyond it. Perhaps another vika sea mile or two lengths away but no more." I felt relief come over me at this news. Battling the oceans currents had left the crew weary and I feared many had thought us lost at sea. Soon, we passed the outcrop of rocks and clear as day I could see the island straight ahead. The waves crashed hard against the pebble laden shores and this would once again be a difficult landing.

The storm began to clear as rain drops gave way to streaks of sunlight that cut through the cracks in the clouds above. Dancing lights could be seen darting the beachhead, fires perhaps to light our way to shelter. We rowed slowly towards the dark shore until the waves took over and carried us in. There in the distance stood a tall and slender beauty unequaled by any I had seen in my life. She stood ankle deep in the frigid frothy waters, her hair braided and draped down the front of her chest. In her presence my heart began to race, my arms grew weak and I spoke through a sigh of quiet relief.

"Sada..."

Four
Starting Over

The Drakkar slid smoothly against the wet stones and came to an abrupt stop jerking our bodies forward. I stood quickly and jumped downward from the front prow into the icy water below and rushed towards Sada. She ran to me and jumped into my arms, knocking my weak body to the ocean floor. I stood and pulled her from the water carrying her to the shore in my arms. Trudging through the rocks, I gently placed my love down still holding her tightly in my embrace.

"I thought I would never see you again." Sada sobbed quietly and then pulled away to wipe her tears of joy from her soft cheeks.

"We barely made it through the storm. Our mast snapped in two and took a young thrall down to the depths of Aegir's kingdom. We are fortunate to be amongst the living." Sada held me tighter and splashes erupted from behind as the rest of the ships occupants began to depart eagerly for land. She placed her hand gently against my face and ran her fingers through my brine soaked beard.

"Your lips are purple, your skin as cold as ice. We best get you inside and warm you up. Come with me." Sada guided me to the front gates of Uncle Valdemar's village, which stood only one hundred paces or so from the shoreline up a steep walkway. We soon reached the top of the climb that was guarded by two large wooden figures of the All Father; another thirty paces beyond that lay the massive front gates. Nearly every able-bodied man was posted outside, no doubt fearing that Freya and Fenrir may have followed us to finish what they had started. It was an impressive display of arms with every man, even the archers were clad with leather cuirass, helms of all manner, and various bladed weapons attached to their long belts. They would prove formidable to any foe that threatened us from the sea.

"Open the gates!" a guard called out in a coarse voice. The walls eked open with a loud bang, followed by the creak of iron hinges. The many warriors, appearing weary and injured, all acknowledged me as I slowly walked through the guarded entrance. Planked wooden walkways led through the center of the village lined with many huts, inhuss homes and several large longhouses adorned with the shields and colors of their owners. Despite the Finn raid on Valdemar's village, he had been busy rebuilding his home and further entrenching his forces. The village itself was a flurry of activity. The forge hut was bright hot with a gathering of men working iron and steel tirelessly sending embers into the air. Merchants of all types sold and traded their wares such as fur, meat, and rare metals. Most of the women tended the injured and cleaned blood-stained cloth. Large fires lined the streets with great iron pots of boiling hot water to clean the soiled linens. The strong smell of woodbine, a most fragrant flower collected in the southern part of our lands wafted in the air as thralls mixed the dried leaves into the pots. Orbrecht was amongst the healers stoking a blade in a fire beneath an iron vessel. His body was wholly covered in blood not of his own. A black bear fur was draped over his shoulders to keep out the cold and in his free hand, he carried fresh linens to tie off wounds.

"Orbrecht, my brother," I called out softly. He looked up from the fire through his messy hair and for a moment seemed in shock, as if he had seen an apparition. The linens fell suddenly from his hand and he released the handle of the dagger in the flame then walked towards me.

"You made it?" he asked in disbelief. "You made it!" A smile came over Orbrecht and he embraced me tightly, nearly knocking Sada off my arm. He pulled back, holding my shoulders and looked over my figure. "By the gods. You made it after all. We lost sight of Valdemar's ship and feared him lost at sea. When the storm blew in, we thought it was certain that you would not return."

"I did not plan returning however the gods will not have me this day. It is not yet my time." I smiled and slowly began to walk towards Valdemar's longhouse.

"Audan?" I stopped and turned slowly back towards my old friend. "I'm sorry for the words that I spoke at our village. I know this is not all you're doing. Please know that you are my brother and I only want what's best for you and the people." I looked long at Orbrecht's face; his eyes were soft and wet, black circles formed around them showing his tireless efforts of treating the many wounded. He was sincere in his apology and for that I felt a sense of renewal.

"I gladly accept your apology, Orbrecht. I hold no ill will towards you. These are dark and terrible times that will test all men. We need to stick together and not let this evil come between us." Orbrecht gracefully lowered his head and I slowly turned and headed for the main hall. Valdemar's home rested at the end of the planked walkway surrounded by another set of palisade walls and even more guards. The walkway branched off to the left another one hundred paces passing several hovels until another gate was reached. This gate was left wide open and beyond it led outward to the many farmhouses and stables outside the village walls. Merchants and townspeople freely traveled through this gate past another large gathering of warriors. It bothered me to think of one of the village gates being unsecured but Sada would not allow me to linger and quickly guided me to the front entrance of Valdemar's hall.

The short entry way was now before me and the familiar smell of warm stone brought back the memory of my first visit when I was forced to land upon these shores. I lowered my head and entered the magnificent stone hall to be pleasantly surprised by a roaring fire, casks of mead, and long tables crowded by hungry Norseman eating at the many fine foods generously provided by my uncle. Sada opened the door wider to let us both in and the cold breeze blew swiftly across the hall and over the faces of the warriors. The famished Norsemen turned their heads appearing annoyed that someone had left the door open letting out the heat from the fire. Then their eyes set upon me and they stood slowly from their benches leaving their food on the tables.

"Audan," a voice called out quietly. Mumbles and faint words bounced about the hall until a drinking horn was raised in the air.

"All hail, Chieftain Audan!" Drinking horns and arms of steel and iron rose above the warrior's heads.

"All hail, Chieftain Audan!" A warm hand found its way to my icy shoulder and I looked back to see Valdemar gazing happily at me with rosy cheeks and a horn full of mead.

"These men know what you did for them and the people of Bjorgvin. You were a dead legend amongst your people and my followers. And now, you are a living legend!" Valdemar lifted his arm and rigidly pointed at his stone throne. "Tonight and as long as you stay here, you will sit on my throne. From now until the Ragnarok, so it shall be!"

"Hail! Hail! Hail!" The room erupted once more with the calls from the warriors at the tables. Several thralls emerged from the back of the hall carrying fresh linens, a pair of leather boots, and fur.

"My lord, my name is Maarit; if you would come with us we will help you change into something warmer." Sada released her grip of my forearm and I looked back, quickly fearing that I would somehow lose her. I gripped her arm and pulled it back towards me. Sada looked back at me with a comforting smile.

"It will be alright." She nodded. "I will be right here when you are dressed and warm. Do not worry yourself." I nodded back and slowly released my grip of her arm. The thrall gently took my wrist and guided me through another doorway to the hall living quarters. I was taken back to the small room where I had stayed once before. An older women fair of hair and skin walked in carrying an iron rod draped in wet steaming cloth.

"Your clothes, my lord. Take them off, if you please. We will cleanse your body before donning your new linens." I reached for the bottom of my tunic and slowly pulled the wool cloth upward until a searing pain ran through my back. The arrow wound would not cooperate with even the simplest of tasks and I found myself unable to lift my arm.

"I..." I hesitated to say it, feeling hopeless and perhaps even less of a man. "I can't lift my arm." Maarit nodded and approached me gripping the bottom of the tunic and lifting it for me.

"I will help you, my lord. All will be well." Despite having the aid of a caring thrall, the pain was still unrelenting as the cloth rolled over my face pulling my arms upward. I gritted my teeth and groaned as quietly as I could until my body was free of the cloth. I breathed a heavy sigh of relief and sat down on the bed that had been laid out for me.

"Just rest, my lord. We will take care of the rest." The thrall grasped the steaming linens from the iron rod and rubbed them about my body. The heat slowly burned away the ice in my veins and relaxed the muscles. My weariness felt heavy on my brow as my eyes began to close. The thrall pulled the hot cloths away and reached for another one to dry my skin. Once she was finished, she paused for a moment gazing intently at my back.

"What is it?" I asked curiously.

"Your wound, my lord. You will need some fresh linens and proper treatment. I shall call upon the healer to see to it." The woman turned to walk out of the room and I quickly grabbed her wrist. She looked down at her arm and then back up at me.

"No. Leave him be." I ordered. The thrall turned back and bowed her head downward.

"I insist, my lord. Without the proper treatment you will become ill and catch fever." I loosened my grip of the woman and nodded my head.

"Go then. But see to it that he does not come to me until the more serious wounded are treated. I'll not have others die while Orbrecht licks my wounds." The thrall bowed her head slightly.

"Yes, my lord. As you wish." She turned and left the room gently closing the wood door. The iron latch fell hard striking the metal lock sending an echo in the silent room. In the distance I could hear the faint hum of celebrations and drinking. My weariness was catching up with me again and so I slowly laid down on my side against the wool blankets of the bed. Steam rose upward from my arm and I could feel a chill run across my spine. I pulled a black fur from the bottom of the bed and draped it over my body. The heat of the bed was comforting; allowing my eyes to shut, I let the warmth pull me down into the darkness. Just a moments rest was all I desired. As I drifted into the black, the darkness soon began to fade to a soft grey, mist appeared before me at my feet and in the distance an ash tree. My gaze flew skyward, searching for the top of the tree but there appeared to be no end as the canopy faded away into the star filled sky. I walked slowly towards the base of the tree that stretched the length of several longhouses. In front of the tree lay a large log and atop the log a small curious creature. As I approached, the creatures figure became that of a small boy. A chill suddenly ran down my back as I recognized this creature, not as a boy but as the foreboding warning I had only a year ago.

"Specter?" I said quietly. The boy turned to reveal his ghastly appearance, a face as plain as the still waters with no eyes, nose, or lips to speak of. In one hand he gripped a dark blade and the other a piece of wood to whittle upon.

"So, Audan, you have returned to the middle place." He turned away again and exhaled loudly. "Come, young man. Sit next me. I have something of great importance to show you." I did as the specter said and approached the log, climbing to the top of it and resting next to him.

"Why have I returned, specter? Am I dead?"

The creature laughed deeply and began to whittle away at his stick with his ghoulish black and purple hands.

"Dead? Dead you say? No, no, Audan. I'm afraid the stink of death has not yet fallen upon you. As it was before, it shall be today. I am not your keeper, nor shall you remain in this realm of eternal nothingness. Odin has seen to it. No, I am once again your guide to the will of the gods. The All Father has called upon me once more to meet with you to bestow my wisdom on your immature youth." I felt some relief in knowing I would not be imprisoned in this place, but why was I brought back?

"You have spoken with Odin?" The specter laughed again but this time in the soft voice of a child.

"I always speak with Odin. Odin is the sky, the land, and the water. Odin is everywhere and speaks to us through everything. Do you hear that?" I sat quietly and turned my ear outward but all I could hear was the deafening silence of the middle place.

"I hear nothing, specter."

"Exactly. That is why you need me. This is why you must be taught to listen and not just hear. Your mortal mind is not attuned to the spirit world." I scooted closer to the specter to show my willingness to learn his instructions. Looking at his head, I noticed something about him had changed since we last met. His once midnight black hair had begun to grey and yet his body still appeared to be that of a young boy, an able-bodied boy.

"Specter?" I asked.

"I know what it is you wish to ask. Do not think on your questions. Spit them out," he said coarsely.

"How old are you? When last we met, your hair was as black as the night sky. It has been no more than three or four seasons since last we met." The specter turned to me and nodded several times as he pushed his blade forward against his stick sending wood dust all around.

"Three or four seasons on Midgard? Has it been so long? No, no, Audan. Perhaps for you the leaves have turned to crimson red, fallen and returned in our absence but here in my realm it has been eons since your return. I have already seen the past and the future. I have even seen your life in its entirety and your death." I felt anxious and swallowed nervously at this revelation. "You wish to know how you die, don't you?" I turned away and looked upward at the great ash tree.

"No. When death comes, let it come swiftly and without warning. I do not wish to dwell on the day it will arrive but to live without care of these things."

Specter moved the blade and stick to his left hand and patted me gently on the back.

"That's a good lad. Wise beyond your years already, but still you have so much to learn of the things which you do…not…know." Specter waved his hand in front of us and sparks appeared in front of the massive tree. A fire grew in its place and slowly rose upward as the wood began to crack under the heat. I heard an awkward sound from behind me and I turned to see shadows traveling quickly towards me. Startled, I stood atop the log and reached for a dagger on my waist but my weapons were nowhere to be found.

"What are they?" I asked urgently.

"Calm yourself, Audan. They are but the past and can bring no harm unto you." The shadows traveled up the log and over my body until they descended upon the fire. "Pay attention and understand the truth I am about to impart upon you." The dark spirits rose from the ground and took on the shape of cloaked figures dancing around the flame. Their shadows stretched high upward against the great ash tree appearing as giants swaying in the mist. I slowly sat back down and crossed my legs to watch the display before me. They hummed and chanted wildly as they danced around the fire until suddenly they stopped.

"Who are they?" I whispered.

"They are called the Norns. Sisters of great and powerful magic that weave the fabric of destiny for all that was and all that is." The shortest of the three sisters began to wave a hand gently in front of her and the top of the flames followed her every movement. The spell was mesmerizing as she made the flame dance and bend to her will. She pulled her hand back and then quickly threw it outward towards the great ash tree. A ball of blue flame erupted from the fire and soared toward the tree, striking its bark. Smoke and ember flew asunder obstructing my view of the tree. The tallest of the three sisters leaned forward, extending her hand and blew a powerful gust of wind to clear the air. The great ash tree shook violently, sending leaves and branches crashing downward. I covered the top of my head for fear of being struck but I could see the specter worried of no such thing. He just stared downward still whittling away at his wood which had begun to take the shape of a ship.

"What are they doing?" I asked. The specter raised his hand and gently covered my mouth.

"Shut up and listen." The smoke and ember cleared from the tree and a bright blue glow emanated from its bark. A large rune appeared seared into the trees skin. The third of the sisters, one of average height, took one step forward and stopped. She reached upward and gently removed the hood of her cloak exposing fiery long red hair that fell downward tied in the most elegant braid.

"Well, Verthandi?" called out the shortest of the sisters.

"What is it?" The red-haired Verthandi approached the tree and stopped just short of touching it. She reached up once more and untied the front knot which held up the tunic releasing the wool cloth exposing her naked body to the wild. A light now shown upon her from above and I gazed upward to see the shine of the moon now focused upon her.

"I do not yet know sister Skuld. There is something strange about this rune, something unseen." Skuld stepped forward removing the hood of her cloak revealing a bright head of long white hair.

"What do you mean, 'unseen'? In all of time, in all of existence, we have never seen anything we could not explain." Verthandi looked back towards her sisters and for a moment I thought her gaze caught mine. She turned back towards the rune lifting her hand upward and tracing the symbol slowly with the tips of her fingers. The rune glowed all the more brightly when she touched it until removing her hand and placing her finger tips on her lips. Verthandi's eyes grew wide and a nervousness appeared to come over her.

"It is a mortal..." Verthandi whispered.

"What was that?" The tallest of the sisters called out. Verthandi gazed at her sisters, appearing anxious, perhaps even scared.

"Urd, I don't understand. The rune... it is a mortal." The tallest of the sisters, Urd, stepped forward quickly and traced the rune with her hand. She slowly placed her finger tips upon her lips and exhaled loudly. Turning towards her sister, she removed her cloak's hood. Urd's hair was cut short to her shoulders and black as the night. She placed her hand on Verthandi's bare shoulder.

"It cannot be," she said in disbelief. "The reading, do it again!" Urd urged of Verthandi. The red-headed Norn once again reached out and ran her fingers along the rune. The rays of the moon shone even more brightly now and her skin was glowing in the darkness of the night. She placed her finger tips on her ruby red lips and inhaled deeply with her eyes closed. Complete silence fell over the sisters as they waited on Verthandi. Suddenly, her emerald green eyes opened wide and she quickly knelt down, picked up her cloak and donned it once more. Verthandi stormed off back towards the fire and stopped at the base of the flame with her sisters in tow.

"What does it say?" demanded Skuld.

"What did you see?" asked Urd. The sister Norn stood there silent, the flames and embers reflecting brightly from her eyes as she watched them dance.

"The unspoken rune; it is a mortal. But how can that be?" The other sisters stomped in place and clenched their fists in frustration. Skuld gripped Verthandi by the shoulder and pulled her close.

"There are no unspoken runes, not even for the gods themselves. If this is a mortal, then its destiny can be woven. No mortal can create their own twine or escape our weave." Skuld reached into her cloak and removed a crooked dagger carrying it back to the tree. She buried the dagger's blade into the tree and scraped away at the bark as she caught the ashes in her hand.

"We shall soon find the truth of this!" she bellowed. The blue bark floated downward into Skuld's palm like embers until the last of the rune was removed from the tree. Skuld brought the tree shavings to Urd, who gripped a wooden bowl. The shavings were placed into the bowl and Urd spit atop it before placing the bowl on a rock near the fire. The bowl bubbled and boiled over until golden twine spewed out. Verthandi gripped the end of the twine and walked backwards until the thread was completely stretched out. With her dagger she cut at the end of the twine and split the end into three pieces, handing one to each of her sisters. Together, they pulled, twisted, and overlapped the twine. As they did so, the twine would slip out from their work, again, and again, and again. No matter how fast they weaved or how tightly they pulled the thread would not bend to the will of the Norns.

"This is the one," remarked Verthandi. The red haired Norn looked upward and once again it seemed as if she was gazing upon me. "The one the prophecies have spoken of." I leaned in to hear Verthandi's soft voice. "He who shall be our greatest savior, or the destruction of all. It is him..."

"I don't understand? Why can they not weave the twine?" I asked. The specter looked up at me and gripped my hand pulling it towards him.

"Open your hand, Audan." I released my fingers and the specter placed his whittle work within them. A ship bearing the same markings of my Drakkar had been expertly crafted.

"The twine they speak of, Audan, is you."

"Me?"

"You see, all mortals and creatures of Midgard have their fate spun by the Norns and the Norns see all. But in your case, they could not spin your destiny nor could they see within it."

"But why? What makes me so special?"

"You were hidden from them."

"By whom?"

"By the All Father himself. With the Ragnarok approaching, Odin would need an ally not of his realm and not under the influence of his kin. A man with no destiny. To be such a man is to be one of the most dangerous weapons against the powers of the dark queen."

"Freya. So that is why she tried to turn me; to make me an ally."

"So, you see, your friends and family are all well known by your enemies. Their life and death is predicted by the Norns. Their fate has already been woven in the twine of destiny. But you, Audan, you may yet be our salvation."

"So, what shall I do next?"

"You will return to the world of the living. You must stop Fenrir and in doing so, you will slow Freya's advance."

"How do I stop the demon dog?" The specter laughed in a deep and unnatural voice.

"Through sheer iron will. The life of your brother will depend on it. Use your hatred and anger. Let it fuel your fury. Do not hold yourself back, do not tire, and do not weep. Unleash yourself against those who would see you dead. Hate is your ally, anger your sword and you must bury it deeply." The fire of the Norns faded away and so too did their shadows once more vanish from sight. The great ash tree that stood before me swayed slowly in the howling winds on high.

"If the Norns cannot see my fate, then neither can you."

"No, Audan, I cannot. I can see how you die but not the quality of the death. But I can see the same thing that the All Father sees in you."

"And what is that?"

"Potential. Now, go." My body gently lifted from the log and the specter vanished in the mists until my sight slowly returned to the darkness.

* * *

"Audan," A hand shook me by the shoulder and I opened my eyes to see Orbrecht standing before me. "Did you rest well, brother?" I blinked several times until my wits returned and I sat up slowly from my resting place allowing the black bear fur to slide off my body.

"I think so. Was I asleep long?"

"A few hours perhaps. Your thrall came to fetch me but there were many wounded to attend to." In the corner of the room, a spearman stood clad in a leather cuirass and leather helm.

"Who the hell is that?" Orbrecht looked back as he pulled out supplies from his leather satchel.

"Valdemar insisted on having guards posted outside your quarters now that you are Chieftain."

I fixed my gaze upon the guard and pursed my lips. "Get the fuck out!" Without saying a word the guard nodded and left the room gently closing the door behind him.

"I have no need of guards," I complained.

"There are rumors, Audan." My eyes nearly went cross at Orbrecht's remark.

"Rumors? What rumors?" I asked sharply.

"That Freya has placed her spies in our midst, perhaps even assassins." My brows raised upward as this was the first I had heard of such things.

"How could that be possible?" I asked. Orbrecht stood closer placing a jar next to me. A putrid smell wafted towards my nose and I shook my head to flush it away. "What is that smell?"

"Remedies. You will need them if you want to heal faster. Now, turn around so I can take a look at this wound." I shifted my body facing my back to the door. Orbrecht ripped the cloth away sending a stinging pain throughout my shoulder. I flinched but held back from making any sounds. "Once again Audan, luck or dare I say it the gods themselves have found you. A flesh wound and nothing more." I looked back to see Orbrecht dip his finger into the jar, retrieving a green paste. He placed it directly on the wound and packed it in deeply. "That should do it." He placed the jar down and reached for the fresh linens. "Lift your arm." I did as he said and he wrapped the linen around my shoulder and under my arm before tying a knot directly on top of the wound.

"Well?" I asked impatiently.

"You'll be well enough to fight by the next new moon. If you do not reopen your wound that is." Orbrecht pulled the knot tighter and then slapped me on the back. He stepped away and sat down in a wooden chair across from my bed.

"So what of these spies and assassins? Who's speaking of these rumors?" Orbrecht looked downward as he repacked his satchel with his medicinal goods.

"No one in particular that I know of. I think the people are just scared, leaderless. You need to show yourself, brother, and make it known that their welfare is your greatest concern. Think of what your father would do." Orbrecht was right. I needed to keep the morale of the people well and good if we were to maintain any kind of order at Valdemar's village.

"What time of day is it?" Orbrecht finished packing his things and stood to his feet.

"Nearly sundown. You should get dressed and show your face." The healer headed out and opened the door.

"Where will you go?" I asked. Orbrecht looked down at his blood-soaked clothing.

"First to get cleaned up, and then, I will join you for a long round of drinks in the hall." I smiled and nodded in agreement. Orbrecht left me to my devices and I looked about the room for my tunic until my gaze fixated on a small object on the floor. I bent down and picked up the wooden statue and placed it on the bed next to me.

"The specter..." I said under my breath. The small wooden Drakkar he carved had traveled with me from his realm to mine. Perhaps a reminder that I in fact was not merely dreaming or having a vision. I stood once more gazing at the small statue for a moment remembering clearly his message. *Hate is your ally, anger your sword and you must bury it deeply.* To my left, I found neatly folded cloths that had been left behind for me and I dressed quickly as my stomach rumbled for food. "Guard," I called out. The door opened quickly and a young heavily armed man peaked inside.

"Yes, my lord?"

"I need those who are able to gather outside the hall. I have a message for my people." The guard nodded.

"Straight away, my lord." He closed the door and left quickly as his footsteps echoed loudly outside. A short moment later another set of footsteps, much heavier and louder made their way towards my door. A knock sounded against the entrance.

"Audan, it's Eygautr."

"Come in, brother." The short, fat man entered slowly and extended his hand for a hearty handshake. "It warms my heart to see you rested. I hear that you are to give a speech to our people."

"Yes." I said softly.

"Well, then, come right away and I shall be happy to announce you." I nodded and quickly finished donning my cloths.

"Audan." Gunnar opened the door slightly and peeked his head inside cautiously.

"Yes, Gunnar, come in. What is it?" I asked. Gunnar slowly removed a wool cap from his head and held it gently in front of his chest. He kept his gaze toward the floor only looking up at me briefly.

"They are ready for you. All has been prepared as you requested."

"Thank you, Gunnar. We will be out shortly." The young warrior bowed his head slightly and returned quietly outside. We left the room and the two guards outside my door followed us from behind. We entered the dining hall that was now empty of its celebrating warriors. We reached the main door to see Sada still waiting inside. An overwhelming sense of love came over me and I felt compelled to do something I should have done a long time ago. "Please, go outside without me. I shall be there in a moment." Eygautr and Gunnar appeared perplexed by my request but none the less stepped outside taking the two guards with them. When they shut the door, I gripped Sada by the wrist and guided her to a bench.

"Sada, sit next to me. I have something I want to ask you." She took a drink from her horn as she walked toward me and placed it down on the table. I suddenly felt nervous but excited but all at the same time.

"Audan. You're as pale as a ghost. What is it you want to ask me?" She gently pushed the strands of hair from in front of her face and tucked it behind her ear.

"With everything that has happened, you have always been there for me. No matter the cost. You are the best friend that any man can ask for." Sada smiled.

"Just your friend?"

"Of course not. Sada, you are the love of my life. I do not know how long my life will last but what I do know is that I want to spend the rest of it with you." Sada leaned back slightly, her smile faded and her head tilted down staring at me intently.

"What are you saying, my love?"

I stepped down from the bench and took a knee on the stone floor.

"Sada, will you do me the honor of being my wife?" She covered her face and tears streamed down her cheeks. For a moment, I thought she was unhappy by my invitation but when she removed her hands I could see the great smile that was concealed underneath stretching to each side of her face. She was overwhelmed with joy.

"Yes, Audan! A hundred times yes!" I stood from my knees and she jumped atop me holding me tightly. I was relieved by her answer as I could not see going on without the love of my life. She was my better half, my bridge to Valhalla, my answer in the stars.

Five
Ascension

We departed Valdemar's hall holding hands tightly as the cold air quickly greeted our skin. The snows began to fall heavy and the wood planks of the walkways became icy beneath our feet. The entire village had gathered just outside the hall. Valdemar, Gunnar, Kenna, and Eygautr waited patiently at the front of the crowd for me to deliver a word to the people so they could escape the cold. Eygautr walked towards me and shook my arm firmly.

"Are you ready?"

"I am, my friend." The short fat man raised his arms in the air to quiet the many warriors and villagers who had patiently gathered outside. Despite his stature, Eygautr was an imposing figure in a bright red tunic lined in gold piping. He appeared a king amongst the common people. Knowing his personality and general flair, he would not have it any other way.

"People, my good people! Much has transpired the last two days and in that short time, we have faced many hardships. The good people of Bjorgvin are no strangers to discomfort and loss. I am honored to be amongst you and to have my remaining warriors within your ranks. Though you have lost your home, know that as long as we can work as one, we shall never be without. My good people, the Chieftain of Bjorgvin would like to share a word with you." Eygautr stepped back and motioned me to come forward. The outdoors became utterly silent and I could hear my heart beat within my chest. I stepped forward, slowly looking down at the ground to mind my step. When I stopped, I looked up to see dozens and dozens of eager eyes set upon me. They were weary, tired, and in many cases wounded. These were my people now and I would give them strength.

"The hour grows late and I shall not keep you here longer than is necessary to say my peace. Family, friends, brothers, I want to thank you for all you have given, all you have sacrificed to this community. I know that we face challenging times ahead and that we all have lost our homes. My dearest Uncle Valdemar, the long lost brother of Rurik has opened his home willingly to us. We will one day return home to Bjorgvin and reclaim the ancient lands of our forefathers. Until that day, Fani shall remain our home." A young woman in a torn blue cloak stepped forward and raised her arm into the air.

"What of our families, our children, our husbands and sons that have come back wounded? What shall you do for them? For everything they have done?" I lowered my head and stared back empathetically at the young woman who had clearly lost much in this struggle.

"All who have served; their families shall be cared for." I turned my head to my left to see a gathering of thralls who had fought with us at the top of the palisades. Many still wore the ragged and bloodied clothes from the day they had spilt the blood and cut the flesh of our enemies. It was time for some drastic change to improve the moods of the people. "For that matter, all thrall who fought at the battle of Bjorgvin shall be free!" A rumble of voices erupted in the crowd, the thralls, of course, showed great approval and joy for this decision. The free warriors and villagers seemed surprised and some even angry.

"But who will labor?" a voice called out. I clenched my fists in frustration at the selfish nature of the question.

"All shall work and contribute to the greater good of this village. The thrall have spilt blood alongside us, have fought and killed in our name, and many sacrificed themselves so we could survive. They deserve much more than our admiration, they deserve freedom and a fair claim in what we do here." I gazed upon the many faces to find those that disapproved and remained quiet for a moment to drive home my point. "Should anyone disagree with me, I call on you to challenge me, here, now, in honorable combat." The crowd fell silent once more and I was pleased that no more blood would be spilled this day.

"Here, here!" Gunnar called out enthusiastically. Other calls of approval rang out from the village growing louder and larger in number until those who may have still disagreed with me faded into nothingness.

"My love for you all is great, but none loved you as much as my father, Rurik! Now he drinks and feasts in the great halls of Valhalla with our ancestors and tomorrow we shall give him a proper ceremony to ensure his entrance into the gates. He gave us the greatest gift a man can give, he sacrificed his well-being, his safety and when the time came, he gave up his life in service to you." I pointed across the crowd and found as many eyes as I could. Their hardened looks had softened at the memory of my father and now was the time to end it. "To you... Tonight my friends find a home, sleep in the Great Hall if you must, light a fire, eat, drink and rest. For tomorrow we will celebrate the legend of Rurik!" Arms and fists raised into the air and my father's name was called out in celebration. "I bid you all a warm and safe night." The people slowly went about their business and I turned away to see Valdemar standing just behind me. He smiled and opened his arms wide.

"I am proud of you, nephew. Tomorrow, your father will gaze down upon us and drink hearty knowing that the fate of his people are in your hands."

"Thank you, uncle, and thank you for opening your home to us, to all of us." Valdemar shrugged off my remark.

"Think nothing of it, little nephew. Now, let's open the doors to my hall and let the people in from the cold. There is not enough rooms in the homes for all of them. Many will need to sleep on the floor but they shall be warm.

* * *

The next day came and went quickly as many preparations were attended to for Rurik's final passage. I spent most of the day quiet in my own thoughts of anger until I picked up my father's sword and headed outside.

"Where are you going?" Sada asked.

"To get some fresh air and work on my sword swing."

"May I join you?"

"If you wish." Sada quickly grabbed her sword from the corner of the hall and followed me outside. We walked to the backside of the hall where a tall wall of stone stood with the wood palisades atop it. The small courtyard provided the perfect place for some practice. I gripped Sada around her waist and pulled her in close giving her a gentle kiss on the back of the neck. I leaned in to her ear and spoke softly, "Are you ready." She gently pushed me away and drew her sword from its scabbard pointing it straight at me.

"The question is, my love, are you ready for me?" Sada smiled from ear to ear and I matched her move by drawing my sword as well.

"Begin." Sada stepped forward and brought her sword across her body. I blocked the sword stepping forward with the bladed edge facing her. "One!" I called out and Sada stepped back then struck again this time striking from the opposite side. Once again, I stepped forward and blocked the blade. "Two!" I called out. Sada stepped back and then stepped forward with an overhead strike. I stepped in quickly grabbing her hand at the pommel of her blade before it could descend. "Three!" Sada broke my grip stepping between my legs and then placing her blade against my throat. "Good, again!" We repeated the shield-less drill over and over again until sweat fell from our brows.

"You're getting faster," I remarked.

"Or perhaps your getting slower!" Sada jested and I quickly jumped in, smacking her ass with the broad side of my blade. She winced and swiftly withdrew. "I didn't mean it!" she said, laughing through her teeth. I smiled and sheathed my sword. Sada came at me like the wind kicking my foot out from under me. I fell to the ground quickly and before I knew what happened her foot was on my chest and her blade pointed at my throat. "I am ready."

"Ready for what?" I asked, not knowing what she meant.

"To go to battle with you. To go Viking. I do not wish to be left behind another moment more while you risk your life for our people." I smiled and leaned forward to sit up but Sada pushed me back down with her foot staring angrily at me.

"You want to go Viking?"

"It is my right and my choice. You're taking me with you." I laughed and placed up my hands in submission.

"It looks like you have left me no choice."

Sada stared at me intently. "Say it!" she demanded placing the blade closer to my throat.

"Alright. When next we set sail with the warriors you will come with us as a Shield Maiden." Sada pulled her sword back quickly and buried it in the grass next to my face. I watched the glint of the blade bouncing back and forth until she jumped on top of me. I grabbed her quickly and rolled her to the ground beneath me. She kissed my lips and then pulled away, staring into my eyes.

"How much do you love me, Audan, son of Rurik?"

"More than all the mead and all the treasures of Valhalla," I responded without hesitation. Sada pulled me in between her legs for another kiss. I felt a presence leaning over us. I turned to see Gunnar, Orbrecht, and Njord dressed in their very best tunics. Gunnar approached me and smiled at the display of affection in front of him.

"It's time, Audan. All has been prepared." My smile faded as I was reminded of more serious affairs.

"Thank you, brother. We will join you right away." Sada and I stood and followed the trio of warriors to the front of Valdemar's hall. The bottom of the sun gently kissed the top of the ocean and slowly began its journey beyond our realm. Torches lined the path from Valdemar's Great Hall to the beachhead down below. Rows and rows of torches led to the body of Rurik, my father who lay in repose atop a Drakkar. The thrall had done their best to prepare the vessel for its final journey to Valhalla. The ship's hull was in pristine condition as the wooden beast shined brightly against the fiery light of the torches.

"Audan," Mother called softly from across the walkway. I turned my gaze to see her standing brilliantly in a bright blue dress adorned in embroidered flowers.

"You look wonderful, mother. Father would have blushed at the very sight of you." Kenna walked towards me and opened her arm wide for a warm embrace. She leaned her head on my shoulder and spoke gently into my ear.

"He can see us, my son. I am sure of it." She gently pulled away and looked me over. A hand rubbed against my shoulder and Sada stepped in front of me.

"Are you ready?"

"I am." With Sada on my left and my mother at my right, I held both their hands as we walked solemnly down the beach. Valdemar stood just ahead with a line of warriors standing proudly behind him. He nodded and waited for us to walk past before proceeding forward behind us. A decorated gangway adorned in flowers and tree branches had been built leading to the top of the ship and so I climbed it, watching each step pass my gaze until the top raze fell below my sight and my father's body lay motionless before me. I did not stop as I wished to greet him one last time before I departed the ship. My mind was fixed on the words that would pass my lips in the next few moments and the message I would use to honor a man of such greatness. Walking to the front prow, I climbed up the dragon's head standing atop the railing and gripping the beast's head with one hand.

"My people! My family! Let us not despair in these dark times for there is light ahead. Rurik, my father, ensured at least that much. So today I shall tell you a tale and it is my hope that you shall share it so that his memory shall never fade from the lands of Midgard." I paused for a moment looking back at father's silhouette and then returning my gaze to the field of torches below. I cleared my throat and took a deep breath to hold back the great sorrow that weighed heavy on my heart. "I want to tell you the story of a man who chose to be more than what other men told him to be. Even at a young age, my father saw injustice in this world. He saw cruelty in man and he saw that evil men would stop at nothing to stomp out righteousness, honor and friendship. And so in seeing these things, instead of playing his part, instead of being content with this darkness, my father took on a life of action. He started by rescuing a girl from a fate almost worse than hell. That girl would one day become my mother and together they built a family, they built walls to shelter that family, and they built a community. A community of good-hearted people, of people willing to work, sweat, and bleed for their kin. For they saw the quality of the man that was my father. The character of which all good men and people aspire to be. You see, when an evil man who stood over my father in position only, demanded the worst of him, my father rose above it. Men of position and power became our enemies." I paused again for a moment wiping the spit from my mouth. My heart was running wild and my anger and hate for Steinar, for Freya was overpowered by the love I had for my father. "So, here we stand, united! Un- afraid! Unspoiled! Because of him!" I paused and looked back at Rurik's body. "Because of him..." I pointed back towards my father.

"And so a good man did not choose safety, he honored himself and his people by choosing what was right! And even though we were outmatched and half the house of gods had turned against us we did not cower! We did not falter! We fought!" The people cheered and a great roar erupted in the village as the fiery torches bounced in the night time air. "We fought not for riches, or fame, we fought for something better than ourselves. We fought to honor our ances- tors, and to honor Odin. And in that journey, Rurik sacrificed himself so you could be here this day. So you could witness the ultimate testament of love that he held for each and every one of us! Look upon the body of our leader, our Chieftain, and ask yourself what you would not give for him!" I stopped again and looked down at my feet, trying to once again organize my thoughts. My hands shook and I held them together to stop the nervous tremor. "Rurik was a great Chieftain, a loving husband, and a dedicated father. May his passage to Valhalla be assured and may Heimdallr guide him across the Bifrost to the halls of Odin where he may drink, feast, and fight amongst his brothers."

I stepped down slowly from the prow and walked back towards father. The flames from the torches seemed to bring some warmth back to his cheeks and for a brief moment I thought he may open his eyes and rise once more, as if to awake from a long slumber. Kneeling down on one knee I placed my hand on Rurik's hands, which lay atop his breast; his sword secured beneath them. Tears ran down my cold face and I allowed them to fall where they may.

"I will miss you, father. Please watch over me as I try to guide our people. I shall see you soon in Valhalla." I stood and leaned over kissing his cold hard forehead and walked back down the makeshift steps, returning to Kenna and Sada's side. Mother gripped my hand tightly and pulled me towards her with a tear streaming down her cheek.

"Thank you, son. Thank you." I nodded and signaled to Gunnar to finish the ceremony. Warriors moved forward and pushed the Drakkar onward as it was pulled by its front prow by another Drakkar. The warriors aboard the front ship rowed hard and fast pulling Rurik's vessel from the hold of the beach. Slowly they made their way out to sea until reaching a position some three or four home fields from the shore. The front Drakkar cut its ropes and turned to its port side, clearing itself from Rurik's ship that continued slowly forward into the darkness.

"Archers!" I commanded. Warriors stepped forward lifting their bows and drawing their strings back. A newly freed thrall carrying a lit torch walked from warrior to warrior setting fire to the arrow heads covered with twine and oil. The arrows burned brightly in the night time sky and roared in the silence of the evening. I turned my gaze away from the arrows back toward Rurik's ship.

"Goodbye, Father…" I would miss him terribly. "Loose!" Bow strings snapped forward sending the arrows flying overhead like streaking stars reaching for the heavens. One by one, they fell upon Rurik's Drakkar and quickly lit the oil soak decks. Within a matter of moments, the flames grew to great height and engulfed the entire ship. The sun had completely descended below the horizon and found its magnificent brightness replaced by the blinding light of father's ship.

The Seer walked away with his bow and from the flames that he had fed eagerly and approached me with a stern look upon his face. "Kin, family, dearest friends and allies! With the passing of one great man Odin gives us the honor of placing another in his place. Today's sorrows will pass with overwhelming good news. Today we name Audan, son of Rurik, to the post of Chieftain!" Seer removed a seax blade from his waist and lifted the blade into the air. The knife shone brightly in the darkness against the light of the roaring fires. "Through blood we are kin, through blood we are unified, and through blood we lead." The old man took my right arm and pulled it towards him. He lifted the sleeve of my tunic and placed the blade against my skin. Looking up at me with wide eyes, he asked, "Are you ready to lead your people? To be the voice, body, and soul?"

I nodded.

"I am." He ran the blade across my arm spilling blood that trickled quickly down my hand and between my fingers. Cupping his hand around the wound, he caught much of the crimson liquid and rubbed it into both hands. He lifted his arms and smeared the blood across my face.

"Raise your arms and take your proper place amongst your people!" I stepped forward raising both arms high into the air despite my wounds for all to see.

"All Hail, Audan, Chieftain of the people of Bjorgvin!" The people raised their hands, weapons, and torches into the air repeating after the Seer.

"All Hail, Audan! All Hail, Audan! All Hail, Audan!" The Seer lowered my arm and held my hand tightly.

"This concludes the ascension! Now, let us celebrate!" The people cheered and quickly flocked towards the great hall leaving the beach a deserted place. I watched solemnly as the fires ate away at the ship in the distance. The flames mesmerized me with their seductive dance. I shook my head to pull myself from my stupor and slowly turned to head inside. Kenna's hand pulled hard on my fingers.

"What is it, Mother?"

"Will you stay with me? Until the ship is gone? I want to ensure he makes it to Valhalla." I nodded.

"Of course, Mother. I will stay with you." I turned back to the ocean and quietly watched the fire rage on.

"You know, Audan, you are Chieftain now. And a Chieftain needs a wife by his side." I smiled without turning my head and replied to mother's implied motive.

"I have already asked Sada and she has agreed to marriage." I turned to see mother's reaction, and her face lit up brighter than the torches that surrounded us. She rushed me and pulled Sada in squeezing us tightly. "I had planned to wait to tell you. I did not want to distract you from this." Kenna placed her hands on our cheeks and kissed us both.

"Oh the gods will bless this union. Why would you try to hide such happy news?" She pulled away from me and squeezed Sada tightly. "My dear, you will be a most beloved daughter. What joyous news this is! The two of you have made me happy even on this, the saddest of days." Kenna wiped away her tears and looked up at the sky lifting her arms into the air. "Thank you, Odin. We have so much to do. When do you plan to have the ceremony?"

"I was going to leave the planning up to you, Mother. I thought perhaps sooner rather than later. These are perilous times and none of us know how much longer we will be amongst one another. Can you make it happen tomorrow evening?" Kenna covered her mouth, her eyes grew wide and her face was flush with excitement.

"Absolutely! Oh, I love you two so much. Rurik would have been proud of both of you."

"I know, Mother."

"So shall I call you, 'Mother'?" Kenna pulled Sada in again for a hug.

"Of course, my dear. From now on, that is all you shall call me. You have always been family but now, now it will be official!" We all held hands and continued to watch the Drakkar which was no more than a bright light in the distance, a floating specter. Time passed quickly as the veil of stars was pulled over the sky and soon the Drakkar disappeared. I closed my eyes and had a vision of the ship lifting up from the sea, the water dripping from the hull onto the ocean below. It would fly upwards like a bird leaving a trail of ripples below in the moon lit tides. Father would be awoken gently by Odin's Valkyries and he would ask Rurik to pilot the ship one last time until reaching the shores of Valhalla. A tug on my left hand pulled me away from this merry vision and back to the quiet beach.

"We should get inside. The warriors will be well into the casks of mead by now," said Sada.

"We could give them the good news! Do I have your permission to share with the others?" asked Kenna.

"Of course, Mother. You will need to make preparations. I'm sure you will find plenty of volunteers this night." Kenna hugged both of us again before ushering us back to the Great Hall.

"Thank you, both of you. Come, come, we must make an announcement." We walked off the beach up the gradual incline to the gates of Valdemar's home. The openings closed slowly and loudly behind us with the guards keenly on watch. The cheers and sounds of the Hall grew louder as we got closer. Kenna stepped in front of us and pushed the door open. We lowered our heads and walked through the entry to see Kenna waiting impatiently for us to stand still. "Are you ready?" she asked excitedly.

"Go ahead, Mother," I said as Sada squeezed my hand tighter.

"Good people of Bjorgvin! Can I have your attention?" The hall quieted down and all eyes were now fixated on Kenna. Her happiness was written all over her face, unable to conceal the joy she felt in this moment. "I have the most joyous of news to share with all of you. My son, Audan, our Chieftain, has asked Sada to marry him." The room now fell deathly quiet as the good people waited the rest of the news. "And she has agreed!"

The chamber erupted in shouting and cheers. Mead flew in all directions and suddenly Sada and I were surrounded by kin that lifted us into the air. There was dancing, singing, and merriment all around. A horn of mead was forced into my hands and I drank heartily, the golden honey spilled in my beard and onto my tunic but in this moment I cared not. The night of drinking and merriment carried on for several hours until most retired to their homes. I sat on the floor next to the fire with Sada leaning against me. I turned to see my love passed out from excess of drink. She began to snore in that quiet way that women do.

"Sada," I said gently, as I rocked my shoulder. She did not move or give any sign that she would wake. I nudged her shoulder and spoke louder this time. "Sada." She lifted her head and through her messy hair looked upward at me.

"Did I fall asleep?"

"Only for a little while." She moved the strands of hair from her face and tucked them behind her ear. "Go to bed my love. I will join you soon." Sada leaned in and squeezed my arm before standing and stumbling to the back side of the hall, where the living quarters resided.

"Don't be long. If I'm still awake I might give you some much needed release." I grinned and Sada blew me a kiss before she turned and stumbled away. A door slammed and now I knew she had made it to our chambers. I slowly rose up from the ground and stared down my drinking horn where half a horn of mead still remained. I lifted the horn and drank it quickly tossing it to the ground. The fire before me had turned to hot orange embers and I watched them glow and flicker in the dark hall with much enjoyment. The hall had fallen completely silent and in my peace I took a deep breath, hoping to release my demons.

"Did you think it was over?" A tall, dark and slender man stood in the shadows wearing a purple tunic with gold trim along the edges. A fine looking piece of cloth in a very poor setting.

"Do I think what is over?" The tall stranger stepped out from his dark resting place revealing a handsome but odd sort of man. His face was nearly as pale as the glaciers themselves with piercing dark brown eyes and a long slender nose. The man's face was rigid, a square jaw and pronounced cheek bones. To look at this man was like staring at a wood carving, something unreal yet there standing in front of me.

"You are a naïve breed of creature. Always with your heads in the clouds, hoping for a better world while you continuously have one foot in the grave." The stranger reached into his pocket and pulled out a silver coin that he twirled between each of his fingers, back and forth.

"I will not stand here and be insulted by a stranger. Now, tell me who you are and what your purpose is here. You didn't come with our ships so how did you get here?" The stranger grinned, his smile was wickedly sharp and wide. He ceased twirling the coin and placed it back into his pocket.

"I came here alone and of my own accord, so don't worry about warriors falling from the sky and knocking down your doors. You have been a very naughty boy, Audan. You see, I've been watching you, your escapades across the frozen landscape." The stranger extended his finger at me bouncing it back and forth. "You have been getting into a lot of trouble. Now, in most instances, I like trouble, in fact I live for it." The stranger slowly walked closer to me standing no more than three steps away placing his hands on his hips. His presence unnerved me but he had no weapons to speak of so I saw no immediate threat other than not knowing his intentions. "You see, I'm kind of a rebel myself. My family loves me greatly although they often misunderstand me." I became frustrated, as the stranger spoke in circles and I would have none of it.

"Stop speaking in riddles, stranger. Tell me who you are and why you are here or I will call out the guard." The man looked down towards his feet and without lifting his head gazed upward at me with a sort of mischievous grin. What the hell was he up to?

"Fine, Audan, have it your way!" The stranger became angry, crossing his arms and taking another step forward. "I am not of your kind but your people know my name well." The stranger rushed forward and snapped his fingers in front of my face, suddenly disappearing in thin air. In a panic, I drew my seax blade and looked about the hall for the missing man. The room was deathly silent save for the sound of a crackling fire in the background. "I am a trickster." I turned around to see the stranger sitting on a chair across the room. I rushed towards him with blade in hand, but before I could reach him he disappeared again.

"Show yourself, magician!" I turned about the room quickly trying to find him. Something from above lightly struck my head and I looked up with blade extended to see the stranger sitting in the rafters kicking his feet back and forth while eating deer meat.

"I am also a father." I pulled back my arm and threw the seax up towards the rafters. The blade flew quickly towards its mark but again the stranger disappeared without a trace, his deer meat falling to the floor below and the blade sticking to the rafters above.

"Coward!" I yelled in anger. "Fight like a man! Show yourself!" I pulled another blade from behind my belt when suddenly the door burst open and several armed men led by Gunnar rushed inside. They looked about the hall and then back to me.

"Audan, we heard yelling. Is everything alright?" I looked about the room again and there was no sign of the stranger's presence. I gazed back at Gunnar who seemed concerned. "Audan? Why is your blade drawn?" I looked down at my hand to see myself still gripping the blade handle tightly and then gazed upward at my friend. His face said it all, he thought me mad, crazed and bereft of sanity. I slowly tucked my seax back into its sheath and placed my arms down to my sides.

"I'm sorry to have alarmed you, Gunnar. I, um, had a bad dream. I think perhaps the drink has gone to my head." Gunnar's serious look waivered and faded to a smile. He laughed quietly and lowered his arms with the men behind him following suit.

"Well, then, get some rest. I'll get back to my post." I waived them off and nodded repeatedly.

"Very well. Good night men. Be safe." They departed slowly and Gunnar watched me carefully as he closed the heavy wooden door behind him that led outside. The entrance closed with a dull thud and I listened quietly waiting for their footsteps to fade away in the distance before making another sound. I took a deep breath and found a seat nearest the fire. A burst of laughter erupted from the corner of the room and there stood the stranger holding himself tightly as he cackled uncontrollably.

"Did you see the looks on their faces?" he said pointing towards the door. "They all think you're crazy!" He continued to laugh and I just sat there quietly waiting for him to compose himself. The stranger wiped away the tears of laughter from his eyes and breathed outward loudly. "Nothing beats a good laugh. I don't care who you are."

"It seems we are at an impasse. I cannot catch you and you will not get to the point. So I will sit here and listen if you are still willing to speak?" The man cocked his head to one side and smiled widely.

"Well, I don't know, Audan, after you flung your knife at me my feelings were rather wounded."

"I apologize for that. I have many enemies these days and when a stranger shows his face and behaves as you do I can never be too careful."

"Very well. As I was saying, I am a father. A father of many creatures, one of which you hurt deeply." A father of creatures? Was he referring to...?

"You don't mean..." I couldn't let the words pass my lips, for if it was true than this stranger was not as strange to me as I had thought.

"So, there is a torch burning brightly in that thick skull of yours after all. Yes, Audan, Fenrir is one of my many children. I so love that beast. Did you know that when he was a mere puppy, I fed him wayward wanderers? Oh, how he loved to play with his food, always capping them at the legs first so they couldn't get away. What a joy it was to watch him relish his meals."

"Loki?" I said under my breath. The stranger continued to speak and regale me of his tales of Fenrir.

"When he became large enough to hunt on his own, I would often take him to Midgard to hunt for himself. Bear and elk were by far his favorite meal and so he would stay away from the villages to chase the heard of creatures in the wilds. Now and then, we would come across a hunter and he would eat them, too. Not a very particular child with concern to food. Then, one day in Asgard Fenrir escaped his cage and ran amuck. The Aesir found out and despite my fierce disagreement had him tied and bound against his will. That's when that fool Tyr lost his hand. A one-handed god, how embarrassing."

"You are Loki, a god of Asgard," I said aloud. The man stared me down placing his hand in his pocket he removed the silver coin once more and threw it towards me. I caught the coin and held it upward to see the face of Loki on both sides.

"Yes, Audan, it is I. I heard that my dog had been released from his bonds and your name seems to keep coming up in conversation. Audan, the deceiver of Freya. Audan, the slayer of a child of Jormungandr. Audan, the mortal right hand of the All Father Odin." Loki stood and walked towards me with a heavy look on his brow. He leaned forward, resting his hands on the wooden table across from me. "What pride you must feel knowing that you above all men on Midgard are favored by the gods."

"Not all gods, Loki," I responded sharply.

"That is true. Freya seems to have a special hatred for you."

"So, now I know who you are but not why you are here. What is it that you want from me, Loki?"

"Just like a warrior, always straight to the point. You know, Audan, now that you are Chieftain, you will need to become better at politics. This means showing your guests some courtesy through casual conversation." I reached across the table gripping a wooden jug of mead and handed it to Loki. "Thank you." Loki lifted the jug and drank heartily. He pulled the jug down slightly for air and then continued to drink and drink and drink until the jug was empty. That jug alone could have filled seven horns of mead and Loki drank it all in one sitting. "A fine brew! Now then, the point. Why am I here? I am here to collect my dog."

"Fenrir, you came from Asgard to get your dog?"

"Of course. I care for that dog deeply and I want him back. Freya let him out from his binding, which I appreciate, but she should not have unleashed him on Midgard. Odin will have him put down if he gets into too much trouble."

"So, go get your dog. Why is it that you consult me on your child?"

"It's your fault that he's out. You and that brother of yours!" I stood fiercely drawing my dagger that held at my hip.

"What do you know of my brother?" I yelled. Loki leaned back in his chair and laughed at me.

"What's wrong, Audan? Do you miss your companion in arms? If he had been a better fighter perhaps he would still be with you today instead of rotting in Freya's torture chambers." Torture chambers? He knew something, that son of a bitch Loki knew more than he was letting on.

"If you know where my brother is than let it slip loose from your tongue or I will find a way to loosen it for you!" Loki did not appear intimidated by my threats as he just sat there smiling at me with his eyes frantically looking me up and down.

"You're mad. I understand. I will come back another time." Loki stood and began to walk away.

"Loki stop." The slender figure ceased his movement forward and turned his head back slightly to hear what I had to say. I placed my dagger back in its resting place and opened my hands in a gesture of peace. "My rage is not for you Loki but for Freya. If you know something, anything, please tell me. If you can help me get my brother back there is nothing that I would not do in return." The room was silent and the fire pit once again crackled loudly in the background. Loki's grin reached wide along the side of his face and he slowly turned his body towards mine.

"Anything? You would do anything to get your brother back?" I suddenly realized the gravity of what I had said. Loki the god, Loki the trickster would no doubt have some nefarious goal in his mind just waiting to be unleashed. All he needed to carry out the deed was a willing participant, a puppet.

"For Jareth, I would climb the walls of Valhalla and kill the gods themselves, if I must. But I have to ask Loki, why a god such as yourself cannot do this task on your own."

"I am not much different than my one-eyed brother. Just like him, I must not linger very long on Midgard. My power wanes here and although I can still perform my magic, its strength and endurance fades as the days pass. Fenrir on the other hand is not impacted in the same way. His strength is much more primordial, much like the elements of rock and fire. The longer Fenrir runs about Midgard, the stronger he will become. The stronger he becomes the more death and destruction he will bring unto man."

"What is your role in all of this, Loki? Surely, you are not an innocent by-stander? After all, you are one of the Aesir and have a stake in the Ragnarok."

Loki rubbed his cleft chin and smiled warmly.

"Freya's aspirations are much harsher than my own. It is true that I to would wish to rule in Odin's place. After all, who would not wish to sit on a throne of gold plated skulls? However, my plans for rule are far less violent than Freya's. I want the people to love me, to respect me as they do Odin. Freya wants to rule over realms of corpses, weak and meager people. For a swindler such as myself, I see little amusement in so much darkness, so much hatred."

"So, that's it, then. I capture the wolf monster for you and you in turn will tell me where I can find my brother?"

"Yes, Audan, that is the agreement."

"There are no other demands you have?"

"Well, not a demand, more of a personal request."

"Go on then." I knew it! I knew there was something else.

"Freya can know nothing of our arrangement. She is depending on Fenrir to cause havoc and mayhem in your realm. Without him, I think she would lose a great deal of her ability to move so quickly across your lands."

"Is that all?"

"That is all, Audan. Oh, and you will need this." Loki reached into his pocket and removed a curious ball of twine.

"Do you expect me to knit a cloak?" I joked.

"This is no ordinary thread Audan. This is gleipnir, the strongest material in existence. It was forged by the dwarves themselves. Impossible to break, but light as a feather."

"You must be joking?"

"I joke about many things, Audan, but the quality of dwarven metals is something I take very seriously. When you use the gleipnir, you must be swift and stout. Fenrir will not be capable of breaking it but he will still be very dangerous until he has been tied down. So, do you agree to help me in this?"

"Agreed." I reached outward and shook Loki's hand. His grasp was like ice and stung the skin at the touch. However, I did not flinch or let him see my weakness. Loki released his grasp and stepped back from me. "When I capture Fenrir, how will I find you?"

"You won't. I will find you."

Loki turned his back to me and stepped forward towards the door.

"Now, son of Rurik, prepare your men and make your ships ready to sail. It is time for you to hunt a monster." Loki unexpectedly shrank to a very small size growing fur, a tail, and a long snout with whiskers. As he did so, I watched with great wonder as Loki became of all things, a black rat! He turned towards me, squeaked and then scurried off across the hard floor, disappearing through a crack under the door. I felt suddenly full of dread. A deal with Loki to return Fenrir? What had I done?

Six
A Union

The next morning, I awoke to a terribly cold breeze rushing into our chambers. I wiped my eyes and opened them quickly to see the window wide open. Snow had piled up on the ridges of the stone opening, littering the floor beneath me. I quickly pulled the wooden slat shut. The wind subsided but the chamber itself was bitterly cold. I turned back to see Sada curled up tightly underneath several dark bear furs. Wishing not to disturb her slumber, I quietly grabbed my clothes and headed straight for the door, hoping to find some breakfast prepared in the main hall.

I pulled on the door gently as it let out a low and long creak. Sada shuffled her feet but did not remove her face from under the covers. Stepping outside quietly, I shut the door behind me and began to don my clothing. Further down the hall, I could hear the quiet shuffle of feet and the faint smell of fresh bread and eggs. A happiness came over me and I quickly straightened out my clothes and hurried in the direction of food.

The other doors in the hall remained closed as their occupants still slumbered quietly. Warm air from the halls fire rushed over my cold my body. The main chamber appeared bright, clean, and orderly; no doubt well cleaned after last night's supper. Several ladies of the hall appeared near the kitchen entrance and set food in varying arrangements, while a small boy stoked the fire and stacked logs.

"Audan," a gentle voice called out. "I'm pleased to see you rising so early this morning." It was mother, who was already finely dressed.

"Good morning, Mother. Did you rest well?" Kenna placed a plate of bread down on the table and rubbed the back of her neck coarsely. She smiled wide, but sighed very deeply.

"Honestly, I don't think I slept at all." Dark circles ringed her eyes, which appeared red and puffy, no doubt from weeping over the loss of father and Jareth. "Sit, son. Eat. You must be famished. We have much to do before the day is over."

I leaned against the dark wooden table and sat down carefully on the bench. Kenna placed her hands on my shoulder and leaned against me, kissing the back of my head. "Today is a very big day! I hope you are ready!" Through my hard night's sleep and the uneasy encounter with Loki, I had nearly forgotten that we planned to have our wedding ceremony today. I rubbed my eyes coarsely and smiled with great anticipation.

"Do you have everything planned?" Mother stopped in her busy tracks, pulling an apron off her waist and placing it on the table. She raised her hands high into the air, smiling brightly.

"Oh, son! It's going to be the grandest event our people have ever seen! There will be torches and fires, food and song and dancing! I will adorn every inch of the hall in great banners and green branches. But we haven't got much time. The day moves quickly and I won't waste any sunlight."

"How can I help?" I asked. Kenna quickly swayed her head from side to side in objection as she quickly swallowed a small piece of bread.

"No, no, no!" She pointed at me. "You, my dear son, will remain here in the hall. I have our best seamstresses coming to measure and fit you for your ceremonial dress. So I just want you to sit here and relax and the ladies will come to fetch you when it is time. Is that understood?" I laughed quietly while chewing on bread and nodded in her direction. "I'm proud of you, son. Your father would have been proud of you as well. You have become a fine man and soon you shall become a great Chieftain with the love of your life at your side."

I swallowed my bread and cleared my throat.

"Thank you, Mother, for everything you do. It does not go unnoticed. I think the gods would have been hard-pressed to plan such an occasion in such a short manner of time."

"Only the best for my sons..." Kenna trailed off, looking stricken. Suddenly, she began to weep, placing her hands in her face and I stood quickly from the table to come to her aid.

"Mother, what is it? What fills your heart with so much sorrow on such a day?" I gently helped her to a chair and pulled back her long finely brushed hair.

"Your brother..." Kenna wept loudly and I wrapped my arms around her stroking her hair gently. "I wish he could be here to see this."

"I know Mother but I promise you, I will find Jareth and bring him home." Kenna lowered her head and swung it side to side.

"No, my son. Don't make promises you can't keep. If what you said is true and Freya has taken him, then he will not return. She will kill him or worse, turn him to her own will."

I stared blankly up at the rafters, not knowing what to say or do. I just held her tightly to give her some form of comfort. "Everything will be well, Mother." Kenna patted my shoulder and lifted her head as she wiped away her tears.

"I know, son. I know. Enough of this sadness and back to happier things. I'm headed down to the docks to purchase some goods. A ship came in early this morning with supplies I could use for the feast."

"A ship?" I was intrigued. With everything going on, I was suspicious of any strangers who unexpectedly appeared on our shores. "What sort of ship?" I asked.

"Traders from further south. Danes, I think." I stood upright, tense.

"Did they give a name? Why are they here?"

Kenna looked up at me and smiled.

"So many questions, Audan? They are just traders, nothing more. Your uncle is down at the docks as we speak, seeing to their needs. There are guards all about the island, so I wouldn't worry so much." Kenna kissed my forehead and gazed at my face. "Now, I best be off. Rest yourself and do not wander off."

"Yes, Mother." Kenna donned a dark green cloak, placing the hood over her head and stepping out the door with a woven basket in her hand. The door slammed shut loudly and I was left alone with the large hall, a crackling fire, and a mug of mead. I closed my eyes and watched the battle of Bjorgvin play in my head over and over again. Jareth's face, lifeless, motionless as he was carried off on the back of Freya. I could not remove the image of his face from out of my mind and it haunted my honor so. Footsteps then came up from behind me and a warm hug quickly embraced me.

"Good morning, my love." Sada kissed my cheek gently and took a seat next to me. "Today is the big day. Are you ready?" I gazed at her lovely face with a morbidly serious look.

"What do you think?" I kept my face stoic.

Sada glanced at me, panic crossing her features.

"What is it, my love? What's wrong?"

A smile crept over my face and I lunged at her, tumbling to the ground and taking our chairs with us.

"I'm overjoyed!"

Sada laughed wildly and we caught our breath before kissing on the floor of the hall. Sada punched my chest and pushed me away.

"My gods! There's so much to do, so much to be done! Where is your mother? Has she risen yet?"

"She went down to the docks to meet Valdemar. A ship came in early this morning with many provisions. She was going to procure what she could for our ceremony." Sada pushed me away, smiling, and jumped to her feet.

"There's no time to waste!" She ran out the door, leaving it wide open letting in the wind and snow. Suddenly, she burst back into the room retrieving a brown hooded cloak. "I love you!"

Before I could reply, she slammed the door shut and I was once again alone in my thoughts. I took a deep breath and closed my eyes as I lay my head down on the table.

"Jareth..." Suddenly, a loud bang erupted and the doors to the Great Hall swung open. Three women dressed in simple clothing entered, one of them, an older woman I recognized from before. "Maarit, is that you?" She looked different since last I saw her, her clothing much cleaner and her hair neat.

"Audan, my lord." Maarit bowed her head slightly before gazing back up towards me with woven baskets dangling from her hands.

"What are you doing here?" I asked curiously.

"I am the best seamstress on the Island. I am here to fit you for you ceremonial gown."

I smiled, thinking how small the world was.

"Well, I'm glad to have you here once more and I wanted to thank you again for the care you gave me when I first arrived. It was a dangerous voyage and you were most welcoming."

"And I, Audan, well—we— would like to thank you."

I felt puzzled, as the three women looked at me with great big smiles and tears welling in their eyes.

"I don't understand? What have I done?"

Maarit placed her hands gently on my shoulders. You have freed us, all of us. We were thrall nearly all our lives. We knew nothing other than what our masters had set forth before us. Now the world has been opened to us, thanks to you. You are our savior and from this day forth I shall treat you as a son." Maarit leaned in and kissed each of my cheeks, and then the other women followed suit. I was deeply humbled by their gesture.

"Thank you, Maarit. I only hope that I can live up to your expectations of what a son should be." The old woman nodded.

"You will, Audan. You will. Now let's see about your clothes." She turned back to her friends who set down baskets filled with linens. Maarit pulled out brightly colored pieces and laid them out on the table. "For your ceremony, you will need an under garment, tunic, pants, a fine leather belt, cloak with broaches, and the best leather shoes. For your tunic we have blue, green, brown, but I recommend the red. It's bold, vibrant, and quite lovely for such an occasion."

"Red it is, then." One of the women grabbed a long twine and approached me.

"Lift your arms, my lord." I did as she asked and she quickly wrapped the twine around my waist, chest, and neck. With each measurement, she took a piece of coal and marked the twine. She then patted me firmly on the back. "Spread your legs." My face suddenly felt flush.

"I'm sorry?"

"Your legs, my lord. I need you to spread them so I can get your proper measurements."

"Shouldn't any pants do?" I asked. She smirked and giggled allowed. Maarit stepped in front of me.

"Not all men are built the same," Maarit said. "We want to make sure your clothing is a perfect fit for a perfect day"

"Understood," I replied. The woman with the measurements handed them to another woman who then in turn repeated them to Maarit. They seemed to be quite the team as they quickly unfolded and folded cloth while making markings on the linen.

"Excellent!" Maarit exclaimed. "We are done here for now. We will leave you to your duties while we prepare your clothing. We shall return shortly before your ceremony to try it on and do a final fitting. Thank you for your patience, my lord." The three women bowed slightly, gathered their belongings and turned to leave.

"Thank you, ladies." The door opened sending in a strong cold breeze. Puffs of snow blew into the room and rolled along the floor until the ladies secured it behind them. I sat back down and returned to my bread and mead. Footsteps echoed down the hall once more and a short fat man appeared.

"Audan," Eygautr said as he adjusted his pants and tunic. "I did not think that anyone else would be up at this hour. Did you not sleep well?"

"I slept fine, old friend. The window was open and the cold breeze awoke me." Eygautr sat down and grip the bread eagerly breaking off a piece and shoving it in his mouth.

"Winter is a brutal mistress and her icy kiss can be the thing of nightmares." Thumbing at my mug, I looked up at Eygautr as I slouched over the table.

"Do you have nightmares?" Eygautr grabbed another piece of bread and then reached for my mug, pulling it from my hands. He look down the wooden cup to see that it had been emptied.

"I think I'm having a nightmare now, young man. My cup has run dry of mead." I stood and walked towards the fire pit where a large container held large quantities of the golden honey and filled two mugs, bringing one back to Eygautr. He took a deep drink and then raised his mug into the air.

"There, that's much better! Now, you were asking me about nightmares?"

"Do you have them?"

Eygautr cleared his throat and coughed several times. "Of course, young lad. All men have nightmares but in all honesty, my nightmares now pale in comparison to the things we have seen that lie just across the water."

"I think I would have to agree with you, old friend. Freya and Fenrir are the thing of nightmares."

"How much longer do you think we will stay here?"

"Not much longer. We need to regain a foothold in Bjorgvin, but we have not the men, nor the weapons to take on a beast such as Fenrir."

Eygautr leaned in, his eyebrows raised high and he gave me a most somber look.

"There are those we could call upon to aid us in another raid."

"Who?"

"The Danes to the south are fine warriors, but the fighters I'm most interested in are the ones we know and hate the most."

I thought for a moment and the wicked look upon Eygautr's face made clear to me his intentions. "You know those of which I speak of."

"Finns! You want us to go to the Finns and ask for aid?"

"What's a matter, boy, haven't you the spine to know when you need help and must beg others?"

"The Finns are not just any people. Even if I could convince them to fight alongside us, they would run us through the moment our backs are turned." Eygautr stood, pointing his thick hairy knuckled fingers at me.

"You need to learn when you are defeated and now you are defeated! This plague that carries on the wind is plague that affects us all. Freya and Fenrir will take over the land of Norge and then move on to Lade, More, Vestfold, and the smaller realms until all has been conquered in our lands. Then, she will swell her ranks and move on the Danes and Finns. Our fates are intertwined. Do not be a stubborn old fool like you father."

In a rage, I reached across the table and gripped Eygautr's tunic by the collar pulling it inward with my other fist pulled back ready to strike.

"How dare you speak of my father this way; how dare you speak of your greatest ally in this manner."

"Your father was a good man, Audan, and my greatest friend, but he did not do well to unite the Viking realms. We have been raiding Finn villages for decades, perhaps longer. Why do you think they hate us so? To them, we are the plague of Midgard. Now more than ever, we need to mend broken alliances and move together as one." I shook my head and wiped the angry look from my face. The short fat man was right. If we wanted to stand any chance of defeating our foe we needed new and powerful allies. "Release me, boy, and I'll forget this ever happened." I released my gripped of Eygautr's tunic and sat back down.

"Apologies, old friend. These are dark times for me." Eygautr adjusted his tunic and leaned back in towards me.

"I understand, Audan, but these are dark times for us all. It's time to put aside your emotions and start acting like a Chieftain. Learn from your father's mistakes and maybe, just maybe, we will get out of this with our lives."

"So when do we sail?"

Eygautr laughed.

"You're the Chieftain not I. That, my friend, is for you to decide. Command me and I shall see it through." I nodded my head several times and smiled.

"Thank you for your counsel, old friend." Eygautr raised his mug into the air.

"Think nothing of it." We slammed our mugs together and finished our drink. An hour or so passed by as we quietly watch the fire and the citizens of work about tiding up the hall. The door opened once more with Kenna and Sada standing outside.

"Audan, come see some of the wares the ship brought." I smiled and stood gazing at Eygautr.

"Will you come with us, old friend?" Eygautr stood, finishing his drink and slamming the cup on the table.

"Why not. Perhaps I have some coin to part ways with." We headed outside on a cold but bright and clear day. Snow had piled up to our knees and the walk past the ramparts to the dock was a treacherous one covered in ice. The guards had gone to work early this morning clearing paths and light fires along the way to melt the frost. After trudging through muddied snow, we reached the dock where an old and worn looking trading ship had moored. Two hooded men stood at the end of the docks, presumably the ships traders. Uncle Valdemar was just ahead of them and walked towards us when he spotted us coming down the hill.

"What do we have to trade?" I asked Uncle Valdemar.

"Iron ore and furs mostly."

"What do they bring?"

"Timber from the south dried grains. We could use the timber to build some better structures when spring arrives."

"Tell him about the other wares." Sada said excitedly. Valdemar held out a leather cloth and removed the covering to expose the most elegant golden jewelry. Rings, necklaces, and earrings.

"Impressive," I said as I walked towards the tradesman. "Good morning. My name is Audan." The traders nodded and announce themselves.

"We are brothers Skald. We bring many fine wares for you and your people if you have other valuables to trade." The tradesman rubbed his clean-shaven chin when I noticed a fresh cut across part of his face.

"That's a nasty cut. Have you been in any battles recently?" The man laughed and pulled down his hood further.

"The only battle I lost was with the ships rigging. A line snapped and smacked me in the face when we hit rough seas." I looked over the tradesman's shoulder to see a small handful of men aboard his ship moving goods and cleaning up the decks. "How much for the gold?" The tradesman rubbed his chin coarsely and extended his open hand towards me.

"What are you willing to pay?" The scoundrel, he wanted me to overbid, but I would have none of it.

"I have iron ore and furs." The tradesman shook his head vigorously.

"Iron ore is easy to come by and furs and plentiful in our lands. What else do you have?" I walked back to Valdemar.

"He does not want iron or furs." Valdemar looked over my shoulder at the tradesman.

"Weapons?" Valdemar called out. The tradesman turned to his brother whispering in his ear. He turned his gaze back towards us and nodded.

"Let me see what you have." Valdemar placed his fingers between his lips and whistled loudly. A guardsman ran back to the top of the hill and retrieved several other warriors carrying a larger leather bundle supported by a log carried upon their shoulders. The men step in front of the traders and opened the leather covering revealing swords, daggers, axes, and spears. The traded picked up a sword and swung it around examining the weight and feel. "These are fine blades, good quality. How many do you have?"

"For you entire stock I'll give you twenty swords, thirty axe heads, forty spears and fifteen daggers." The tradesman turned back to his brother and whispered in his ear.

"Thirty swords." Valdemar shook his head.

"Twenty-three," replied Valdemar.

"Twenty-eight." Valdemar shoot his head again and removed his hands from his pockets.

"Twenty-five."

The tradesman spoke privately with his brother once more and then nodded his head.

"Deal!" The tradesman approached Valdemar and shook his hand. The other man approached me and extended his arm as well.

"Congratulations on your purchase, my friend." I shook his hand.

"Thank you."

"Your name is Audan, is it not?" I suddenly became uneasy.

"Perhaps. Who is asking?"

"I have a message for you. It was written in blood!" The tradesman pulled out a knife and thrust it towards me. I stepped back but tripped on a rock and fell. The tradesman lunged down towards me with a crazed look in his eye. He descend upon me, when a hand gripped his hair pulling his head back and cutting his throat. Valdemar released the tradesman, letting his body fall to the ground. Something struck the ground near my head and I looked up to see an arrow shaft. An archer was posted up at the top of the sail and screamed at me.

"Get up, boy!" Valdemar yelled. I rushed to Sada and pushed her in front of me as we ran up the hill.

"To arms, to arms!" Eygautr yelled. Warriors rushed down the hill and when Sada and Kenna were out of harm's way, I rushed back down with the men to assault my would-be assassins. Valdemar reached the other tradesman and knocked him in the head with the broad side of the sword. He turned back to two of this men and pointed downward.

"Keep him alive! I have questions for him." We rushed down the planks of the dock where the other tradesman attempted to flee in their ship but they were too late. Several warriors boarded the ship while Valdemar and I pulled it back towards the dock and secured the lines. We jumped aboard the ship and I swung my sword from side to side. Only four men remained aboard, including the archer up above.

"Drop your weapons and you may live! Do not and you will die!" The archer atop the rigging pulled out a sword from its sheath.

"Long live the dark queen!" He ran the blade through his gut and fell into the water below. The other three men followed suit, running to the far side of the ship and sinking blades into their bellies. I rushed to the railings and looked down to see their lifeless corpses sink into the icy waters below.

"What the hell was that?" Eygautr exclaimed.

"Assassins! Where is the other tradesman?" I looked back toward the beach where the remaining Skald brother sat upright on his knees while a guard pressed a blade against his back. We ran off the ship and back down the docks until reaching the treacherous bastard.

"Who sent you?" He spit on me and I struck him with my fist and pulled his head back by his hair. "Who sent you?" I yelled.

"The dark queen is coming, Audan. She has spies everywhere and now she knows where you are…" I pressed the tip of my blade against his chest and plunged it in deeply. The tradesman gasped and coughed up blood. I stepped back and then kicked the blade further into his body. Again a steam of blood came shooting forward and he gazed at me with a most sinister stare, laughing aloud. Rushing forward, I grabbed the blade and removed it from his chest. I pulled my sword back and swung at this neck, severing his head clean off and watched it roll along the pebbles.

"They know where we are!" Valdemar exclaimed.

"No, no they don't," Eygautr disagreed. "They were a search party, that's why they were trying to get away. They didn't know Audan would be here. They were going back to tell their masters. Now, they will never speak again." I gazed out at the open ocean's horizon and buried my blade in the rocks below.

"There must be hundreds of them out there. It's only a matter of time before they find us." I felt a panic come over me, but I closed my eyes and took a deep breath, before acting out on my emotions. "Double the guard at the shore, reduce the torches and flame at night. We need to stay invisible to the outside world."

"Agreed," said Valdemar. "I'll have my men empty the ship of its provisions and pull it ashore to keep it hidden."

"Thank you, uncle. Let's head back inside and get cleaned up. We have a wedding to attend to." I lifted my blade and walked calmly back to the hall. I now planned to drink more mead and rest before the ceremony.

* * *

A knock erupted at my door. "Yes, who is it?" I said, rubbing the sleep from my eyes.

"Maarit, my Lord. We have returned with your clothing." I quickly walked to the door and opened it to see the three ladies waiting patiently outside.

"Come in, come in."

"Thank you, my Lord. We will need to undress you. Is that acceptable to you?" I nodded in agreement.

"Of course. Do what you must." The three women quickly helped me remove my clothing and then fitted me with the ceremonial gown. The material was the cleanest and finest I had ever felt against my skin. The red tunic was bright and vibrant with gold piping lining the sleeves, collar, and bottom edge.

"Do you like it?" asked Maarit.

"It's wonderful. Thank you, Maarit." The old woman smiled brightly.

"Then, I shall leave you to help prepare for the ceremony. It is nearly time." As quickly as they arrived, they then departed.

"Audan," my uncle called out from the other side of the door.

"Yes?"

"May I enter?"

"Of course. Come in." Valdemar walked inside holding two horns of mead in his hands.

"I thought I would bring you something to calm your nerves after our melee at the docks." I laughed and reached outward for the horn.

"Do you think me weak, uncle?" I gripped the horn tightly and took a deep drink.

"Weak? No, dearest nephew, but if there's one thing I do know it's that marriage can do funny things to a man's constitution. I've seen the bravest of warriors faint during their union ceremony and I have seen others run into the woods like crazed men, never to be seen again."

"This has been a long time coming, uncle. Sada is the one for me. The one the gods themselves made for me. I would never do anything to dishonor her." Valdemar slapped me on the shoulder and raised his horn high into the air.

"That's a good lad! So when do we head into the hall?"

"I'm waiting for Kenna. She planned the entire event and I will do her the courtesy of telling me when and where to move." Valdemar wiped mead from his chin and burped loudly.

"It's best you do it that way. Let the women have their fun. They live for these sort of things." Another knock came at the door.

"Come In!" I called out and finished the last of my mead. Kenna quickly peeked in and stormed inside. She reached over me and pulled the horn from my hand.

"Drinking before your ceremony? You need to have your wits about you, son, not crawling on your face!" Before I could say anything, Valdemar stood, handing me his horn of unfinished mead.

"Leave him be, woman! I gave him the mead. Here, lad, take this and drink up. It will give you strength." Kenna crossed her arms in protest, while I dumped the last of the mead down my throat.

"Valdemar, I should have known. I'll expect you to ensure he makes good on this day."

Valdemar laughed heartily and cleared his throat.

"I'll be standing behind him with my steel in hand. The young man won't be going anywhere except his chambers with his betrothed." Valdemar hit me in the shoulder again. "Am I right, my boy?"

"To right, uncle!"

"Stand up, my son, let me have a good look at you." I stood and turned slowly with my hands out to my sides. I turned all the way around and saw my mother with her hands over her mouth.

"Mother? Does this not please you?" She pulled her hands down to reveal her hidden smiles as tears streamed down her face.

"You're such a handsome young man. I'm proud to call you my son! I only wish your father and brother were here to see this." Kenna leaned in to kiss me on the cheek. "Now, are you ready, son? Your bride will be along shortly and we don't want to keep her waiting." I placed the empty horn down on my bedside and straightened my tunic.

"I'm ready, Mother. Will you walk with me?" I extended my arm and Kenna wrapped hers into mine.

"Of course, son."

"Well, then, what are we waiting for?" Valdemar held the door open for us and I allowed Kenna to leave first. As soon as I entered the hall, the overwhelming smell of burning herbs filled the air. Guards lined each end of the hallway and we walked towards the entryway to the hall when Kenna had me stop.

"Wait here. I'm going to go check on your bride." Mother squeezed my hand and walk to the opposite end of the hall departing through the outward door. I gazed to my right to see Gunnar and Eygautr finely dressed with one hand on their swords waiting at the backside of the hall near the stone throne. A beautiful archway made of branches and adorned with dried flowers had been erected. Just beyond the archway stood large wooden statue with the likeness of Odin carved upon it. I smiled, wondering if the old man would approve of his likeness on this piece of wood. No doubt he was watching me now, protecting us, helping to shelter us from Freya's all seeing eyes. A hand gripped my shoulder from behind and I looked back to see an unfamiliar face.

"Are you ready, young Audan?" The man that stood behind me wore the robes of the Seer but I had never seen the Seer's entire face before. Half of his face was terribly disfigured with burns covering most of his skin and a sword cut that ran across his forehead to the bottom of his nose. I hesitated to reply and now felt embarrassed as I gawked at his disfigurement. "It's alright, Audan. You know I never did tell you why I always where a hood. And I'm sure your father never told you how I came to acquire these scars?"

I shook my head.

"No, Seer, he failed to tell me the tale." The Seer reached back gripping the hood of his cloak placing it gently over his head.

"I was once a young man like yourself and in those days I was even less cautious than you were before you met the gods. One day atop a hill, I called a man a liar and a cheat simply to force him into a duel. You see, I wanted his lands and his woman. The man agreed to my challenge and so we fought and in no more than three swings of my blade, I ran my steel into his flesh and ended his life. All that belonged to him was now mine. But, the story does not end there. For many days and nights, I spent my time drunk, boasting of my great victory and the woman that I now spoiled at will. Then one evening in my drunken slumber, I was awoken to the cut of a blade across my face. When I attempted to cover my wounds I could not move my arms.

My limbs had been tied to each side of the bed. Standing above me was the scorned widow covered in my blood. She leaned over my body and whispered into my ear, '*This is for my lover*,' and she lit the wool linens ablaze. The flames soon reached my right arm eating away at my flesh and spread quickly to my chest and face. The twine used to hold me down also caught ablaze and soon splintered. In my greatest moment of pain, I summoned all my strength and snapped the twine freeing my limb. I untied the others as the fire continued to eat at my body. At long last, when the last of the twine was undone I fell to the floor and rolled about until the flames subsided. With only one eye, I managed to run outside to the oceans water to quench the pain but only found more from the sting of saltwater. My body went limp and I fell lifeless into the waves. It was not for a great many days that I awoke under the care of a young woman and her family some distance from my home lands. For many weeks, they nursed me back to health through pain, fever, and many times near death.

"When I could walk again, I made it outside in the light of day down to a small river where I could see the monster that lay before me. I was now as ugly on the outside as I was once on the inside. So it was from that day that I swore to the gods to serve them and their people. To only do good unto others and to spread Odin's message until the end of my days. So there you have it, young man. Now you know my story. I hope for your sake that you gleamed something from my misfortunes."

My eyes were wide open and I now found a whole new respect for a man I once thought so little of.

"Thank you for sharing it with me. I won't forget it." Without saying a word, the Seer stepped in front of me and walked towards the archway. He turned and stood in front of it facing the crowds of well-dressed family, friends, and visitors. Suddenly, a loud knock came at the exterior door and the guards gracefully opened the entrance. My eyes now beheld the most stunning site in all of creation. Not on Midgard nor in Valhalla would one find such a beauty that I now beheld before me. Those not yet standing, quickly rose in the hall and as Sada stepped gracefully forward in her embroidered white dress. The room fell silent. She looked up at me, blinking to adjust to the torch lit light of the hall. Her hair was straight and fell gracefully on each side of her shoulders. The top of her head was adorned with a white crown made of shining fabrics and in her hands she held a small branch with three bright green leaves.

I felt frozen in place. Sada walked down a padded walkway of white linen towards the center of the hall. I felt a hand push me gently from behind and I walked forward to meet my love in the middle. I stopped about a half a step away from Sada, fearing that if I came too close, I might trip and knock her over. She looked me up and down, her face lighting up as if all the world were right.

"You look quite handsome," she said to me.

"And you are the envy of all the realms." I extended my arm and my love gladly took it, walking down a center aisle past our many family members and dearest friends. Njord stepped out in front of me, holding what appeared to be brand new sword and sheath.

"Is that for me?"

"We can't have our Chieftain carrying around a relic, now can we?" Njord smiled, placing his hands on his hips and gripping his polished hammer. He then reached around my waist, removing my blade and replacing it with the new one. "I'll make sure this one gets cleaned up and returned to you."

"Thank you, brother." Njord quickly melded back into the crowd and we continued forward until stopping in front of the Seer. The old man raised his arms into the air, holding a large wooden staff.

"Before I begin, I would just like to say that it's about damn time, Audan, son of Rurik!" The room erupted into laughter and the Seer raised his hands higher to calm down those in attendance. "Family, friends, brothers and sisters, in these dark days, the gods have truly blessed us with one such day that can be filled with light and love. Like the god Sol shining light down upon us, Audan and Sada have decided to shine their own light this day and share it with each of us, so that we all may be reminded of the beauty in the love between man and woman." My heart raced and I rubbed my hands as my palms began to sweat. Sada glanced over at me and smiled, but tried her hardest to keep herself fixated on the Seer. "So it is with great privilege that I am here today to ask the gods to bless this union of our son and Chieftain Audan and our beloved daughter, Sada."

The Seer extended his hand outward. "Audan and Sada, give me your hands." We extended our arms and the Seer placed our hands one on top of the other. He pulled out a brightly-colored piece of twine and began to wrap it around our hands. "This twine represents to binding of two destinies as the Norn's would weave your fate. What once was two shall now become one. By the power of our ancient gods, I now pronounce you husband and loving wife."

Sada and I reached out to one another and kissed passionately. The onlookers cheered loudly and we turned with smiles to greet our family and friends. A perfect union in an imperfect world. That night was filled with much dancing, mead, and celebrations the likes of which the Isle of Fani had never seen until my bride and I disappeared into our chambers for a night of warmth.

* * *

"Why have you not left yet?" a mysterious voice whispered. I opened my eyes and looked about the dark room to see nothing there. Cautiously, I lifted my head and reached for the dagger beneath my pillow. Gripping the handle, I slowly pulled the blade from its hiding place and held it outward, the metal reflecting the small bit of light that came in through cracks in the window.

"Who's there?" I asked quietly. All was silent, all was quiet and not even my love who lay peacefully next to me, stirred. Thinking it was a dream, I relaxed and placed the blade down next to me. I shook my head, but heard the voice once more.

"Audan!"

"Loki? Is that you?"

"It's been two weeks, Audan. Two weeks since we made our arrangement and still your ships have not sailed back to the mainland to fetch my dog." I rubbed my eyes and then placed my dagger back beneath the pillow.

"So, it is you. Keep your voice down or you will wake Sada." The outline of Loki emerged smoothly from the shadows of my entryway towards the foot of my bed.

"She will not wake this night, Audan, I assure you. I have given her dreams of spring, warm fields, and flowers." I turned to see Sada smiling and sound asleep.

"Why are you here?"

"To ensure you have not forgotten our pact."

"I have not and I will maintain our bargain."

"Then why have your ship not yet sailed?"

"Because peace is not something that we people of Bjorgvin have tasted in many years. My people needed time to rest, my men need time to gather supplies and I needed time to be a husband to my wife."

Loki paused for a moment, turning his head away and taking a deep breath.

"I see. So while you are resting on your island paradise people of Midgard are being slaughtered. Do you not hear the screams from the mainlands? Have you not seen the blood running through the inside passages? Midgard is dying, kingdoms are falling."

"Loki, I..." He lifted his hand.

"I understand your needs, Audan, and now I need you to hear mine. Make sail for the mainland by tomorrow or I shall find ways of making island life very uncomfortable."

I felt a hard pit in my stomach. I knew he spoke the truth. I nodded slowly several times.

"I understand. I shall have a ship ready and leave as early as possible tomorrow."

"Good. I leave you to your rest then." The silhouette of Loki pulled back and merged into the shadows.

"Loki?" He did not respond and I no longer felt his uneasy presence lingering over me. Slowly, I laid back down and let my head sink into my pillow. Sada shifted slightly leaving one of her hands against my cheek. I closed my eyes and, although unnerved, I let myself drift back into a deep slumber.

* * *

I awoke the next morning to the sounds of many footsteps walking past our door. Sada remained fast asleep and I wished not to disturb her dreams. I quietly stood, donned my clothing and headed out the door with my axe in hand. As I stepped into the main hall, I quickly stopped when I saw that nearly all my warriors had gathered inside fully dressed with supplies on their backs.

"What's all this?" I asked curiously. Eygautr approached pulling his belt up under his stomach and removing a small wooden statue.

"We received knocks at our doors this morning, each of us, but when answered, there was no one there. Just this." I held the statue to my face and gazed upon a wolf's head eating a ship. I looked up towards my men and each of them raised their arms in the air holding the very same statue. "And something else, a voice carried in the air leaving a message."

"What message?"

"Ready the ships. Go fetch my fucking dog." I rolled my eyes in frustration and looked down at the small wooden statue.

"Loki…" I gripped the wooden statue tightly and turned about throwing it into the fire in anger.

"Was this your doing, Audan?" asked Eygautr suspiciously.

"No, Eygautr, it most certainly was not." I protested.

"Then who was it?" I gazed upward from the ground and hesitated to utter these words for fear of seeming foolish to a man that I respected.

"Loki. It was Loki."

"Loki? You mean to tell me that we were visited by the god himself?" Eygautr said in utter amazement.

"Did you ready the ships?" I asked in frustration.

"We are nearly ready to depart. The last of the provisions are being loaded as we speak. Two Drakkar with a compliment of nearly fifty men each. The remaining warriors will stay behind to provide security and maintain order on Fani while we are gone."

"That bastard!" I was furious that Loki had taken it upon himself to rouse the men, but my warriors were more interested in the god himself and not his actions.

"So, it's true then. It was Loki that did this."

"He visited me last night when I slumbered." I stopped to scratch my forehead and realized that nearly one hundred men were there to listen to my ramblings. "Back to your duties, all of you. I would speak with Eygautr, Valdemar and Gunnar in private." The many warriors nodded their heads and shuffled out the main door loudly while bantering on about what had just transpired. I walked towards a row of tables and dropped my axe loudly on the surface. Sitting down I waited patiently for the remaining warriors to leave the room until the door slammed loudly. Two warriors guarding the doors remained inside. "You as well."

"My lord?" the guard asked.

"The two of you, outside. I'll not have my private discussions become idle rumor." The guards nodded and quickly headed outside slamming the door behind them. My counsel sat quickly at the table and waited patiently while thoughts swirled around in my head.

"Audan?" asked Uncle Valdemar. I met his gaze and nodded without speaking a word. "Are you going to tell us about our visitor? About Loki?"

I ran my fingers coarsely through my long hair pulling it out of my face. Opening my eyes wide, I reached outward for a wooden mug of mead quickly pressing it to my lips and drinking heartily. As the golden liquid passed my throat and into my gut, it warm my body and for that matter, loosened my lips.

"I have an agreement with Loki," I muttered. Gunnar reached outward grabbing a mug as well.

"What sort of agreement?" Gunnar asked. Suddenly Sada walked into the room clad in leather armor with dagger, sword, and shield.

"What the hell are you doing?" I asked.

"I'm going with you. What does it look like I am doing?" I placed my hands on Sada's shoulders and stared deeply into her eyes.

"I cannot allow you to go. I could not bear to see you hurt or even killed." Sada did not stop and continued securing the belt and sword scabbard to her waist. She was determined and when Sada set her will to something she would not be deterred. Not even by me.

"I am your wife, Audan, but I am also a free woman. I will not stand idly by and let you run off to face danger without me again. This is a family affair and we should see to it together. You promised I could go! Are you not a man of your word?"

Sada was right, I did promise her and no matter my objections there would be no changing her mind now.

"Very well, but you stay with Gunnar and don't ever separate from the group. Do you understand?" Sada nodded but still appeared very angry with me. I left the men to pack their affects and stepped outside for some much needed fresh air.

"Audan" a coarse voice called out and a shadow approached from the side.

"Hilgrid?" My old friend stood beside me with his face mostly covered but there was no mistaking his sharp eyes. "I have not seen you for some time."

"I'm not coming."

"Not coming? But why? You are family and I need your bravery by my side." Hilgrid took a deep breath and exhaled heavy in the cold air.

"I need to leave Audan." The tone of his voice had changed, something sad and lost within him. A desperation but for what? Reluctantly I bowed my head in acceptance of his wish.

"Even if I could I would not keep you here brother. You are a free man and have earned the right to do as you will. I am in your debt for the times you have saved my life. But may I ask, where will you go?" Hilgrid looked out to the east back towards the mainland.

"Something calls me brother, something wild. I need to find what it is." I extended my arm and Hilgrid did the same. I gripped his large hand wrapping my fingers around his claws.

"Go brother. Find what it is you seek. May Odin watch over you and bless you on your journey. Should ever need anything come and find me." Hilgrid nodded and marched off in the snow of the streets without uttering a word. I hoped that I would one day see him again but wondered if he would be anything like he is now. No more than an hour later our party boarded the ship and Sada sat at an oar opposite of me with an angry look about her face; still angry at my objection of her joining the crew. It was going to be a long voyage.

Seven
Asunder

An uneasy feeling sat in the pit of my stomach that morning as we pushed the Drakkar off from the rocky docks. There would be no farewell gathering this time, no mass of loved ones to wave goodbye as our ship carried us off into the dark waters. We were alone, utterly alone, in this journey towards our end. I gazed back at the guards standing atop the wooden palisades and watched as the wind-swept banners of Valdemar's home danced in the breeze. Although we sailed for my home village of Bjorgvin I knew in my heart of hearts that it would not be the childhood home that I once knew.

"Clear sailing!" Eygautr called out. He walked towards me and motioned with his head to join him at the rear prow. I stood from my rowing chest and slowly walked down the aisle minding my sea legs. Reaching the rear I sat down next to the short fat man and waited curiously for him to speak, but he did not. I squinted, as he sighed loudly and looked about the horizon. "Your father would have loved this. Sailing off into the high seas to almost infinite peril. Nothing made him feel more alive than when he knew he may die."

I chuckled and rubbed my beard fiercely. "He drinks in Valhalla now. I doubt he laments on the troubles of mortal men." Eygautr gave me a sour look and scoffed, crossing his arms over his belly.

"The dead never forget the living. You father watches over you, and your mother and your brother. Just as mine still watches over me."

"How did your father die?"

Eygautr shook his head and smiled. "Oh, it was many, many years ago, lad. When I was a young boy, not even of fighting age." Sea spray gently wash over our heads and I wiped the salt away from the corner of my eye.

"Tell me."

"There really is not much to tell. One day, a neighbor of ours was cutting wood from a tree that was clearly marked on our lands. My father objected, and the man took insult. To this day, I can't remember his name or the look of his face. My father, Darragh, was challenged to a duel, single combat, to settle the dispute. Father being the man of honor that he was would never turn down a challenge such as this. And so he brought the request before the clan's Chieftain and it was accepted. The very next day their duel would commence. Father spent that evening just with family staying close to me, Mum, and my sister. The next day when he awoke, Mother dressed him in his finest tunic, sharpened his axes and helped him don his shield. We walked together through the forest until reaching the town square where a great many people had gathered. The Chieftain welcomed each man into the center circle by embracing them and then addressed the people by describing the grievance that could not be settled." Eygautr paused for a moment looking down at his beard and then back up towards the sky.

"What happened next?" I urged curiously. Eygautr turned towards me with his left eye now watery.

"He fell..." Eygautr took a deep breath and blinked several times before speaking. "It was a good fight that lasted longer than it should have. Father just could not keep up with the other man. Soon, he tired, he waivered, and he was struck in the back. The blade cut deep and his legs gave out on him. Face down in the mud he lay until his challenger approach from behind pulling a tuft of his hair to lift his head. Father gasped and stared at me with his cold blue yes until a blade met the side of his neck. Blood fell all around and the other man hacked at this neck until his head came clean off. I'll never forget that day as long as I live."

"I'm sorry for your loss, old friend. It's never easy to lose the ones that we hold dear."

Eygautr shook his head and opened his eyes wide. "Well, enough of sorrow. We have troubles of our own to worry about." A shadow approach from behind.

"That we do," said Valdemar. "It's time we figure out what we're going to do when we get to Bjorgvin. I'm not one for jumping into the fire. We need a plan and quickly."

I glanced back to see Sada approaching and she quickly sat down in our circle. "I agree. We do need a plan and it better be a good one."

Eygautr scoffed and waved his hand at Sada. "Go back to your post woman. This is men talking, speak not suitable for the ears of women." Sada's eyes were fierce like a predator and the corner of her lip raised into a mischievous smile.

"That's right, Eygautr, I am a woman but on this voyage I have as much stake in the matter as you. Besides, you will need someone that is fast to cover your fat arse." Eygautr's face turned bright red and he raised a finger to Sada.

"You're a shield maiden and hardly that as it is. Stick to what you know, my dear, and leave strategy where it belongs."

"Oh, and where is that?"

"With real warriors, with the men."

Sada rose to one knee and opened up her arms.

"Do you wish to fight me, old man? I'll show you what a real warrior fights like."

I stood and parted the two with my hands. "Calm yourselves. There will be enough fighting for all of us when we get home."

Valdemar laughed and threw a piece of hack silver in the middle of us. "Let them fight, Audan. I'll bet that piece of silver that your wife wins in three moves." Eygautr rose to his feet shaking his fist at Valdemar.

"Why you!"

"Sit down!" I yelled. "All of you need to just calm yourselves. I know were all anxious for a fight but we need to get our heads together. Now, I agree with Sada. I think she participates. She may need to do this herself one day."

Eygautr sat back down crossing his arms in defiance.

"I'll allow it, but I don't like it!" Eygautr relinquished himself from the argument and I looked around the circle of friends to notice that Gunnar was missing from the group. I turned back and saw the young warrior securing some line against the rails.

"Gunnar! Get over here!" He quickly finished his work and hurriedly met with us.

"Yes, Audan?"

"Join us. I need another fresh warrior to hear our plans and provide insight." Gunnar smiled and nodded enthusiastically.

"I'm honored." He quickly sat down and patiently waited for us to continue.

"We five are the core of this voyage. We must lead these men and the manner in which we do will take them to victory or death. When we reach Bjorgvin, I expect our village to be mere ash and splinters. We will approach the shore cautiously before disembarking."

"And are we all to depart or is someone going to stay behind and watch the ship?"

I shook my head. "We can't afford to be without any arms. Every man will need to be worth many more of Freya's Draugr if we wish to succeed."

"But if we leave the ship, we may be stuck on the mainland with no way to escape Freya," said Sada.

"I'm aware of that, but we have no choice. Fenrir is wreaking havoc on the countryside, laying waste to all in his path. If we allow him to continue Loki will turn on us and we will have one less favor from the gods." I crossed my arms and gazed at the deck beneath my feet. I was taking them to their deaths, all of them. How could any of us survive this task? Eygautr leaned forward extending his arm toward me.

"So let's say we make it to Bjorgvin, we land and find no trace of the enemy. How will we know where to find Fenrir? How will we know which way to go?"

"We follow the ash and corpses. Fenrir with create a path of destruction and we shall follow it." Valdemar placed his hand on my shoulder and looked at the others in the group.

"Nephew, if we do find Fenrir, how will we stop him?" I reached back into a leather satchel and pulled out the bundle of silver thread given to me by the trickster himself.

"With this," I replied. My family and friends look at the bundle of twine in awe as its silver essence glimmered in the daytime sun. Valdemar, being the fondest of treasure, reached out first and touch the twine.

"What in god's name is that little nephew?"

"Loki gave it to me. He called it gleipnir, a dwarven metal spun into thread." Eygautr burst into laughter and snatched the thread from my hand.

"Dwarves! Dwarves! They are a legend. Have any of you ever seen a dwarf before? Have anyone seen a dwarf in one thousand seasons?"

"It's true, Eygautr. See for yourself." I pulled my seax from its sheath and extended my hand outward with the handle facing my friend. "Cut the thread, if you can." Eygautr snatched the blade from me and quickly placed the dagger against the thread and pushed it hard into the deck.

"We shall see the truth of this!" Eygautr mocked. He pushed and pushed the blade against the thread but it would not cut. He turned back to me in disbelief. "What have you done, boy? This is a trick, is it? A game of sort?"

I shook my head. "No, old friend, it's no trick or game." Eygautr looked up at Gunnar who stood now.

"Quickly boy, get me my sword." Gunnar uncrossed his arms and retrieved Eygautr's sword from his belongings. He handed the sword to the short, fat man who eagerly removed it from its sheath. "Your seax is just dull. Watch!" Again, Eygautr pressed a blade into the gleipnir but the thread would not cut. He pulled the sword back and forth in a sawing motion sending up wood dust from the ships deck. Stopping every so often he would see that his blade only dug into the Drakkar. He quickly stood nearly falling down in his frustration and raised his sword over his head nearly hitting Sada who quickly leaned out of the way. "Stand back while I make short work of this!" Eygautr fell his blade heavy on the thread and when he pulled his sword up the thread had not even splintered. Only Eygautr's sword shown any wear from the pit that now lay in the blade.

"Do you believe me now, old friend?"

Eygautr was furious, his head had turned blood red and sweat dripped down from his forehead. He threw his sword down to the ground and reached for a pole axe that lay secure against the railings.

"Nothing is invincible. Nothing!" He raised the pole axe high into the air and gracefully chopped at the thread bring down all his might. The axe shattered into a thousand pieces and Eygautr fell to his back releasing the handle of the axe. "By the gods!" he exclaimed. Valdemar walked to the thread and picked it up examining where the axe had fallen.

"There's not a single scratch on it. This is the finest metal in all the land." I reached over Valdemar's hands and removed the thread from his grasp. Wrapping it back into a bundle, I placed the thread into the leather satchel for safe keeping. Eygautr still lay on the ground, his head cocked upward in disbelief. I stood over him and extended my hand.

"We have seen the undead, Valkyrie's, trolls, Fenrir, and even the gods them-selves. Yet, you doubt the existence of dwarves in the mountains?" Eygautr took my hand and slowly stood upright.

"I'm sorry that I ever doubted you, my boy. With things so bleak I was not expecting the gods to grace us with such a needed gift."

"So, that's it then. We're just going to tie up a giant wolf?" exclaimed Sada. "I don't think he will let us do it so willingly."

"Exactly. We will need to scout ahead and find his resting place. We can bind Fenrir as he sleeps."

"And if he awakes, dear nephew? What then?"

"Then, we fight for our lives and hope that one of us are quick at tying knots."

* * *

The hours passed quickly as the sails gently pulled us towards Bjorgvin. It wasn't long before we could see the harbor in the distance and the bleak re-mains of our home.

"There she is! Home!" Gunnar yelled excitedly. The other warriors stood from their resting place and looked out on the horizon to see get a glimpse of Bjorgvin.

"Keep your voices down." I commanded. "We don't know who still may be out there." I walked towards the center of the Drakkar to help unlash lines from the sail. "Drops the lines. We're bringing the sail down. It's oars from here on in." If someone was waiting for us, I didn't want them to spot the sail so far in the distance. We needed some concealment on our side. It was late in the day and as I looked behind us, I could see that the fog was forming but still far out to sea. There would be no hiding our ship for long.

"Alright, lads, you heard him. Get that fucking sail down and get to your oars. Let's go!" barked Eygautr. The men moved swiftly and without question. It was good to have such a veteran as Eygautr aboard the ship. Despite being Chief I was still more comfortable commanding smaller groups of those I know well and trust. Half of these men belonged to Valdemar, perhaps a quarter were what remained of Eygautr's mean. The last quarter were warriors of Bjorgvin, my men, my trusted fighters.

"Audan," called out Sada as she leaned over the rails, while holding onto a line. She pointed out into the distance. "Look there." Smoke rose high into the air but this was not coming from Bjorgvin. This smoke was nearly a day's march away.

"It must be another village. I told you it would be easy to find Fenrir." Sada leaned back and kissed me on the cheek.

"Let us hope that we are the ones to find him and not the other way around." We left the rails and took position behind the oars. Eygautr slowly stomped his right foot against the deck to help us keep pace. It wasn't long before the edges of the Fjord encircled us leading us straight to the docks.

"Slow..." Eygautr commanded. "We're nearly there."

"Gunnar, climb the mast and get a better look." The young man pulled his oar in and set it to the side. He quickly climbed atop the base of the mast and began his ascent. As the waves came upon us, Gunnar would wait for the lull before heading further up, so he would not fall. As he reached the top, he placed his hand above his eyes to block out the sun and surveyed what remained of our home.

"I don't see anyone," he called down to us.

"Are you certain?" I asked. Gunnar looked again and then turned back down towards us.

"I am certain. Not a living soul." I looked away from Gunnar and gazed at the faces before me.

"Very well. We make for a landing. Oars, make for home!" I sat back down upon my chest and pulled an oar alongside the men. Slowly and cautiously we rowed as the sound of debris now hit our ship, remnants of a masterful dockyard that no longer existed. We would make a beach landing this day.

"Row, row, row!" Eygautr commanded in an even tempo. Looking down at my feet as I rowed I was anxious to stand again to see Bjorgvin. "Row, row, row! Keep it steady, you dogs. This is still our home, let's show some pride!" Eygautr straightened out his tunic tucking in the loose cloth behind his leather belt. "Brace yourselves! Oars in!" The Drakkar slip smoothly against the pebble laden shore and came to an abrupt stop. Quickly we rose from our posts gathering our arms and shields ready for what may come. "Audan?" Eygautr raised his eyebrows at me clearly waiting for orders. "Well, Chieftain, what say you?" I smirked and lifted my arm in the air.

"Disembark, form up at the beach head." Without hesitation bodies leapt over the front prow splashing down into the icy water. I waited my turn following the warriors in front of me until Sada looked back at me smiling wildly. "What is it?" I asked her. She raised her axe hand and wrapped it around me.

"I love you, Audan." I happily took in her embrace.

"And I, you. Now get off my ship," I joked. Sada leapt down to the waters with a smile on her face and trudged forward to the beachhead joining the other warriors in a makeshift shield wall. I could already hear Eygautr critiquing the men at their sloppiness and the gaps in the wall. Taking a deep breath, I leapt over the side and let the water rush over me. I stood quickly and for a moment thought I saw Jareth reach out his hand to help pick me up. "I'm coming, brother," I whispered under my breath. I met the shield wall and looked forward at the burnt out hovels and fish shacks; there would be no fighting on this hallowed terrain.

"What do you think nephew?" Valdemar asked with shield raised high. I lowered my weapons and casually walked ahead of the formation.

"Let's go. Stay close to one another." My feet dug loudly into the hard pebbles until the ground softened and turned to soil. I passed a large wooden beam laying on the ground that was once a pulley for the dock and walked up a small incline until reaching the base of Bjorgvin. Ash and soot littered the once fertile grounds and as I gazed upward I was not prepared for the devastation that lay before me. Sada's hand met mine and gripped it tightly.

"Oh, Audan, what have they done? Look at our home." A tear fell down from her face and I stood stoic as my warriors walked slowly ahead of us. With each step they lifted the soot with their boot, leaving behind black trails of footprints. Smoke still rose from some of the heavier piles of destruction and with a gaping mouth I took account of what remained.

"It's gone. All of it. The dock, the forge, even the great hall. All of it, destroyed." Sada released my hand, wiping the tears from her face and stepped forward, gripping her axe tightly.

"Come on, love. Let's have a look around." I lifted my bearded axe onto my shoulder and cautiously walked forward. The ground beneath foot crunched and cracked from what lay underneath.

"Audan!" Gunnar called out from the other side of a burnt out hovel. "Quickly, come see this!" Gunnar's voice was unsettled and I ran towards him around the pile of wood until I could see the back of his green cloak and bow in hand. He looked back at me, fearful, with blood shot-eyes filled with tears. "Audan, look what they have done to our kin." I stood next to Gunnar and to my surprise found a gaping hole in the ground where once there was none. My eyes beheld a horror so terrible that I closed them tightly and opened them again to be sure of what lay before me. Bodies of our loved ones laid strewn about covered in ash. Their corpses had been stripped of all clothing, their heads cut from their bodies and placed on their genitals. Their flesh had been cut, flayed, and mangled on their limbs down to the bone. They were tortured before they were killed. As a final insult, their own weapons pierced their bodies, pinning them to the ground. Their final moments shown clearly on the expressions upon their faces. Such horror and pain the likes of which I had not seen. Gunnar turned away and began to throw up. Sada rushed to his aid patting his back but Gunnar pushed her away and stood upright, embarrassed in his moment of weakness.

"Audan." Uncle Valdemar stood on the other side of the ditch and motioned me towards him. "There's a message for you." I stepped forward straight through the ditch past our comrades stepping in piles of muddied blood until reaching the other side. "Have a look." Valdemar pointed with his blade just ahead and in that direction stood a timber standing upright and against that timber stood a man, a dead man.

"I know this man," I said softly. "He was once a guard in the great hall. He was a good man, an honorable man." The man was heavy set and very, very young. It was Feitr, or as many knew him, Feitr the fat. His back had been cut wide open, his ribs pulled outward from his spine and set in the shape of wings. A blood eagle as it's called, meant for traitors and the worst of criminals. Not men of honor, not Feitr.

"Was he close to you?" asked Valdemar. I placed my hand on the lifeless face of the young man and stared into his open, bleak eyes; running my fingers down his face, I closed them for the last time.

"No, but he was loyal to my family. Last I recall he took the place of another young warrior, Tibor." I closed my eyes for a moment, lamenting at the loss of Tibor to the troll Gymiran. "So many terrible deaths, so much senseless loss." Valdemar placed his hand on my shoulder.

"Nephew, it will do you no good to bear the burden of death. She comes for us all in the end and no man, no matter his position in life, can prevent that." I shook my head in anger and placed my hands against my ears.

"No! They were my responsibility. All of them. I let them down and I let these monsters devour them." I dropped my bearded axe to the ground and removed my Seax from its sheath.

"What are you doing?" asked Valdemar with concern.

"What's right!" I cut at the ropes that bind Feitr to the timber until his corpse fell heavy to the ground. A cloud of ash flew upward as his body settled into the soil and then something caught my eye sticking out beneath a large wooden plank. A tiny hand rested quietly against the ground pale as snow and dry as the ash. "No!" I bent down placing my hands beneath the great plank and lifted upward but it was too heavy.

"Quickly, everyone, give Audan a hand!" Valdemar ordered. My family and friends surrounded me and together we lifted the massive timber and threw it to the side. The hand led to the body of a little girl, dead and cold still clutching a small cloth doll in her other hand. Her face was serene and peaceful as if merely asleep. The pain and anger inside became too great; the world around me spun as the blood boiled in my veins.

"Who's child is she?" asked Gunnar. "Everyone should have been cleared out to the ships before the battle began." Sada removed her hands from her hips and placed them over her mouth.

"She must have hidden herself out of fear before the battle. The poor thing." I swept downward, picking up my axe and began cutting back and forth at a timber screaming and yelling in shear fury. Wood splinter flew asunder and soon the timber gave way to the might of my blade as it snapped in two. My bearded axe buried itself in the ground and I fell to my knees; spit and tears ran uncontrollably down my face. Falling forward I braced myself with my arms and screamed at the ground, arms wrapped around my back and stomach pulling my body upward.

"Audan, calm yourself." I fought back pulling away swinging my body forth and Gunnar and Eygautr came to subdue me.

"Calm yourself, lad. They're all dead. There's nothing you can do!"

I continued to yell uncontrollably until the weight of my comrades pulled me to the ground. Gunnar held on tightly and exhaustion came of me. Breathing heavily, I swallowed my spit down and rolled over on my belly.

"Freya! Freya! Freya, you witch, you cruel beast! Look what you have done! Was it worth it? Was all this misery and destruction worth your black crown?" Sada rushed to me gripping my face with both hands.

"Love, you must calm yourself. We need a leader right now, a chieftain, not a crazed mad man. Come back to us. Get your senses about you and stand." I closed my eyes and took a deep breath; when I opened them, I could see everyone standing around me, some with looks of concern and others with looks of shame.

"Apologies," I said as I slowly stood to my feet. I surveyed the rest of our former home, but nothing remained. Even the palisades that once stood tall had been flattened and burned to the ground.

"Gunnar," Eygautr called out. "Take three of your men and scan the outer village. Find out what direction are enemies have traveled."

"And if we should see anyone?" Eygautr shook his head.

"Make no battle with the enemy. I need your men to be shadows, light of foot and quiet as the grave." Gunnar nodded and picked three men to follow along. They pulled off their shields, armor, and anything that would weigh them down before they departed east.

"Bury them..." I said quietly. Valdemar turned to the group and repeated my orders.

"You heard your chieftain. We're going to give these people a proper burial. Every last one of them. Use a shovel if you have one; if not, dig with your hands." A broad and fit man with a deep black beard named Ivar stepped forward and threw a large leather bag to the ground. Unlashing it, he removed shovels and picks.

"Here you are, my Lord." Ivar handed me a shovel and I gladly took it and began digging graves with the rest of the warriors. Sada found a pick axe and worked the soil next to me. I gazed upward at my wife who stared at me with great concern.

"Are you going to be alright?" she asked softly.

"I'm fine."

"You don't look it. You nearly went mad back there," she argued.

"I'm fine, woman!" I replied sharply. "Now, leave me be. We have work to do." Sada grimaced and went back to her work. As holes were finished warriors would help each other move bodies to their final resting place. With nothing to spare at the gravesites, we left small offerings of stones and beadwork. I finished digging and angrily plunged the shovel head into the dirt. It was time to bury the little girl. Slowly, I walked to her and knelt down to her motionless body. For a moment, the clouds parted and a soft light shined upon her. I gently brushed her hair out of her face and tucked it behind her ear and then carefully lifted her fragile body. She weighed almost nothing, like a feather in my arms. Reaching her grave, I gently placed her down into her final resting place placing her little arms over her chest. So peaceful she seemed, like she was just sleeping there. I knelt down and removed a dried piece of cod from my satchel placing it next to her body. "For your journey. May your passage be safe and may Odin watch over you for eternity."

Several hours passed and now the remaining bodies of the fallen had found their resting places. We sat and rested while several men took up watch around the outside of the village.

"Eygautr!" a warrior called out.

"What is it, lad?"

"The scouts!" he said, pointing outside the village remains. "The scouts return and they are running!" Valdemar looked up at me worry.

"That can't be good, nephew." Uncle stood quickly donning shield and sword. "Arm yourselves! Something's coming!" Gunnar and his three warriors reached the watch and sprinted towards us.

"Audan!" Gunnar called out bereft of breath. "Audan!" He reached me and braced his body against his knees looking down trying to catch some air. "Riders! Riders are coming in from the east."

"How many?" Gunnar stood and looked at me dead in the eyes.

"Maybe thirty or forty men."

"Villagers?" Gunnar shook his head.

"No, my lord. They are well armed. Light cavalry at best. We remained out of their sight, but they are headed this way." Valdemar gripped my shoulder and leaned into my ear.

"We have no time to get back to the boat. We need to stand our ground here and meet these men."

"Shield wall!" I called out. Quickly, we formed in the center of the village. A face I had not noticed since we debarked took up position next to me.

"It's good to see you, brother," Njord called out.

"You as well, brother." The ground began to tremble and shake and soon the column of horseman could be seen coming down from the nearest hill outside the clearing of the forest. They carried no standard, no flags and rode with spears bent forward.

"Hold your ground!" Eygautr ordered. "Let's show these bastards that this is our land!" The horses wailed and cried out wildly and the riders whipped them forward in a frenzy.

"Steady, lads!" Valdemar ordered. "Steady! Don't blink until your spears are in their belly. Dig in your heels. Take out the horses, but kill the riders if you can." The column now entered the village and stormed towards us closer, closer, and closer. My heart raced in my chest and I braced for the impact of a charging steed against my shield and spear. The faces of the riders were clear as day, the white of their eyes bearing down on us, all thundering hooves and bristling spears.

Eight
Dark Heart

"Here they come!" We let loose our war cries and just before they reached our wall, the horses and their riders slowed. Spears were raised upwards and their riders circled us.

"Cover the rear!" Eygautr ordered. Several men shuffled back now, creating a circle formation. Horse after horse galloped past us and their riders looked down upon us not with malice but with a tired look on their faces. The rear of the column approached with a center rider wearing a bright helm clad in full chain mail and flanked by two other riders. He stopped his horse and pulled back on the reins making the beast step back several paces.

"Who's in charge here?" the man called out. I lowered my shield and stood upright.

"I am!" The mounted warrior removed his helm and held it in his arm.

"And who are you?" he asked.

"I am Audan. Son of Rurik. This is our home and our lands." The mounted warrior looked about the piles of splintered wood and ash covered lands.

"I don't see a village here." My blood began to boil and I stepped forward.

"Do you offer insult?" The mounted warrior slowly stepped down from his steed and approached me.

"No, my fellow warrior. Merely stating the obvious. We, too, have lost our home to this pestilence that infects our lands. We barely escaped with our lives as it is."

"Might we have your name?" Eygautr asked.

"Apologies. Customs are something we are shot on in these dark times. I am Tormod, Chieftain of the people of Valestrand; or what remains of it, anyway. It's good that you have come back to your homelands, Audan, but I'm afraid that news in this region is bleak to the east and the south."

"What news have you?"

"A large force of the undead have headed east. They march from village to village under the orders of a queen."

"Freya..." I mumbled.

"Freya? You mean the goddess? How can that be?"

"She has been plotting and attacking our land for some time. Bjorgvin was the strongest of the clans on the western shores. We lost her when her army attacked our walls. She released the beast, Fenrir." Tormod's jaw dropped and he looked down at the ground in dismay.

"So the rumors are true."

"We returned from exile to hunt down the beast and bind him so he may be returned to his cage." Tormod laughed deeply placing his hand over his belly. "What do you find so amusing, brother?"

"There's no binding Fenrir, not by your hands anyway. The Draugr have slaughtered tens of thousands of Norse warriors across the countryside. What makes you think we are a match for the hound of hell?"

"It can be done, Tormod, but we need more men." It was clear that Tormod did not like agree with our quest and thought it a failed endeavor.

"It seems you have your mind set on it."

"I do."

"Well, then, we shouldn't linger here much longer. When the sun goes down, things become a bit more precarious. There's more than Draugr running around these woods. I will take you to our leader."

"You are not the leader of this band of men?" I was suspicious now. Why would he take charge if he did not lead these warriors?

"No, merely another old warrior. Most of these men did not come from my lands but we have slowly swelled our ranks to build a foothold against this evil. Have you horses?"

"No," I said reluctantly.

"Very well. You can follow us. We will keep a slow pace; just try and keep up. These lands are crawling with the undead. The dark queen's scouts and spies are everywhere."

Eygautr leaned into my ear and spoke softly.

"How do we know we can trust these men? They could be mercenaries for Freya."

"I understand your concern, old friend. If we are to track down Fenrir and catch him I think Tormod and his men are our best chance at that. We need alliances now more than ever. We don't have a choice."

"But we do! We can go it alone," Eygautr pointed out.

"Is everything alright?" Tormod asked.

"It's fine. Just talk amongst warriors. Lead on, Tormod, and we shall follow."

"Two horses to the rear!" Tormod commanded with an outstretched arm. "Keep an eye out for anyone coming from behind. We don't want to be caught off guard." Two horses quickly pulled off and galloped behind our formation. We grabbed the rest of our things and quietly marched forward, leaving behind Bjorgvin and its many dead. As I took my first steps just outside the village beyond the main gate, I looked back at our hallowed out home and swore to myself that one day we would return. One day, the people of Bjorgvin would come back and claim our lands, rebuild the great village that once stood as a proud symbol of our family name. One day, one day could not come soon enough. The march ahead was long and bitterly cold as the snows began to pile up and the frost-bitten wind nipped at our bodies. The horseman at the front appeared to fair no better as they fought off the winds that roared higher above our heads. Just ahead, a little respite came as we entered another forest; the winds died down behind the wall of trees and the snow had not risen so high beneath the tree branches. We marched for several more hours through the deep wood, always keeping an eye out for the enemy who may be hiding in the shadows of the wood. We soon came to a grouping of large boulders amongst the trees when the front of the column had us stop. A welcome rest as most of my men threw down their arms and lay down against the side of the hill.

"Audan!" Tormod called me forward. I turned back to Eygautr, Valdemar, and Sada, who all seemed concerned that I would leave them behind.

"It's alright, friends. Stay here. I'll go see what Tormod wants."

"Audan, I don't trust them," Eygautr snapped.

"Nor do I," Valdemar replied. "You should take someone with you." Admittedly, I agreed with them but did not want to upset our new comrades with any show of distrust.

"Gunnar." The young warrior ran ahead past several warriors with bow in hand.

"Yes?"

"Come with me. I need a bodyguard." Gunnar nodded and followed me to the front of the column where Tormod appeared to patiently wait.

"Who is this?" Tormod asked. I lifted my arm and placed in on Gunnar's shoulder.

"This is my most loyal of warriors. Where I go, he goes." Tormod smiled.

"Very well. Come with me." We walked around the large stone boulders to the other side beyond the view of my men or the other riders. Tormod stopped just in front of a clearing next to the largest of the boulders covered long vines.

"So?" I asked. "Where are we?" Tormod grinned from ear to ear.

"Do you not see it?" I looked around at the trees, stones, and snow covered leaves.

"I don't see anything." Tormod pursed his lips and whistled a bird call loudly. The sound of moving brush became louder until wood planks pushed themselves outside of the vines. Two lightly armed guards stepped outside and motioned us to enter quickly.

"Not everything is as it appears, Audan. Follow me and watch you step."

"What about my men?"

"My warriors will be sure to escort them inside. They will have food, water, a warm fire and a place to rest. I assure you, all will be well." I nodded and followed Tormod through the long green vines into a long and dark tunnel. The path winded in many different directions and every so often we would pass torches that were evenly spread out. Soo we reached an opening where wooden posts had been erected, a stable with fresh running water along a channel carved out of rock. The horses made noises as we walked by and a young boy came to calm their nerves. Tormod stopped before a large door and knocked seven times. The sound of wood slats moving behind the door echoed in the cavern and the door opened slowly exposing the light of the fires on the other side. As we left the passageway, we entered a giant open cavern filled with tables, chairs, even a kitchen. There were five levels to this underground hall, two below and two above the one I stood upon. Ladders extended upward to each level and pulleys were erected to move heavier goods when needed. In the very center of the cavern was a natural well filled with fresh water.

"What is this place?" I asked.

"Welcome to our home, or as we like to call it, Skerheim. Our rocky home beneath the forest." No sooner did we arrive that the rest of our forces along with Tormod's men entered as well. Some stayed in the main cavern, others were lead to other passageway where living quarters had been setup. "Our leader awaits you."

"You're Chieftain?" I asked.

"We don't have any Chieftains here Audan. Not that we wouldn't pay you the respect due to one. He's more of a leader of rogues and helped build this safe place. Come." Tormod led Gunnar and I up a ladder and after we reached that level he brought us to the next up another ladder. The part of the cavern was less crowded with only a handful of men and their belongings. We were brought before a man sitting solemnly in a wooden chair with his back to a lantern. "Go on, present yourself."

"I am Audan, Chieftain of Bjorgvin and son of Rurik." The thin man with long blonde hair stood and quickly turnaround.

"Audan? Audan of Bjorgvin?" I knew this man.

"Fiorn? Chieftain of Myrlende; is it truly you?" Fiorn walked up to me and embraced me patting my back. He pulled back gripping my shoulders.

"By the gods, it's good to see you. I had word that you had perished at the assault on the Finns. We never heard from you after that battle."

"Reports of my demise were greatly exaggerated."

"And what of your brother and father? How fare they?"

I took a deep breath before handing out poor tidings.

"My father drinks with our ancestors and my brother has been taken by the dark queen. I do not know about Jareth's well-being and have not heard from him for quite some time." Fiorn's face turned to concern and he quickly reached for a skin pouch.

"I'm sorry to hear of your troubles, brother. I truly am. Here, drink with me and I will share with you the secrets of my enterprise here." Fiorn pulled two chairs from the wall and set them out for Gunnar and me.

"Will that be all, Fiorn?" Tormod asked.

"Yes, Tormod. Thank you for bringing them to me. Get some food and much needed rest. I'm sure you and your men are tired."

Tormod bowed his head slightly.

"Thank you brother, Fiorn."

"And who is the archer that stays so close to your side?"

"I am Gunnar."

"Well, Gunnar, I'm pleased to meet you. Now, on to business then. Skerheim is a collection of clans, at least what remains of them. We have several much smaller caverns spread throughout the realm. The dark queen and her forces know nothing about them and we'd like to keep it that way. Most of the men you see here belonged to strong Norse families in one way or another. Unfortunately, each of us lost our villages, our Great Halls and our lands. The dark queen came for us all and she brought that must and the undead to finish us all off."

"So how did you escape?"

"Some took to the sea, some disappeared into the mountains. I knew of this place long ago when I was a child so naturally I brought what was left of my men here. We raid on Draugr positions to the east and west. From time to time, we meet warriors such as yourselves and add them to our ranks. Odin knows we've lost many men over the summer. Now with winter dropping its heavy snows, I would expect to lose more men. The good news is that Freya has slowed her march east. Her army of undead do not seem to manage so well in the cold. And what of you, Audan? Your war band was clearly on the path to something."

I trusted Fiorn whole heartedly but hesitated to speak the truth. "We are on a mission of sorts to collect a bounty."

Fiorn nodded and leaned forward. "A bounty? And who is it that you will be collecting?" I looked back at Gunnar who gave me no sign of resistance.

"We are here to collect Fenrir on the orders of Loki."

Fiorn spit out his mead and placed his up on the table in front of him. "Come again?"

"We..."

Fiorn stood and interrupted me. "No, no brother, Audan. I heard you. I just don't believe what it is that I'm hearing."

"My lord!" A simple warrior with a face and clothing covered in mud barged in lowering his head.

"Eerik, what is it?"

"We returned from our eastern patrol and found a large farm ablaze but there were no corpses to speak of. There's a rumor that the people are hiding in the woods no more than an hour's ride from here."

"What of the undead?" Fiorn asked.

"None have been sighted this day, my lord."

"How many lived on this farm?"

"One of our brothers who once lived near hear said nearly fifteen men, women and children dwelled at the farm." Fiorn turned his gaze from Eerik back towards me.

"We have made it our calling to rescue what people we can from this darkness. We send women and children south and enlist the men to fight with us. Are you well enough for a ride?"

"I am," I replied.

"Good. I could use a warrior like you. Join us to search for the villagers. You may bring one other rider with you. The rest will remain behind."

"We are traveling light?" I asked curiously. I would think that a greater number of warriors would only increase our chances for success but I was not about to question the man who had been fighting and holding this ground.

"The Draugr are sensitive to noise. We like to ride quietly and in small numbers to keep them from finding us."

I nodded my head. "Very well. Gunnar will stay here to mind my warriors. I will bring Sada along for the search." Fiorn seemed surprised.

"Sada? Your woman? She is here?" I turned and pointed down the cavern to the lower levels.

"My wife. She is, indeed. Ready to fight by our side."

"I don't mean any disrespect, brother, but the dark wood is no place for a woman. Every time we leave this cavern there are no assurances that we will return."

"I understand, but Sada is ready and has been waiting to join in the fighting. Besides, if we do come upon the frightened villagers, it may do us well to have a women's touch." Fiorn pulled his hair back behind his ears and smiled.

"Very well, brother. Do as you wish. Gather your things and we shall see you at the cavern entry way."

I stood and bowed slightly before heading back down the ladders to the main level where most of my warriors along with Sada had gathered. She sat in the center of the room with Eygautr and Valdemar eating some smoked fish and drinking fresh water. I walked up behind her placing my arm on her shoulder and whispered in her ear.

"Get your things. We're going on a hunt." Sada placed her wooden cup down and looked back up toward me.

"To where?"

"Just get your things and walk with me to the end of the cavern. I'll tell you all about it."

"What's going on, nephew?" Valdemar asked.

"Sada and I are going to help Fiorn with something, build some good will between our clans."

"Do you need more warriors?" Eygautr stood as he spoke. I gently raised my hand and smiled.

"No, brothers. Eat and take rest in the refuge of this hallow. We're travelling in a small group and should be back before too long."

"And if you don't return?" Eygautr asked.

"Then Uncle Valdemar will take charge." Eygautr reluctantly sat back down and as I walked away with Sada I could see my men whispering amongst themselves. No doubt curious about the task I was about to undertake.

"Why such secrecy?" Sada asked.

"I didn't want them to worry. You know how Valdemar and Eygautr are. They're never happy unless we're travelling with a heavy contingent."

Leaving the main hall, we entered the dark passageway and made our way forward. Sada kissed me on the cheek and leaned into my shoulder.

"What was that for?"

"For thinking of me. I would have thought you would take Gunnar or your uncle."

"I know you're eager to get your blade wet. This might give you that opportunity."

"So, what are we doing?"

"There's a farm not too far from hear that was burnt out and destroyed. One of Fiorn's scouts heard a rumor that the former occupants were hiding in the forest nearby. We're going to look for them and if we can, rescue them."

"It's nearly sundown. Didn't Tormod warn against evening travel?"

Sada was right and I had a bad feeling that what lurks in the darkness may come to find us.

"He did, so best be on your guard."

Sada placed her hand on the pommel of her blade and walked just ahead of me with a smart strut about her. "I was born for this, my love."

We reached the stables where the stable boy was waiting with two fresh horses.

"Fiorn said you were to take these two. They have provisions to last you a day." I took the reins from the boy and handed Sada hers. Sada smiled and approached the head of her horse, stroking its long neck gently and placing her face against it.

"Oh, you're a sweet thing, aren't you?" Sada reached into her pocket and removed some dried root that she had been keeping for long trip. Placing her open hand in front of the horse the beast happily nibbled on the food and pressed its head into Sada's shoulder.

"I think she likes you," I said.

"I think so, too." We walked our horses several more paces to the end of the cavern. Four men waited for us, Fiorn, Tormod, Eerik, and a much older warrior with a grey beard I had not yet met.

"Only six of us? You were serious when you said we were traveling light."

Fiorn nodded. "I was, indeed. Men, for those of you who are unacquainted this is Sada of Bjorgvin. She is wife to the Chieftain of Bjorgvin, the man standing before you, Audan. So mind your eyes." The men laughed under their breath and happily welcomed her to the group. The older warrior approached me and extended his arm.

"Grim of nowhere."

"Grim of nowhere?"

"That's right, my lord. I have never been from anywhere because I have lived everywhere."

"Very well," I replied.

"Enough with the pleasantries. We have a ride ahead of us and if we're lucky some Norse people to bring home safely." Fiorn turned to the two guards and the entrance and waived them to open the gate. Quickly, the guards unlatched the door and removed the wood planks that block the entry. We headed forward with our horses through the long vines that gently ran across our bodies until we were free of them and into the woods. The guards wasted no time in securing the entrance once more and making the cavern of Skerheim disappear. "Follow me, and don't make a sound unless you see a Draugr or the villagers." We heeded Fiorn's warning and for the ride forward no words were spoken. Fiorn lead us to a soft dirt path through the woods at a slow pace. The horse hooves were nearly silent and the sounds of the forest now echoed in my ears.

Every snapping twig, every rustling bush and falling snow against the leaves was a Draugr to me. I gazed in all directions feeling very alert and very alive.

Sada road just ahead of me and every once in a while would glance back towards me. I would smile and then nod in another direction to keep her eyes ahead. Soon, the smell of smoke and ash filled the air and Eerik, who led at the front, lifted his arm for us to stop. I pulled gently on the reins and my horse did as command. I patted the top of his neck to keep him calm as we quietly waited on Eerik to signal us again. Suddenly, he sat upright and slowly dismounted, motioning us to do the same. We descended from the horses and quickly tied their reins to trees nearby. Eerik walked to the center of the column and had us gather around him.

"The farm is just beyond that rise there," he said, voice low. "We're going to circle around it, split into groups of two and meet back here. Whatever you do, stay quiet and if you find the villagers, don't yell. Just bring them back here." Naturally, I chose Sada to walk with me, Grim left with Tormod and Eerik walked with Fiorn. We made our way slowly around the farm through the thick trees, ferns, and snow covered floor. On our left side, smoke slowly rose into the air sending bits of ash to land on our cloths and hair. The snow crunched under foot and I stepped delicately to keep as quiet as possible. Soon, the horses and other warriors were beyond my sight; only Sada wearing her black fur hood remained at my side. My love stopped me pressing her hand delicately against my chest. She pointed out in the distance to a rising mound of earth and stones.

"Look there," she whispered. "If I was to look for a place to hide that would be the one."

"Alright, then, let's have a look." We ventured further from our companions into a depression in the forest floor. The snows were much lighter here and soon we found only patches of sleet amongst the green ferns and brown soil. Something dark suddenly caught my eye and I knelt down; it was a footprint the size of a man's.

"Sada," I called out quietly. "It looks like you were right. Look." I pointed ahead where more footprints led ahead to the backside of the mound. There were no children's steps to speak of and I became wary that perhaps we were walking towards a Draugr nest.

"Is it them?" Sade asked.

"I'm not sure." I stood slowly and readied my bearded axe. Sada pulled her shield from her back and unsheathed her sword. We approached cautiously, moving into the shadow of the mound. The air became colder here and I felt ice running through my veins. It felt like a warning, it felt like death. I froze when I heard the sound of a small rock falling. The stone appeared falling down from the other side of the mound and now I knew that someone or something was there. We stood next to each other and took our steps together, inching closer and closer until the edge of a cavern could be seen. I stopped Sada and looked into her beautiful eyes moving my lips, *are you ready*? She nodded and together we stepped out to the other side of the mound where a pile of leaves lay atop many sticks. Sada stepped forward and slowly pushed her sword into the leaves and pulled back the sticks. The leaves and twigs rushed forward knocking Sada to the ground!

"Audan!" A body stood atop her and as she tried to pull away I lifted my axe and placed the blade against the man's neck.

"Get off her or I'll end you!" A young man holding a hatchet turned to see my bearded axe gleaming in his direction. He dropped the blade and held his hands up. "Stand up. Slowly." With terror in his eyes, the young man stood. Sada pulled herself from the ground and pointed her sword point at his throat.

"Please don't!" a small voice called out. A little girl rushed out from the hiding place and wrapped her hands around the young man. "Please don't kill my father. He was only protecting us." I pulled my axe back from the man's neck and Sada lowered her sword.

"Is that your farm?" I said as I pointed in the distance. The man nodded.

"Yes, it is my lord." I smiled and rolled my eyes.

"These are the farmers we were looking for." Sada stepped towards the concealment and pulled all the leaves back revealing the rest of the farmers and the family.

"Fourteen. All but one," said Sada.

"Who are you?" The young farmer asked.

"I am Audan and this is my wife, Sada. We came with a group of warriors to retrieve you." The farmer walked up to me and shook my hand vigorously.

"Oh, bless you, sir, bless you. The gods will favor the both of you, I'm sure of it." Sada helped the others out of their hiding place and one by one men, women, and the smallest of children popped out of the dark cavern.

"Who did this? What happened to your farm?" Sada asked curiously. An old women approached us. Blind, she walked with the help of a cane.

"It was the dark one." the old woman said.

"The dark one? You mean the dark queen? You speak of Freya and her Draugr?"

"No, my lord, the dark one. He came in the night, the smell of smoke and Sulphur stinking up the air all around. We were gathered in the great hall when the roof set ablaze the whole of the village ran outside." The old women began to cough violent and bent over at the waist. The young farmer braced her and helped her stand upright.

"What happened next?" I asked.

"The village ran outside to the center courtyard and there stood a man. Tall and black of skin. His flesh was cracked and filled with fire. We just stood there and stared at him for fear of what he may do. He opened his eyes and smoke rose up above his head. When the dark man opened his mouth, fire spewed forth, engulfing our stables and great hall. We cowered in fear but one of us stood against the dark one. A young warrior of the farm, Bjarke, charged forward with dagger in hand and plunged the blade into the dark one's chest. Liquid fire drip out from his wound and engulfed the boy's hand in flame. The dark one lifted him by his throat into the air and said, *you shall bear witness to the flame and tell others that I am coming.* He opened his mouth and spit fire upon the boy; he screamed in great agony and was dropped to the ground and burnt to ash. The dark one turned and walked away leaving behind the destruction or our home. We ran for the forest and did not turn back." Sada wrapped her arm around the old woman.

"I'm sorry for your loss. Come, let's get you out of here."

"Who was he? The dark one, I mean? Did he give you a name?" I asked. The old woman shook her head and looked up towards me with her snow white eyes, a look of terrible fear upon her face. Her lips shook and trembled in terror.

"The dark one will return. We dare not utter his name." The fear was contagious and Sada now appeared nervous and gently pulled the woman forward. Then, we head the snapped of twigs and the rush of footsteps. I raised my axe and stepped ahead of the group.

"What is it?" Sada asked. "Draugr?" I took a deep breath. The air was clean and sweet. It couldn't be the Draugr. Dark shadows emerged from above the mound and atop I spotted the figures of our comrades. Tormod recognized us first and the look of panic was painted across his face.

"You found them?" Tormod asked hurriedly.

"We did. They are safe." Fiorn followed behind Tormod and gripped my arm.

"We heard the scream from some distance. We must away from this place quickly before we are found." Quickly, we helped the group up to the top of the mound. The horses could be heard, spooked by something in the wood they made loud noises followed by terrible cries; then silence.

"Stay here." Fiorn urged to the group. I ran with Fiorn just ahead and crouched down behind a tree. In the silence of the wood a foul smell ran across my nose. The smell of death, of rotting flesh and the coming terror. Fiorn saw the dread in my face and asked,

"What is it, Audan? What's out there?" A twig snapped not far away, then another, and another.

"Draugr," I whispered. "Run." We sprinted back to group that waited at the top of the mound. Tormod waited with sword at the ready.

"What is it, brother?" he asked.

"Draugr. Everyone get back down into the cavern. Go!" The famer's family quickly rushed back down into the hole in the ground.

"Can any of you fight?" Grim asked. Two young men raised their hands. "Good lads. Fight with honor and maybe I will share a drink with you in Valhalla." Grim pierced the ground with his sword and hand each man a hatchet. Suddenly, in the distance, a great howl erupted, first one, then two, then three.

"By the gods!" exclaimed Fiorn. The sun set beneath the mountains of the forest and the dark shadow covered us entirely.

"I know that sound," I said with a trembling voice.

"We will have more than the Draugr to tangle with!" Tormod warned. Grim beat his sword against his shield loudly three times and then pointed his blade just ahead where the glowing eyes of the undead approached.

"Prepare for battle! It's a glorious day to die!"

Nine
Blood and Bone

The farmer's family hid tightly in the cavern at our backs as the glowing eyes of the undead slowly descended upon us.

"Stay together!" Fiorn urged. I counted the number of undead closing in on us. First ten, then twenty, then thirty. Their numbers swelled as more stepped out of the trees. Six warriors and two farmers were all that stood between the slaughter of an entire family. The Draugr moaned in the twilight and dragged their weapons across the ground scratching loudly against the dirt and stone. They stopped no more than twenty paces away and made a loose formation.

"Why do the wait?" asked Grim angrily. The foul smell of their rotting flesh filled the air all around us. The young farmer men standing next to us in line gagged and spit, the stench was so horrid. Then another Draugr stepped to the front of the formation. His skin, although a deathly pale white, was intact save for the sword gash across the left side of his face that left his eye hanging from its socket.

"Why do you come here warm blood?" the Draugr asked.

"Sigmund?" Fiorn uttered softly. I turned to our old friend and witnessed the look of shock and doubt across his face.

"You know this creature?" I asked.

"I do," Fiorn replied as he lowered his sword and shield. "Sigmund, what happened to you, old friend? Where have you been?" The Draugr took another step forward in his ragged brush-torn cloths and quickly jerked his head from one side to the other.

"Sigmund..." he said. "There is no Sigmund here. Sigmund is in hell. The same place you are going, warm blood." The Draugr formation released a terrifying ear-piercing shriek that caused my teeth and bones to ache. Sigmund the Draugr lifted his sword in the air and then quickly dropped it, signifying an attack. The Draugr rushed into the narrow fighting ground, first slamming their bodies against shields. I reached my axe high over Sada's defense and pulled a Draugr in close with the claw of my bearded axe. Sada swung her blade from the side, quickly relieving the beast of his head. The body fell heavy before us. Grim and Tormund worked the line, sending Draugr after Draugr falling to their final demise. Soon, a wall of corpses had amassed nearly waist high. The Draugr Sigmund jumped over our defense and pulled one of the farmer's men down to the ground with him. The boy swung his hatchet in desperation but Sigmund pulled on the boy's leg and pierced his crotch with the tip of the sword. The boy screamed in agony and his brother came to his aid, mounting the top of Sigmund and pulling his hair back, cutting wildly from behind until Sigmund's head came free. The boy farmer lifted the head into the air and threw it at the Draugr that still pressed against our defense. The slight did no phase them as they continued to hack and whittle away at our shields. Eerik took a slash to his shoulder and in his frustration lunged forward, bashing a Draugr down with the edge of his shield. One fell, then two, then another when suddenly a spear flew in the distance, piercing Eerik in the gut. Blood spilled forth and Eerik dropped to one knee.

"No!" Fiorn yelled in anger. He side-stepped, still taking hits from weapons against his shield and dragged Eerik to the rear of the formation. Two of our injured now whimpered and moaned behind us while only six continue to fight off the decrepit killers. I picked up the pace, now swinging my axe faster and faster above the insignificant shield wall taking down what beasts I could until a Draugr with a large hammer came down on old man Grim's shield and completely shattered it. The noise sounded like thunder and echoed loudly in the little valley. Grim fell backward and I helped him up just in time to parry a sword thrust. Our defense was split now with three warriors on each side and the fighting had turned to utter chaos. Demon spawn rushed forward into the gap quickly grabbing the farm boy and Eerik. Above the melee I saw limbs and flesh strewn about as the field muddied into a dark pool of human bile. The Draugr feasted on their bones and screamed in pleasure at the fresh meal.

"You fucking bastards! I'll have your heads! I'll have all your heads!" Tormund yelled and he went mad with rage hacking and slashing, ferociously cutting Draugr down like insects. It became impossible to step without slipping on wet flesh. Sada screamed and gripped the front of her thigh where a bleeding gash had appeared. She lunged forward, stabbing the Draugr that had wounded her. He laughed deeply and pulled back for another swing when I hacked off his arm. Sada bashed his body with her shield, knocking him to the ground. The job was not yet done and so she stepped up to the creature and stomped in his head with her feet until nothing but a muddied mess lay below.

We finally closed the gap between us and once again created a united front against our foe. Sada hopped to the center, locking her shield just behind Fiorn's as she was too weak now to take a hit alone. With bodies strewn about, I looked below to see Draugr spears and picked up three, throwing them ahead into the crowd. The missiles slowed them down but did not cease their onslaught. More eyes appeared just above and beyond the fighting. The forest seemed to swell with creatures of the night as we tired and our defense once more began to wane. Exhaustion was now our biggest enemy. Bereft of breath, we pushed on. The farmer boy screamed in terror as a sword point slipped past the shields and entered his chest. The boy gripped the sword with his hand, slicing it open and knocking it away. He lunged forward and hacked the creature until it fell just to be replaced by another. A small axe flew towards us and split the skull of the farm boy, knocking him backward. Not a scream, barely even a sound was uttered as the axe had pierced him so deeply. Only five us of remained as the hordes continued to push and now the farmer's family in the cavern behind us screamed in desperation knowing that we to would soon fall and that they would surely die a gruesome death.

The trees then erupted with the sound of a great horn blowing loudly. The Draugr stepped back, ceasing their tireless onslaught and they gazed upward at the top of the mound. The horn blast stopped and the forest was eerily quiet. For the first time I saw something in the eyes of the undead I had never seen before: fear. Then, the horn blasted once more and the air filled with snaps and quiet shrieks in the darkness. Iron stingers fell from atop the mound and blasted the Draugr horde back from our fighting position. Dark shadows above jumped and bounced between the bases of the trees, unleashing arrow after arrow.

"The warriors of Skerheim have come to our aid!" I called out. "Fight! Fight for your lives!" We charged forward, releasing a war cry and while the Draugr in front of us focused on the archers above, we cut them down like the dogs they were paving a path of utter destruction. Shields of every color now descended down into the trench and a hasty shield wall erected in front of us.

"Audan!" It was Gunnar with bow in hand.

"Thank the gods you have come, brother. I thought we were all dead men for sure."

"Stay behind the wall and take rest while we handle these brutes. These bastards won't escape the vengeance of our swords!" Gunnar tucked away his bow on his back and swapped it for a shield and hand axe. He joined the formation and we watched from the rear with the farmer's family as the horde was pushed back into the dark forest. Archers covered the top of the mound and continued to slow the Draugr forward movement in the distance. Chaos now only resided with the undead as our organized fighting formation unleashed blow after blow of merciless conquest. Fiorn gripped my arm and pulled me towards him.

"We should get the farmer's family out while we still can." Sada sat on the ground neck to me still clutching her wound. It still bled heavily and I grabbed a pinch of dirt in my hand and moved her fingers.

"This is going to hurt," I said. Sada looked away and I packed the dirt into her wound. She winced and I felt the muscle around my fingers press hard against my skin. I removed my hand to see the bleeding had stopped. I helped my love to her feet and pointed to the farmers.

"Can you get them to the horses?" Sada looked at the farmer's family.

"I can."

"Good, the go! Ride fast!" Sada hobbled quickly to the famer's family and urged them out of their hiding place amongst the terrible din all around. One by one, they lifted themselves from the cavern and Sada led them up the mound under the cover of arrow fire back towards the horses.

"Grim!" I called out to the old warrior.

"What is it, boy?"

"Help Sada get the farmers back to Skerheim." Grim shook his head.

"I am old and full of hate. If this is my chance to die in battle and ascend to Valhalla, I will not forsake it." Grim left from our safe place from behind the shield wall and joined the fray. Tormod stood.

"It's alright, brother. I will go with them and ensure their safety!" I nodded in thanks to Tormod's warm gesture.

"Thank you, brother. Keep my wife safe. See to it she has her wound treated!" Tormod grabbed his things and headed up the mound quickly, catching up with the back of the column. The farmer's family disappeared and were hopefully on a path to safety. Only Fiorn and I still rested behind the melee and soon we caught our breath and stood to our feet.

"Are you ready?" Fiorn asked.

"I am, brother." I walked up to the formation, the sounds of grunts, groans, iron and steel deafening to the ears. Eygautr and Valdemar had found themselves at the center and I tapped their shoulders to make space for Fiorn and me. Valdemar smiled wildly.

"It's good of you to join us!" he said after plunging a spear into the skull of a Draugr.

"Did you think we would let you have all the adventure to yourself?" Valdemar stepped to the side and let me into the wall. Eygautr made room for Fiorn, but instead of stepping to the side he stepped to the rear of the melee yelling at the top of his lungs on where to direct our efforts.

"Get into line!" Eygautr commanded. "Get into line, you stupid bastards! Handsomely now!"

Slowly, the shield wall straightened and became tighter. No spear thrust could penetrate and we waited for Eygautr's next command. "Alright, together. Step!" We stepped forward and thrust our weapons outward as we did so. A line of Draugr fell to our feet. We stepped over them and several warriors to the rear made quick work removing their heads with swords. With each step, we felled another line of Draugr and then another and another. Nearly fifty Draugr in all had fallen to our arms and now the remaining forty or so began to waver and step further back. We did not rush forward, we did not chase them down, but stayed close to one another and let the archers do their worst to those who would not confront us at the wall. Victory it seemed was all but assured as the rotting beasts began to flee back into the darkness of the woods.

"We have them on the run!" Eygautr cried out in victory. Then, the dreadful sounds of deep howls filled the dark forest. Every warrior and undead stopped in their tracks and listened patiently. The howls erupted again, this time much closer. Trees limbs snapped and cracked in the distance and now the nearby brush could be heard be trampled and torn apart. Only one thing in all of Midgard could make such a sound. Only one thing in all of Midgard could move with such speed and ferocity.

"Ulfhednar!" I yelled with a warning. Large dark shadows emerged at the top of the mound and began attacking the archers. Stingers flew wildly and we drew swords when bows became useless. One by one, the creatures took down our cover, sending warriors flying through the air and down into the ravine. A body rolled past and stop just ahead of my feet. The warrior had been disemboweled, cut from the belly button up like one would clean a deer. His guts were strewn about the forest floor and steam rose from his fresh corpse. Those archers not at the front of the columns fled down into the ravine to join us in the shield wall. The Ulfhednar growled and snapped as they slowly crawled down the mound to the flat small valley below. Six in all, they stood no more than forty paces from us. The Draugr no longer under the hail of stingers now seemed encourage by the arrival of their allies. The remaining forty or so amassed once again just behind the Ulfhednar and slowly approach us.

"Keep the rocks to your backs!" Eygautr called out.

"Don't let these hounds frighten you, boys. Their bark is worse than their bite! Let's show them who is master and who is pet!" With my men now in the formation, it was time for our rallying cry.

"Sons of Bjorgvin! What makes the grass grow and the rivers flow?" they replied in fierce unison.

"Blood! Blood! Blood!"

"And how do we get blood, my brothers?" I asked.

"Kill! Kill! Kill!" I pointed my bearded axe outward at the sharp-fanged beasts now bearing down on us.

"For glory!" The Ulfhednar howled and dug their claws into the dirt, leaping forward at our shield wall. With all their might, they jumped straight into blade, buckler, and brawn. Shields shattered, shafts snapped in two and the beasts buried themselves deep with our ranks. As our wall gave way, the Draugr took the opportunity to move in and work the flanks. A fellow warrior knocked down by the wolf demon sent my flying to the ground face down. I lifted my body and turned to see the sharp menacing eyes of an Ulfhednar leaping towards me. My bearded axe had fallen out of my hands and I could not reach for it. The beast leapt with open jaw, bearing his gleaming teeth. I flinched and closed my eyes when the creature fell before me. A warrior had jumped in front of me and buried his blade into the furry creatures beating chest; it was Eygautr. The short fat man wrestled with the beast as he turned and twisted the blade the Ulfhednar clawed and ripped at Eygautr's flesh. The old man yelled in anger and continued to press on his attack. The beast let out a final scream and fell motionless atop the old man.

"Eygautr!" I ran to him and pulled the beast off his body. Eygautr bled from head to foot, his back covered gashes so deep you could see the white of his ribs. He shook and coughed up blood while his hands covered his chest. "Eygautr, no…" His shaking stopped and he looked at me with cold eyes and a blood-stained smile.

"I will tell your father about the man you have become." His head fell gently to the side and the old man breathed no more. A leg brushed violently up against me and I jumped to my feet, returning to the fighting at hand. Two of the Ulfhednar had been defeated but now the Draugr picked off unsuspecting warriors who had fallen beneath the beast. I licked my dried lips only to have my mouth filled with the rock-like taste of blood. An Ulfhednar pressed forward against Gunnar's shield and I stepped in with a mighty blow of my bearded axe, landing in the foul creature's shoulder. He let out a scream and pulled away. A flood of undead filled the void, smacking the dull weapons against our shields. Fiorn pressed his assault, thrusting his sword low and cutting at the lower limbs of the undead. Shredding their tendons, he knocked down the creatures, yet they crawled after us with sword or dagger in hand. When the beasts lost their weapons, they used the bony fingers and teeth to inflect harm on us. A Draugr leapt over the shield wall and gripped one of Fiorn's warriors by the hair, biting directly into his neck. The creatures ripped out a chunk of flesh, sending blood shooting everywhere. The warrior succumbed to his wound, falling heavily on the ground. Grim ran in and smashed the beast's head in with the pommel of his sword.

"No!" I yelled out. I suddenly found myself lying on my back. Something had grabbed my leg and pulled me with great speed underneath the shield wall. My back and arms became covered in bile and blood. Then, the creature released its grip. I sat up only to be pinned back down by an Ulfhednar. He rushed in to bite my head and I pressed the blade of my axe into the corners of his mouth. His fangs dangled just a few inches from my fingers but he could not move his mouth. The axe head had become completely lodged in his flesh and so I leaned to one side pulling with all my might until the blade ripped through his mouth, severing part of his lower jaw from his head. The Ulfhednar gripped his face in pain and I swung my axe back around and dropped it squarely into his skull.

The monster let out a terrible cry and then fell silent. Feet and shields rushed around me and a hand pulled me back into formation.

"Get up, boy!" Uncle Valdemar yelled. He brushed me off and turned back towards the fray. "Go to hell, you fucking..." A spear squeezed between the shields and lodged itself in Valdemar's neck. He stepped back two paces, gripping the spear with sword still in hand and then calmly stepped forward. "Let me through!" he ordered. The men saw the shaft protruding from his body and quickly moved out of his way. Valdemar leapt into the horde and ran straight for an Ulfhednar. The beast jumped atop him, knocking Valdemar's shield from his grasp. Valdemar plunged his sword into the beast's side and twisted it. The wolf beast struck Valdemar's arm, causing him to loose grip of his blade. As the beast swung from side to side in agony, Valdemar gripped the shaft of the spear in his neck. Holding tightly, he pulled it out and then buried the spear into the beast's stomach. The creature wailed in horror and fell over as it trembled and shook in agony. Valdemar coughed loudly and blood shot violently from his neck. Soon, he coughed no more and the pulse of blood slowed to a trickle until he passed on.

"No! Uncle!" My rage consumed me and I turned away from my fallen comrades to wage unending war. Three Ulfhednar and a handful of undead remained. The shields at the front of the line were cracked and they began to splinter and fall apart. A wolf beast leapt over us but impaled himself on a long spear, snapping the shaft under his weight and falling over to die.

"We can't hold them much longer!" Gunnar cried out.

"We must hold or we will all die this day! Fight, fight for honor, fight for your lives!" cried Fiorn. More of our valiant warriors fell to the random sword or axe swing. More of our valiant warriors fell to the tooth and claw of the Ulfhednar. What once was many was now only a few brave warriors amongst a field of corpses piled high. Exhausted, weak, and worn out from the blood lust our defense began to waiver once more and the undead slowly pulled the shields aside and pushed themselves into our ranks. Then, the skies began to hum and sing loudly. A raging wind blew sending leaves and dirt in our faces, narrowing our vision. The sky seemed to turn from night to day as it cracked loudly with thunder and lit brightly with lighting. No sooner did I blink that bolt of light streaked downward striking our foes. Theirs bodies catching fire on impact.

"Thor!" the undead cried out. "Thor!" They ran from the battle, leaving behind their weapons. The last two Ulfhednar remained defiant at the blasts of lightning as the leapt from side to side of the ravine. We huddled together closely and pushed our backs hard against the rocks for fear that the light may strike us. Then, a final bolt struck the ground before us. A man emerged from the fire, tall and muscular. The warrior carried no sword nor shield. He only carried a large hammer, a hammer that sparked with the light of lightning and hummed with the rage of the clouds. The man in the green tunic was Thor himself!

"By the gods! We are saved!" Fiorn called out. The Ulfhednar rushed in, leaping at the Asgardian god. The first wrapped his teeth around Thor's arm biting furiously. Thor shook him off and threw the beast across the small valley into a tree. The second beast went for Thor's neck but he gripped the beast's upper and lower jaw and pulled with all his might until the jaws snapped. The creature fell to the ground and Thor bludgeoned him with his mighty hammer. The last of the Ulfhednar howled loudly and ran into the night. Thor pointed his hammer in the distance and a bolt of lightning fell after the wolf beast, striking it and knocking over several trees.

This day the battle had been won. We lowered our weapons and as Thor approached us dropped to one knee.

"You are Norseman, not slaves. Get up my brothers and rejoice this day in our victory!" The men cheered and chanted Thor's name as loudly as they could. He gazed upon me and approached. "Audan, son of Rurik. It has been a long time since you and I last spoke." Thor extended his arm in a friendly handshake and I gladly returned the gesture. "Last time we met you were a pawn in Freya's game and a thief in my hall. Now you are an honored warrior amongst your people. I'm proud to fight alongside you."

"If not for you, we would have won the battle with far less men to celebrate our victory. I thank you for helping to spare the lives of so many." The color red caught my attention against Thor's green tunic. Blood dripped down from the wound that the Ulfhednar had inflicted on Thor's forearm. "You're bleeding?" The smiling god lifted his arm and surveyed his wound.

"It would appear so."

"But how?" I asked. Thor stepped forward, gripping my shoulder.

"A friend of Odin such as yourself should know that our powers wane on Midgard. As the Ragnarok approaches, we become more like you each day. It's a strange thing you mortals face, fearing death and the sting of pain."

"Audan!" Gunnar called out. "We have wounded. We need to get them back to Skerheim and treat them, otherwise they may die of infection." I gazed back at Thor.

"We are weak and exhausted from battle. Can you help us carry our wounded comrades back to our cavern?"

Thor nodded.

"I can do more than that." Thor approached the four wounded warriors and looked carefully at their wounds. To the first one he said, "Don't move. This is going to be very painful." The Viking warrior nodded and grit his teeth. From his hammer, he released a small flash of lightning that burnt and cleaned the wound. The warrior screamed out in pain and then looked down to see his wound closed by fire.

"Thank you, my lord," the warrior said. Thor did the same with the second and the third warrior. When he reached the forth, he shook his head and made a disagreeable sound.

"What is it?" the warrior asked.

"You have the bite marks of the Draugr. I cannot heal this. Tomorrow, you will catch fever and die. Then in the evening you will be reborn a mindless flesh eating corpse." The warrior was overcome with dread at the sound of this news. "Or…" Thor uttered.

"Oh, mighty Thor, please tell me you can help me?" the warrior pleaded.

"You can pick up your sword and spend your remaining hours hunting Draugr until you die honorably and join me in the hall of Valhalla. For if you turn, it will not be so." The warrior stared at the group for a moment and then gazed upward with determination in his eyes.

"Help me stand." Thor lifted the man upright and handed him a sword.

"Give me your shield," Thor said. "Where you are going, you will not need it." Without hesitation the warrior handed Thor his shield and began to walk towards the fleeing Draugr. "Go with honor."

The warrior walked proudly into the darkness of the forest, the sight of him becoming dimmer until he finally disappeared, never to be heard from again. We quickly went to work, helping the three wounded out of the ravine and to the horse trail that lay above. Thor lifted two men alone on his shoulders and carried them at a fast pace. With the god of lightning on our side we had no fears of the Draugr rallying for another attack. The walk was long and agonizing as our every wound, cut, and scrape stung and burn. My muscles cramped terribly.

It had been nearly half a day since I drank any water. Some men slowly fell behind but Fiorn and Grim urged them to move forward leaving no man behind. The darkness consumed the forest floor and soon we could not even see our feet. Thor stopped and placed the two wounded gently down to the ground.

"Why have we stopped, my lord?" asked Fiorn. Thor knelt down and gripped his hammer in front of his face.

"Everything in the mortal realm and the heavens is always better with a little light." Thor blew softly against the hammer and it began to glow bright blue. The ground lit up brightly and all could clearly see their feet.

"That's amazing," I said. Thor nodded.

"There are all manner of finer things in Midgard. Great and powerful weapons, magic and spells the likes of which you have not even dreamt about." Thor secured his hammer to his belt and lifted the two wounded once more and carried on with the march. A little more than an hour had passed and finally we reached the outside entrance of Skerheim. "Is this it?" Thor asked. Fiorn stepped forward and knocked on the secret passageway five times.

"It is, my lord." The guards from the other side quickly unlatched the entry-way and opened the gate. The first of the guards popped his head out.

"Fiorn! Thank the gods you have returned." Fiorn placed his hand on the guards shoulder.

"No, my friend. Thank Thor." Thor walked past the guard and he watch in complete awe as the glowing hammer was carried into the cavern.

"Thor?" the guard asked in disbelief. We followed Fiorn and Thor down the cavern to the main hall. Another guard had been sent ahead to let the others know we had arrived. Soon, voices erupted from the open cavern and as we entered the bright lights of fire and the sounds of cheers erupted. Those that stayed behind quickly took control of the wounded and moved them to a separate room to be treated, while the rest of us collapsed loudly in the room discarding our gear anywhere we saw fit. Sada immediately recognized me despite being covered in mud and blood.

"By the gods, what happened?"

"Water," I pleaded. Sada rushed back to the fresh water well and filled a mug bringing it to me. I eagerly drank the enter contents of the cup. "More," I asked. She took the cup from my hand filling it once more at the well and returning it. I finished drinking my water and took a deep slow breath.

"There are so few of you?" I nodded.

"The Ulfhednar," I replied.

"The wolf beasts? They were here?"

"Yes, my love. We had the Draugr on the run, but the Ulfhednar came after you and the farmers escaped. It rallied the undead to continue their assault." Sada looked about the room.

"Where is Uncle Valdemar and our friend, Eygautr?" I looked up at Sada and shook my head. My eyes teared up and I lower my head in shame.

"They didn't make it, my love. Eygautr died protecting me from the bite of an Ulfhednar. Valdemar was killed by a Draugr, a spear throw to the neck. Both men took an Ulfhednar with them before they died. It was a good death for both of them." Tears ran down Sada's face and she sat down quietly next to me. She held my bloodied hand tightly and rubbed her thumb atop it.

"And Gunnar?"

I pointed to the other side of the cavern.

"Gunnar is fine my love. He fought bravely this day."

"Thank the gods. And who is that man who brought in two of the wounded?" Sada said as she pointed across the cavern.

"That, my love, is the hammer wielder. The only reason we are all still alive this day. That is Thor."

Ten
Paths Unwanted

With night falling well upon us those that survived the devastating battle now rested. Sada and I lay upon a wool cloth atop a stone floor. It was not the most comfortable place I had ever slept but after the terrible fight we had just finished I cared not where I rested, only that I did so. Sada ran her fingers gently through my beard and kissed my cheek gently.

"Good night love," she said to me. I turned and wrapped my arm around her to keep her warm and quickly fell into a deep slumber.

* * *

The next morning, I woke and found Sada gone from our bed. The smell of fresh food wafted in the cavern and I slowly sat upright, leaning against a wooden crate.

"Did you sleep well?" Fiorn walked into my sleeping quarters and sat down on the floor next to me. I nodded my head and yawned deeply.

"Better than you, it would seem." Fiorn smiled, closing his eyes.

"We don't sleep much here living in the cavern. With no sun and moon to keep us on course, we tend to lose track of time. Your woman is an early riser. She is in the kitchen helping prepare breakfast for the men." I rubbed my eyes and pulled my hair from my face, still not ready to rise from bed.

"The injured?" I asked.

"They will recover. The light of Thor cleaned their wounds and sealed them almost instantly. I suspect they will be a little slower for a few days."

"How many?"

"How many what?" Fiorn asked.

"How many dead?" Fiorn looked down and then scratched at his face.

"We lost sixty-one men. Twenty-seven of these warriors were of your own party. The three injured belong to me."

"Sixty-one Norse warriors for fifteen farmers? Was it worth it?" I asked. Fiorn shrugged his shoulders.

"We would have met the Draugr and their dogs on the battlefield one way or another. We just happened to meet them while rescuing a family. I for one am glad we were able to destroy such a large number and take out the nearby Ulfhednar. They have been giving us problems for some time and have limited our evening activities. Now, we came move unimpeded in the twilight hours."

"And how do they fair? The villagers?" I asked.

"Well, they lost one at the farm and two of their young men to the melee, but the other twelve are well. It has been long since we had women in our presence. They have quickly gone to work cleaning, cooking, and repairing linens. I had half a mind to send them south today like the others but I think I will keep them around for a while longer. If I allow them to linger for too long, the men may start to fight over them like wild animals."

I nodded, understanding. Slowly, I stood and walked out of the sleeping quarters with Fiorn by my side. The light of the fires were bright and provided ample light for the room. Sada and several Norse women stood side by side preparing food and drinks for the warriors. The cavern was still mostly quiet as many men continued their slumber. Our victory left a sour taste in my mouth and I wished to no longer speak of it. A young warrior walked quickly up to Fiorn and whispered in his ear.

"Very good," he said to the young man who briskly walked away. "Audan, come with me. Someone is waiting for you outside." Without question, I walked just behind my comrade making our way into the caverns hallway. We reached the entrance and the guard quietly unlatched the door and opened it for us. The vines lying over the doorway were stiff and frozen. My feet crunched loudly under the piles of fresh snow. Bereft of my cloak and fur, I took in a deep breath and let the cold into my body. The ice chilled my blood and cooled my soul. Breathing outward, I watched the hot breath dance in the icy morning air. Fiorn stopped and pointed in the distance. "He's out there."

Confused I asked, "You're not coming with me?"

Fiorn shook his head.

"Men are meant to respect and fear the gods, not to walk amongst them." I looked out in the distance to see Thor standing in a clearing covered in fresh powder as he stared out into the forest. I began walking forward when Fiorn placed his hand on my shoulder.

"Audan, you have chosen a dangerous path, my friend. I hope you know what you are doing. Either way, I wish you the best of luck." Fiorn slowly extended his hand and I gripped it firmly, returning the gesture with a handshake. Fiorn turned away quickly and made his way back into the cavern. I walked towards Thor and exaggerated my steps so he would hear me coming. No more than ten paces from him, he turned his head slightly.

"You don't have to be so loud, mortal. I could hear you and Fiorn stomping your way through the cavern." I stopped in my tracks, resting one hand on my sword handle and the other on my hip.

"You called for me?" The giant of a man turned slowly with the great hammer Mjolnir in hand.

"I want to show you something," he said quietly in a hoarse voice.

"Very well." Thor held his hammer in front of him: a very plain thing, a metal pure as black and a handle made of iron. He dropped it to the ground and the snow below it shot outward, creating a clearing. All around us the falling snows ceased their descent and floated in place. The snow drifted and swayed, beginning to take form, the form of a man. He seemed an imposing figure, tall and muscular with a square jaw and sharp features in his face. His eyes were intelligent and unnerving, but there was something else to him. A look that I've only see in certain animals, the look of a predator.

"Do you know who this is, Audan?" I cautiously approached the figure and examined it carefully.

"I do not. Who is this man?" I said as I shook my head.

"This is no mere man. This is creature the old lady from the farm spoke of. This is the man who will set your world a flame and leave nothing but ash and ember in his wake."

"Surt?" Thor nodded his head. He knelt down picking up his hammer and the imposing figure fell apart, the snow falling to the floor. The winds again began to move and the snowflakes fell gently on our heads.

"The first of the elementals has returned to Midgard despite our best efforts. The ravens tell me he quietly roams the countryside, sometimes slipping out of our sight."

"If Surt is here that means the Ragnarok is here as well. The world will end soon."

"The forces that diminish our powers on this realm are weakening; I can feel it." Thor's eyes lit up blue as they cracked and snapped loudly. He looked upward at the cloudy sky. "It won't be much longer before all of Asgard can descend to Midgard for the final battle. Before we do, we have another task for you."

"I'm happy to serve, Thor, anything for you and Odin, but if the world is indeed coming to an end why should I do anything?"

"Because there is still time."

"Time for what?"

"The signs of the Ragnarok are approaching, this is true, but you can help reverse their current path, perhaps even bring peace back to Midgard. Odin has great faith in you, my friend, and if he places so much trust in you, then I, too, will support you." I rubbed my forehead in frustration and looked away out into the empty forest. I still had a task to complete, and Loki would still hold me to my vow.

"Do not worry about him," Thor said.

"Get out of my mind, Asgardian. My thoughts are my own," I snapped.

"Not when you work for Loki. The trickster is up to no good."

"He wants his mutt back. That is all."

"And how many men will you lose trying to find and capture such a beast?"

"I don't know, but I can't turn my back on him. He's too powerful. At a moment's notice, he could show and slit our throats in the night. He is a clever and shrewd god."

"No more clever or shrewd than you and I. Besides, we still need you to muzzle the hound, so it would seem that nothing has changed. We need you to amass an army to march on the Draugr hoard that roams to the south."

"A most heavy burden and you ask this of me now as my ranks are thinning and as well as those that we can trust."

"Trust is exactly why we ask this of you. After you capture Fenrir, you will travel every corner of the north, make allies, create friendships, and gather the forces of men to your will."

"I don't think you understand. The world of men is weaker now than ever. It's about survival. The Draugr out number us, the Ulfhednar pick us off in the night one by one and we make great sacrifices for little gain."

"You have..."

"It's about survival!" I yelled. "That is all. Every man will be out for himself to make it just one more day and then another day after that."

Thor was frustrated with me and he closed his eyes, taking a deep breath.

"If the people of Midgard do not unite there will be no survival. Your families, your friends, everything that you love and once knew will be gone. Surt needs time to gather his strength and build his forces. He knows that once the barrier is broken the soldiers of Asgard will fall upon him like a tidal wave."

"And what of Freya and Fenrir? If Surt is not yet a threat what will I do about them?"

"Freya's time will come. The dog, on the other hand, is your problem. Bury your dead, Audan, mourn for them and then find the beast. We need you now more than ever. I must return to Asgard and help prepare our forces for the fight to come." At this point, I was used to the gods leaving me in our time of need.

"Well then, farewell." I extended my hand and Thor gripped it, shaking it enthusiastically.

"Until the Ragnarok." The air around me suddenly felt warm and the hairs on my arm stood upright. A bright flash erupted before me and just like that Thor was gone. Loud crackles of thunder echoed above in the clouds and I looked skyward, hoping to catch of glimpse of his light streaking across the clouds.

"I hate it when they do that," I said quietly. I stood there for a moment, staring at the bright white snow beneath my feet and let my mind wander. Freya and Fenrir were on the loose, a Draugr army marched southward and now Surt had finally appeared on Midgard. I imagined a map in my mind and watched the pieces move about and pondered how I might intercept each one. No matter my move there would always be one or two opponents who would move freely or out maneuver me. I wanted to wrap my arms around the land and protect everyone and everything from this evil. No matter what I did, it would never be enough. I would always be one step behind and many more innocents would die. A fire now raged in my heart and in my veins. The cold of the snows seemed to leave me altogether. There was nothing to do now but move forward and capture Loki's hound. I ventured back into the caverns where I could once again feel the warmth of the fires against my skin. Breakfast was prepared and I quickly swallowed my portion before climbing the ladders back up to Fiorn's chambers. When I approached, I saw the man leaning back in his chair with his feet up on the table. His hands rested behind his head as he gazed up at the ceiling. I looked up to see what he might be looking at but there was nothing there.

"I take it the meeting was brief?" asked Fiorn without moving his eyes. I nodded my head and smiled.

"Yes, very brief. As is Thor's way." Fiorn kicked down his feet to the floor and turned his gaze to me.

"So, you finished your meeting with Thor and you already ate your breakfast. I'm assuming there is something you wish to discuss? Perhaps something from Thor?"

"Thor's plans change nothing for me. I still go to capture the beast."

"So, you're going to do it then? You're going to catch Fenrir?" I shook my head and raised my brow.

"Aye, I am. Loki has commanded it and Thor has no objections. The hound has caused too much chaos and destruction already. He must be stopped." Fiorn stood from his chair and turned to his sword that leaned against the wall. He gripped the handle and partially removed the blade from its sheath, staring briefly at the glint of steel until slapping it shut. He wrapped his belt around his waist and secured the blade to his side.

"Very well, my friend. What do you propose?"

"Gather three of your best men to join myself, Gunnar, Njord and Sada. The rest of my men will remain here to help protect the cavern."

"Tormod!" The young warrior rushed up the ladders and stood before his leader.

"Yes, my lord?"

"Go find Grim. I need you and that old bastard to come with me on an errand." Tormund bowed his head slightly.

"Right away." He ran off back down the ladders and disappeared into the caverns.

"You're going to come with me?"

"Of course. You need the very best men to capture this beast, do you not? I just happen to be the very best of my men."

"Who will lead if you are to fall?"

"They will figure something out. I would not be the first leader they have lost while fighting off this darkness. I will certainly not be the last." Fiorn was a good fighter and a great friend, indeed. These days I seemed to be running low on companions and now I needed trusted allies more than ever. A few moments later, the young Tormund returned with a sleepy-looking Grim. His silver hair was in disarray and his beard pointed far to the left, no doubt from sleeping on his side.

"This had better be important," Grim exclaimed as he wiped the drool from his lips. "I was having a good dream. One of *those* dreams, you know." I laughed quietly. "No, Grim, I don't know. Please tell us."

"Well, you see I was in a tavern with the largest horn of mead you could possibly imagine. I mean, it was so huge it had to touch the ground and sit against my lap just to stand upright. So the mead was flowing, good music and a roaring fire. The ladies were running about with their breasts exposed and then this one lass, she had hair the color of fire that ran down to her buttocks in great beautiful braids. This lass sits on my lap and whispers in my ear that I, Grim am the manliest of men she has ever beheld. She pulls back her head and stares at me with bright emerald eyes and then stands, asking me to take her out back. So, what's a man like me to do? I stand and follow this woman outside ready to give her the business end if you know what I mean. Just as she kneels down to suck my cock..." Grim paused and looked at us intensely. Tormund leaned forward with great interest, no doubt due to a lack of experience in this area.

"Then what?" Tormund asked enthusiastically.

"Well, you see this hand here?" Grim placed one hand in front of him just below his waist. "I placed this hand on top of her head." Suddenly, Grim lunged forward and struck Tormund in the face sending the young man to the ground. He stood quickly gripping the handle of his sword and Fiorn restrained him as we all laughed at the boy. "Then, this little cunt woke me up!" Grim reached over to Fiorn's table grabbing a wooden mug of mead and drank it quickly.

"Fight me, old man! I'm not afraid of you." Grim slowly placed the mug down and wiped his chin.

"Young lad, you would have a chance in all the nine realms of kicking my ass. You forget one thing."

"And what's that?" Tormund asked sharply.

"I'm old for a reason. I fuck hard and I fight even harder. You'd do best to remember that the next time you want to wake an old warrior." Tormund was not amused and he gave me a look of disgust.

"You think this is funny?" I raised my hand slowly to try to calm the boy's fiery nerves.

"I'm sorry, Tormund, but, yes, it is amusing to say the least. I mean, pow, he just knocked you flat on your arse. You never saw it coming." Fiorn gripped Tormund by the shoulders and forced him to sit down in a chair.

"That's enough fucking around. Now calm yourself. You're lucky he didn't take a battle axe two you when you woke him." Tormund crossed his arms and looked away.

"Next time, I'll wake him with a battle axe." Fiorn sat atop his table and pointed to a burnt leather map held down to the table by rounded stones.

"Alright, enough. Let's get down to it. Audan has need of us. We're going to join him in capturing his beast." Grim crossed his arms.

"Beast? What beast?" Fiorn replied unblinking.

"We're going to help Audan catch Fenrir the mad dog." Grim erupted into laughter.

"You must be joking?" The old man slapped my shoulder and laughed even louder. "No one binds Fenrir, no one except Tyr." Grim turned his head from side to side looking intensely about the cavern. "I don't see Tyr amongst us, so I don't see how we're going to bind the beastie." I reached into my satchel and removed the gleipnir rope. The silver shine reflected off of Grim's eyes and for the first time the mouthy old bastard was speechless.

"This is…" Grim lifted his hand and snatched the gleipnir from my grasp.

"I know what it is, boy, by the gods I do." Grim wrapped it around his fingers and looked the rope up and down in utter amazement. "How did you get it!" he yelled.

"It was given to me." I didn't understand why Grim was so upset. He seemed almost furious that I held the gleipnir in my possession. What could possibly upset him so?

"By who? Who gave it to you?"

"The trickster, Loki." Grim took a step back.

"Loki? And you would trust him with your life? That bastard is known to trick men, lead many to their deaths he has."

"Why do you doubt Audan? He is a loyal and trustworthy friend," Asked Fiorn.

"I don't doubt him, only the person who would so willingly hand over such a precious gift. Do you know where gleipnir comes from lad?"

"I do."

"Do you now?" Grim doubted me. I could hear it in his tone. Something about my confidence he did not like. "You see Audan, I have been down to the mines, I have lived amongst the Dwarves."

"Grim?" Fiorn asked.

"Oh eye, many a years ago when I was just a pup like yourself. Dwarves don't just give away their precious metals, especially not gleipnir. A gift for Kings of men perhaps but Dwarves often keep such a thing for their own needs. When gleipnir trades hands in the mines it is always from one dwarf to another and always for a purpose."

"What are you getting at Grim?" Fiorn asked. He threw the rope at me and I caught it quickly tucking it back away into the satchel.

"I'm saying Loki is a lying piece of shit. That there is stolen."

"Why would a god steal gleipnir? They could probably have however much they desired." Grim shook his head quickly.

"No, certainly not. Not even the gods would have gleipnir without trading it for something of great value. That rope you have in your satchel in particular is worn."

"How could it be worn? Nothing can break it." Grim nodded and stepped back towards me reaching in the satchel and putting the gleipnir close to my face.

"Do you see that? Scratches. This rope was used to tie something up, something big that didn't want to be bound." I don't know why I didn't see it before but the old man was right. Loki was up to no good.

"You're saying this was the gleipnir that Tyr himself used to bind Fenrir?"

"It just may be lad. If Loki had that and gave it to you that would tell me that he unbound the beast himself; set him free on Midgard and all this misery is his fault."

"Audan?" asked Fiorn. "What do you want us to do? I think Grim is right but Thor seems to think we should continue onward with Loki's plan." I didn't like it, this path that the gods were setting me on. Things were only going to get worse and going in after Fenrir sounded more and more like a trap.

"Odin trust Thor and therefore I will trust him. If Thor says we must bind Fenrir before we can raise an army then so be it. I'll not forsake their counsel." Fiorn rubbed his chin and stared back at Grim and Tormund.

"What?" Grim asked.

"Well? Are you coming with us?" Grim laughed and now smacked Tormund on the shoulder.

"I don't know why we are still here talking about it when that mutt is out there causing so much havoc. This might be my one chance to not die of old age. So, what are we waiting for?" Fiorn smiled and turned to the youngest of our party.

"Tormund?" The young warrior smiled and puffed out his chest.

"You have my sword, from now until Valhalla."

"Good lad. Then it is settled. Audan, when do you wish to leave?" asked Fiorn.

"We leave at dusk. The night will our cover, the darkness our friend. We can't let the Draugr know of our movements. We need to find Fenrir asleep or all will be for not."

"How will we find the evil mutt?" asked Grim.

"We follow the path of destruction. Fenrir is not staying off the beaten paths. He's moving from town to town. Follow the terror and there you will find the beast."

"Very well. We meet at the stables at dusk. Get some rest and ready your things. I will see you all soon." We left Fiorn to his tasks and I returned to Sada and Gunnar filling them in on our task at hand. Both were well aware of the danger that lay before us and neither showed any worry on the matter. Njord the blacksmith would be left to lead the few warriors we left behind. Bereft of veteran warriors Njord was the closest thing to a trust worthy and competent commander. As for those who died fighting off the Draugr and Ulfhednar to rescue the farmer's family; it was time to give them a proper burial. Their bodies lay outside in the snows. By now their bodies would be frozen, completely covered in the frost bitten forests. I headed outside the caverns followed by Sada, Gunnar, and Njord. When the guard open the gate and let me outside I could see what remained of the farmer's family outside. They had already buried the bodies of Eygautr and Uncle Valdemar and surrounded their graves with stones in the shape of a ship to mark their final resting places. The old woman who warned me of Surt slowly approached and reached her hand out for mine. She gently gripped them and pulled me in closely to her.

"I know your warriors are weary so we decided to bury the dead for you. It was the least we could do to say thank you for saving our lives." I nodded and gently shook her hands.

"Thank you for caring for our friends and family. They will be greatly missed." The old woman pulled her can up and walk it up my side.

"Come down here young man. Let me see you." The blind old woman extended her hands upward and I gently guided them to my face. She moved her hand up and down my face running her fingers around my nose, eyes, and through my beard. "Hmmmm." She muttered.

"What is it?" I asked curious about what a blind woman would think of the feel of my face.

"Your handsome, yes, very handsome." My cheeks became flush and I smiled. "Thank you."

"No wonder the warrior girl loves you so. Brave, handsome, and kind. You will be a fine leader for your people, if you can stay alive, that is. Not all clans are so fortunate. Most are ruled by hard men who care little for the worries of their people."

"What is your name?"

"I am Vigdis, grandmother to the family you see before you and the two slain sons that we have buried this day."

"You are blind. How is it that you were able to see Surt?" The women snapped her head back and shot he head from side to side, as if she was listening to something in the forest.

"We mustn't utter his name, dear. He can hear us." My heart began to race in my chest and I looked about the forest floor for any signs of our enemies.

"Is he here, now?"

"He is everywhere, my dear, he see's everything, hears everything and knows all."

"Tell me, how did you see him?"

"My sight has been gone for many years. A fever took me and the days that followed my eyesight was less and less until one day only the darkness remained. That night when the dark one came I could see him, I could see the fire that surrounded him and the embers in every step he took. It wasn't like other times where a sound created a faint shape in the darkness. No, I could see him clear as day and when I looked into his eyes, it felt as if his eyes burned a hole in my very soul."

"You said you could see his footprints. Do you know what direction he headed?" The old women turned her body and pointed.

"He went north, to the Fire Mountains."

"You cannot see but you can find north?" I began to think that perhaps the woman was mad or worse, a witch.

"Not all things are done by sight, my dear. Some things are felt in every breath, in every thought, in our very bones. There is a great force that comes from the Fire Mountains. I can feel it growing stronger each day. Perhaps that is why the dark one ventures there, perhaps he seeks power in the great fires." I paused for a moment and thought of the movements of our enemies. The Draugr to the east, Surt venturing to the North.

"What is it, love?" Sada asked.

"Our enemies are trying to separate us. That is why their forces are so far from one another. They want us to thin our numbers. It's the only way they can destroy us." I turned to the old woman, who gazed with her white eyes in my general direction.

"Vigdis, do you know where I am going?"

"Oh, yes, you go to find the great wolf."

"Do you know where the wolf is?" The old women smiled lifting both her hands into the air and taking a deep breath.

"I can smell his foul breath southeast of here; and something else. A bog..."

"A bog?"

The old woman nodded enthusiastically, grabbing my arm and pointing me in the direction.

"Follow the path of destruction until you reach a great bog. There, you shall find the beast has made a home in pits of muck. Follow the smell of death and there you will find him slumbering after he feasts on entire villages."

I leaned down and hugged the old woman.

"Thank you, Vigdis. I shall not forget you." I began walking towards the grave of my comrades when Vigdis grabbed the bottom of my tunic.

"Audan, just remember that not all of us who practice magic are evil. The Vulva, the Witch is what she is by action, not by name alone. Good luck, young man. You're going to need it." I bowed slightly and left her and her family to their grieving. The air outside was still and silent, not a creature stirred in the wood this midmorning and the graves of our comrades seemed almost surreal as if they had stood for centuries.

"It's a beautiful place to rest. I think Valdemar and Eygautr would be happy," said Sada. I looked up at the tops of the trees and all around and nodded my head.

"It is beautiful. I don't think they could ask for much better. Uncle Valdemar would have preferred to be buried on his island. Nevertheless, this place shall do." I knelt down, placing my knee in the wet cold snow removed my seax dagger from my hip. "I swear on my life that I shall not stop until I honor your memories and your deaths are avenged." I made a small cut in the palm of my hand and dripped the blood onto both grave mounds. The crimson liquid shone brightly against the white of the snow. Gunnar and Njord stepped in front of me and they two made their oaths to Eygautr and Uncle Valdemar. A blood oath that we would not take lightly.

Eleven
Between Dreams
and
Nightmares

Dusk approached quickly as the winds picked up and the frost rose steadily from the ground, biting at our faces. I had an inescapable feeling of dread in what we were about to do knowing that somewhere out there a sleeping beast waited for us with tooth and claw. The morale of the surviving warriors wavered. It had been long since our numbers were replenished and even Fiorn, whose personality was normally quite joyful, slowly began to turn hard. No longer full of love for life, Fiorn's exterior had been worn down like a rock in the river: beaten smooth and bare by every loss of life. Perhaps he agreed to join me on this task only to end his misery or perhaps he wanted to see if there was still something worth living for. You are never quite as alive as you are the day you barely escape death, nothing comes close. The cold air whips over my neck and I shudder for a moment before lifting the fur, draping the wool hood over my head. My ears immediately feel warmer.

"Are you ready?" asks Sada as she walks towards me. I held the reins of her horse in my hand.

"I am. Are you?" Sada looked out at the forest and over the snow covered graves of our fallen comrades. From this place you would never know there was a war going on. It was quiet, peaceful and sometimes you could fool yourself into thinking that there was nothing at all wrong in Midgard. If only that were true.

"I keep telling myself that I'm ready for whatever comes our way. Now, I think fear has gripped me."

"What do you fear, my love?"

"Failure. We are all going to die soon and I don't want to die before I can complete the task that the gods have set before me. I don't want to die knowing I failed our family, our loved ones."

"So you don't fear death?" Sada breathed deeply and exhaled her hot breath into the open winter air; her gaze was hard like iron as she peered out into the forest. Gently taking the reins from my hand, she mounted her horse and adjusted her sword pommel at her side.

"Death would be a reprieve from all that we have suffered. No, my love. It is failure." The sound of hooves echoing against stone projected from the caverns and now our remaining allies joined us in the clearing. My faithful warrior and guardsman, Gunnar, the young warrior and servant to Fiorn, Tormod, the old veteran berserker of a man Grim, Njord the legendary blacksmith of Bjorgvin and, lastly, Fiorn himself.

"A fine gathering this is!" Grim yelled out enthusiastically. "I'm sure the gods will see fit to keep the wolves from gnawing at our bones after we die on this quest. Or at the very least keep the Draugr from fucking our corpses!" Grim broke out into laughter on his own. It was difficult to find humor in these dark times but Grim seemed to manage it well.

"A poet and a warrior, Grim? I never took you for a learned man." Grim's face became stern as he shot a steely gaze towards Fiorn.

"There are many things, Fiorn of Myrlende, that you do not know about Grim the Berserker of the North." Grim stuffed some freshly baked bread into his mouth chewing loudly for all to hear.

"Aren't there many Berserkers in the North, Grim?"

Grim laughed and pointed up to the sky.

"No, boy, what remains of my brothers now look down upon us from the heavens. Many were devoured whole by the Draugr and those who were not became the undead themselves." Grim spit on the ground. "So you ask me, how can I be Grim the Berserker of the North? Well, that's an easy answer, young Chieftain. Because I have spilled more blood, crushed more skulls, and severed more limbs than any man alive." Grim lifted his worn round shield upwards and sunk his thick teeth into it. He bit down harder as he pulled his head back, taking wood shavings and splinters off his shield and spitting them to the ground.

"Are you done, Grim?" Fiorn asked. Grim pulled a splinter from his lip and a small drop of blood followed. He licked his lips and closed his eyes, breathing heavily for a moment.

"Aye, I'm done. For now. So, we go to fetch your wee beastie. This is it, then? Just the five of us?"

"Six!" Sada said fiercely. Grim lowered his eyes and shook his head.

"You're a fine lass, I'll give you that much, but I still don't think you're going to be much in a fight."

Sada pulled on the reins of her horse causing him to stir and buck in place.

"That's enough!" Fiorn yelled out. "If we do this right, there will not be any fighting. That's why we're traveling alone and in such small number. The old woman, Vigdis, said the beast is to the south east so that is where we ride. I have seen this bog, many years ago while on campaign. It is vast and has many passages where horses may not go. We will have to leave them at the base of the bog before continuing. What's more, the mist is every present in this place and we will need to stay close lest you wish to get lost."

"He forgot to mention haunted," Grim remarked.

"Haunted?" I asked curiously.

"Oh, aye, there be far worse things in the bog and mists of this place than Draugr or Ulfhednar. At least with those monsters and be seen and smelt from a distance. You will not see the things that kill you here, boy."

"Enough, Grim. I don't need you rattling their nerves any more than they already are."

"Oh, no? You don't think I should tell them about the mess they are getting us into? How about the specters that creep up out of the ground and ponds, or the deadly mist that can infect your lungs and cause a man to choke on his own blood."

"Grim!" Fiorn was losing his patience, but Grim would not be deterred.

"Audan, I tell you this because I think you are a good man and I think you are trying to do the right thing. I really do, but you need to know what is out there. Entire armies, legions of brave warriors have lost their minds in the mists and disappeared. There was no trace of them, no arms or armor, no banners, no streaks of blood. They were gone, poof, vanished."

"Is that all?" Grim was upset by my cool demeanor. He clenched his fist and punched his shield. I cracked a small out of the corner of my mouth finding his displeasure somewhat amusing.

"There it is," said Grim pointing at me.

"That smile, that bit of light in your soul. I might not be able to knock it down a peg or two but the bog will suck that light out of you I swear it, but when you're screaming for your mum, holding your guts in your hands and crawling to your own death, don't say that good old Grim didn't warn you."

"You sound like a scared little man." Sada did not like Grim, mainly because he did not approve of shield maidens.

"Are you telling me you're not scared, little girl?" Sada pulled back on her reins jerking the horse from side to side.

"No, old man, I'm not scared."

Grim laughed loudly.

"Then, you will be the first to die."

"Grim, take point. I don't want to hear you speak unless you're slaughtering our foes. Do you understand?" I grew tired of this.

Grim smiled picking something out from between his teeth. He pulled on his reins and kicked his horse hard to move him forward while muttering something as he passed us.

"Njord, I want you up there with Grim. You're used to breaking old rusty metals so I'm sure you can handle Grim."

Njord nodded.

"Of course." He kicked his horse and headed forward, alongside Grim. Fiorn and Sada took the center and I pulled back to the rear with the young Tormod. We rode forward at a light pace trying to keep our horses from making too much noise. Shortly ahead, a fork in the path appeared, one turn well beaten and the other that led to broken tree limbs and branches that stuck out into the path.

"Audan, which way do you want to go?" Grim asked. I pointed to the left away from the well-worn trail.

"Vigdis said to stay off the beaten path so that is what we shall do." Grim pulled his reins to the left with a reluctant look upon his face. No doubt hoping we would run into some trouble on the way. Valhalla was close for Grim, you could see it in his eyes. He just needed that one final battle, that one moment of violence to go out in a blaze of eternal glory. Whether he believed it or not, he was probably in the right company to make that wish happen. Dusk quickly fell away to darkness and now our march forward had slowed to a crawl. The path ahead was littered with branches and tree limbs spread about the forest floor. One wrong step and our horses could break their legs, making our journey even longer than anticipated. I could hear owls crying out in the distance and the squeal of mice as the feather creatures ripped into their flesh. Fiorn had remained quiet for much of the journey but now hummed an unfamiliar tune. It was a beautiful sound but it was also sad.

"What are you singing, old friend?" I asked. Fiorn shook his head.

"Nothing you would be interested in, brother. Perhaps a bit too dark for your liking."

"No, please tell me. The air is cold and the darkness consumes us. I need some distraction." Fiorn looked over his shoulder at me as his horse stayed a few paces ahead.

"Very well. It's a song my mother used to sing to me when I was a child. It's about a brave warrior, of course, heading out into the wilds to fight an evil dragon in its dark lair to rescue a beautiful woman, the love of his life."

"It sounds like a great tale," I remarked. Fiorn lifted a finger into the air.

"Ah, but just wait. The warrior rides into the dragon's lair to find his love already slain. Burnt to a crisp against the stone walls. All that the warrior could recognize of his love was her fiery red hair and brown riding boots he had given her as a birthday gift.

"So he slays the beast?" Fiorn shakes his head.

"No. So overcome by grief, the warrior walks into the lair straight up to the dragon, its fangs still dripping with the blood of the one he loves. The warrior drops his arms and removes his armor and willingly lets the serpent burn him to ash."

"He did not take revenge on the dragon? But why?"

"If you lost Sada would you still want to be here in Midgard wandering the wilds without her beauty at your side?" I shook my head. "I didn't think so. Life is so short and when we find someone we love, truly love so deeply that we are willing to give anything for them, well, we die inside when it cannot return. There is no point in living without love. We become empty shells, and we might as well become the Draugr that we fight so desperately."

"Who do you love, Fiorn?" Fiorn sighed, I could tell that I struck a nerve and perhaps he would not be willing to share.

"I have loved many in my time. I once loved a woman as you do now but she was taken from me, not by a dragon but by sickness. I thought of finding my own dragon lair and ending my life, but as I came to rule my people I found love in caring for them. Have you ever worked the land and raised crops, Audan?"

"I have."

"Good, then you know what it is to care for something, to raise it until it can bear something wonderful for the people. That is what it is to rule, Audan. If you love your people, give them the things they need and not necessarily what they want, you can help them grow to do great things. I fell in love with my people and since that time I have not yearned for the kiss of cold steel against my neck."

"You're a good man, Fiorn. If we make it out of this alive, I hope to rule my people as you have. I hope to be an honorable man."

"That is my hope as well, brother." The ride was long and soon light began to return to the skies. Morning would follow quickly and we needed to reach the bog before it did otherwise Fenrir may be on the move once more. In front of us the trees began to thin out and clear out of our way. A small hill lay just to the left and Grim dismounted from his horse.

"Grim? What is it?" I asked. Grim pointed just ahead in the distance.

"The bog lies ahead. I'm going up the hill to scout the valley. Is anyone coming with me?"

"I'll go," I said as I climbed down from my horse.

"I'm coming too," Sada said. I placed my hand on her leg and stopped her before she could dismount.

"No, my love. Stay down here with the others just in case we are attacked on the hill. If something goes wrong you'll have a better chance of escape from down here." Sada grabbed my beard and pulled me in closely.

"I don't want to leave you." I wrapped my hand behind her head and pulled her in to kiss her lips. She pressed against me firmly and released her grip.

"All will be well. Stay here. I will be right back." Grim was already a quarter of the way up the hill and I ran after him as quietly as I could carrying only my bearded axe. We marched up the leaf-covered hill under the cover of trees and darkness until reaching the peak. Grim tightly grabbed my tunic with his leather glove and pushed me down. He pointed just above a large boulder no more than a few paces from us. A faint smell traveled on the winds passing my nose: it was rot, decaying flesh.

"Draugr," Grim whispered. I nodded and we started removing anything that may make noise from our bodies. Once discarded, we slowly walked and crawled towards the boulder. We approached so quietly that all I could hear was my heart beating inside my chest. Louder and louder it pounded like a hammer against an anvil. For a moment I worried the Draugr would hear my heart but I closed my eyes for a moment and listened to the wilderness around me. As I heard the tree limbs shake and leaves move in the wind, I heard my heart beat less and less. When I opened my eyes, Grim was staring at me seeming concerned he had picked the wrong man. We continued forward on our hands and knees until we reached the back of the boulder. Nodding at each other, weapons in hand, we climbed to the top and peered over the other side. First, there was a banner of blood red adorned with the face of a house cat and crossed spears behind it, the banner of Freya herself. Even slower now, we inched forward and there below us sat three of the undead overlooking the bog valley below.

They made no noise and very little movement, save for the swaying of their heads as the surveyed the horizon, but what were they watching? I looked outward in the distance at the great bog and the many mists that lay below. Then a faint sound caught my ear, at first I thought it was the find or perhaps even the swaying of the trees as it repeated itself over and over again. But it was not the wilds making this noise, it was the sound of snoring. Far out into the bog, the outline of a hill appeared only it wasn't a hill. The outline moved slowly up and down, up and down in line with the sounds of snoring. The hill of the bog was no hill at all, but Fenrir the great wolf!

He had grown three times his size since devouring Bjorgvin no doubt from swallowing countless warriors and villagers on the northern trail.

I cautiously pointed out in the distance and Grim himself caught the outline of Fenrir in his eye. We found what we were looking for and now we knew why the Draugr were here. They were watchmen for the beast as he slept, keeping an eye on all that moved in the bog. We scooted forward and could see two swords, a hand axe and shield, and a horn. In the middle of the three lay of pile of random clothing, tunics, and something else: limbs. No doubt the body parts of wayward travelers or warriors that may disturb the slumbering hound. If we were to make any progress in binding Fenrir, we would first need to subdue the undead watchmen. I set my sights on the one nearest the horn for he could send an alert that would sound for miles and miles. A small group of Draugr we could defeat on our own but if they awoke the beast that now slumbered peacefully we would have no chance of escape.

We stood slowly still staying out of side from our adversaries and looked at each other without blinking. Grim was ready. I was ready. We bent our knees and as we were about to jump Grim slipped.

"Shit..." Grim exclaimed quietly. He fell on his back and rolled down the other side of the boulder, knocking down two of the Draugr warriors. The third stood in a panic and at first leaned towards Grim but hesitated and went back for the sounding horn. I threw myself on top of him, landing squarely on his shoulders we fell hard to the dirt and rolled about. The rotting beast moved quickly and straddled me on my waist. Unable to lift my axe, I reached for my seax dagger at my side and lifted it upward into his dead cold jaw, clamping his mouth shut. I twisted the dagger and pulled the handle to the side with the beast following. Down to the ground he went and upward I rose lifting my bearded axe dropping the blade on his face. His head practically exploded with dark blood that splattered my face. I did not linger in the moment and turned to see Grim still struggling his both Draugr. Rushing to his aid, I nailed one in the back. My blade stuck and I pressed my foot against him, kicking him to the earth and freeing my axe. The creature turned quickly and stood upright, swinging his sword side to side. He lunged in with a heavy thrust that sent him off balance. I hooked his sword with the axe's claw and spun all the way around, removing the blade from his hand and landing my blade on the other side of the creature. He moaned and I swung once more, severing his head from neck. Grim had been struck in the shoulder but gripped the sword handle of the Draugr whilst sending his pommel into the vile beast's face. The Draugr was stunned and fell backward with Grim pressing on, slashing and hacking wildly until the beast succumbed to his wounds and fell silent.

"That did not go as planned," Grim remarked.

"Are you alright, old man?"

Grim over looked the small gash in his shoulder that bloodied his tunic. He knelt down gripping some snow and packing it into the wound.

"Aye, I'm fine. I'm lucky this is the only injury he inflicted. That was quite a stumble down the rock. I thank you for coming to my aid."

"You would have done the same thing." Grim nodded as he wiped blood from his face.

"I would have, but I don't think I would have been as quick." Suddenly, a rush of footsteps came up from behind us and we lifted our blades, keeping our backs to the cliffs. "It appears that they were not as alone as we thought!" Blades came around the corner and we braced to fight off our foe no matter the number until warm and familiar faces presented themselves. It was our companions coming to our aid. In a sigh of relief, Grim and I looked at each other and lowered our blades.

"What happened?" asked Fiorn. "We heard a fight break out and thought perhaps you had been ambushed." Tormod and Gunnar looked about the still corpses on the ground and gathered their weapons. I reached down and gripped the sounding horn handing it to Fiorn.

"They were watchmen for the dog. Look there." I pointed out in the distance at a slumbering Fenrir, the mists rolling over his body and the sun now coming down gently lighting the way.

"By the gods," remarked Sada. "He's enormous. How did he get so big?"

"I don't know, but we are running out of time. The mists will give us a few moments more but sols light will wake the beast and he will return to slaughtering innocent people. If we do not wish to waste another day, now is the time." Without much more thought, we marched back down the hill to where our horses waited. We mounted them once more and rode for a very short period until reaching the edge of the bog. Dismounting once more, we tied our horses to the last of the trees before the clearing. Tormod handed out spears to each of us.

"I already have a weapon. What do I need this for?" I asked. Tormod smiled.

"Your axe won't keep any distance between you and the hound. Bring it, but you will want the spear should he awaken." The young warrior was wiser than I had imagined and I gladly took the spear from his hand. I strapped the axe to my back, discarded my shield and then reached for one final item, my leather satchel. I opened it gently and a bright light emanated from inside. The gleipnir, no matter how many times I saw it was still impressive. I removed the thread from the leather case and wrapped it tightly around my hand and elbow, making a large loop.

"Will it float?" Grim asked.

"What?" I wasn't sure what Grim meant.

"Will it float? Because if it doesn't, then do not drop it in the bog or all will be for not. I would tie the end to one hand and hold it with the other. Just in case." Without delay I did just as Grim suggested and tied the end to my hand and held the loop in my other hand.

"Are we ready?" asked Fiorn. We looked at one another and nodded one by one. Fiorn led the way with spear in hand as we left our horses behind. Marching forward, the mist lay before us and the sight of Fenrir had all but disappeared. He was not terribly far off and we could still hear his snore and feel it shaking the air all around us. The ground was wet and soft, with small paths darted by larger ponds. The air was foul and smelt of bile. As we marched forward, I saw the skeletons of many deer, wolves, and smaller animals strewn about the ponds. Soon, the air became warm and thick, the taste of the air stuck to the roof of my mouth and stuck to my skin. Bubbles popped up from the ponds and each time, they did, a faint noise erupted, like a scream. Sada stood just behind me her eyes wide and alert.

"I'm fine," she whispered. "Just keep looking ahead." I turned back forward to see nothing but mist.

"Fiorn?" I could not see, nor hear my companion. "Fiorn?" I said just a little louder. The others gathered behind me and we waited for the mists to clear. Sounds came from the distance and I thought I heard the voices of men. The voices were erratic, speaking softly and then loudly in a fast manner. I could not make out what they were saying, nor where they were. I looked left to right and saw nothing but the floor of the bog and the moving mist. Then, suddenly a terrifying scream erupted from in front of us.

"Fiorn!" I yelled. We rushed forward through the mists, not knowing what may be in front of us. Clumsily tripping and falling, I scrambled up once more. I saw a dark shape in the distance and ran as fast as my legs could carry me. As I came closer, I recognized the clothing of Fiorn. He was on his knees, leaning slightly back. Dread washed over me. I saw the long point of the spear protruding from his stomach. "Fiorn!" I reached my old friend and kneeled down next to him. The spear had been plunged into his stomach with the spearhead resting in the mud, keeping Fiorn sitting upright. His eyes had been removed from his face leaving behind bloody empty sockets. He gasped violently for air as blood ran out of his mouth. He reached outward with one hand for something to grasp and kept his other hand on the shaft of the spear against his body. I gripped his free hand and held it tightly. "Fiorn, I'm here!"

"Audan..." he said weakly. "Audan it came from nowhere." Grim pressed against my back with his legs looking outward with sword in hand.

"I told you, boy, the spirit world is out to get us here. Not even Odin can watch over us now." Fiorn released his grip and reached out to my face with his bloodied hand and pressed firmly against it.

"It ate my eyes. It took my spear and struck me and then it made me watch it eat one of my eyes."

"What Fiorn? What was it?" Fiorn began to scream relentlessly. He must be mad. Then, a sword point pierced his neck down into his spine. I followed the blade upward with my gaze to see Grim standing over him.

"He didn't need to suffer anymore and we don't need him to give up our whereabouts." Grim removed his blade quickly and then wiped the blood on his sleeve. I closed my eyes for a moment and let my head drop; when I opened my eyes I noticed Fiorn's arm was still extended outwards and as I followed his arm I saw his finger pointing in the distance. I looked behind us and as the mist cleared and ghoulish green figures emerged, popping in and out of the bog.

"Look," I said quietly. Our party turned to around and lowered their weapons in utter shock when they laid eyes upon the manlike figures that floated in the mists. The largest of the creatures swiftly lifted its arm in the air and dangling from his hand was the other eye of Fiorn. The ghoul laughed deeply and I rose to my feet, lifting my spear and advancing towards the specter. As he cackled, the mists became thicker, concealing our foes until at last it cleared and the ghosts had all but gone. Grim stepped forward grunting and breathing heavily.

"Where did they go?" Grim asked as beads of sweat fell from his brow into his beard. "By the gods, I warned you, boy. This evil shall be the end of us!" A hand gripped my shoulder and I turned quickly to see Sada with fear in her eyes.

"Audan, look!" I peered over her shoulder and stepped past her to see that our friend Fiorn was gone.

"What sort of evil is this?" I muttered. Every trace of our comrade had disappeared. All that remained was the spear still sticking out of the dirt.

"How could they have moved him without making a sound? How could they do it without moving the spear?" Sada exclaimed. I shook my head in disbelief at the empty ground before me.

"We need to leave, boy," Grim urged. I was afraid, there was no doubt about that. How could we possibly fight an enemy we could neither see nor hear? But if I turned back then all the men that had died and even Fiorn's death would have been for nothing. We needed to find Fenrir. We needed to bind the beast.

"No. Fiorn would have wanted us to move forward." Grim shook his head.

"I'm with you, Audan, but I don't like it."

"Everyone stay close, no more than an arm's distance from each other." I led the way into the mists and the bog became more unbearable as the path was now waist deep in water. We quietly sloshed forward until I saw the water in front of me move and then stop. I froze and the others did the same. The water moved again as if the wind were pushing it and then stopped once more. Hot air blew all around me and the smell of rotting flesh filed my nose. I looked up and saw the mist clear before me. It was the mouth of the wicked hound, Fenrir.

We had found him at long last. I pointed ahead and my comrades silently spread out around the beast. I placed my spear on the ground and untied the gleipnir from my hand. Carefully and quietly, I stepped forward until reaching the massive left paw. I gently wrapped the line around his paw reaching under and over twice until I was confident the line would hold. I handed it to Sada who moved to the right front paw and began doing the same. As she finished wrapping her line the stepped off to the side to hand the line back to me when she slipped on a moss-covered stone. I reached out to catch her, but it was too late. Sada fell into a small hole and a splash erupted cutting the deafening silence. I looked up at Fenrir's face to see a startled yellow eye gleaming down upon us. A growl emerged from his throat.

The beast had awoken.

Twelve
The Might of Tyr

"Audan look out!" I could hear Tormod rushing headlong behind me in a frenzy as Fenrir's massive jaw inched closer to my face, fangs dripping wet with anticipation of the meal to come. At last, the beast would have his vengeance on the mortal that split his lip in two and at last I would meet my final fate. As I was about to close my eyes and accept what was to come a spear point flew over my shoulder and with it followed Tormod in a mad dash to save my life. A quick jab to the face was all it took and the beast jerked back, barking and snapping furiously as dark blood trickled down to the ground.

Fenrir grimaced as he generously licked his fresh wound. The angry hound lifted his hind legs in the air and stopped as he spotted Sada in his massive eyes. I could see her face in the reflection of the beast's eye, the look of absolute terror; her skin turning a pale white. I reached for her and pulled her up from the pool of water and dragged her aside before Fenrir could make his move. Without warning, the hound wailed and screamed in pain and when he turned his head I could see Grim hacking and slashing violently at his rear legs, left, right, left and right he swung mighty blows. Fenrir strained to stand on his snarled front paws so he could turn and finish off Grim the Berserker but the gleipnir held strongly in place.

"Pull the rope! Pull it!" Grim urged pointing at me frantically, his beard whipped over his shoulder. I ran from Fenrir, pulling the silvery gleipnir over my shoulder with all my might. My heart pounded heavily in my chest. I worried that the beast may come at me from behind and take my head. The air whipped over my hair and the bog's water splashed in my face as I made a death run for it.

"Sada, give me a hand! Pull!" Sada joined with me and we gripped the silver line and pulled as hard as we could until it squeezed mercilessly at Fenrir's already-knotted paws. The hound reached down with his massive jaws, pulling and tugging at the gleipnir with his teeth only to make his foul gums bloody and raw. With each bark, he spat great waves of blood and bile the likes of which only seen on epic battlefields. The smell was foul and rank with death and I yearned to wipe it away. Out of the corner of my eye, I caught Grim climbing desperately up Fenrir's spine pulling and tugging at the beasts midnight colored hide until he stopped lifting his arms into the air and dropping his sword deep into the beasts back.

"Take that, you fucking mongrel! Go back to that dark place from whence you came!" Grim twisted the blade back and forth laughing hysterically at the monsters agony. A yelp erupted from the beast's throat so loudly that it made my bones ache and I reached for my ears, expecting them to bleed. Suddenly, Fenrir shifted his frame and he rolled on his back, knocking the veteran berserker face down in the mud. The gleipnir jerked away from our hands, leaving a burn against my palms and was now swinging freely at the end of Fenrir's front paws. He gazed at me angrily as he gnawed at the line once more. No doubt, he remembered me from the scar I left on his lip. The healed gash left a scar that ran long and deep. No creature, no matter man or beast would forget such a slight. Tormod tapped me on the back and ran past me and underneath the hound. He stuck a spear violently into Fenrir's gut. Tormod let out a war cry over and over. The beast howled in pain, pulled back a rear limb and struck Tormod squarely in the chest. He let out a gasp as the wind was knocked from him and he flew backward with great speed past Fenrir's tail landing in a shallow pool where he struggled for air. The beast's front legs shifted to the right when I saw Njord gripping the gleipnir and running between Fenrir's paws. Tormod had distracted the beast just long enough for Njord to grasp it without Fenrir knowing and now the hound was trying to catch up.

"Njord!" I called out, but he did not hear me. So panicked in his mad rush, Njord moved quickly to wrap the line around Fenrir's rear legs. The beast turned about and lunged for Njord when Gunnar let loose arrows into the side of Fenrir's neck. So small were the iron stingers to Fenrir they must have felt as flea bites do to dog. Nonetheless, they stung and Fenrir was now enraged.

"Audan!" Gunnar called out as he let loose another arrow and lowered his bow. "Get on his back! I'll keep him busy." Sada and I ran forward directly under the beast's massive blood-soaked jaw. Preoccupied with Gunnar and Njord, Fenrir did not notice us until we were directly beneath him. He pulled his head back and then lunged downward but Sada had a spear point waiting for him. The long thin blade plunged deeply and stuck just under his chin. Fenrir tried to lunge down but each time the spear point pushed further and further into his body with Sada bravely holding it under his weight. She stepped forward pressing her attack and screaming with the fury of all the Valkyries.

"Die beast! Die you fucking animal, die!" Blood showered down in buckets onto the fierce shield maiden as she jabbed her blade further and further passing Fenrir's jaw and pressing against the bottom of his tongue. Gunnar's arrow continued to fly without interruption as they made a dull smacking sound each time they landed, sinking deep into Fenrir's hide. Njord now finished wrapping an end of the gleipnir around Fenrir's back legs and urged the mud covered Grim to join him. Without delay, the veteran lent his muscle to the line and together they pulled and pulled with all their might, yelling aloud. The beast flopped from side to side when at last a wail let out and finally Fenrir came crashing down to the earth once more. A loud thunderous din erupted in the bog, sending mud and water all about. Dirt flew into my eye and I was blinded. I bent down and quickly wiped the mud out from my eye and charged forward at Fenrir's flank, gripping his wet muddled hide and climbing on his back.

"The gleipnir! Throw it to me!" Njord whipped the line upwards but it missed its mark, falling down in front of Fenrir's dreadful face. Njord and Sada ran forward with spears in hand thrusting ruthlessly and keeping the hound's bite back while they retrieved the line. Undeterred by the threat of sharp iron, the beast rolled on its opposite side, knocking me face first into the soil and sending the rest of my comrades scrambling for cover. Gunnar picked me up from the ground and quickly ushered me out of harm's way. Fenrir struggled violently upwards and soon the gleipnir began to come loose. Our knots did not hold in place. In a panic, we lifted our weapons upwards ready to defend ourselves, but I knew if we could not secure the line we would not be able to fight off the mad dog.

"Get the rope! By all the gods of all the realms, get the bloody rope!" Njord yelled. He picked up his spear and charged forward. He jumped in the air and plunged the blade into the hound's front left paw, putting all his weight behind the wooden shaft. The spear head went clean through his foot pinning the monster to the ground. Fenrir leaned forward, gripping the spear shaft with his teeth and snapping it in two. He spat the splintered wood from his mouth back at Njord. Gunnar followed Njord and leapt over the beast's paw, plunging another spear into Fenrir's jaw. The hound jerked backward and shook his head in anger, pulling the spear out of Gunnar's hold. Then Fenrir turned away pulling the gleipnir loose he removed one paw from its magical grip.

I ran under the dog looking up to see the scars and broken arrows and spearheads from his many slaughters. Dropping to the ground at a run, I slid until reaching the line, gripping it in my hand and wrapping it around his loose paw. Like a falling tree, Fenrir swiped at me, sending my body up into the air still grasping the gleipnir in my hand. For a moment it seemed that time stood still as my body flew upward and almost weightless at Fenrir's strike. I fell hard on a small patch of rocks in the bog and then rolled down into a watery pit, the muddied liquid rushing over my face deafening the sounds of battle above. Without much thought, I pulled myself from that hole and gasped for air as my lungs struggled to breathe. My every bone ached terribly and now my ribs felt bruised, perhaps even broken. It hurt to breathe and, as I opened my eyes, all I saw before me was tooth and fang bearing down upon me. Fenrir opened his mouth and lunged forward at me before I could muster a defense. *This is it,* I thought to myself. I had no weapons with which to defend myself and not the strength to leap out of the way.

"Audan, no!" Sada stepped bravely between Fenrir and I, her long braided hair whipping behind her. She swiftly swiped her sword from side to side cutting away large chunks of flesh from the hound's upper lip. He pulled back, licking his wounds with his massive black tongue. He barked several times and lunged forward again. Sada bravely pressed her attack with the ferocity of our ancient heroes. "Stay back! Stay back, demon!" she yelled.

Reckless and wild she moved forward, beating back the bite of the hound with no thought of her own safety. Love now stood between Fenrir and his next meal and for the moment it seemed that Sada's love for me was greater than Fenrir's urge to feed on mortal flesh. I stood slowly, gripping my left side and breathing shallowly against the relentless pain of my rib cage. I was in awe of Sada as she cried out as only a shield maiden could in the heat of battle. Fenrir swiped at her with his paw, knocking her blade out of her hand.

Arrows and spears flew forward striking Fenrir on his flank and Sada made a run for it directly under Fenrir's jaw. She retrieved the gleipnir running light of foot. From paw to paw, she wrapped the line around his legs until a tangled mess was weaved beneath him. I knelt down and retrieved my bearded axe from the mud. I charged forward to give her more time to finish the job. I lifted my arms and let the weight of my axe sink its blade deep into the hound's right leg. The beast whimpered and snapped savagely at me. I ducked and rolled away, but his fangs glanced my lower leg leaving a small gash in its wake. The fresh cut alleviated some of the pain from my ribs and I took a deep breath ignoring my great discomfort.

"Grim, Gunnar, help me!" Sada pleaded from the rear of the beast. She held the line tightly but Fenrir twisted and pulled, trying to escape the gleipnirs impossible hold on his body. Grim and Gunnar ran to her aid. They dropped their weapons and pulled relentlessly on the line.

"Pull!" Grim yelled. "Pull dammit or we're all dead! Pull, you sons of cunts!" The tangled mess of wet gleipnir under Fenrir slipped and rapidly tightened against his flesh cutting in deeply and turning the rope into a rosy silver sheen. Njord stepped in front of Sada, gripping the gleipnir closest to the hound and pulled with his tattooed arms until his veins bulged.

The ground was wet and slippery but Fenrir had claws to dig in with. He resisted us with the strength of one hundred wolves pulling in the opposite direction. I joined in as well, gripping the line at the rear and pulling over my shoulder. Soon, we were at a standstill and neither Fenrir, nor our party could make the line move in any one direction. I released one hand from the gleipnir gripping my bearded axe in the other and threw it at the hounds back legs. The axe swung high and fell quickly under its weight, spinning over and over through the air until a lucky glance of the blade struck the beast. Fenrir winced and the line gave way on his end. I pulled and wrapped the gleipnir around my waist and dug in with what strength I had left. Fenrir's paws began to slip and the mud and earth beneath his feet tore under his claws. Closer and closer they came together and I felt the odds begin to shift slowly in our favor.

"Pull him!" I called out in desperation. "Pull, my brothers! Pull!" Fenrir growled and snapped ferociously until an unexpected wail let out, cutting away at the fog. Fenrir's massive body gave way to the combined strength of our party, slipped in the mud and fell over on its side. The ground shook and rumbled underfoot like the sound of a thunderous lightning storm, but we did not delay in doing what needed to be done.

"Pin him down! Pin him down!" Njord cried out, running for the spears discarded about the bog. Njord quickly pressed the blades into the thick, soft ground and one by one grabbed loose line securing it to the spears. Soon, the beast was secured to the bog's floor and we pulled the line even tighter cutting deeply into his flesh. Fenrir's mouth was still free as he snapped upward and presented a very real danger. We had to bind his mouth.

I walked back through the thick reeds where I found Tormod sitting upward holding his hand against his head.

"Get up! We need you!" I urged in encouragement. I gripped Tormod firmly by the forearm and helped him to his feet, holding him in place until he regained his sense of balance. Tormod helped to tense the lines while I moved to confront Fenrir head on. It took some time to walk around his massive body now that it was stretched out against the ground. All was peaceful until I reached his menacing face. The hound's fierce bright yellow eyes focused in on me, his dark pupils became small, needlelike points focusing in on me. He breathed heavily, shooting hot air that rushed over my body. He growled deeply as I approached. He bared his teeth at me and I smiled lifting my bearded axe to my shoulder.

"Do you remember this?" I flipped the blade back and forth, moving a piece of sunlight into Fenrir's eye. His growl became deeper, more intense and he pulled his body upward to turn from me but the gleipnir would not give way. "Your reign of terror is over, pup! You're lucky that Loki wants you alive otherwise I'd skin you and roast your body on a spit." Fenrir growled again and looked away, clearly frustrated being bound. I walked down to his paws, searching for the excess line and found it sitting between his feet. I reached in between his muddied pads and pulled the line out until I could walk with it. Sada walked to Fenrir's face and fiercely placed her sword point to his eye.

"Move and I'll cut it out!" Fenrir did not growl or whimper. The beast had at long last been beaten down and was now obedient to our demands like any good dog should be. I gripped his hide from the flank and carefully climbed up until straddling his neck. Tormod and Gunnar waited anxiously down below for me to throw the line back to them. I let the Gleipnir fall between Fenrir's fangs and before he could close them, Gunnar gripped the free end and threw it back to me, whipping the line around the top half of Fenrir's snout. I pulled tightly, slipping the line between Fenrir's teeth all the way back to his gums until the flesh pulled back and bled profusely. Fenrir did nothing more than growl and wince with each tug of the line. I dropped the loose end once more between his fangs and Gunnar sent it back up to me after wrapping it around the lower half. I pulled the gleipnir until Fenrir's jaws snapped shut. I breathed a sigh of relief as his teeth would no longer threaten our lives. Leaping down into the mud, Tormod helped me to wrap the line around his snout several times until we pulled tight and tied it off. Fenrir had at long last been bound.

I thought back to the god Tyr who sacrificed his hand to achieve such a feat and although our limbs remained, we had lost many good men on this journey. Mortals were capable of achieving the same greatness as gods, but at a much higher price. Perhaps, we were not so different; as Odin once said, they were mortal once. "How will Loki know his hound has been tied up?" Grim asked wiping the blood from his forehead.

"He has eyes and ears everywhere. I'm sure he will be here shortly."

"So are we to just wait in this cursed place?" asked Gunnar "You saw what happened to Fiorn. Fenrir is not the only monster in the mists." I understood the berserker's concern but we could not leave Fenrir unattended lest the Draugr arrive to free their greatest weapon and unleash him once more.

"Start a fire and get comfortable. If you wander off into the mist, you will surely die." We all breathed a sigh of relief and sat down next to Fenrir's belly to stay warm until the fire was built. The midnight black fur would have made enough winter coats for an entire village but Loki would punish me with death if I killed his precious pet. I pushed myself firmly against his belly and Fenrir growled but quickly ceased his moaning, knowing there was nothing he could do about it. Tormod and Njord grabbed pieces of dried peat from the bog while Grim knelt down between us digging a small hole into the ground.

"Damn!" Grim exclaimed.

"What is it?" I asked.

"Water everywhere. I can't dig any more than a hand's length deep or the water just rises straight up." I looked down the small hole Grim had dug and watched as he wiped the water and mud from his hands.

"It will have to do. Get the kindling going and we can pile the peat high. Find anything dry you can use." Tormod and Njord returned, breaking the dried peat into small pieces and spreading them around where Grim had settled in working his stone and steel. The old veteran stuck his stone over and over again with the band of metal wrapped firmly around his think worn fingers. Sparks flew in every direction and Grim pulled himself in closer to the bundles of peat, changing his striking angle each time. The sparks flew straight into the peat and soon, smoke billowed. The old man wrapped his hands under and around the smoking piece of bog and blew on it in his cupped hands. The embers ran up and down the many small fibers glowing bright orange until they became flame. The fires grew quickly and danced upward over Grim's hand. He rolled the peat around, leading the fire to pieces that had not yet been lit. He quickly placed the burning mulch into the pit and pulled his hands away hurriedly as the heat became too much to bare. "That'll do," he said with a proud song in his voice.

"How's your head?" I asked Gunnar. He laid down next to the fire with one hand under his head and the other gripping the pain on his brow. He rubbed his fingers back and forth while squinting, the wrinkles of his forehead sinking deeply into his skull.

"It's been better, brother. I never saw that paw coming for me. Everything just went black and I woke up face down in the mud. I thought perhaps I had perished but knew I was amongst the living when everything still smelled like shit." We laughed quietly. "What does Valhalla smell like, Audan?" Gunnar asked. I thought about it for a moment and all I could remember was the sweetness of it all.

"Valhalla smells like mead, roasted pig, and fresh air. It's not foul like most of our villages." Gunnar smiled.

"That sounds quite nice. It makes me wonder why we bother staying alive at all." He started to nod off, his eyes rolling to the back of his head. Grim threw another piece of bog on the fire causing the flames to rise higher.

"Where were your gods when we took down this beast, Audan? They can protect us from rotting Draugr and deadly Ulfhednar but not from Fenrir himself?"

"Do not mock the gods!" Njord yelled. Njord had remained quiet for most of the journey, but now he grew angry. His upper lip curled and shook uncontrollably. "If you dare to question the gods then we shall lose favor on our journey. Is that what you want, old man?" Grim threw his sword to the ground and stepped forward squaring off with Njord.

"What are you going to do about it, smithy?" He pushed Njord in the chest and took another step forward. "Are you going to pray to the god's smithy? Hmm? Are you going to ask Thor to throw a bolt of lightning at me, cook me right before your eyes?" Grim pushed Njord again but this time Njord gripped the old man's wrist, twisting it and sending him to his knees.

"Go fuck a swine!" Grim's face turned to rage. He swept his leg under Njord, sending him crashing to the ground. Before the blacksmith could rise Grim stood atop him with a dagger at Njord's throat.

"Insult me again, boy, and I'll gut you like the little fucking worm you are." I stood and kicked Grim in the side, stealing him of breath. Grim rolled to his side, dropping his dagger on the ground and now both men lay on the dirt gasping for air.

"That's enough!" I yelled. "What the hell are you two doing?"

Njord stood first gripping his side.

"I'm sorry Audan, I don't know what came over me."

"And you, Grim, you draw a dagger against your ally over a simple insult?" Grim stood coughing gripping chest where I kicked him.

"The boy needed to be taught a lesson. He should be whipped for his impudence!" Njord stepped forward, his head leaning over my shoulder.

"And you should be hanged for being a useless old man." Sada stood and slapped Njord across the face. Njord clearly in shock of being struck by a woman said and did nothing in response. He just stood there, eyes wide with astonishment.

"What the hell is wrong with you, Njord? I've never known you to behave like a child." Njord rubbed his cheek and looked around the bog in shame.

"It's these damned mists, Sada. This place is cursed. We shouldn't be here." Njord was right, this was an evil place. I could feel it down to my bones. Everything here just somehow felt wrong. My very gut felt ill and the air sickened my lungs. Nothing was right about this place but we needed to stay just until Loki collected his dog. Still, I feared if we stayed too long the bog would be the one to collect us.

"And you, Grim?" Sada asked.

"What do you want?" he said extending his hands outward. Grim clearly felt he had done no wrong in antagonizing Njord. The old man was stubborn but not stupid. He knew what he was doing.

"Njord is your comrade and fellow warrior in arms. You might be dead if it was not for him. Make amends! Or do you two wish to duel?" Njord and Grim looked each other over and soon their anger faded back to exhaustion.

They shook their heads and then extended their arms to call a truce. Sada then stepped towards Gunnar and slapped the back of his head.

"Gunnar!" Sada yelled, startling the injured warrior. Gunnar quickly sat up-right.

"What? Why did you do that?" he asked startled.

"Do not close your eyes, at least not for a few hours."

"Why not?"

"You took a good knock on the head. If you close your eyes you may not come back. I've seen it happen before to other men."

"What happened to those men?" Sada looked down at the fire placing her hands closer to the flame to soak in the warmth.

"They would not wake no matter what we did to them and after several days they just stopped breathing and died."

"That's a terrible way to go. Certainly not a death for a warrior." Sada nodded in agreement.

"Stay awake, friend. We'd like to keep you around just a little longer." Gunnar sat up some more and scooted closer to the fire. We sat there for some time, sharing stories and retelling days of peace. The fire began to die away and I grabbed more peat, stoking the coals and piling on more moss. Flames quickly jumped upward and the cold was once again melted away from my body. The warmth sank in and we began to succumb to our exhaustion. Grim still stood to his feet keeping a watchful eye on the grey abyss still gripping his side.

"Are you alright, Grim?"

"It's not the first time someone kicked the wind out of me. It won't be the last." Grim's pride was hurt more than his body. A warrior as old as he was old for a good reason. He was numb to most types of pains, but every person, no matter how strong, is not invulnerable to ego. I thought of apologizing to Grim but worried that being overly soft with him would create a lack of respect. I needed him to follow my orders and guidance, but I also did not want him to hate me.

"Take some rest friend." Grim scoffed at the idea and scratched at his grey beard.

"I'll take the first watch. I will wake one of you when I am tired," he said without looking back.

"When are you tired, Grim?" Grim looked back shooting me a steely gaze.

"When I am dead. Until then, I will remain awake." Stubborn old man. I left him to his watch and let my senses dull. The dark warmth came over me as I tucked my cloak and fur around me, the fire warming my clothes. My body twitched and before I fell asleep, I opened one eye to see Grim still on his watch, like a stone statue he did not move. I watched him silently for a moment until letting myself fall back asleep. With aching ribs and heavy eyes, I slipped under the covers of my consciousness and faded to rest.

* * *

A light hand gripped my shoulder and shook me awake. "What?" I asked with my eyes closed.

"Audan, wake up," Grim said softly. "There's something in the mist." I opened my eyes to the bog before me, the smoky fire still going. I rolled over and grabbed my bearded axe and winced when I over extended my arm; my ribs were tight and sore. It would be several weeks until they healed properly. Ignoring my discomfort, I stood quietly and looked between the empty spaces of the moving fog.

"I see nothing."

"Just listen," Grim urged. I let my ears do the looking and I listened intently until I heard something overhead. The sky above vibrated as air rushed above our heads. Suddenly, it grew louder, the clamor beating down on us relentlessly until it was all we could hear. The noise woke the others. We stood in a circle with our backs to one another, weapons raised in the air. Sada stood next to me with worry painted across her face.

"What is it?" she asked.

"I don't know but I'm sure it's nothing good," I replied. The sound grew to such strength I could hear nothing around me. Gunnar yelled something, but the sound drowned out of his voice.

"What?" I called back. Gunnar pointed up towards the sky.

"Wings!"

A dark object descended and carried Gunnar off into the fog with him yelling in anger. We closed the gap left by our comrade.

"Stay together!" Grim commanded. Then, another dark beast descended, and another, and another, knocking everyone down to the dirt in the blink of an eye.

"It's an ambush!" Tormod called out with dread in his voice. I could not see the beasts that attacked us clearly. They were nearly silent and impossibly fast.

Grim looked up at me and began to scream as something dragged him through the bog behind the veil of the mists. I felt the wind move quickly behind me and before I could turn I was pulled into the sky by claws that dug tightly in to my shoulders. I yelled and winced at the pain and tried to wench myself free, but to Below, Sada reached out for me, but I was pulled far into the mists above, her face vanishing as her voice cut through the haze. "Audan!"

Thirteen
Kingdom of Chains

At some point I blacked out as the wind whipped past my face and I now awoke to the cold against my face. My outstretched finger tips ran across something hard and familiar, stone I think. My eyes were closed and I did not yet wish to open them, as I worried at the horrors that might confront me in my waking state. So I lay there face down against a hard floor, my cheekbone digging heavily into ground. The stinging sensation in my shoulders returned, as I remembered the deep gashes left by a Valkyrie's talons as she lifted me high into the air. I remembered nothing but Sada's terrified face as I was carried away and then the rush of fog all around until the world went dark. I listened intently to my surroundings for some familiar sound or indication of where I might be. The silence was deafening and my ears began to ring loudly. I lightly shuffled my hands on the ground just to drown out the silence, but kept my noise as low as possible so as not to alert anyone.

The air was humid and stale in this place, which might have been an old long house or stable that had not been used or rarely visited. I slowly opened my right eye that lay against the floor. The room was dark, too dark to discern size or color, but distantly I saw the outline of iron bars that stretched upward to a solid ceiling. There was no roof thatch or wood planks to be made out, just a hard, smooth wall as far as the eye could see. Beyond the bars, a faint light emanated. I twisted my torso slightly and was quickly reminded of the broken ribs that Fenrir had inflicted upon me. I pressed my hand gently against them and breathed slowly through my nose. The sharp sting traveled upward and tugged violently at my chest. I closed my eyes again and listened but still could not hear anything.

Perhaps it was evening and all that dwelled in this place slept but in this dark hole how could I know if it were night or day? I reached down towards my belt and seax dagger to find that they had been removed. Someone took my cloak and boots as well. I opened my eyes once more and looked about the small dark room to look for provisions, but found none: no blankets, water, food, or warmth to speak of. Only my tunic remained and I was left alone in the dark. It was apparent now more than ever that I was a prisoner. The Valkyries had brought me to this place but were they my jailers? I would need my strength if I were to face the things to come with the daylight. I did not know how long I had slept, but my body ached something terrible. I needed to heal. I needed to be strong now more than ever. I let my eyes shut again and despite the cold and discomfort sleep soon came over me.

* * *

My senses returned to me once more. I felt plenty rested but my body had become terribly sore and stiff. I slowly opened my eyes only to see the same barren dark prison cell. There was no sound, no trace of anyone nearby, so I thought it safe to have a look around. Slowly, I lifted my body upward, bracing my rib cage with my hand. Rising to my feet, I took my first step forward only to feel a sharp pebble under my foot. I jerked away quickly and paid the price with a burning and stinging chest. Clenching my jaw, I moved forward slowly looking around the corners of my cell wary of catching the eye of any guards that may be nearby. If they knew me to be awake, they may enter my cell and beat me to keep me weak and pliable to their demands. As I approached the iron bars, I saw no force guarding my cell or the stone room outside it. There were no doors or windows to speak of from my vantage point. To the far left, a bright torch lit against the wall roared quietly lending the meager amount of light. The corridor outside my cell was long and appeared unending, but I could only see a small portion of it. Just below the torch sat a large wooden barrel. There was nothing striking about the barrel and I could only guess to its contents. Below the barrel, the floor of the corridor was faintly lit. A stone walkway that looked as if it was carved rather than laid in place. Was I in a cavern of sorts like Skerheim? The room was deathly silent again and so I waited quietly for my jailers to arrive. Hours passed or at least what seemed like hours and still no one came. I saw no one. Heard nothing. Why would they leave me here so long unattended? Surely, I would be brought before my jailers to be tortured or at the very least executed? I slowly paced about the room walking from side to side, counting my paces. Six paces exactly, six paces across and six paces wide. Just enough room for me to lay down with my outstretched body but not nearly enough to enjoy and freedom. I paced for some time and then ceased only when my ribs burned once more. Several more hours passed and I became terribly thirsty with no water or sustenance for nearly two days. I laid down to sleep once more, hoping that rest would absolve me of my hunger pains and that perhaps closure would come in the form of a voice or a blade.

* * *

Something startled me from my slumber. I sat up in my cell, patiently listening. This silence echoed loudly in my ears and I rubbed my finger inside it to drive it out. I opened my mouth and my dry lips cracked horribly as I ran my fingers gently down the crevices. My cell was still bereft of food, water, or any sort of provisions. Had my jailers forgotten me? Had they been killed? Or had I been left here to die a slow and painful death to be starved like a mere beggar or die of thirst as a sailor lost at sea?

I slowly stood and cautiously approached the iron bars, this time resting my hands on them firmly when there were no guards to be seen. There it was again! The noise! Like a tapping of some kind. Metal on metal? I wasn't sure. I desperately needed to hear it again. A sound, a voice, anything to cut the mind numbing silence I now endured.

I looked back to the torch that still lent its meager light. The silence was so overwhelming that my heart beat seemed to thump loudly in my chest. I breathed deeply and slowly, hoping to calm my racing pulse, but now my breath became louder in the darkness and I feared it would drown out the sound once it returned. I closed my eyes, calmed my racing heart and made myself still.

Again, the sound came. Now, I knew: it was a small tap against a stone surface. Something metal, perhaps? Striking stone. It was faint, but distinct, sending a faint echo through the corridor. This time my ear caught the impact very near the barrel and torch. I followed the light upward to see a dark line that rose up high to the ceiling, disappearing into the stone. I did not move and I did not blink. What was it? Was someone there? I considered calling out, but again feared the reprisal of a nearby jailer, even though I'd never seen one. My obscurity could possibly be my greatest asset and despite my thirst and hunger I was not yet about to give it up.

Again, the sound came and went and I guessed it was coming from above the hallway outside my cell. I closed my eyes again and patiently waited until it returned.

When I opened them once more, I saw the faintly lit surface of the stone floor. The sound came, and with it, a ripple on the floor near the barrel.

Water! It was a water drop. The noise that tortured me so was nothing more than drops of water coming from a crack in the ceiling. The thought of a deluge in the cavern nearly sent me over the edge and I licked my parched lips in an effort to ease their pain. Oh, what I would give now for just a single drop of water.

My hunger pains came on again and now my stomach was upset. I had not relieved myself in nearly three days. Bereft of a bucket or hole in the ground I squatted down nearest the right side of the cell bars and relieved my there. Nothing solid came out of me, just liquid and I feared that death would follow very soon. With nothing to clean myself with I ripped a piece of cloth from the bottom of my tunic and made good use of it before discarding it outside my cell. The smell was foul as my bowels had emptied what was left inside them. My stomach moaned loudly as I sat in my corner thinking of anything I could hold onto. Scurrying sounds came from the far end of the corridor, perhaps rats or some other vermin had joined me in this pit after all but I paid no mind to them at the moment. Sada was my only saving grace and I longed for her warmth and care at this moment. The darkness of this place was beginning to close in on my mind and my thoughts began to wander. Terrible thoughts lingered and left a bad taste in my mouth. I wanted to wash them away and so I lay down to sleep once more hoping they would be gone by morning or thirst would take me and I would be in a better place. As the time passed the hunger and thirst pains became too much. I moaned in frustration and curled up on the floor in a tight ball gripping my stomach. I couldn't take it anymore, I pounded my fist on the floor and pushed myself from the stony ground.

"Guard!" I called out. My voice echoed against the wall and bounced through the corridor. The iron bars vibrated and hummed at my call for help. "Guard!" I yelled louder this time leaning against the cell door with only the echo of my voice as a response to my cry. The echo faded to silence and I slid down the iron bars back to the cold floor. In my defeat a small tear escaped my eye and I looked to the ceiling for one last call. "Anyone?"

* * *

Something disturbed my sleep once more but it was not the sound of dropping water. My hand was freezing cold and I rubbed my fingers together to warm them only to feel them wet and covered in mud. I scrambled to sit upright and saw a dark muddied puddle before me. The water must have been dripping for hours, perhaps even days to have reached my cell. Without delay I dropped to my face and pursed my cracked lips outward slowly sucking the water into my mouth. Dirt quickly met with my tongue but the water was clean and fresh. I clenched my teeth together and let the water fall in between the cracks of by teeth before swallowing it and then removing the dirt from my gums. I followed the puddle to the edge of the bars and stuck my head out as far as I could to access the largest part of the puddle. Despite the dirt, I could swear it was the best tasting water I had ever had. Not a drop was wasted and I drank until the puddle wasted away to nothing. I could still hear the water drops in the distance and it would be at least another day before the water would reach me. I ran my finger through the dirt and built a small berm for the water to follow and build up. My spirits lifted at this new development, a small victory in an otherwise bleak situation. I looked out at the torch just above the barrel looking for anything different since I last laid eyes upon it. That's when it came to me, who was replacing the torch? The torches should only last for a day, perhaps less. Were its care takers arriving during my sleep and silently tending to the flame?

I was determined to wait out the torch until it reached its end and catch a glimpse of its caretaker, and so I waited. I leaned against the iron bars and kept my eyes fixated on the flame but after a time I found myself becoming comfortable and nodding off. It wasn't enough to just sit and watch, I needed to stay busy. I lifted myself upward and climbed two rungs of the iron until reaching the top rug. I gripped the bars and gently released my feet letting my body hang down. My back and neck cracked something awful and let my muscles stretch as far as they would allow. My ribs, although tender, no longer stung the way they did the day before. Rest, it seemed, had slowly begun to heal what had been broken but it would be many more weeks before I was ready for a good fight. I placed my foot back on the rungs and gently lowered myself to the ground, stretching my neck from side to side. I could feel my body warm as my blood flow improved and heart pumped steadily. I raised my arms upward only to catch a whiff of the stench beneath them. Captivity was unforgiving in so many ways and now it seemed my body had turned rotten. Quickly, I lowered my arms and shook my head to relieve myself of the smell. I paced about my cell quietly for a time, but even that did not occupy my mind long enough.

So, I sat back down and watched the flame once more. Soon, its dance mesmerized me and I was lost to the flame as a spellbound prisoner. Hours had passed, how many I could not say but what I did notice was not the flame of the torch was reaching its end. I suddenly became anxious in anticipation of the caretaker of the flame to arrive and tend to the light. I gripped the iron bars tightly, looking down each end of the corridor and keeping my ears ever alert to any sound that may make itself known. As the torch reached its end, the flame became loud almost whipping the air around it. The light became dimmer than usual and I feared that no one would come to relight the torch.

Perhaps, this is it? They would first deprive me of my freedom, then my sustenance, and now they would even rob me of the light. What monsters could leave me here for a fourth day? How long would my captivity last before the hunger took me? Or the puddle water would soon run out? Suddenly, a loud bang rang out, the closing of a door. My heart raced and I leaned my face outward to catch a glimpse of what was to come. Jailer or not, I no longer cared. I needed something, anything, to keep me going. The sound came from the left of the flame and in the darkness, I saw a bright light approaching, followed by the echo of footsteps. Not the footsteps of an armed guard, but those of a light-footed peasant bereft or weapons or the keys to my freedom.

The figure approached the not-yet extinguished torch and reached upward, quickly replacing it with a fresh one. The light above the figure's head quickly extended outward but the figure's back was to the flame, obscuring its face from view. I could see a simple brown cloak and hood that was draped over his head. This person appeared to stand slightly taller than myself and turned, pulling the lid up from barrel. It reached behind the barrel grabbing a small wooden spoon and dipping it inside the barrel pulling the spoon back up and taking a drink. Water! There was water in the barrel! The figure placed the spoon back down and secured the lid back into place. It lifted another torch to the flame, lighting it and turning away back down the corridor to walk away.

"Wait." Like a reflex I could not hold back my desperation. The word just flew out of my mouth and now the figure stopped in its tracks. I thought perhaps the figure would advance on my quickly or call out some insult but it did nothing of the kind. Without any sign of aggression, I took a chance to ask for help.

"Please, come closer." The figure turned its head towards me and then looked back down the corridor, perhaps to see if anyone had heard my quiet call for aid. The figure walked towards me, the light of the torch shining so brightly I held up my hand to block it from my eyes.

"I thought you were dead," the figure said to me in a warm but cautious voice, the voice of a man. I looked out from under my hand to see the face of a Norseman with brown eyes, gaunt white cheeks and a long blonde beard.

"Water?" I asked quietly. The man placed the torch on the ground near the bars and walked back to the barrel retrieving water with the spoon. He gently placed it to my lips and helped me drink. The man made several more trips until he placed the spoon down and retrieved his torch from the ground. "Thank you."

"They don't keep anyone back here. They never have," the Norseman said to me.

"Where am I? What is this place?" The Norseman looked back down the corridor and then turned towards me. I could see a look of fear and hesitation in his eye. Something or someone was keeping an eye on him.

"You are in dungeons of the dark queen but we just call it the dark keep. We are deep underground."

"Freya? This is Freya's keep?" I asked weakly. The Norseman nodded. "How long have I been here?"

"Nearly a week. Have you been fed?" I shook my head. The Norseman reached into his clock removing a small piece of bread and handed it to me through the bars. "Eat this now. Do not save it. If the guards come for you, they will search you." I quickly shoved the bread into my mouth savoring the flavor as long as I could before swallowing it whole. It wasn't much, but it would have to do for now.

The Norseman turned away from my cell, clearly not anxious to stay.

"Who are you?" I asked him. The Norseman looked back down the hall. He appeared startled and pulled his hood back over his head.

"My name is Dagrun but around here they just call me Dag. I must go." I reached out and grabbed the Norseman's tunic pulling him towards me. He gripped my wrist firmly and then loosened his hand.

"Please, don't leave me here." Dag shook his head.

"I must go. If I don't return, they will become suspicious and come looking for me. If they find me talking to you, they will kill us both. I will return once each day to relight the torch. Stay alive." Dag stood and walked briskly down the corridor. I leaned against the iron bars and watched in desperation as the light of his torch faded. I heard a distant door slam. Dropping my head in disappointment, I leaned back down into the wall and slid down to the floor. My head swirled with this new information. If I was indeed in Freya's keep then she knew I was here, and she wouldn't forget what I'd done to her. Not after everything that has transpired. She would want me weak and begging on my knees before she plunged a dagger in my heart. I did not wish to think on it longer and hoped that perhaps Dag would return tomorrow and maybe I could learn more about my captivity and the whereabouts of my captors.

The small piece of bread and servings of water fell heavy in my gut and my stomach gurgled with happiness, hoping to receive more. The water drops in the ceiling had slowed but the puddle had built up and was not far off from my cell, perhaps another day. I felt some hope in my heart but quickly buried it deep down so not to be crushed when things became difficult. I laid down, counting the cracks in the floor: one, twenty, eighty-seven, and one-hundred-fifty-two. My eye lids became heavy and I let them fall, but then panicked at the thought of Dag returning and I being asleep. What if he could not wake me? I'd have to wait for another day before getting anymore answers. I sat upright, but my meager meal worked its way further into my body and coaxed me to sleep. I laid back down once more, rolled to my side and closed my eyes, and let images of Sada pass in my mind. I would get out of here. I would return to her.

* * *

I awoke to what I perceived to be early with the torch light my only method of measurement. Once again, I waited for hours watching in great anticipation as the torch burned through its thick, oil-soaked rags. Soon, the torch reached its end and the light extinguished. Dag should be here soon. He wouldn't let the torch light stay out for long. I had questions, questions that needed to be answered and the only one who could answer them for me was Dag. I waited there quietly in the complete darkness. This darkness was not like the dark that comes upon the forest each night. This darkness was oblivion and all-consuming with only your thoughts to keep you company. My thoughts had begun to turn sour once more, my hope stomped out by Dag not returning. I began to question myself and wondered if I had gone mad? Was Dag even real? Did I truly see him and speak with him or did I merely conjure up his image in a dream? If he was real what kept him from returning? Did my jailers learn of his indiscretion and murder him? These thoughts consumed my mind and ate away at what hopes I had left. I swept these thoughts from my head and tried not to give up hope. I waited, and waited, and waited in oblivion. Dag did not return that day and I was left to lie alone in eternal darkness.

* * *

"Stanger…" a soft voice called out. With my eyes closed, I thought perhaps I had heard something in a dream and did not think on it. Then, it came again. "Stranger, awake." I opened my eyes only to be blinded by the overwhelming brightness of a torch. I blinked rapidly and let my eyes adjust. It was Dag! He had returned! I sat up quickly and scooted my body towards the iron bars.

"You came back. Why do you not come yesterday?" I asked.

"They had us working day and night in the mines. One of the slaves died, so they pulled me from my duties to replace him for the day. Here, take this." He handed me a larger piece of bread and I happily took it taking a bite.

"You are slaves?" The Norseman laughed under his breath.

"We are all slaves here." He lifted his arms, showing the iron shackles around his wrists. The chains were not there but he had clearly been marked as a thrall.

"How long have you been here?" I asked. Dag looked upward, appearing to count the number in his head.

"Nearly seven years now." I stopped hewing, confused.

"Seven years? Has Freya been upon Midgard for so long?"

"Longer. There are many thrall here much older than I. We work the mines, digging tunnels between realms, kingdoms and digging up precious metals for her armies."

"How many in number are you?" Dag rolled his eyes.

"Thousands, perhaps even ten thousand. I still have not met everyone in our ranks. The caverns are vast beyond imagination. Dwarven folk once lived here, but they were driven out by the Draugr and Freya's dogs."

"The Ulfhednar?" Dag nodded. He stood and collected water from the barrel, bringing the spoon to me several times until my thirst was quenched.

"The Draugr are her soldiers, the Ulfhednar her hunters and scouts. In here, it's the trolls we fear."

"Trolls?"

"The Trolls are our jailers. Twice the size of a man and twice as strong. They whip us, keep us in chains and make us work until our bones break. So, I have to ask you, why are you forgotten here?"

"What do you mean?"

"There are others levels to the prison where many men are kept. They are starved and deprived of water until they are broken. Then, they are clad in chains and fed only enough to keep them working in the mines."

"Where is Freya?"

"She is on campaign but should return soon." I nodded.

"And where does she stay?" Dag pointed back down the corridor.

"Only three caverns over in the main throne room. She has her own chambers guarded by a troop of Valkyries." Dag extended his arm placing his hand on me. "I must go soon, stranger. Tell me, what is your name?"

"I am Audan, Chieftain of Bjorgvin and son of Rurik."

"A Chieftain. Well, you best keep that to yourself. Many have come before you, and now their heads perch on spikes that line the mining paths, a reminder to the thrall not to look to men for leadership, but to only obey Freya. I will return tomorrow if I am not pulled from my duties."

"Is there a way out?" I asked urgently. Dag shook his head with a disappointing look.

"There's only one way out of here, friend, and that's the mercy of the blade." Dag stood and walked back down the corridor once again disappearing behind the far door. I quickly ate what remained of my bread, but left one crumb behind. The bread would not sustain me long. I needed meat and if I was going to get any, I needed bait. I placed the bread crumb in the corner of my cell and sat down quietly in the opposite corner. Time passed in the darkness and I felt warmed by the glow of the torch in the corridor. I leaned my head against the iron bars and waited for my prey to arrive.

Hours passed and my head began to nod to sleep but I fought it flexing my arms and gritting my teeth. I shook my head, forcing myself awake. Then, a shadow appeared across the corridor, running along the wall's edge. It stopped and then ran across the hall towards my cell. I kept as still as possible watching a giant rat slowly make its way to the iron bars. Its small, beady eyes glowed red as they reflected the light from the torch. The creature knew I was there but walked into my cell, anyway, perhaps thinking I was asleep or too weak to do anything about him anyway. Cautiously, he walked along the wall until reaching the corner to snag the bread. As soon as he grabbed it, he ran back for the iron bars, but I jumped outward, laying on the ground, blocking his path. In the blink of an eye, I swept him up in my tunic and wrapped him up in the fabric, twisting it until I could get a firm grasp of his neck. He squealed and fought frantically until I snapped his little neck like a twig. The pop was quick and his more than likely painless.

I unraveled my tunic revealing the dead rodent sitting lifelessly in the fabric. I gripped his head and twisted until it came clean off and held its body above my head drinking the blood as it flowed into my mouth. The taste was unsettling, an overpowering taste of rocks and minerals with a faint bitterness. The blood slowed to a trickle and I stretched out his little body, squeezing out every last drop. When the blood finally stopped, I breathed a sigh of relief at my fresh kill. Perhaps, the best meal I had in weeks. I skinned the rat, starting at his neck back to his tail and threw the hide far down the right side of the corridor. Its bare white flesh just inches from my teeth, I sunk in and ripped a piece of flesh from his back thigh. The meet was moist and warm and not entirely unpleasant. The taste of the rat's meat was less gamey than I had anticipated and the meat sat well in my stomach. For the next hour or longer, I spent my time picking every bone clean, throwing away the bit I could not eat. The thigh bones were thick and sturdy, perhaps making a sturdy weapon. I tucked the bones between my thighs to hide them until I could fashion a poor man's knife. The meal quickly settled in and after several more hours passed I went back to sleep hoping to wake only when Dag returned.

* * *

"Audan." It was Dag. I yawned and felt strangely tired. Wiping my face, I noticed the blood from the rat was still wet upon my lips. Dag had not been gone long.

"Why have you returned so soon?" I asked suspiciously.

"Is that your blood?" I shook my head.

"No, I found a rat. Why have you returned so soon, Dag?" The Norseman seemed more fearful than usual as he turned to look back down the corridor several times. He did not carry a torch this time and perhaps came here without his masters knowing.

"I have spoken your name to some of the other slaves, the newer ones. They know of you."

"Who, who does!" I said loudly. Dag extended his finger placing it up to my lips urging me to remain quiet.

"Freya has returned this night from her campaign, and your name has floated throughout the cavern on whispers." Dag stopped talking and listed to the corridor and then returned his gaze upon me.

"Yes, what is it?"

"Freya will summon you tomorrow to the throne room."

"For what?" I asked.

"I don't know, but most men do not meet with Freya in person. Those who have do not return." Dag sounded panicked now, but I needed him to stay just a bit longer.

"What of my fighters? Is there a woman warrior here? Named Sada?" Dag shook his head.

"No, women do not stay in the mines. We have not received any new slaves since your arrival." A slight glimmer of hope. Perhaps Sada and my warriors had escaped with their lives after all. Dag paused and rubbed his beard coarsely.

"So it's just me then." A strangely comforting feeling but I knew that no rescue would come from outside this place. "If only my brother were still alive."

"You have a brother?" Dag asked.

"I had a brother." I said reluctantly. "His body was taken by Freya in the midst of battle. He is most likely amongst the ranks of the undead now."

"I to had family. It's difficult to let go, I know." I shook my head and laughed under my breath.

"The silver tongue fool. He could talk his way out of anything but could not keep from being dragged away by the corpse goddess. It's been several seasons since last I saw his face. I miss his never ending ramblings and reckless need for danger." Dag looked back down the corridor and then at me again.

"How long has he been gone again?"

"Several seasons at least."

"There is another down here that's sound an awful lot like the man you describe. The guards have been especially harsh to him. You're looking for Jareth aren't you?" My heart dropped and I pulled back gasping under my breath.

"Jareth. He's alive?"

Fourteen
Wither

A loud bang erupted from the end of the hallway and Dag appeared terrified.

"Tell me Dag, my brother is he alive?" Dag took several steps from me and looked down the corridor.

"I believe the one you speak of still lives and works the mines. I cannot linger here any longer. The others will come for me. I must return." Dag left quickly leaving me without all the answers I sought. At least now there was a small glimmer of hope. At least now I could rest knowing my brother may still live. I had to find a way into the mines and out of this cell if I was going to meet with Jareth. I laid down, my head brewing with plans of escape and decided to sleep on it so I could once more be fresh of thought.

* * *

When next I awoke, the puddle of water had finally reached my cell and so I knelt down, stretching out my lips and consuming the muddied liquid hole. It satisfied my thirst and would keep me at least another day.

The torch at the end of the corridor burned brightly, so Dag would not be here anytime soon. As I sat there cleaning dirt from under my long nails, a loud crash erupted at the end of the hall. Excited to see Dag, I rushed to the bars and peered outward, but the figure lit underneath the torch was large, much larger than any man. It moved slowly towards me with a thunderous footstep and terrifying large eyes glowing blue in the darkness. As it approached, I moved away from the bars and sat against the wall of the cell. The shadow of the figure approached, blocking out what little light I already had and when it stepped in front of the iron bars, it blocked the entire entrance. He looked down at me and I knew from the stories told to me as a child he could be but one thing;

A troll.

"Are you my jailer?" I asked. The troll did not speak, nor did he give any sign that he understood my words. A familiar sound came from his hand: the jangling of keys. The troll shuffled his fingers through the many keys on an iron ring until reaching the one he sought. He placed the key in its lock and turned. A loud knock erupted through the corridor as the lock gave way and the troll grasped the iron bars slowly pulling it open, creaking loudly as he did so. I stood still, waiting for some direction but the troll gave none.

"Well?" The beast lifted his massive arms and extended a finger pointing towards the end of the corridor. "You want me to walk?" The Troll grumbled unintelligibly and so I stood slowly and cautiously left my cell. It had been over a week since I had walked any further than six paces and so my legs felt weak and even shook as I stretched them outward. I was suddenly startled by the slamming of my cell door. The Troll moved up behind me and I lengthened my steps to stay at least a pace or two ahead of him. I looked back up at him over my shoulder before reaching the large wooden door and he stared down at me grumbling in his low tone. Quickly, I looked away fearing that too much eye contact may upset the brute who seemed to see so clearly in the darkness.

We reached the large door and the Troll placed his massive hand on my shoulder, pulling me back and stepping in front of me. He lifted up his collection of keys, searching for the right one and then unlocked the door. He pushed it open and a flood of light blinded me from the other side. I shielded my face with my arm; it had been so long since I had seen such light that I felt staggered backward. I looked upward at the troll, whose face I could see clearly now. A well-built creature of muscle and brawn, his skin was grey like ash. His face was chiseled with a stone-like square jaw. There was no hair to speak of, no moles or scars. In fact, the troll did not appear to have any of the physical imperfections of men. His eyes were very large and round and appeared black in the light. When he turn his face, I noticed large tusks that protruded from the inside of his upper lip and curled downward just above his chin. He grumbled and turned his rear to the right. Without delay, I followed his directions and walked just ahead of him as he slammed the door behind him.

As my eyes adjusted to the bright light, I saw the room ahead was enormous, far larger than I could have imagined. Great stone walkways and staircases extended as far as the eye could see. The walkways and walls were adorned with fine Norse decorations, depictions of great battles of men. I slowed my pace to examine all the carvings but the Troll did not permit me to linger and pushed me forward with his fingers. We reached a stone bridge that arched upward and back down the other side. Looking over the edge, I saw an endless oblivion down below, a great chasm so dark, it must have led to hell itself. The Troll pushed me ahead again and we reached the end of the bridge to a large iron-banded wooden door. Large metal rings held fires in place on the ground to light the way and were spread out every ten paces or so. Entering the doorway, I followed a corridor that was long and narrow, which reached upward to an unfathomable height. This truly was a remarkable place and like nothing the lands of Midgard had ever seen. Men could not build this. At the end of the corridor, two Valkyries stood guard with spears and shields in hand. They did not move, nor did they shift their eyes to watch me. They merely gazed forward, ever watchful and clad in their leather armor. Beyond the guards lay a great hall with red and black banners depicting a black heart with a bloodied spear run through it that draped the walls. A red cloth secured to the ground now lay before my feet. It ran to a massive stone throne adorned with precious jewels. The stones caught light from the torches and as I approached, the light became brighter and nearly blinding. Suddenly, my jailer grumbled and I stopped in place, waiting for his direction. He gripped the back of my tunic firmly in his hand and lifted me in the air to the height of his shoulder. He knelt down on one knee, still holding me up.

"What are you doing?" I yelled.

"Is that any way to speak to your queen?" a voice called out.

Not just any voice, but a voice I knew well, a voice that lent to the death and destruction of many lives. Freya. I hesitated to turn my head and gaze upon her, knowing that this would be my end but the Troll would not have me deny his queen. He swung me back behind him and then threw me into the air. I landed on a number of stone steps then rolling downward. My ribs struck the corner of one of these steps and I gripped them in pain before something kicked me down to the ground. A boot pressed my face down and dug deeply into my cheek. A figure bent downward, quickly pressing its lips nearly against my ears.

"You know it an offense punishable by death to not acknowledge your queen." Freya stood and then quickly removed its boot from my face. I turned my head and standing above me was the flawless goddess herself. Her long blonde hair shined brightly in the light of the throne room and her blue eyes were warm and welcoming and showed no malice towards me.

"However, you are new to my realm and so I shall show you a kindness and allow you to correct your mistake. Now, stand Audan, son of Rurik." Freya turned and slowly walked to her throne with a long fur cloak trailing behind her. I stood cautiously to my bloodied and worn feet and watched as Freya casually sat down in a white robe and draped her legs of the arm rest.

"It has been some time Freya." I did not know what to say in this moment but knew not to offend her or meet my fate sooner than I wished. Looking about the hall, there were no doors or windows with which to escape, so I banished the thought and decided to confront the dark queen head on.

"Has it? Last I remember my Midgardian allies killed your father and my monsters destroyed your village. What a failure you have become, Audan." I nodded only to remain on similar ground with Freya.

"You are right, my queen. I have failed my people. They have no home to go to. I have failed my father and let him die at your hands and now I am your prisoner. I submit to your will." Freya tapped her finger loudly against the stone and then stood quickly wrapping her cloak around her.

"I must say, Audan, I did not think you would bend so quickly. I mean, after everything you have endured, everything you have been through, only to make it here at the foot of my throne. I could have Kruc throw you off the bridge at the snap of my fingers." So that was the name of the Troll. I turned back to see a glimmer of a smirk at the corner of Kruc's mouth, but it did not last long and quickly faded away. "You even completed the task after chaining my dog for me. He was useful in digging Surt out of his rocky tomb, but afterwards it became quite troublesome to control him." *Her* dog? What did she mean *her* dog? That was Loki's dog, or was it?

Torches lit from the back corner of the throne room and at the center of the torches was the hound, Fenrir, chained to the stone floor by the gleipnir. What was Fenrir doing here?

"I'm sorry, my queen, I don't understand." Footsteps emanated from the walls behind the thrown and around the corner walked a tall and slender figure that clapped its hands together and laughed in a deep and maniacal manner.

"Are you really that thick, Audan?" It was Loki. My blood came to a boil and rage set in as I clenched my fists. "What a gullible fool you are! I mean, to sacrifice your own people just to catch the world-eater. Even you knew it would have been easier to kill him, but no, you put your trust in me."

"Loki, I should have known you were up to no good. So what did she promise you? A kingdom? Eternal glory?" Loki shook his head and approached me, stopping about five paces away.

"No. I got something much better than that. Shall I tell him Freya? Shall I divulge our unfolding plan to the one Midgardian that could have stopped it all? You see, Audan, when Midgard falls, so, too, will the other realms and when Surt burns your precious rock ash, I will remain to rule."

"A kingdom of chains, a kingdom of corpses. Nothing more."

Loki reached outward and struck me hard against the face. My head turned but I stood firm.

"Still, he doubt us. He doubts our clarity of foresight. We cannot build a new realm from the ones that exist and so, we must start over. Midgard shall burn in flame eternal. Those loyal bloodlines that remain shall stay to rebuild and create a new realm. Freya shall rule as its benevolent queen and I, well, I shall be and do whatever I want. So long as the people of Midgard bow to me."

"And what of Odin, Thor, Tyr, and Baldur? What of the other gods? Will they merely allow you to do thus?"

"The power of all the gods in all the realms combined could not equal the ultimate power that Surt wields once he is replenished. As we speak, Surt heads north and soon will be at full strength. It is inevitable. All your struggles, all your sacrifices, for nothing." Loki turned to Freya and bowed slightly. "My queen, I leave you to your duties."

"Where will you go Loki?" I asked.

"That is for me to know. Oh, and Audan, enjoy the end of the world." Loki walked past me and left the throne room through the main entrance. Freya gripped a bright green apple in her hand and sunk her ivory white teeth into them biting deeply. She wrapped her lips around it, pulling a piece away. She chewed loudly with her mouth open gazing at the fruit and running her fingers gently along the skin.

"So now that the world is about to be mine the only question is: what do I do with you, Audan, son of Rurik?" Freya stood gracefully from her throne and walked towards me, looking as beautiful as ever. A dark and evil temptress she was. Even now, only moments from death, it was hard not to gaze upon her and admire her visage. A deathly beauty and only my love for Sada kept me from her. She stopped her face just short of pressing against mine speaking softly. "You know, you had such promise, Audan. The Norn's may not know what to make of you, but when I look into your eyes..." Her gaze pressed deeply into my eyes and under her spell I could not turn away. Her lips parted slightly and she exhaled a sigh. "When I look into your eyes... I see a greatness in you, like no other mortal before." A tear escaped her eye and ran down her cheek, smoldering against her skin. She reached upward to wipe it away, but it had already burned away. She turned away and walked back to her throne sitting down properly this time, regal, as a Queen would.

"So?" I said with certainty in my voice. "Let us say we get the sword and get this over with." Freya seemed perplexed, cocking her head to one side and leaning her head against her hand.

"The sword? Do you think I am here to execute you?"

"Is that not what you do with traitors in your realm?"

"You are a traitor, Audan, there is no doubt about that. However, I have a special place for you in my heart. A kind of fondness. Perhaps it's the love you once showed me or just simply the fact that when faced with battle, you simply won't die. No, Audan, I think you are too good to simply fall to a blade while imprisoned. It's like killing a farm animal: you keep them caged all their lives and then one day instead of feed, you bring the knife. It's all very undignified."

"So, what would you do with me then?"

"Kruc." The hulking Troll let out a short grumble. "Take our friend, Audan, to the mines. He will make an excellent addition to my children."

"And if I refuse?" A false show of defiance. I needed Freya to put me in the mines and I wanted her to think it was what I dreaded.

"Refuse all you want, Audan. Your life is mine from this point on. You will work the mines and as you beat back the rocks, they will beat back wearing you down and rob you of your will. And one day, when you have work the mines long enough you, will come back to me and you will love me. Take him away!" Kruc grabbed my shoulder and pulled me back but I fought falling to my back but he simply dragged me away.

"You crazy bitch! I'll never submit to you! Never!" As Kruc dragged me away, Freya raised her hand into the air.

"And Audan." Kruc stopped in his tracks and waited for his queen to finish speaking. She shot me a terrifying smile and I feared what words would escape her mouth next. "You brother, Jareth… he died, like a coward. Did you know that?" Freya stood from her throne and walked away to her chambers.

"You stupid bitch! I'll kill you! I'll kill you!" As we left the throne room, the large wooden doors slammed shut on their own and the guards posted continued their watch. Kruc picked me up, throwing me atop his shoulder, we crossed the stone bridge once more but instead of going straight, he turned right down another equally long and narrow hallway until the chamber opened up to insurmountable heights. A clamor of tools clattered in the air and along every wall and every crevice for miles on end were men clad in chains, working shovels, pick axes, and carrying bails of precious metals. Kruc dropped me in front of another equally large Troll who slapped iron bands around my wrists and ankles with a chain connecting each. He threw a pick axe in my hand and pushed me forward. So, my work began.

* * *

Months passed since that day in the Throne room with Freya and Loki. I had not heard or seen from them since. The work in the mines was hard and each day I would see men fall from thirst or hunger. Those who could no longer work were thrown off the stone bridge and into oblivion. Those who refused to work were impaled onto long spikes and left out for the others to see. Each night, when our work was done, Kruc would retrieve me and throw me back into my cell block. No prisoners ever joined me in this section of the prison and so my time not in the mines was spent alone with only Dag to visit me to relight the torches. I tried to speak with other men while working the pick axe in the mines but they had been there so long that they feared the wrath of the Trolls. With each visit, Dag would give me my share of food, water, and most importantly, information. Then one day, Dag returned, seeming more rushed than usual.

"What is it?" I asked curiously. Dag breathed heavily with sweat dripping from his brow. He must have run the length of several caverns before reaching me. Dag lifted his hand into the air.

"Let me catch my breath," he said weakly. Soon, he took in a deep gust of air and then breathed out slowly. "I have a message for you."

"A message? What message? From who?"

"From your brother, Jareth." How could it be? Dag had mentioned Jareth months ago but Freya said he was dead.

"How can that be?"

"Your brother, he lives. Many, many caverns from here?"

"But Freya said he was dead." Dag shook his head.

"Dead? No. Not dead. Badly beaten and scarred, perhaps, but your brother is very much alive."

"How can I be sure it's him and not one of Loki's tricks?"

"He said your mother is name 'Kenna,' you wife to be is named Sada, and that you had a very small cock. He laughed after that last part."

"That son of a bitch is alive. How does he fair?"

"Just as any man of the mines. You may not recognize him as you once did."

"What message did you bring?" Dag looked back down the corridor to be sure no one was coming and then proceed to extinguish his torch on the ground.

"A message of escape." I laughed coarsely.

"No one escapes this place. The only way out is up." Dag smiled.

"You may be right, but your brother seems confident. In his cavern, the roots of Yggdrasil are exposed."

"The tree of the nine realms? It cannot be?"

Dag nodded.

"It is. Precious metals are not the only thing the dark queen seeks in the bowels of the mines. She harvests sap from the roots night and day and has done so for years."

"But, how is that possible? It is said that no tool of man can pierce the bark of the great tree. What instrument do they use if not an axe?" Dag smiled widely his eyes warm and bright.

"Nidhogg." I had never heard this word before.

"What is a Nidhogg?" I asked. Dag leaned closer against the bars and spoke softer.

"Not what but who. Nidhogg is a dragon of the mines. He has lived here for a millennia feasting on the roots to sustain his hunger. Your brother proposes to use the dragon to reach the peak of the mines and enter the world of men." I shook my head. The whole plan sounded crazy.

"There must be another way?"

"I'm afraid not. Freya and her Valkyries fly up through this skylight anytime they leave on campaign. They have never used another path."

"What lies above?"

"A plain far to the north in Midgard, a land of rock and fire. To the south lies and west lies lands you are more familiar with but there is more. I have found out that Freya and her guards leave in a fortnight."

"Where do they go?"

"I have heard rumors of a battle. Freya consulted with her captains just last night about a massive force of men gathering nearby. They seek to strike at the heart of Freya and her forces. Their forces number nearly ten thousand and they are led by none other than a woman."

"A woman leads ten thousand Northmen? That's not possible." Dag shook his head.

"I know it seems strange, but I only share what I have heard. When the Valkyries leave, only a small contingent of Trolls will be left behind." This concerned me. The trolls, despite their small number, could easily fight off thousands of weak slaves with nothing more than digging tools to defend themselves.

"How will we fight off the trolls?" Now a fear took over Dag's face, his eyes turning away from me. "What is it?"

"When the time comes, I will take the keys from the jailer and free you. We shall trade places and under my guise you will make your way to the throne room and release Fenrir. I fear that dog more than any creature in this pit."

"Release the hound! Are you mad?" I yelled. Dag cupped his hand over my mouth and urged me to be quiet.

"I cannot do it Audan. You have tangled with the beast, it must be you. Fenrir will be the distraction needed to occupy a good number of the Trolls. Without him, you will face the Trolls head on and surely fail. You will need to take gleipnir with you to tame Nidhogg and ride him to the surface." There was something more to this plan, something I did not see.

"Why would all the slaves sacrifice themselves for Jareth and I? What is in it for them?"

"You're not stupid, Audan. This is why I like you. No, it's not just for you. Jareth has been here for much longer than you. His silver tongue and brave heart has earned him the loyalty of the entire mine. Your brother commands nearly seven thousand men and in private they call him 'General.' You and Jareth will carry ladders of rope to the surface and secure them for the miners to escape. Without the ladders, they will not support you." Dag stood quickly lifted his extinguished torch and relighting it over the one on the wall. "I must go. You will not see me again until it is time." Dag turned away quickly to rush back out of the corridor.

"Dag," I said. He stopped and turned. "You are a good friend. I hope that you survive to meet me again on the surface. I could use more good friends." Dag nodded.

"So could I." Dag left and I returned and I lay back to return to sleep with a glimmer of hope and the promise of blood. As I sat there contemplating the many ways in which our plan could go awry, I hoped with what little hope I had left in me that it would not. If what Dag said was true and Jareth had nearly seven thousand men by his side then perhaps we could overwhelm the Trolls. I dreaded the thought of releasing the hound. What would keep him from bypassing the Trolls and attacking us? Was it really worth it to retrieve the gleipnir to reign in Nidhogg? And what of the dragon? Could Nidhogg be so easily overtaken and controlled? The whole thing sounded mad and very much like my brother. My stomach ached again. I was still getting barely enough to eat to sustain me. My tunic had become loose, hanging over me like a blanket. I was withering away and if we didn't do something soon, I would fade into nothing.

* * *

"Audan." A voice called out quietly. "Audan, awake. It is time." Slowly lifting my head, I saw the torch-bearing Dag standing outside my cell. Two weeks had come and past and now he stood before me just as promised. My eyes burned, my every bone and muscle hurt terribly and I struggled to even sit up right. I needed rest, food, and water. "Audan, what are you doing? Get up." Keys jingled above my head and Dag unlocked the iron bars and swung the door open rushing to my side he shook me. "Get up!" I sat up slowly and looked upon his fearful face.

"Why do you look scared, Dag?" Dag reached back and slapped my face.

"Because if you don't get up this is all for not. Now, rise to your feet." My senses quickly came back to me. The famine had worn me down, but Dag's hand to my face sent the blood rushing about. He helped me up and put a gourd full of water to my mouth. I drank heartily until he pulled it from me. "Are you ready?"

"I am." Dag removed his robe and I removed my tunic. We traded out cloths and donned our new outfits. Dag handed me the torch and then sat down in the corner of the cell wiping dirt on his face.

"The hood, don't forget the hood," said Dag, pointing at my back. I lifted the hood, placing it over my head. Dag had been much better fed than I and his cloak hung loose on my body, his hood weighing down on my head. "Good, now shut the gate but leave it unlock." I stepped outside and quietly closed the gate. I gazed at Dag who turned his body keeping his head down. "Good luck, Audan. I'll see you at the end of this."

"Good luck, Dag. May Odin watch over us." I was hesitant to leave Dag behind, but if the guards came looking and saw an empty cell our ruse would be found out. I quickly made my way to the end of the corridor, opening the door and leaving it cracked on the way out. The stone bridge was not far off and not a troll was in sight. All was quiet in the caverns as its many slave and prisoners slumbered in their cells. Cautiously but confidently, I walked forward with torch in hand, keeping my gaze low and my face out of sight. I reached the base of the bridge and quickly scaled it to the other side without any resistance. Just ahead, lay the corridor and at the front of the throne room a single troll stood guard with a large double bladed axe in hand. I continued to walk forward despite being worried he may recognize me. The Troll's feet was covered in leather wraps. This was not Kruc and not a Troll I had seen before. As I passed him, he did not grumble or make any movement towards me. He acted as if I was not there.

I reached the center of the throne room easily enough and now I spotted Fenrir just beyond the throne. Tiptoeing my way towards him, I was careful not to make a single sound. If he barked or growled it would alert the Trolls and a battle would break out before I could free the beast. Fenrir breathed heavily as he slept against the stone floor; the gleipnir secured to six iron rings on the ground. I began with the ones in the front placing my torch on the ground, untying the knot and slowly moving the line to the next ring. The gleipnir slipped through the loop and I made my way to the other side of Fenrir. I repeated this several times until reaching the last two rings. My brow was sweating profusely and as I wiped the sting from my eyes, I saw that the gleipnir was not just loop through the rings. The second to the last ring loop under and then wrap around Fenrir's right rear leg. The last and final strand was tied in a knot on his ankle and at last tied to the final ring. *Of course it couldn't be simple.*

I reached under Fenrir's leg to undo the loop before pulling it through the ring when suddenly Fenrir grumbled. I leapt back as his back leg kicked and I was about to run until I realized the hound, was dreaming. Fenrir whimpered like a tiny mutt, kicking his legs and scratching on the floor. I had to hold back my laughter at seeing this beast of a monster acting out as a mere pup. When Fenrir's fit ceased, I wiped the smirk away from my face and quickly whipped the line around his leg to undo the loop. Finally free of his leg, I pulled it though the ring and slowly walked it toward the final ring. I reached down and lifted the iron ring from the floor but it slip from the grasp of my sweaty fingers. The ring landed loudly with a knock that echoed in the hall and my heart jumped in my chest in anticipation of the hell that would follow.

I swung my head up expecting to see the beast bearing down upon me, but all I saw was the hound slumbering silently. I exhaled deeply in relief and quickly took two steps forward, as I was crouched down and reached for the final knot around his ankle. My legs were thin and weak and as I inched forward they burned terribly but I did not allow it to slow me down. The knot was tight and filled with thick mats of black fur. I worked the line piece by piece slowing pushing the far end through the loops and tucking the fur out of the way so not to pinch it. I approached the final loop when the hairs on my neck began to stand upright; something was watching. Gazing upward, I spotted a grey figure in the distance looking at me, the Troll guard at the entrance spotted me and growled loudly. I pulled the final loop loose and as I did Fenrir awoke to the Troll's roar and sprinted towards him, leaping in the air and jumping at his throat. They tumbled and the Troll battered at Fenrir with his massive fists while the hound snapped and clawed at him. I took the chance to run!

Sprinting around the fighting goliaths, I swiftly passed the entrance, my hood falling off my head. I stopped in my tracks just before the bridge when I spotted two more Trolls with spears in hand standing at the ready on the other side. It was now or never. "For Valhalla!" My war cry echoed in the halls of the mines and a faint roar followed that grew and grew to a tremendous din. The prisoners of the dark keep had moved against their jailers. The Trolls before me looked around in a panic and then charged towards me. I looked back at the hound who finally spotted me after making his first kill and waved my arms in mad desperation.

"Here, Fenrir! Come and get me you stupid mangy dog!" The beast roared and charged forward and I ran from the Trolls toward the dog until I closed the gap between the two. I stopped, turned and ran back towards the Trolls who shifted their focus to the dog as it leapt forward. Sliding beneath the legs of a Troll, I stood and ran for the mines to the right. Just before entering the cavern I had spent so many months in a hand grabbed me from behind. I turned and swung my fist to meet my foe and the figure ducked and quickly back away.

"Audan!" It was Dag. "Audan, it's me." He handed a pick axe to me and pushed me forward. "Do you have the gleipnir?" I pulled the silvery thread from my cloak and showed it to him. "Well done, my friend! Follow me. I will take you to your brother!"

We ran through the first cavern to be confronted by a wild melee between prisoners and jailers. With Fenrir not far behind, we did not linger to help the others in their battle. As we charged from cavern to cavern, we saw men being slaughtered by the dozens but as the prisoners surrounded the Trolls, they fell one by one. A most violent death came as they were pummeled by dull pick axes and dented shovels. Blood covered the walls and floor of nearly every hallway until we reached a cavern unlike the ones I had seen before.

"Is this it?" I asked urgently. Dag nodded.

"It is, the cavern of Yggdrasill, the world tree!" As we ran, I looked above to see a sky light high above. Massive roots covered the ceiling digging into the walls and floors and traveling into other corridors. From the large roots much smaller ones hung down from the ceilings like massive vines covering everything in green. A large wooden platform extended upward to the roots where large stone bowls stood collecting sap from spears that had been pressed upward into the tree. We climbed up the stairs of the platform until reaching a band of men armed with crude handmade knives. At the center of this group of men was a thin and frail looking young man who stood upright with his hair running over his face and beard down to his waist. The man approached me quickly and stood back raising my pick axe ready to defend myself when he dropped the knife and opened his arms.

"Brother..." The man wrapped his arms around me and held me tightly. He gripped my shoulders and pulled back from me looking at my eyes.

"Jareth?" I asked. He nodded his head and a sort of happy and sad laughter erupted from our voices. "By the gods, it is you!" I reached back in and returned the embrace. "I thought you were dead!" Jareth shook his head.

"I died many months ago, brother. Now nothing can defeat us."

"Much has changed in your absence; it's time for you to live again." A loud roar from the ceiling of the mine on the opposite side of the vines. "Is that?" Jareth nodded and smiled exposing his dirty teeth.

"Nidhogg. Did you bring it? Did you bring the gleipnir?" I pulled out the line once more and handed it to my brother. He gripped it eagerly, his eyes wide with excitement as he twirled it in his finger.

"I pulled it from the hound, himself. It's real." Jareth looked around at the men that surrounded him.

"You know what to do. Circle the dragon, force him down to the platform." The men quickly dispersed carrying their tools and grabbing torches on their way up the stairs. I turned to Dag.

"I could not have reached you if not for this man." Jareth extended his arm to Dag and they shared a hearty handshake.

"You shall be the first to ascend the ladders." Dag nodded in appreciation. Far below us the melee continued and in some caverns the fighting had ceased as the jailers had be quelled.

"Jareth, what do you need from me?"

"Are you ready to ride a dragon, brother?" he said, smiling wickedly at me. I shook my head and grimaced.

"No."

Jareth laughed loudly and slapped my shoulder.

"Good, neither am I. Come with me." I followed Jareth up the platform until a we reached a set of ladders. "Climb with me and wait. When Nidhogg gets beneath us we jump and reign him in. It was a mad plan but hope was now on our side. I nodded and climbed upward nearly to the height of a longhouse and we waited. In the distance, I could hear men yelling and shouting, while the beast Nidhogg roared. Louder and louder, the noises grew until the glow of flame could be seen and the shadow of the beast revealed itself. A long, brown tail appeared covered in scales and dirt, attached to a body that extended like a worm. The head had a long and broad snout with a row of uneven fangs jutting out in all directions. His eyes were pale white like the snows of the highest peaks and his horns jutted out like branches from his head. I looked to Jareth for when to jump but he gave no sign of nervousness, no indication of anxiety. Imprisonment had made him hard as a stone and as fearless as the gods themselves.

Soon, Nidhogg's tail was directly below us and the men waved the tools and flame back and forth, pushing the beast further back until his head and neck were beneath us. Another group of men approached from the rear of the platform and now Nidhogg was surrounded, swinging wildly back and forth and knocking several men down and sending several others over the edge to their deaths.

"Now brother!" We jumped down from the ladders each holding one end of the gleipnir. I landed on the beast's midsection while Jareth fell squarely on Nidhogg's neck. I jumped down, running beneath the worm-like dragon until reaching his fangs. He snapped his jaws at me and I threw the line between his mouth. The line landed firmly on the other side and Nidhogg lunged forward and just as his teeth were about close his head lunged back. Jareth rode atop the dragon pulling the reins of the Gleipnir back. "Jareth! You did it!" the men cheered and chanted out his new name, "the General."

"Climb up, brother! We're not through yet." Jareth pointed upward at the skylight, escape was very near. I gripped the cold scales and climbed them like a ladder to the top, grabbing the spike that protruded from his back. I waved down Dag and urged him to climb upwards as well. The Norseman moved towards us carrying three very long ropes over his shoulders.

"Catch, Audan!" One by one, he threw the ropes upward and I caught each, wrapping them around a larger spike further up Nidhogg's spine. Dag climbed and the beast shook and bucked and Jareth pulled back on the reins pressing a small dagger into his neck. Nidhogg complied and shook no longer. Dag reached the top of the beast and gripped the horns in front of him. Jareth turned back and nodded.

"Are you ready?"

"Ready!" we replied in unison.

Jareth let out a war cry and snapped the reins. Nidhogg charged forward, digging his claws into the wood planks and running past several warriors until reaching the roots. He leapt from the platform and my heart sank. Rocks and trees rushed passed me faster than I could count them. The scaling beast ascended upward, climbing and leaping from root stem to root stem. The long lines behind us followed and down below neatly piled ropes unraveled followed by a neatly stacked piles of rope ladders. Dag held on tight and looked as if he was about to be sick. Round and round Nidhogg went around the tree until finally the skylight was near. Jareth whipped and yelled at the beast until the dragon stopped at the crest of the rocky window; the bright light blinded him as he tugged his head away.

"Why have we stopped?" Dag called out.

"He won't climb!" Jareth exclaimed. He kicked and shouted at the beast but he would not budge. Dag and I joined in kicking and punching the beast. Nidhogg let out a roar and at long last made the final ascent, running on the final root stem until reaching the rocks and scrambling to the top. Jareth stopped the dragon only a few paces from the hole in the ground while Dag and I quickly jumped down grabbing the lines and securing them around heavy boulders. When my line was fixed. I looked up expecting to see the great tree Yggdrasil but above there was nothing but cloud covered skies.

"You expected to see the tree. Didn't you?" Dag asked.

"Of course, its roots lay just beneath this ground. Where is it?" Dag laughed.

"The tree connects the realms and its roots stretch further than our minds can possibly imagine." Dag pointed high above. "It's somewhere out there but I don't think we would ever reach it." A question still lingered, something I had wished to ask Dag but had not the time.

"The sap, what does Freya use it for?" Dag shook his head.

"It's poison to mortals but I have witnessed Freya drink it on occasion. In the darkness, it appears red but in the light a colorful sheen like the rainbows of the Bifrost can be seen. What effect it had on Freya, I know not but she kept her stores well stocked." I breathed heavy, my first breath of fresh air in months and threw my arms into the air.

"Freedom!" I yelled. Jareth leapt down from Nidhogg pulling the gleipnir from of the beast's mouth.

"Get out of here!" he yelled at the dragon whipping him with the line. Nidhogg whimpered and quickly scurried back into the hole, beneath the ground where he belonged among the roots. I reached outward and grasped the gleipnir from Jareth's hands tucking it back into my cloak.

"We should go. Freya's scouts could be all over this valley and with no arms, we're no match at all against even a handful of Draugr." Dag pointed out in the distance towards a stretch of mountains.

"Beyond those hills lie your lands and forests and rivers. Quickly, this way."

"What of your seven thousand men, Jareth?" I asked. He shook his head and smiled as he reached for the ropes and secured them to the heaviest of rocks for his men to climb up.

"They all know where to rally. Let's find shelter first before dusk arrives." We agreed and moved onward following Dag. Climbing down a steep ravine we reached a river with a path that led back to the hills.

"What are you doing?" Jareth asked me. I stopped to relieve myself at the side of the road when suddenly a loud snap whipped passed my head. I stinger lodged in the tree next to my head and the wild call of savages filled the rocky ravine. It was an ambush!

Fifteen
A God Emerges

The ravine came alive with the yells and war cries of savages running down from the hillsides. They wore thick grey cloaks and had covered themselves in the soil of the rocks. Their concealment was so well done that they could have killed us whenever they wanted. I raised my hands in surrender as nearly twenty men encircled us while more stood on the hill bows at the ready.

"Well, what do we have here?" A tall man with a long, black beard called out with sword drawn. "Spies of the dark queen? Scouts?" Jareth took half a step forward and was quickly met with sword points no more than a hairs length away.

"We bear no love for Freya."

"Is that so? My men tell me you came out of the hole in the ground. They say you rode a serpent." The warriors around the dark-bearded man burst into laughter.

"Aye, we did. Nidhogg!" Dag spouted out. The warriors suddenly became silent, whispering back and forth to one another. The name of the dragon had clearly been familiar to them but now the black-bearded man seemed more skeptical as one brow lowered and the other raised.

"Well, that may be but I say they are spies!" The warriors of the ravine shouted in agreement, raising their arms high into the air. I stepped forward with my hands open to stay their anger.

"We're not spies. We escaped from the dark keep!" I yelled in protest. The black-bearded man approached me face to face and then struck me in the face with his sword handle still in hand. My weak and frail body fell under the weight of the blow and when I hit the dirt my head rang with pain.

"And they're liars as well. Hang them all!" The men cheered and a rush of shadows came over me pulling and pawing at my clothes, limbs, and hair. They stood me up and marched us towards a nearby tree bereft of leaves, just a dark oak skeleton against a grey hillside.

"Wait, wait!" Dag cried out. Ropes were thrown over a large branch and the warriors quickly made a hangman's noose. Kicked from behind, I fell once more and when I turned my head, I saw Jareth trying to fight off his attackers but there were too many. They kicked and punched him mercilessly until his body went limp. Dag gave no fight other than protesting but his cries of innocence fell on deaf ears. They stood us up again and placed the ropes over our heads and around our necks. I swallowed back the lump in my throat and did all I could to forget the hope of freedom I had breathed for such few precious moments. The rope became taut as men pulled them from the other end and now the black-bearded man stood before us with a wide smile.

"You poor bastards picked the wrong day to crawl out of your hole. So, have you any last words for the world of men?" Jareth spit on the man's face landing squarely on his cheek. The warrior merely wiped it off with his glove.

"No last words for you. Very well." He moved to Dag standing face to face with his hands on his hips. "And what about you? Any last words."

"We're not spies. We escaped the dark keep! I swear it to all the gods! I swear it!" The black-bearded man removed a cloth from his belt, no doubt something he used to blow his nose into. He jammed the cloth into Dag's mouth and punched him in the face.

"A liar to the very end!" He then walked in front of me his eye fixed keenly on mine. "And you? Do you have anything of significance to say before I take you from this world?" I thought for a brief moment what I might say to change the dark-bearded man's mind, but I cared not to die sound like a sniveling coward. I would let my convictions stand.

"Death to the dark queen! Long live Midgard! Hail Odin the All Father!" The dark-bearded man smiled and stepped back.

"Raise'em up, lads!" The rope squeezed on my neck tightly and I was pulled into the air. I felt as if my head would pop right off and my legs below swung uncontrollably. The warriors cheered and yelled in excitement washing out the sound of my struggles. My vision began to blur as a rider atop a large steed appeared.

"Magnus, who are these men?" My rope spun and soon my body faced Dag and Jareth and I could see them fighting back the impending death as well.

"Spies. They came up from the dark keep." The rider jumped down from his horse.

"They don't look like spies to me. Have you questioned them?" The world became darker around me and my leg began to feel cold as my blood slowed.

"What would be the point, my lord? Only lies would fall from their tongues." The rider shook his head and pointed upwards at us.

"Let them down. The Marshal will be the ones to decide their fate." The world faded to black and now I could only faintly here voices.

"But, my lord!"

"I said get them down!"

"Yes, my lord." My cold stiff limbs struck the ground. Light flooded my eyes as I looked up at the day's sky and gasped for air. Dark figures came over me, lifting me up by my arms. I tried to stand but I could not feel my legs and I fell downward though the warriors bracing my fall. The rider approached me gripping the tuft of my hair and pulling my head back.

"If you are a spy, I will cut you down myself. Take them back to camp!"

"As you wish, my lord," said Magnus. My sight went dark as a cloth was wrapped around my eyes and tied behind my head. I could hear Jareth and Dag breathing heavily as they carted us away and lifted me on the back of a horse lying face down.

We traveled for quite some time as I listened intently to the horse's hooves striking the ground. We rode over rock and dirt, through mud and crossed no more than two rivers. The warriors did not speak much, but soon I could hear a flurry of activity. Horses could be heard running by quickly, men joked and laughed around crackling fires and steel was being sharpened over whetstones. The smells were all too familiar, the smells of a large war camp. The aroma of hot soup wafted in the air accompanied by the scent of horse manure and piss. This camp had been occupied and waiting for some time. No doubt a campaign was in progress, or about to begin. Our horses stopped and a pair of hands grabbed my shoulders pulling me down.

"Alright, you bastard. Get the fuck off my horse!" I slipped down and fell into the frigid mud below. I stood slowly and was once again set upon by a warrior who pushed me forward. "Walk!" he commanded. I marched forward until the warrior tugged back on my arm. "Stop here and don't fucking move." He took three loud steps away from me and stopped abruptly. "Prisoners for the Marshal. They're to be questioned."

"Very well," a voice called out. A hand gripped my arm and pulled me forward then another pair of hands worked around my waist, legs, and back. "He's clean. Get him inside."

I was pushed forward again, and the room became darker but the warm of a fire was very apparent. Then, a leg pushed against the backside of my knee. "On your ass. Do not speak unless spoken to." The warrior let go of me and stepped away. I ran a finger on the ground feeling a cloth beneath me. We were inside a tent. Then, I heard another person slump next to me. A shoulder brushed against my body and without my sight I knew it was either Jareth or Dag.

"Do you know who I am?" the deep voice of a man said. I simply shook my head and did not speak.

"I am the man who kept the three of you from hanging this morning. If you are truly spies, we will find out. If you lie to us, you will die slowly and painfully but if you are honest and true, we will show you mercy." The man paced back and forth for a time and then stopped in front of us. I am Trygve, Lord Commander and right hand of the Marshal. You are to be questioned by the Marshal personally. Do not speak unless spoken to and if you attempt to escape I will skin you like a deer. Is that understood?" I nodded once more and we sat there quietly for a time until more footsteps approached from behind and walked around to the front of us.

"Is this them?" a woman's voice called out. It had been many months since I had heard the voice of a woman and despite the fierce tone, it comforted me somewhat.

"It is, my lady. These men were seen leaving the great hole in the ground, the dark keep," replied Tyrgve.

"The dark keep, nothing comes crawling out of the dark keep except for Valkyries that fly and Draugr that spring forth from the ground. Curious that three Norseman should be seen leaving such a place." The woman walked back and forth and then a creaking noise erupted as if she had sat in a well-worn chair. "I'm going to ask you some questions and I want you to tell me the truth. If you are lying to me I'll have you cut up and fed to my dogs. Do you understand?"

"I do, my lady," I said.

"As the Marshal of this army, I am entrusted with the protection of its men as well as the people of the North. So tell me, are you spies?"

"No, my lady," I replied.

"No," replied Jareth and Dag.

"You, the one with dark hair. Where did you come from?" The Marshal asked.

"A village outside of Aarhus my lady," replied Dag.

"A southerner. How to you come so far north?"

"My village was sacked many years ago by the very creatures you fight. I was brought beneath ground and forced to work in the mines."

"And where does your allegiance lie?"

"With you, my lady, and the people of Midgard. I was a slave for many years. I do not wish to be so again." The Marshal fell quiet for a moment again.

"This one speaks the truth. Take him to a tent and place him under guard. See to it that he is cleaned, clothed and properly fed. I may have need of him later." Footsteps moved forward towards Dag and I heard them leave the tent. "Your friend is truthful but that does not mean that either of you are not spies. What of you?" Her voice drifted to Jareth. "Where do your allegiances lie?"

"To myself and those who would fight with me."

"A bold statement coming from a man on his knees. Would you not wish to pledge your allegiance to me?"

"To my captor? No. I will have no more masters, in this life or the next."

"I would watch your tongue unless you wish to lose it," the Marshal replied sharply.

"If I am to die then so be it. I have nothing more to say." The Marshal sat back down in her chair and snapped her fingers.

"Take this one to an open air cell. We will torture the truth out of him later." Footsteps came from behind, grabbing Jareth. I could hear them dragging him out of the tent as he kicked his legs.

"Farewell, brother," he said to me.

"Brother?" the Marshal said with a curious voice. "If you are his brother, then you must both be working together."

"We escaped the dark keep and were searching for companions to aid us. Nothing more."

"And what about you, where do you hail from?" I shrugged my shoulders and sighed deeply.

"I once came from a small village but we to were attacked by Freya and her hound."

"Fenrir? So you saw the beast yourself and survived. Few can say such a thing. This village of yours, did you have many kin there?" I nodded slowly.

"I did once, I had a father who was slain by a jealous Jarl, a mother who could now be anywhere, an Uncle who was killed by Freya's forces, and..." I paused for a moment, I could feel the lump in my throat beginning to form at my sorrow and I swallowed it back.

"Yes? You were saying?" My weak and frail voice struggled to find the words but I cared not to upset the Marshal.

"I had a woman once, the love of my life."

"What happened to her?"

"I do not know. I was taken and the last thing I saw was her face."

"Where did you say you were from? Your voice sounds strangely familiar." The Marshal stepped closer to me and I could now see her shadow looming over my head.

"It does not matter now. My home was destroyed."

"What is your name?" My heart pounded in my chest, I didn't know who this woman was and if she represented the wrong alliance, even my name could get me killed. I thought for a moment to give her a false name but knew that she may find the truth of it and that my death would come moments later instead of sooner.

"My name is Audan, former Chieftain of the people of Bjorgvin and son of Rurik the slain." A gasp filled the tent and the Marshal took a step back then forward again, crouching in front of me. Fingertips touched my forehead along the blindfold and I jerked back for a moment thinking she would do me harm, but her touch was soft and warm. I stilled myself as she ran her fingers to the back of my head and untied the knot. The blind fold came down and the light of tent blinded me. I blinked rapidly until a blurred figure before me came clear.

"Audan?" she said to me. "Is it really you?" The face before me shined brightly and a tears ran down her flawless face.

"Sada..." She moved the hair out from over my eyes and lunged forward wrapping me in her warm embrace.

"By the gods, I thought you were dead." She pressed her sweet lips firmly to mine and I gripped the back of her head pulling her in tightly. It felt as if our embrace would last an eternity and I never wished to leave it. Sada helped me up from the ground and looked me over. "What did they do to you?"

"I was their prisoner and slave. Living conditions were difficult, my love."

"You're so thin, your hair so long." Sada turned her head towards the entrance. "Guard!" A young leather armored warrior walked in to the tent. "See to it that this man is clothed and fed immediately. I want him to receive the best care." The guard bowed slightly.

"Yes, my lady."

"Sada?" I asked.

"Yes, my love?"

"What about Jareth?" Sada gasped again placing her hand over her mouth.

"Guard, one more thing!" The young man returned. "The other two prisoners, do the same for the immediately. They are no longer our captives, they are our honored guests. Also, find Tyrgve and send him to my tent." The guard bowed again.

"Yes, my lady." Moments after the guard left, Tyrgve entered the tent surprised to see me standing on my feet and in such close proximity to Sada. He gripped his sword.

"My lady! Watch out!" Sada raised he open palms to Tyrgve.

"Lord Commander, may I introduce you to my husband, Audan, Chieftain of Bjorgvin." The Lord Commander sheathed his blade and dropped to a knee.

"My lord, a thousand apologies. Had I but known who you are." I approached Tyrgve placing my hand gently on his shoulder.

"No apology is needed. You saved my life this day and for that I thank you." Tyrgve stood and smiled humbly.

"It is good that you are here. We need more people we can trust now more than ever. We have been at camp for nearly a month gathering every lost warrior to our cause." Tyrgve walked over to the map, pointing to large groups of wooden figures that stood opposite of each other. "Our forces lie here, the plains just before the Fire Mountains. Surt's forces are here just beyond ridge line you see here. His scouts line the hills and have been keeping an eye on us ever since we arrived." Sada wrapped her arms around my waist.

"Sada, why are you and ten thousand men so far North?" Sada pointed at Surt's forces on the map and then waved her hand further south. It appeared to be a battle plan of sorts, showing the disposition of many armies throughout the North. The forces of the Norseman were split in two but great in number.

"Freya's forces are marching further south but Surt has been gaining ground daily. If we are to defeat Freya we must stop Surt from gaining a foothold or all might as well be lost. We go to attack the heart of the enemy. Surt and a great numbers of his forces lie near the Fire Mountains. We go to victory or Valhalla."

* * *

Nearly thirteen days passed. Sada said that I slept for nearly two days after my first meal. The most peaceful sleep I think I had in my entire lifetime. Each night, I came to a soft bed next to a beautiful woman. Sada had hardened over time and gained the respect of many clans uniting the North against a terrible evil. She said that when the Valkyries took me that she was continuing my work and that she vowed to not stop until the gods had been sent back to their realm. As the days passed and many of the prisoners of the Dark Keep had made their way to our camp and helped to swell our forces. I awoke early the eve of battle knowing that after all that had transpired, after all we had been through together that I still wanted to live. I wanted to go back to a time long ago, lost when the fields or the farms were bright and green filled with happiness, laughter, and prosperity.

As I lay there quietly I stared at Sada sleeping peacefully beneath the furs. The blanket lay just beneath her shoulder exposing her long, beautiful neck line. Her hair rested over one eye following the line of her nose. I leaned in and kissed her forehead softly but she did not stir.

"My lady/ Audan?" It was the Lord Commander Tyrgve. Sada still did not stir and so I answered.

"Yes, Tyrgve."

"The men are preparing themselves for the march. We will be ready to leave shortly."

"Very well. We shall meet you outside."

"As you wish." Tyrgve walked away and I turned to wake Sada gently shaking her shoulder. She opened her eyes and smiled when she lay them upon me.

"Good morning, my love." I smiled back.

"Good morning. It is time. The men will be ready soon." Sada sat upright and kissed me.

"We had better get ready then. It's a big day." Sada removed her covers and stood in the cold air naked. Her body was fit from the many months of fighting with only a few scars to speak of. I stood and walked behind her, placing one arm around her waist and the other over her breasts. She leaned into my arms, kissing them lovingly.

"I have only had you back for a moment and now the moment has passed. Today may finally be the day we must say goodbye." Sada turned in my arms and faced me gazing deeply in my eyes. The stare was warm and loving as she ran her fingers down my face.

"If we are to die today, then we shall drink together in the halls of Valhalla this night. After everything we have been through, do you really think that death would keep us apart?" She wrapped her arms around me and we kissed passionately for several moments, breathing each other in, tasting one another, until we felt the pull of duty calling to us. She ran her hand though my hair and tugged on my beard, pulling me close.

"I have lost you before, Audan, never again." Sada released her grip and we each began dressing ourselves for the battle to come. Sada had their armorer fit me for new leather armor. The prison of the Dark Keep had made me thin and so I needed something that fit properly. I donned my tunic, my trousers, and leather belt and leather breastplate to protect my upper torso. I sat down, fitting my leg wraps and leather boots then stood securing my bracers. A set of chainmail had been made for me as well and as I lifted it over my head and let it fall on my shoulders, the weight felt cumbersome.

"Here," said Sada. "Try swinging with this." Sada handed me something long wrapped in a cloth. I pulled the corner and let it fall, exposing my father's bearded axe.

"You've had it all this time?" She nodded.

"I kept it safe for you. I thought perhaps you may return to claim your father's blade once more." The blade glinted brightly as I turned it.

"You've had it sharpened and polished?"

"I did." I placed the axe down and embraced her.

"Thank you." Sada returned my affection and then pushed me back.

"Use this axe to help free Midgard. I may be the leader of this army, but you Audan, you are the symbol of hope that all our banners ride behind." I lifted the axe again and swung around several times in the chain mail. The mail made me slow and my swings were off.

"I can't wear the mail," I said, ashamed. Sada shook her head.

"Then don't wear it, my love. Ride into battle free like a raven light of foot and swift of purpose." I removed the mail and lifted my axe once more, I could move and swing freely now. Sada finished donning her armor, leather and chainmail and carried a helm in her arms with a face guard shaped like a dragon.

"You look fearsome, my love." Sada smiled but quickly the wrinkles around her lips and eyes smoothed as the smile faded.

"We shouldn't keep them waiting. They will become restless." Sada walked outside the tent quickly and I followed. Tyrgve was waiting outside with Magnus. To the right were my own personal Captains Dag, Grim, Njord and Gunnar. Despite the loss of Eygautr and Uncle Valdemar, these men had stood by me through many terrible battles and proven themselves beyond a doubt. Grim briskly walked towards me with a shit-eating grin on his face.

"What has your spirits so high, old man?" Grim took a deep breath and looked about the skyline.

"I have waited many decades for a battle such as this. Today, I will fight with honor and die with a sword in my hand. Nothing would give me greater pleasure." He stepped up to my face and placed his hand on my shoulder. "I am ready to die today, Audan, not because I fear the odds that stand before us but because I long to be among my comrades once more. So if you are to die today young warrior I shall count you amongst one of my friends." I nodded humbly and smiled.

"Thank you, Grim." I turned to Gunnar and Njord, two men who had been with me since the beginning.

"And you two?" Gunnar pulled his sword from its sheath and let it hand from his side.

"Today is as good a day as any. I've followed you for this long. I don't plan on turning back now." Njord bounced his hammers in his hands and then secured them to his belt.

"There is no place I would rather be now than by your side."

"You both honor me. I will look for you on the battlefield." I turned to Dag, the newest of our group. "This is not your fight, Dag. You don't have to join us today." Dag stood tall placing his hands on his hips.

"I was in that hole for seven years. This is my one chance redeem myself, to honor the family that they killed, raped, and enslaved. I will be the first to ride into battle." I placed my hand firmly on the side of Dag's face.

"Stay close to us and don't get lost." Sada mounted her horse and we followed suit. Her generals followed closely behind and as we made our way through the camp warriors lined the tents of the path raising their arms into the air cheering their Marshal. She was a sight to behold, the leader of the free people. In all my dreams, I never once thought that the greatest threat to Surt would be the fury of a woman.

As we rode past the warriors of the North, soldiers filed in creating a line that stretched back for what seemed like miles. Endless rows of spears, horses, and shields of every color and design. All the banners of Midgard assembled in one great line. We rode north to the ravine that split between the great snow-covered caps along a river. The road slowly winded upward until reaching a dry plateau of grey dirt and rock. Our horses bucked and whined loudly at the foul stench of sulfur that now filled the air. Not far off in the distance was a dark and never-ending black mountain with a trail of lava that flowed down to its base. The nearer we came, the larger the mountain became. I thought we would have to advance to the base of the mountain to face our enemy but as I brought my gaze downward I spotted the enemy horde in wait.

Sada turned her horse around and pointed to each side, indicating she wanted the forces split from a narrow column to a much wider attack formation. With nearly fifteen thousand men it seemed that we could cover the entire stretch of the plateau from one mountain range to the next. I rode up alongside Sada with my captains in tow. Tyrgve and Magnus were scouting out the enemy position, trying to discern and tactical advantage of attacking such a massive force one way or another. As I was about to speak with Sada, a loud crack erupted from the ground below and the started to shake the earth violently. Our horses panicked but we forced them to stay in their place until the shaking ceased.

"An earthquake?" Gunnar asked. I gazed at the enemy position to see a brightly flaming light waving from the front of their ranks. It began to walk forward leaving behind his forces, it was Surt.

"Sada!" I called out. She fixed her gaze upon me and I pointed outward to the advancing god of fire. "Look there!" Above Surt, the air began to crack and whip in a fury, as dark-winged figures descended from above, escorting Surt forward. Their troops still showed no sign of advancing on our position. It appeared that Surt wished to speak.

"The white flag!" Sada commanded to the generals. A banner man rode forward on his horse lowering his standard and raising a small and plain white flag. "Generals, captains of Audan, follow me." He kicked our horses and snapped their reins riding forward behind our fierce Marshal. The white banner waved gracefully next to Sada as we approached our enemies for a meeting of terms.

Surt ceased moving forward, his sword at his side burning brightly and the Valkyries came down from the sky and stood next to him. One in particular caught my eye, it was Freya! We slowed our horses to a stop some twenty paces from the immortals keeping an ever watchful eye on them.

"Freya!" I called out. "You should have stayed south with your forces. Now your life will be mine!" Surt lifted his sword and placed it in its sheath dousing the fire and sending a plume of smoke rising.

"I heard you had escaped my keep with my prisoners. I'm here to finish you and, look, your little woman." Sada ignored this insult, keeping her focus on the fire god, Surt.

"I am Sada, Marshal of the people of Midgard. I am here to discuss terms." Surt did not blink nor grimace or smile. In fact it did not seem that Surt even breathed. Surt closed his orange burning eyes and then opened them again to reveal of smooth black pearl.

"Terms?" he asked. He lifted his arm that was covered in a long black cloak removing a loose thread with his finger tips that burned to ash at the touch. "There are no terms between gods and men."

"You will refuse to discuss terms?" Sada pressed the issue in an effort to assert her dominance.

"You will surrender your forces to my will or I shall burn you all to ash." Sada turned her horse to her sword side and gripped the blade handle.

"Midgard will never surrender to an illegitimate ruler. Odin is the one true god of Midgard and we will fight to the bitter end." Surt looked over our forces and then turned his gazed upon me.

"So you are the one? Pathetic."

"End this now, Surt. More people do not need to die," I exclaimed. Freya stepped in front of Surt, her dark wings extending wide.

"I'm going to make sure you die slowly, Audan, I'm going to make sure you get to see everything you love destroyed before I take the light from your eyes. This world is mine and shall bow to me and as the Dark Queen. I shall rule for an eternity!" Surt gripped Freya's shoulder and pulled her back towards him.

"You shall rule?" Surt placed his second hand atop Freya's shoulders.

"I freed you, Surt. Loki freed you. This realm belongs to us and you are going to help me take it." I felt the hairs on the back of my neck stand up. Surt appeared far more powerful than Freya and now they disagreed on the rule of the realm.

Freya would not back down so quickly. Suddenly, Surt reached back behind Freya, gripping the base of her wings. His hands caught ablaze, torching her skin in an instant. She screamed out in such terrible agony that she could not even reach for her sword. Surt flexed his arms and pulled outward ripping the wings out from Freya's back. She fell to the earth and writhed in pain as Surt threw her clipped wings at her feet. He pulled his sword from its sheath and flicked the blade lighting it ablaze and pointed it downward at Freya.

"Whoever said I needed you?"

Sixteen
Flame Eternal

"Traitor!" Freya screamed out in agony. I stood and watched in shock as the gods turned on one another. Three of Freya's Valkyries leapt to her aid with clenched teeth and flashing swords. Surt stepped quickly to the side of one and swung his fiery blade through her stomach, cutting her in half. The second leapt over the corpse and came down with a mighty thrust. Surt parried and kicked the corpse goddess to the ground. The third came at Surt's back, swinging down from on high. Her blade fell hard against Surt's fire sword and as she pushed down her blade, it melted and then snapped. Surt's sword broke through, severing her head at the neck. The blood boiled on Surt's blade until it burnt to ash. He then turned his gaze back to the second Valkyrie he had kicked to the ground. She took to the air, flapping her wings. She dropped her sword and transformed into a dark Valkyrie, a winged beast of tooth and claw. She descended faster than the wind, screaming like a wild banshee. Surt held his ground and they collided. The fire god fell hard and tumbled with the feathered ghoul as their fists traded blows and wrestled for supremacy.

The dark Valkyrie ripped her arm loose of Surt's grip and struck down with her claws across his face. A bloodied gash appeared and steam rose from the crimson liquid. In a rage, Surt shouted and gripped the Valkyrie's neck squeezing with all his fury. The corpse goddess pulled at his fingers but could not pry them loose. She raised her legs and clawed at whatever she could reach, tearing at his leather cloak and digging into his flesh. The veins in Surt's neck and forehead bulged and he yelled louder until blood ran from the Valkyrie's eyes and nose. The flurry of her striking legs slowed and her eyes began to roll in the back of her head. Her body ceased to move as the sweet song of death came over another immortal. Surt released his grip and stood cracking his neck from side to side. I leapt down from my horse and rushed to Freya with bearded axe in hand.

"Audan no!" Sada called out, but I ignored her cry and pressed forward placing my blade against Freya's neck. Surt turned and gazed at me with cold eyes.

"Step aside, boy. Freya's life is mine." I slowly lowered the blade from her neck and dropped the handle into Freya's hand. The wingless goddess looked up at me, her eyes showed the confusion in her heart and head.

"Audan, what are you doing?" I knelt down, placing my face over her shoulder. I reached out and closed her fingers over the handle of the axe.

"You loved me once. Now I'm giving you a final curtesy. Defend yourself that I may have the honor to kill you."

"I said step aside, boy! You dare to defy a god?" His voice was loud and echoed across the plain. A tear fell from Freya's eye and burned to steam before reaching her chin.

"In all of eternity, no man has ever offered me arms just so he could kill me himself." She stood slowly and I backed away, keeping out of her striking distance if she decided to turn on me. She lifted the bearded axe with both her hands and glanced at the blade. She raised her eyes through the long blond strands of hair over her face, her lips quivered and her chest rose quickly over and over again.

"Go, fight him and perhaps even a god as evil as you can redeem yourself."

"I'm sorry." The words fell on my ears but I was in doubt that I had heard them in the first place.

"What?" I asked in utter shock.

"I'm sorry Audan. It could have been different." Freya faced Surt. I stared at her back, where her clipped wings bled terribly. She was now more human than ever and the odds against Surt were not in her favor. I stepped backward until reaching my horse to leave enough room for the gods to battle and turned to gaze briefly at my comrades whom still had disbelief written on their faces. Sada pulled her horse next to mine.

"What have you done?" she asked in frustration.

"Bought us more time. If Freya wins, then the enemy we will face will be weaker but if Freya loses we still have one less enemy to face. For now, she fights for us. Whether she knows it or not." Freya stepped forward with axe at the ready.

"Drop the blade, Freya. Why die in a final struggle you know you will lose? Let me release you from your burden of eternity."

"You betrayed me, Surt. I could have left you in that rocky tomb. Now, I will send you to oblivion." Freya charged forward screaming with all the fury of hell. She swung left and then right. Surt ducked out of the way each time. He pressed forward and Freya blocked his blade and struck Surt in the face with the wooden handle. The strike did not faze him. Reaching back, he glanced Freya's cheek with his knuckles. She turned round and swung her axe down. The force was too great and Surt's sword gave way, taking him downward with it. Freya then lifted the axe from the ground, the blade barely missing Surt's face as he reeled backward. Like a wolf, she lunged forward bearing sharp fangs and sank them into Surt's neck. He yelled, but it was Freya who suffered the most. She spat the blood from her mouth and leapt back, as the blood had melted away from her lips and teeth. She cried out in agony and the Fire God struck the back of her neck with his pommel. Freya fell to her face and Surt stood over her with his flaming sword at his side. An icy breeze blew past and heavy flakes of snow began to fall over the plateau.

"You should have let me kill you. Now, you will understand pain." Freya lurched upward on her hands and turned onto her back holding herself upward on her elbows. She spat at Surt's blackened boots and hissed loudly.

"Without me, you cannot possibly hope to defeat Odin. The warriors of Asgard will descend upon you and peel your flesh from bone."

"We shall see." He stepped forward and plunged the fire sword into Freya's heart. She cried out in utter terror, gripping the blade tightly as it cut through her hands. She turned to me with blood trickling though her mouth and staining her teeth. A smile crept up on her face and her head fell limply to the side. Surt pressed his leg against her shoulder and pulled his sword free. Freya, the Dark Queen, was dead.

In some ways, I had felt that justice was done, even though my vengeance would go forever unfulfilled. The fire god reached behind his waist and pulled forward a shining helm with chainmail aventail. He lowered his body and placed it upon his head. When he raised up and opened his eyes a bright white glow burned from inside his helm. Smoke lifted upward above his head and he sheathed his fire sword.

"Go to your armies, go to your Northmen and prepare for battle. There will be more killing this day, much more killing." Surt turned and walked away back towards his battle line, leaving behind the corpses of three Valkyries and the goddess Freya. I gazed at her now still body, a gaping hole in her chest where smoke billowed and a dead look in her eye. Even in death, Freya was almost the most beautiful creature I had ever seen. As I watched the blood trickle into a muddied pool, a white light emanated from the chests of the fallen. Their bodies began to glow and shine bright white, so powerful the light was that we all turned away covering our faces. The light hummed loudly and illuminated the snow covered plateau brightly. Suddenly, the hum and light faded and shot upward. I watched as the balls of light climbed towards the clouds and then disappeared on the other side.

"Where do they go?" asked Sada.

"Back to their realm, I suppose."

"They still live?" I shook my head.

"No, I don't think so. They will go to Yggdrasil to be born again but not as they were. Only the Norns know." I retrieved my bearded axe from the ground and mounted my steed. We turned our horses around and quickly rode back to the army of Northmen at our backs. Warriors stood firm in their formations waiting for orders to move forward. Tyrgve and Magnus approached Sada on horseback.

"What are your orders?" Tyrgve asked. Sada looked up and down the battle line and returned her gaze to her Generals.

"Lord Commander Tyrgve, take up position with the heavy infantry and myself in the center. Magnus, join the auxiliary on the left flank. Ensure your ranks are filled with archers and spearman to breakdown the enemies' defenses.

"And me, Marshal?" I asked Sada. She smiled lovingly and looked over my shoulder.

"You and your captains will that the right flank with the Militia and the remnants of the warriors from Bjorgvin. They will need your leadership to press forward. Push the enemy back and meet us in the middle. We will need your skill and courage to help defeat Surt."

"Any parting words, my lady? I'd hate to start this battle without a kind word from a beautiful word." said Grim. Sada gave him a seductive look and blew the old man a kiss.

"To victory or Valhalla, Grim. May you honor your kin." For the first time ever, I watched as Grim's face and ears turned a crimson red. Even the toughest of Berserkers could be made to blush by a beautiful woman.

"A word to the men before we go. They will need your encouragement. A Marshal is first and foremost a leader and then a warrior," Tyrgve urged. Sada nodded and smiled widely.

"Very well." She unsheathed her sword and raised it high into the air. "If it is speech to stir their souls and bring courage to their hearts, then it is a speech they shall have!" Drums began to beat loudly in the background as Surt's army maneuvered and shifted its forces in preparation for an attack. Sada rode her horse to the very center of the army, pulling back on the reins and lifting the steed on its hind legs and then dropping back down. "Norsemen, Norsemen hear me!"

She pointed her blade across the battlefield. "Out there lies one of two armies that have wrought death and destruction on this land. Your homes, your families have been destroyed and terrorized by the gods. What ruler punishes his people so? What ruler would take so much and give nothing in return? An unjust one, a corrupt and evil ruler. We have many gods and are asked to respect and fear them all, but I say— no more! No more will I pay homage to the beasts that rip children from the hands of their mothers. No more will I bow to the creatures that take the lives of our loved ones and leave the land a barren wasteland."

The warriors cheered in agreement and anger. Sada had struck a nerve with the men and their arms began to clamor loudly. "My brothers, will you fight with me? Will you fight and help me send these demons back to the realms from whence they came? Will you avenge your families and right a terrible wrong?" The men erupted into a deafening roar. No longer could I hear the drums and movements of our enemies across the field. I turned back from Sada to see Draugr moving forward at a light run and soon our arms would clash.

I turned back to Sada who stood tall atop a white horse; she was magnificent as she called out to her warriors. They loved and respected her, each one ready to fight and die under her command. It was a terrible woman that brought this destruction upon us and now a great one would lead us to freedom. In this moment before battle, I loved her more than I ever had before. She turned her horse and gazed at me with a beaming smile and fierce determination on her face. "Sons of Odin, what makes the grass grow and the rivers flow!" she called out our families' battle cry, the war cry of Bjorgvin. Nearly ten thousand men not of our home repeated the call.

"Blood, blood, blood!"

"And how do we get blood?" she cried out above the din.

"Kill, kill, kill!" She lifted her sword and pointed towards our enemy.

"To glory!" Like an earthquake, the charging steeds and warriors shook the earth in a terrible roar. I slapped my horse's reins and kicked his sides with my captains and militiamen following behind me. I pulled my horses to the far right and waved to my forces to follow. They shifted their ranks and swung wide as the center line of Sada's heavy infantry charged ahead. I looked forward to see the bulk of Surt's army comprised of Draugr, Ulfhednar and the remaining Valkyrie that had pledge their allegiance to him. With Gunnar to my right and Njord to my left we rode like the wind to a wall of undead that carried sword, axe, and shield. Closer our armies drew until I could see rotting flesh and standing fur. I cried out in anger, swinging my axe downward as we collided with the wall. The sound of our arms clashing was like thunder. The din rose and rose until all I could hear was a dull roar.

I struck warriors as I charged through the mass of fighters, knocking many down with my horse. Soon, my steed slowed and I pulled to the right, so as not to get too far from the Militia. I hacked and slashed, cutting undead warriors down with great ease. A break in the din brought forth the screams and clashes that surrounded us. High above, I heard the snaps and whips of iron stingers that streaked just above our heads, mowing down hordes of undead.

The militia men quickly pushed forward, hacking flesh and bone and stomping out the Draugr where they stood. I looked to the left to see my captains heavily engaged and turned to ride to their aid. A howl erupted and within the ranks of the undead stood small groups of Ulfhednar.

"Hold the line!" I called out. I didn't want the men to get split up by the Draugr before we engaged the hounds. We needed a tight line, otherwise they would break through and cut us down.

"Hold the line!"

Suddenly, a roar erupted and an Ulfhednar leapt for me, I swung my axe down, but was too slow. The beast threw itself against me, knocking me from my horse. I fell to the ground, the air knocked from my lungs. In a panic, I reached around blindly for my axe as I looked up through a flurry of men and arms. Then, a large hand gripped my shoulder and claws sank in. The Ulfhednar straddled my body, fangs dripping red with blood it lunged down towards my neck and then let out a terrifying shriek. Norsemen from all sides plunged their steel into the flesh of the beast, sending his head back reeling from the pain. Finding my axe, I gripped the handle, stood quickly and buried the blade in the hound's skull, sending him straight to the earth.

"More, over there!" Grim pointed as the furry beasts moved themselves to the far side of their formation. They mead to flank us and pull our men down one by one.

"Lock you shields!" I called out. The Militiamen slowly pulled back creating a hasty shield wall. I fell back into the ranks behind the shields with my axe up high. The Draugr pushed against us and quickly found blades punching into their faces and necks. I reached over with my axe peeling at what flesh I could reach.

"Tighten the line!" I called out. The warriors squeezed together, so much so that not even a flake of snow fell between us. The very warmth of the line from the body heat was enough to make a man sweat. Now Ulfhednar jumped forward, my captains dismounted from their horses and joined the ranks. A hound reached very near me, ripping shields away from Norsemen and then throwing them out to the undead to feast upon. We dropped our blades on him until he became weak and bled out. If we stayed, the Draugr would whittle us down. Another leapt at our formation above the melee. I could no longer see the front of the field and needed a pair of eyes. "Grim!" I called out to the left. "Take command!"

"Alright, you bastards! You fucking listen and you listen well. When I say step, you fucking step!" Grim lifted his sword in the air as an Ulfhednar gnawed at the shields in front of me. "Step!" he called out. Together as one, we moved forward and the front line of enemies became unstable as they were pinned against us. We slashed and hacked as the legions of dead rushed forward. The screams of mortal men filled the air as rusted and bent instruments cut at our skin.

"Step!" Grim called out once more. I pushed my body into the men in front of me, lending to the strength of the shield wall. Spears began to fall from the sky and I looked above to see half a dozen Valkyries dropping the shafts over our heads. One fell directly into the man in front of me. As his body went limp the Draugr pulled him out from the line and another warrior jumped in his place. "Hold the line! Tighten it up!" Grim ordered.

"Archers! Up there! Shoot those bitches down!" I yelled to the back of the formation. The archers turned their focus far above the battle, drew their strings back and let loose a volley of iron. They met their mark with ease. The corpse goddesses fell limp from the sky, falling hard on their allies while the others pulled back with arrowheads plunged deeply into their limbs.

"Step!" Grim ordered once again. We pushed forward and now piles of fallen enemy lay beneath our feet. Their already rotten corpses filled the air with a most offensive odor. The slain Ulfhednar pissed and shit themselves in the already blood-soaked ground. The earth below us was now a terrible mix of excrement, snow, and soil. I tripped slightly, catching my foot on the teeth of a Draugr. I looked down to see his mouth gaping open and a blade wound that capped off the top of his skull. I kicked his face in until there was nothing left but a pile of flesh beneath me and then turned my attention forward once more. I leaned my axe forward and cleaved more flesh while steel and bone pounded against the shields.

"Hold!" Grim called out. "Hold the line! Tighten the formation." Gaps were closed once more the bodies of the undead began to pile up in a wall before us. We held in place as our enemies had to crawl and climb their way over their own dead just to reach us only to help make the wall bigger.

"We need to push forward!" I yelled." Sada's infantry would be in the thick of it and if they were to win we needed to push through this horde and meet them in the center. Time was of the essence and we could no longer delay.

"Alright, you crazy fucking bastards!" Grim called up. "Get up the wall! Charge!" The wall pushed forward and we climbed atop the fallen, bracing our bodies on limbs and torsos. Our footing was terribly unstable but nevertheless we reached the top and came crashing down the other side like a tidal wave against our enemies. The Draugr and even the Ulfhednar could not withstand our fury and four to five lines on enemy ranks fell almost instantly. Our arms cut through them as a blade pushed through air and now the undead made strange wincing sounds and hesitated to push forward. Peering through the myriad of shields, I spotted something I had never seen amongst the ranks of the undead. A Draugr armed with sword and shield dropped his arms and screamed in terror, turned and ran from the battlefield. He was struck down from the back by a heavy set axe-wielding corpse. Then, another began to turn and follow in their fallen comrades footsteps.

"They flee! The undead are afraid! Press the attack!" I called. The men cheered and let out a ferocious war cry as they pressed forward. I shifted to the right and urged the men to push hard, so we could collapsed the right flank inward. With the Draugr on the run our ranks now did as they pleased pushing forward and decimating the right flank. Their forces collapsed and without a solid line, they fought in small groups against our solid wall. My arms had tired from holding the axe above the wall and striking outward but the advanced had lent fire to my spirit and so I pushed on, killing what foes dared to come against us. A snap ripped past my ears. Stingers descended upon us and our shields still faced forward.

"Arrows! Shields up, lads! Shields up!" Many arrows made their mark before the shields were raised and man after man slumped down to the ground. The stingers pounded hard against the shield wall, some even piercing through the timber, ripping into men's arms. Those veteran warriors held in place despite the pain, those who lacked disciplined pulled their shields down at the pain and were mowed down. Njord huddled next to me and Gunnar on my right.

"We have to get to the archers!" Gunnar cried out. The Draugr that had fled left a deep gap in their lines with enough room to run. The Archers were no more than two farm fields away. They could load two, maybe three arrows on our charge but no more. I turned my gaze to Grim.

"We need to run! Take out the archers!" Grim nodded and stared forward with fierce determination.

"Break ranks! Charge! Charge! Charge!" Warriors unlocked their shields and ran forward at a sprint. I hacked at Draugr as I ran past but took no time to engage any one warrior. Arrows flew straight at us now as we neared the line of archers. Without a shield, I charged into an undead, hacking off his axe hand and hugging his rotting flesh tightly. I pressed on using him as a barrier. Stinger after stinger lodged into his back and he screamed helplessly until I reached the line throwing his body into the archers knocking three down. I lifted my axe and swung from side to side, hacking at the legs of others as they reached for their short swords. Quickly, they fell to the ground and my fellow warriors charged into the breach overtaking the archer's positions. I climbed to the top of a small mound and looked down the battlefield to see the center line heavily engaged. Behind Surt's forces was the fire god himself standing tall with the hound Fenrir at his side held tightly by a leash of gleipnir. A hand gripped my shoulder and I turned quickly to see Gunnar breathing heavily, his face covered in dark putrid blood.

"Audan, the right flank has collapsed! We must reinforce the heavy infantry, Sada is counting on us!" Sada? I scanned the battlefield for my love and her white stallion but neither could be seen in the calamity of battle. So thick were Surt's forces that even the banners of the norther clans could not be seen. Gazing upon our column, the men seemed victorious and willing to move forward. I was tempted to move in on Surt and challenge the god face to face, but Sada needed us now more than ever.

"Men of Bjorgvin, my stomach thirsts for more blood! What say you?" I yelled. The men chanted back.

"Blood! Blood! Blood!" Grim wiped the blood and bile from his face, smiling through crimson teeth.

"To battle! Shift the shield wall to the center! Shift! Shift! We have them now, boys!" The men hastily moved on command locking their shield wall together and I pressed myself inward picking up a battered shield from the ground and joining the wall. "Forward!" Grim commanded. We moved forward at a steady pace but Grim kept us from moving too quickly to regain our strength. As we approached the melee of the centerline, the Draugr had their backs to us not giving any sign that they noticed us coming. "Hold!" Grim called out. Our forces stopped in their tracks eager to charge forward. "Do you remember what Freya did to your home?"

"Aye!" the men called out.

"Do you remember what the hound did to your families?' Grim yelled.

"Aye!"

"Don't stop until you see their heads roll! Charge!" We unleashed a great and powerful war cry that cut through the din of battle. Stampeding forward, we shook the ground. It rumbled in terror beneath our feet and as the Draugr turned to see the men of Midgard bearing down on their left flank. They reeled back in an attempt to defend themselves but we cut them down like weeds. I caught a glimpse of the faces of the centerline: they were exhausted and could not push ahead. We quickly worked our way within their ranks and allowed them to fall back. I pressed forward with what little strength I had, but it was more than enough to press back the decrepit adversaries. As our line advanced, a terrible roar erupted from the far side of the battlefield. The Draugr pulled back, ceasing their advance and all men gazed upon the bright shining eyes of the beast cloaked in midnight fur. Surt lifted and removed the collar from the hound's neck and pointed down towards the battle line.

"The beast comes for us! Fenrir the world eater approaches!" a voice shouted from behind. I turned my head to cheer on the warriors when I saw her. Sada stood in the middle of the battle line surrounded by a horde of her warriors covered in blood. Her eyes locked onto mine and for a moment the battle froze all around us. Her lower lip fell slowly and her fierce gaze stared deeply into my eyes. She moved her mouth saying something but I could not make it out. I turned away and looked forward, gazing straight at the hound. Suddenly, Grim broke ranks and stepped forward pointing at the beast.

"C'mon, boys, let's put this dog down for good!" The crazed berserker charged forward with sword and shield. Like the flooding rivers, we rushed forward consuming every enemy in our path screaming and yelling and the tops of our lungs. I hacked and slashed Draugr after Draugr until a path was cleared in front of me. Grim ran atop black stones, holding his sword with both hands over his head he swiped at the beasts face as it lunged forward to sink his teeth into the veteran. The old man left a fine gash across Fenrir's nose sending him reeling backward. Before Fenrir could mount another attack on Grim sword, spear, and axe fell on him from all directions. The beast swept his muzzle across the field striking down lines of warriors only to be attacked in the gaps he left behind. I ran forward as the men climbed atop Fenrir appearing as ants scurrying on a horse. The beast leapt upward and shook the Norseman off and reached back, ripping one man off his fur then snapping him in half sending blood and limbs crashing down atop of us.

Fenrir stomped on many men crushing their insides and sending blood and bile spilling out of their orifices. Arrows and spear shafts protruded from his belly and despite the onslaught that we lay upon him, the beast continued his slaughter. The Draugr were emboldened and turned back to fight. A blood-curdling scream erupted next to me, Njord fell to the ground with a blade in his gut. I ran towards him to rush to his aid but Fenrir stepped forward snatching my friend as he reached his hand out towards me. The hound sunk his fangs into Njord until his bones crunched beneath his bite and Njord's calls for help ceased.

"No!" I was without my senses now and buried my axe into the dogs paw urging him to come down on me. When Fenrir descended, I plunged my bearded axe between his teeth. He reared upward and I held on to the axe handle as he lifted me into the sky. The black of his pupils focused in on me and I swung my body to one side until a tooth snapped out. I fell downward atop fresh corpses quickly grabbing my axe and working at Fenrir's legs until he came snapping down again. I planted my steel behind his ear and ripped a chunk of it away. He wailed loudly and jumped back out of striking distance from our warriors. "I will have my retribution!" The dog ran back to its master and the Draugr pressed upon us once more.

"Audan!" a voice called out from behind. "Audan! You must face Surt!" I turned back to see the voice was Sada. "Only you can stop him! Go!" A hand grabbed my arm. It was Gunnar pulling me forward.

"Let's go, brother. I shall clear a path." Gunnar slashed his way through a minor wall and as we entered the gap, I could see the left flank in the distance with Sada's general still heavily engaged with the enemy. If victory were to come today, it would not come without great loss. Our lines were staggered and the Draugr were gaining small victories.

"Audan!" Gunnar urged. "Let's go!" I ran forward with my up a small slope where the fire god waited. I reached him nearly breathless but ready for what may come. He stared at me with empty black eyes and smoke rising from his helm.

"You leave your men in the field to die?" I quickly caught my breath and pointed my bearded axe towards my foe.

"The people of Midgard will never submit to you, Surt! The Ragnarok is here and with it the warriors of Asgard will descend upon your head and push you back to oblivion!" Surt smirked and slowly shook his head.

"So this is Odin's champion? I am disappointed. No mere mortal can defeat me and you, Audan, are more mortal than most."

"Face me, Surt, and I shall seal your fate." Surt raised his fire sword and walked forward with embers left in the wake of his footsteps.

"Very well. Have it your way." He lunged at me, swinging his sword down from on high. I caught it with the hook of my blade, pulling his tall slender figure inward. As I swung around to hit him with the axe handle, he gripped my forearm and set fire to my skin. I pulled back in searing pain and lunged forward swing over my shoulder at a downward angle. Surt quickly blocked this strike and jumped forward, kicking me in the chest. I fell to the earth, the wind knocked from my lungs.

"Is that all you have in you, boy?" He swung his sword down on me and I rolled to the side catching some of the flame against my shoulder. I reached out while still bent down sweeping at his legs and catching his calf. Surt looked down at the fresh wound that bubbled and steamed. He yelled in anger and rushed forward, swinging from side to side. I ducked and half blocked one strike but each time he would swing the sword behind his head and bring it back down on me. I charged forward, throwing my shoulder into his chest. He fell back only half a step and then gripped me by the neck lifting my body into the air.

"Foolish mortal. Your world has come to an end. I will cleanse this land fire and start anew." Suddenly, a stinger landed in his neck. I tuned to see Gunnar notching another arrows and letting it loose landing right into Surt's ribs. The fire god winced and dropped me to the ground. He turned to walk towards Gunnar only to find my blade in his back. Heat exploded from the wound and Surt fell to the ground. He turned quickly and swiped at my legs. I leapt back and watched as the fire god rose.

"So you do bleed, Immortal."

Surt pointed angrily at me.

"You will pay for that, human!" He came at me again with a barrage of strikes from all sides. The fire nearly blinded my vision and he caught a piece of my shoulder. Leaping back, I pulled the arm away and tried to put the pain out of my mind.

"Long live, Midgard!" I charged and swung furiously and found Surt on poor footing. He tripped backward and was unable to block the might of my strike. The bearded axe broke through his defense showing a piece of his chest through his dark leather cloak. I pressed on, striking over and over while Surt held himself on one knee blocking my strikes. Stepping in, I kicked his face, sending him barreling over with his back to me. Striking down, I quickly left another gash that bubbled and steamed. I removed the blade and pulled it back to strike him down once and for all. As my sword fell, a flash of light passed my eyes and suddenly Surt's eyes were right in front of my own. I felt as if I had been hit by a tree and I looked down to see the fire sword buried deeply into my chest. The pain now flowed to my limbs and head and I screamed out in agony.

"Audan, no!" I could hear Gunnar screaming but could not see him. My arms went numb and I released the grip of my axe dropping it to the earth. Surt smiled wickedly and licked blood from his lips. My vision narrowed and I felt as if I was being pulled to something cold and dark.

"The days of Odin are over. Long may fire reign." Surt ripped the sword from my body and I felt myself fall heavily. When my eyes again opened, I found myself standing on the edge of a snowy cliff. I gazed down curiously at the world below. Chaos and battles raged over much of the frozen landscape and from up here it seemed that someday the world would catch fire. A humming sound caught my attention and gazed down at my arms and body. The blood that had stained my tunic was gone, the scars on my arms and hands had all but disappeared. I felt better now than I had ever felt, healed, rejuvenated and without pain. I suddenly realized...I was dead.

"How did I get here?" I turned around slowly, expecting to see mountain or hillside of trees, but no. Standing before us were several wide steps of stone leading to a massive wooden door that stretched taller than an oak tree. There were no walls or building to speak of, the door stood on its own in the middle of nowhere. In between the cracks of the door faint white light peaked through stretching outward humming an odd tune. I took my first step forward cautiously and planted my foot firmly upon the stone step. The humming became louder and suddenly mysterious runes lit up on the floor and around the frame of the great oaken door. I reached behind me for my axe and swung my hand around for the handle, but the axe was gone. I reached down for my seax, but found it missing as well. That is when I realized that my cloak was not one of mine. It was bright red and embroidered with golden piping made of a material so soft that it slipped off one's skin. "Could it be?"

I stepped forward to the next step, the humming of the light grew louder and brighter still. The runes' glow intensified to a white hot blue. I stopped for a moment for fear of what my next step would do and so I turned back and looked over the cliffside. There was nowhere for me to go except forward. I returned my gaze to the door and quickly took the final two steps. Great torches on each side of the door lit brightly and the glow of the runes subsided. I walked towards the door with an outstretched hand and reached for the iron door handle. I gripped the ring slowly and looked upward as I pulled, but the door would not open. It seemed locked from the other side. I stepped back from the door and placed my hands on my hips, looking the great gate up and down. Surely such a large entrance would be guarded by a fearsome warrior.

"Open the gate!" I called out. I waited for a moment in the cold silence amidst the burning torches until a loud crack erupted from the other side of the door. The door began to press forward as it opened and I stepped back quickly to get out of its way. The light, the utterly blinding bright light, blocked my vision. I placed my hands over my eyes and listened to the hum of the light intensify to a near deafening sound until finally it softened and subsided with the light. I removed my hand from my eyes and saw before me a warrior clad in bright chainmail, a shining helm, at the ready with spear and shield. He lowered his weapon and removed his helm. It was Heimdallr and just beyond him lay blue skies, bright white clouds, and the most magnificent bridge of every color imaginable that reached skyward to a bright and glorious city in the distance.

"We have been expecting you, Audan, son of Rurik. Odin and your father await you in the hall of the slain."

"Valhalla? But I am not ready for the end! I'm not ready for death." The skies ahead shone brightly and though the very air beckoned me to step forward into the light I held back hoping I may return to Midgard and finish my affair.

Heimdallr smirked and approached me placing his hand on my shoulder.

"Death? Death is only the beginning."

THE END

About the Viking

D.W. Roach is a former U.S. Marine and current Physical Security Professional with experience spanning the globe serving several Fortune 500 Corporations.

His personal interests include shooting, fishing, hockey, the outdoors, BBQ's and Military History. He currently resides in the Bay Area with his wife and children.

"I chose to write a book for a number of reasons, and in the end, it was for the love of the story. As I put words to paper the characters came to life for me. I remember at one point going to bed and all I could dream about was the adventures the main characters were going on. It became exciting and very real.

In many ways I incorporated much of my own life experiences into the books I write. I wanted to convey what it was like for the warrior, the guy on the ground, fighting against nature with the odds stacked against him. I also wanted to show readers and fans of Norse mythology something they haven't seen before.

I hope you enjoy the Marauder Series as much as I enjoyed writing it!"
You can find Marauder books and social media at the below links;

Main Web Page
http://marauderseries.blogspot.com/

Facebook
https://www.facebook.com/marauderbook

Amazon Authors Page
http://www.amazon.com/David-Roach/e/B00QBBZDNQ/